They heard about the exploding car on the radio. Barbara steered the Mustang back onto I-10, headed it east. "We don't even know where it happened," Sandobal said.

"The Interstate only runs two ways. Let's see what's ahead."

She followed a sheriff's car until it pulled into a Terry's Tourist Trap restaurant. "That guy will tell us what's up," she said. "Small-town sheriffs love to talk."

She was right. "We got no ID on the car," Deputy Sheriff Enrique Cortes admitted over coffee Sandobal bought him. "No plates," he added. "Motor numbers blown up. All the plastic parts burned. Except for the doors. Blew all the doors clean off."

"Was it a brown Lincoln?" Sandobal asked. He was losing patience.

"Yeah, that's right. New. Nothing left of the chassis, frame, or wheels. Just a black spot. Twisted metal."

"Anybody inside?" Barbara asked, afraid to breathe.

"Barbara," Sandobal said. "Give it up." He reached over and took her hand.

"But if that was the same car. If Vicki was kidnapped, and if . . ."

"They're pretty sure it was empty," Cortes said. "That's why they're thinking maybe it wasn't no accident." He paused. "They found a timer," he added. "Guess somebody blew that car up on purpose."

Barbara leaned forward. "Anything else?"

"Well, this ain't for public consumption," Cortes said, looking around. "Another van—a Dodge, they say—is now involved in the murder of a state trooper over near Tucson."

BOOK YOUR PLACE ON OUR WEBSITE AND MAKE THE READING CONNECTION!

We've created a customized website just for our very special readers, where you can get the inside scoop on everything that's going on with Zebra, Pinnacle and Kensington books.

When you come online, you'll have the exciting opportunity to:

- View covers of upcoming books

- Read sample chapters

- Learn about our future publishing schedule (listed by publication month *and author*)

- Find out when your favorite authors will be visiting a city near you

- Search for and order backlist books from our online catalog

- Check out author bios and background information

- Send e-mail to your favorite authors

- Meet the Kensington staff online

- Join us in weekly chats with authors, readers and other guests

- Get writing guidelines

- AND MUCH MORE!

**Visit our website at
http://www.pinnaclebooks.com**

PLAYERS

Clay Reynolds

Pinnacle Books
Kensington Publishing Corp.
http://www.pinnaclebooks.com

PINNACLE BOOKS are published by

Kensington Publishing Corp.
850 Third Avenue
New York, NY 10022

First Printing: December, 1998
10 9 8 7 6 5 4 3 2 1

Printed in the United States of America

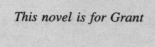

This novel is for Grant

"Organized crime is a contradiction in terms."
—Al Capone

Prologue

The black and primer-gray 1968 Chevrolet Camaro screamed off the blacktop, ripped through a barbed-wire fence, careened over a sandbar, left the ground and bounced hard on the flat expanse of the open desert beyond. For a second or two, the vehicle seemed to hesitate, then roared off, fishtailed, growled, and plowed into the dusty landscape.

A forest-green Range Rover calmly followed the track off the blacktop shoulder, slid through the gaping hole in the fence, climbed the gouged embankment in the Camaro's wake. There it stopped, idled. A man dressed in desert camo and shooting goggles, rifle with a laser-guided scope in hand, left the back seat, scrambled up onto the luggage rack. The vehicle prowled forward, quick, but in control. Four wheels churned yellow sand and green prickly pear beneath them: stalking.

The Range Rover had less trouble with the terrain, but it lacked the speed of the Camaro. Didn't matter.

Inside the Chevy, the driver bounced, wrestled with the steering wheel, tried to hold the car straight, wiped sweat out of his eyes. He squinted through the cracked, bug-caked windshield. A long mesa tinted the distance purple. Otherwise, there was only huisache, skunkweed, sotol, mesquite, and rock. And cacti. Would cacti give him a flat? He didn't know: city boy.

The rearview filled with a cloud of dust. He spun past an arroyo that snaked into a yawning, dry resaca right in front of him, swerved to the right, then left, jerked the wheel hard, nearly turned over, then raced away, ninety degrees off course. A radio tower appeared: hope. A road, he thought, maybe.

He pushed the Chevy hard, wiped his eyes. It stung. He ground knuckles into his eyes, pounded his fists on the steering wheel, then grabbed it before he lost control.

He dodged a boulder, saw a roadrunner dart in front of him, spotted a small knot of lazy Brahmans in the sunny, dusty distance, kept his foot pressed flat to the floor. The car bounced, jarred, swerved. Half the time, only two wheels were on the ground at once.

The Range Rover followed: patient, steady. It tracked the Camaro's golden dusty contrail. The man on top of the rack adjusted his scope.

The Camaro's driver could see the tower clearly now: red, white, silver in the sun. Small building beside it, chain-link fence around it, gravel road next to it. He twisted the wheel, angled the Chevy's nose toward the gravel trail, back toward the highway, aimed to connect just beyond a gnarled mesquite tree. The Camaro was low-slung, badly suspended. Fast engine on a smooth highway. Nothing off the road. All four shocks blew on the first bounce. Lucky the tires held up.

He heard the sharp crack of the rifle, felt the blow shatter his rear window, grabbed the sting on the back of his neck with his hand: blood.

"Mother*fuck!*"

He wrenched the wheel right, then left, then right again: evade another shot. He wiped his eyes, blood now mixed with sweat. Sweet odor, briny sting.

Below the level of the ground, beyond an earthen dam, between the Camaro and the gravel road was a stock tank. Never saw it. The battered Chevy zoomed up the lee side, left the ground for twenty feet, and landed flat on all four wheels in the middle. The water was two feet deep. Every window in the Camaro smashed. The trunk and hood popped open. The overheated engine steamed. Splashed water flowed back quickly down the hard, dry ground, into the swirling stock tank.

"Get him out." The order came from a man who emerged from the Range Rover, stopped on the crest of the dam. He was black, youngish, but already going gray at the temples. He wore dark glasses and an expensive cream-colored suit, held a Desert Eagle .357 in his hand. He scanned the sky overhead: empty. He glanced around clockwise, surveyed the horizon, shook his head. Except for the aroused Texas desert dust, the startled cattle, there was nothing: silence.

The shooter scrambled down the gravel embankment toward the smoking car. The driver also got out. He was older, heavier, grim behind dark glasses, balding with a scar on the side of his face. He, too, wore a suit—black, rumpled, nondescript. He, too, scanned the sky, the horizon. He carried an Uzi. His companion lit a cigar, made his way carefully down to the edge of the muddy tank. The driver stayed behind.

The Camaro's door was open, the driver half out into the water, face covered with blood. A bright wound gaped on the back of his neck.

"I told you to shoot the tires."

The shooter shrugged. "Couldn't help it. Bounced around too much." He pulled the Camaro's driver by the collar of his bloody shirt over to the bank, dragged him out of the mud, turned him over.

The driver's eyes were open, bloodshot. Blood flowed from his neck. One leg stuck out at an impossible angle. His front teeth were broken off, his mouth filled with blood.

"Ought to buckle up, Pancho," the shooter said. He waded back into the water, slogged over to the steaming Camaro. He examined the trunk-well, then pulled the driver's seat forward, searched the back, pulled the seats loose, ripped open door panels. He used a sharp K-Bar to slice away upholstery, the headliner, to dig into every crevice.

He turned to his companion on the bank, shrugged. "Nope." He waded back to where the driver lay, panting, bleeding.

"Where is it?" the well-dressed man asked the driver.

"Fuck you, man," the driver spat out: bloody mist. His speech was garbled, tongue bit through.

The shooter stepped forward, kicked the driver in the ribs. The driver groaned. "I'd answer if I were you, *chico*."

"And the horse you rode in on, motherfucker," the driver said. He tried to spit again, couldn't—too much blood.

The shooter looked at the man, at his cigar, shrugged. The man shrugged back. The shooter kicked him again. This time, he slipped slightly, and his heavy boot struck the driver in the temple. His head rocked sideways, then returned. Blood ran from his nose, eyes. A dark mark appeared on the side of his head. His eyes were open: fixed. His tongue lolled out.

"Dead?" the black man asked.

"Dead," the shooter affirmed.

He threw down his cigar. "We needed him alive. To talk."

"Hey, thought he was tougher than that."

"You're supposed to be good at this."

"Fuck you," the shooter said. "I'm the professional here."

"But I give the orders."

For a moment the two of them stood over the body, watched the Camaro settle into the artificial pond's muddy bottom, listened to the wind.

"Put him back in the car," the well-dressed man said.

"What? Why?"

"Just do it. You're the professional."

The camo-clad shooter scowled, put down his rifle, bent, picked up the body, loaded it over his shoulder. He waded back into the water once more, moved toward the car's open door.

He dumped the body inside, lost his balance. He stumbled back into the swirl, away from the car.

"Set him up. Like he's supposed to be there."

A look: disgust. He turned, bent over, leaned in. The man on the bank raised his pistol, sighted, squeezed off one quick round. The shooter's shoulders humped, his head struck the headliner of the car. He slouched forward across the driver's body. One neat red hole gaped in the left side of his back: direct hit on a camo cloud.

The man holstered the big automatic, picked up the other's long weapon. He opened the breech, removed the bullet, reached into his pocket, and extracted a single, red-tipped cartridge. He inserted it, rammed the bolt home, sighted carefully through the scope, placed the scarlet point of laser light where he was certain the Camaro's gas tank would be—and fired.

The car exploded in a rush of heat. Flames leaped half as high as the radio tower. The water around the car caught fire. The concussion seared the man's face.

"Professional," the man said.

He gathered up the spent shell casing from the pistol, collected his discarded cigar. He turned, climbed up the dam, went back to the Range Rover. Sweat now soaked through his suit. His shoes were covered with a layer of mud and dust.

"Fuck up?" the driver asked.

A nod: "You know where this leaves us?"

"Square one?"

The black man nodded his head. He tossed the long weapon into the backseat, relit his cigar, found a rag, wiped off his shoes. "Now, we have to do it the hard way."

PART ONE
Wednesday

One Month Later

1
Eddy

In Eddy Lovell's opinion, Moria Mendle was not an imposing man. He was a short, fat prick. But he was a player. Moria liked to sit in the back of Bishop's Cafe on Lower Greenville Avenue while he conducted business, eat fried oysters and drink Löwenbräu like he invented the combination. Bob Cole, Mendle's partner, was always there, always on Moria's right: eye sweeping the room like twin electronic scanners, one hand in the pocket of his jacket like it was rooted there. And in the corner, usually in the shadows, there was a steel door with arms, named Hedge.

It was the way he looked.

Hedge was a dark, ugly hulk who wore sleeveless shirts that allowed black, curly body hair to twist out in wiry clumps. The biggest mystery about him was his ethnic origin. He was dark-skinned, his head hair was kinky, cut short, no facial hair, but his eyes were pale green. No one Eddy knew had the guts to ask him about it. In fact, Eddy never heard anyone speak to him. He never heard Hedge speak, either.

Bishop's was one of those places no one went into unless they'd been there before. Even the cops stayed away. It was technically a cafe, but aside from fried oysters, grilled cheeses

Bishop served up from his greasy hot plate behind the bar, no
food was consumed in the place. It was a beer joint. No hard
liquor, no music, no pool. Now and then there was a ball game
on a tiny black-and-white next to the cash register, but Bishop
kept it slanted so it was hard for anyone but him to see. He
never turned up the sound. People who came into Bishop's
came in there to drink or to see Moria: business.

Moria's exact business was another mystery to Eddy. He
knew it was felony-hot, had to do with easy women, big cash,
but it was hard to define, hard to see. He owned a string of
mobile home dealerships—the slick, rip-off-the-rednecks kinds
of operation lining the interstate approaches to most cities—
and he ran four or five tit-and-ass joints out on Harry Hines,
Northwest Highway. One was a glitzy spot for high-rolling
foreigners in town for the week. All the girls had boob-and-
ass jobs, half of them had the clap most of the time. A number
were HIV positive. Foreigners, Eddy believed, were dirty and
full of disease. They hated rubbers as much as they loved pussy.
But they paid well. Where money was concerned, love and
safe sex were blind.

Eddy stayed out of Moria's places. He preferred the other
clubs, dingy, low-light places where girls fresh out of braces
danced naked through smoke and bright lights five nights out
of seven to try to pay for diapers, the payments on the piece-
of-shit metal housing Moria sold. Most had a husband somewhere—on dope or welfare—maybe in the joint—men jealous
as murder who would fuck up anybody screwing around with
their wives. That was safe sex with some punch behind it.

There were other enterprises in Moria's little kingdom: restaurants, gin mills, Adults Only bookstores, a massage parlor
pretending to be a whorehouse up in Carrollton, just down from
the World of God Tabernacle where the Reverend Will used
a more legitimate and more lucrative scam to rip off the same
morons who bought trailer houses, watered booze, dirty magazines, and cheap pussy from Moria.

But Eddy decided long ago that it was all a front for whatever
it was that Moria really did, whatever it was that kept him in
champagne blondes and stretch limos, and whatever it was that
made him wary of cops most of the time.

The only thing Eddy felt sure of was that it wasn't dope. Cole set him straight on that: Moria's daughter had had too much crack a few years before, passed out in her father's Beemer on a parking lot down in Arlington. Somebody came by and set fire to the car. Gangbangers, likely. That was what the cops thought, what the press said. Moria thought different. He figured it was a low-ball player named Sanderson from Fort Worth who was trying to edge Moria out of a couple of his boob-and-bounce joints. He wanted to deal. Moria didn't. Sanderson was now someplace in the middle of Lake Worth wearing about a half-ton of Readimix. Or so Cole said. Moria didn't screw around with that kind of thing. And since his girl's death, he didn't screw around with dope. Actually, Cole said, he never had. Neither had Cole.

"We're into bigger things," Cole said.

Eddy didn't care. He didn't do drugs either. And like Moria, he had a personal reason.

Eddy sat in Bishop's, smoking unfiltered Camels and nursing a beer. It was his first, he'd been sipping on it for more than an hour while waiting to be called to the back room. Business was heavy today. Four guys had been in and out, quick and nervous. Eddy's beer was flat. He signaled to Bishop, a fat ex-Marine with long grimy hair who always wore tee-shirts with names of rock bands from the sixties. He frowned but put a head on the glass. Then he stood back and folded his arms and waited while Eddy fished a bill out. Bishop gave nothing away, not even to regulars, and Eddy didn't feel like a regular. He didn't want to.

A tall, well-dressed man pushed aside the dirty curtain and came out of the back room. He jerked at the fabric of his shirt, tried to peel it away from his chest while his other hand mopped sweaty film off his face. He wore expensive sunglasses, the haircut said money: New Age Yuppie, Eddy thought. Twelve-banger Jag and five-hundred-dollar shoes.

It was cool in Bishop's, but this guy made it steamy. He straightened his tie and took a good look at Eddy, who flexed his hand around the beer glass. It was a big hand, hairy on the back, full of muscle that ran up into the sleeve of his wind-

breaker. The guy wiped himself down again and left. Bad news,
Eddy thought.

Eddy had met Moria in the joint: Huntsville, Texas Department
of Corrections—the TDC. Eddy was in for aggravated robbery:
two-to-five, parole in six months if he stayed clean. He was
also innocent, but not in the way most of the guys in the joint
are innocent. Eddy was away for the wrong gig. He was picked
up in a sweep, and he decided to cop a plea rather than face
charges for what he had really been doing: selling two crates
of virgin M-16s to a bunch of paramilitary nuts from Lufkin.
Eddy didn't like to deal guns, but Tommy Bodine came into
them cheap: working automatics were worth big money.
Tommy was the contact, he needed backup. Eddy was the best
backup in Dallas. It was what he did then. In a way, it was all
he knew how to do: he was a player.

The buyers were strake, all vets, all former commie crunchers
with nobody but the federal government to hate anymore. Eddy
thought: retards. One was a deputy sheriff. Another was ex-
Highway Patrol. The rest were strictly from encyclopedia sales.
Popped uppers all day, .30-calibers all night. The bumper sticker
on their van read: "God packs a Smith and Wesson: No Fear."
They planned to overthrow the government, Tommy said: A
laugh.

Eddy knew candidates for thorazine when he saw them. Still,
if they wanted to run around in the woods and play soldier
with hot guns, it was nothing to Eddy. Twenty-five grand,
though: that was something to anybody.

Their van was tagged for speeding in Kaufman County, and
the local black-and-white found itself in a running firefight
across half of East Texas—two dead, four wounded, including
the ex-state trooper. Eddy thought: Amateurs. The Alcohol,
Tobacco & Firearms suits hadn't yet tied him with them, but
he figured they would rat him out soon enough. They had wives,
kids, weren't players. Tommy came in on his own and dealt
down to accessory: it beat running. He sent word to Eddy that
he would be on the hit parade soon. It was easier for Eddy to

cop to a bullshit robbery rap, drop out of sight for a while, go
to prison.

There's no place better to hide than prison.

He looked like the guy on the convenience store's security
tape, anyway. Six-two, two-thirty-five, ponytail and a mustache,
body a linebacker works for, but something between the ears.
That didn't show up on the tape. Eddy wasn't jerk enough to
hit a U-Sak-It in broad daylight. Cops should have known that.

Guy comes in with a Kmart squirt gun and sticks it in the
clerk's face. The clerk—maybe nineteen, maybe twenty, all
Indian, scared shitless—pisses his pants and hands over two,
three hundred in small bills, hits the alarm. The guy runs down
Lower Greenville Avenue and ducks into a bar. Ten minutes
later every cop in Dallas is all over the day drinkers, and the
sweep brings them all out into the 100°-plus afternoon for a
shakedown.

Eddy had just finished stashing the twenty-five big ones he
took as his cut from the gun deal, and he walked in with two
hundred and change to blow on a beer and a girl—Monica,
probably—so he was picked up. Next thing, he was downtown
in a cell fighting junkies for a chicken leg. A month later, he
was in the piny woods of East Texas wearing prison whites
and glad he wasn't looking out onto the plains of Kansas.

Weapons is a federal rap. Leavenworth is hard time. Huntsville can be done on a handstand.

It wasn't Eddy's first time away. One assault and a bullshit
breaking-and-entering had introduced him to the Dallas County
penal system. More recently, a carrying-a-concealed-weapon
beef drew him two-to-five—which was Raul Castillo's fault,
that moron, wherever he was.

Castillo was like a bowl of bad chili. Good to have around
once in a while, but always came back at the wrong time.

On the convenience store rap, Eddy asked for mercy and got
a deuce with deductions. Not bad for a con with a sheet.

The Dallas County DA's office liked confession. It was
almost as good for clearing the docket as it was for purging
the soul. Especially in an election year.

Eddy first saw Moria in the exercise yard. He was short, not
in the wiry way so many cons have when they're trying to be

tough: just short. Maybe five-two or three. He was also pudgy, soft. There wasn't any muscle. He walked onto the grass all by himself. His arms stuck out from his body, and even from twenty-five yards, Eddy could see the money: manicured fingernails, high-dollar haircut, used to being taken care of. Eddy thought: Wuss.

But it was all a con. Eddy figured he probably owned strip joints and ran crack and pussy out of the back room. He was right about the joints, right about the pussy, but he was wrong about the cocaine.

Moria squinted into the summer sunlight like it was the first time he'd ever been outside: lost. Eddy figured he'd last about ten minutes in population. The hacks probably brought him right out here from processing, then went up to the tower to make bets. Moria's whites still had their creases: two sizes too big. The cuffs were rolled up, and he could hide a Doberman in the shirt. He looked spongy, just the kind of white meat to attract trouble from the Bloods.

Eddy knew about trouble, he knew about the Bloods. All twenty-to-life, all bad-asses. He'd put three in the hospital already. He didn't like being fooled with, and he didn't need help soaping down in the shower. They bothered him for a week or so, until two broken arms and a set of cracked fingers finally got the word out: Eddy Lovell was nobody's boy. He sure as hell was nobody's girl.

Trouble came quick for Moria. Three of the Bloods who always hung around the bench press stood up and added the short, fat guy in the yard to their inventory. They wore sunglasses—although it was against regulations—they adjusted them carefully, pumped up their muscles, then rolled over toward Moria.

Moria saw them coming and glanced over at Eddy. There was something in his eyes: not fear, not hope, something else, something compelling, something sure. But Eddy never knew exactly what it was or why it made him move. He had been clean for three months now, didn't even curse out loud. But then, he seldom did. He was out of the action completely, and that was his ticket home. It was stupid to get involved, but Moria gave him that look. It drew him in. It was like the small man had been searching for Eddy. Now that he found him, Eddy had no choice. His feet moved him across the grass.

"Back off," Eddy said to the head Blood, a bull named Judd. "He's taken."

"Says who?" Judd was big. Strong safety for the Packers, two seasons. It was an old story: too much money, too many drugs, too many women. He hadn't broken training, though. He'd found steroids more common than crack in the TDC. And he'd developed a taste for white ass. Moria looked ripe.

Eddy figured his belt wouldn't quite cinch around Judd's biceps. It might not cinch around his cock, if the stories he'd heard were true.

"Jimbo," Eddy said. "He's Jimbo's."

The name worked. Judd looked at Moria for a long moment, then he shrugged, turned, led his two buddies back to the bench press.

"Who's Jimbo?" Moria asked. His voice was soft, like a woman's. Eddy turned.

"Runs the Bloods. Runs what else he wants to. Gang rape, double murder. Bad dude. Lifer, four times nonconcurrent: Don't give a shit."

"And I'm his?"

"He's in the hole. Won't be out for ninety days. Then, you're on your own." Eddy wanted to move away. Moria's eyes held him still.

"I'm out of here in ninety days." Eddy shrugged.

"I owe you," Moria said as he turned away.

They didn't talk after that. But Eddy started getting regular mail: cigarettes, rubbers, shit he could trade. The return address was a box number Eddy didn't recognize. Moria stayed by himself on the yard, in clear view, and he kept to himself in his cell. He was in for jury tampering. He was cooling out, waiting for a new lawyer, new trial. Half the guys in Huntsville were waiting for the same thing. But they weren't Moria. Two months, he was gone. Eddy was out a week later.

Getting out early surprised Eddy. He hadn't filed a release plan, had only begun getting ideas together, checking angles. But one afternoon he was called from his cell, ushered into a room where the Parole Board glanced at his folder, gave him the ten-cent speech about keeping himself out of trouble, handed him a suit, shoved him out the front door.

Bob Cole was waiting for him in a new green Town Car. He introduced himself as a "friend of a friend," told Eddy to get in. They grabbed a sack of burgers and hit I-45 North. Eddy asked no questions: a ride was a ride, and there was a bottle of Black Jack on the console and hot R&B on the tape deck. They hit Dallas at midnight, and Cole took him straight to the back room at Bishop's, where Moria was waiting: oysters and beer.

"You drive?" Moria asked Eddy from behind his table, no formalities. It was late. Eddy was tired, a little buzzed from the whiskey. He would have asked to go home, only he didn't have a home. Not anymore.

Moria looked fresh, like he'd just gotten out of bed. His eyes had the same intensity Eddy saw in the yard, but not as helpless. Just certain, casual. His voice was still soft, but not feminine. Just sure. He had a folder in front of him, made notes as he heard Eddy's answers. He was a lot more curious than the Parole Board had been.

Eddy nodded. "License's expired." He stood in front of the table, glancing at Hedge. In the joint, guys like Hedge bore watching. They bore watching anywhere, Eddy thought.

"Get it renewed. Commercial. School?"

"Highland Park, SMU." He pronounced it "Smoo."

"Play ball?"

"Two seasons. Semi pro in Canada. Fucked up my knee."

"Position?"

"Missionary," Eddy smiled.

"Major?"

"Cheerleaders," Eddy smiled wider.

"Cut the shit," Cole ordered.

"Service?" Moria asked. He held his pencil ready to mark.

Eddy shook his head. He glanced at Hedge's solid shadow. Bob Cole sat still and stared at him. Eddy felt like every move he made was being recorded.

"Ever kill anybody?" Moria's voice was easy, quick.

Eddy didn't move. It wasn't a casual question. It wasn't something to kid about. "Nobody you know."

"Know what this is?" Moria gestured to Cole, who reached beneath his chair and put a neat black automatic on the table. Eddy nodded.

"Beretta Pistola Automatica Brevetto," Moria said in a smooth Italian accent. "Seven-point-six-five-millimeter automatic. Two extra clips. Box of ammo. We'll get you a security guard's permit. Officially, you work for Bishop."

"I got a rap on that," Eddy said. "CCW. Other shit, too."

"I know. That's fixed. We'll have the permit by Monday." He tapped the pistol with his pencil. "Load it, carry it, clean it if you shoot it, dump it if you use it."

"I don't like guns." He bent his arms and rubbed his triceps.

"Learn. It's part of your job," Moria said. "I'm not hiring you for muscle. I got him for that." He glanced toward Hedge.

"What you got him for?" Eddy returned Cole's scanning stare evenly. It made him uncomfortable.

"Brains," Moria said.

"And me?" Eddy's eyes stayed locked with Cole's.

"Wit," Moria sighed. "You're a wiseguy."

He nodded again, and Cole pulled a large black bag up and put it on the table.

"I don't think I asked for a job." Eddy returned his attention to Moria, kept his voice level.

"You got something better?" Cole asked.

Eddy shrugged. He didn't. He still had the money in a locker at Love Field. That would carry him for a while. But that money was still hot, so Eddy didn't think much about it.

And there was Raul's deal. But he didn't think much about that, either. Raul was gone.

"I told you: I owe you," Moria said. "You got a job. With us." He nodded at Cole. "You're a driver." He looked at Cole. "Give him the stretch," he said. Cole nodded. "White limo out back. $2,500 a week, and a room. You'll like the room. Class hotel." He reached into his breast pocket, pulled out a sheaf of bills. "Get some clothes. One, two suits, some casual stuff. We like to go to the track. Don't want you to stand out."

"That's nigger work," Eddy said. "I ain't a nigger." In the corner, Hedge shifted.

"You got a prejudice?" Moria's head raised and his eyes squinted.

Eddy chewed on the question a minute. His mind flashed on Monica, Tommy, Ramona, others he had let into his life. "No," he said. "Some of my best friends are short."

"I told you to cut the shit," Cole growled.

"You got a prejudice, you leave it home," Moria said. "Work for me, the only color you see is green."

"I don't want to be a chauffeur."

"You're not a chauffeur. You're a driver. There's a difference," Moria said. He stared at Eddy. The same drawing look Eddy recalled from the prison yard appeared in his eyes. "Look. You did something for me. I'm doing something for you. You don't want it, you got something better, that's fine."

"You don't," Cole sneered. "We checked." His eyes gleamed.

"Then why the interview?" Eddy wanted to sit down. He didn't like standing there like a schoolboy before the principal. Even the goddamn cops let him sit down, he thought. He had to admit, though, behind the table, Moria looked bigger than he was, used to getting what he wanted.

"Want to make sure we've got it all right," Moria said. He looked down at the paper in front of him as if pleased that Eddy reminded him.

"You have family here?"

"Houston—brother," Eddy said, then thought. "I got a sister back East."

"New York," Moria confirmed. "Rich bitch. What's the deal? You ain't close?" Eddy shrugged. Moria's eyes dropped to the file. He went on. "Parents dead: car wreck. Ex-wife in Denver. Kid in California."

Barbara, Eddy thought. A cold panic took root at the base of his spine. He knows about Barbara. The cops didn't know about Barbara, where she was. He didn't think anyone outside his sister and brother knew about her. Even Ellen didn't know, and Ellen probably had more right to know than anyone. But she gave up that right a long time ago.

"You and the kid close?" Cole asked.

"No," Eddy said. "Haven't seen her in years." That was the truth. It made him sad.

"Girlfriend?" Moria went on.

Eddy shook his head with finality. At least there was nothing to know there. Monica wasn't his girl. Monica was everybody's girl. Monica was just a place to fall.

But Monica also knew about Barbara. The thought worried Eddy.

"Princess," Moria said to Cole. He rose and left the room. Eddy saw him pull a small telephone book from his pocket.

"Get a bath, a shave, and the clothes. Lose the Fu Manchu."

Moria smiled. Eddy fingered his mustache. He had worn it ten years. "And get a haircut. You ain't no rock star, so keep it short, neat. Lose the earring, too. Take two days. Enjoy. Eat well, sleep, swim, screw. I don't care. Be ready on Monday."

"Where?" Eddy realized he had accepted the job. He didn't feel uncomfortable about it. The stack of bills looked good.

Moria reached out and opened the black bag.

"Know what this is?"

"Phone."

"Cellular, portable. Seen one before?"

"I've been in jail. Not on the moon."

Moria smiled. "Works like a regular telephone, almost. Instructions are inside. There's one built into the Caddy, Cole's car, too. This is the automatic dial button. It's already set to reach me or Cole. Just punch it. Don't call me on any other phone. Don't use this for anything else. Got it?"

Eddy nodded.

Moria fished a black box out of the bag, "Pager. I try you first on the phone, then this. Wear it everywhere. Take it in the shower. Wear it to bed. Don't even take a dump without it. You drink?" Eddy shrugged. "Two beers. That's your limit in a four-hour period. When I call, I expect you to be where I am in thirty minutes, dressed, sober and ready to go."

"Dallas is a big—"

"Thirty minutes. Dressed, sober, ready to go. Keep the car gassed. I might want to go to the Coast, Vegas, or I might just want to ride around." Cole came back in, nodded once, and sat down. His eyes resumed their roaming around the room.

"If I'm hot, I'll tell you, but always come heavy. You never know."

Moria stuck out his pudgy hand. Eddy shook it once. It had a surprising, firm grip. He nodded when he let it go, picked up the money, the gun and the phone and followed Cole out to the car, a new white stretch limo: Cadillac. Cole tossed him the keys and turned back toward Bishop's, walking fast.

"The Sheraton at LBJ and Coit," he called over his shoulder. "Room 414."

Most of the time Eddy spent in the hotel or in one of several clubs in Deep Ellum, Dallas's downscale blues district, where he liked the music, the girls, the leave-my-ass-alone attitude. From time to time, he'd get a call. Mostly it was to take Moria to the country club or to some hotel or a Highland Park mansion: drop him off, hang around the bar, then drive him home, stay visible. No trouble, no sweat. Easy money.

Sometimes they made the rounds of Moria's joints. Eddy would sit in the car, maybe stand outside and smoke. Hedge stayed with him, always close, silent. Cole was never there. Cole ran his own show, Eddy decided.

Sometimes Moria flew out of town: New York, LA, Mexico. Eddy might go a week or ten days without a call, and while he carried the automatic in a belt holster against the small of his back, he never had to show it. A lot of the time Moria had a woman with him, but that didn't bother Eddy. Princess saw to that.

She met him at the door of the Sheraton's room. Low twenties, five-seven, flat belly, tight ass, long legs, a part-time redhead who would never need a push-up bra. All she said was "Eddy?" when he walked up. She wore spandex biker shorts, a peasant blouse, spiked heels: All American Girl. He nodded, they went in. That was Friday. They didn't come out until Monday morning.

The best thing about Princess, Eddy thought, was that she knew when to end a sentence: right after the first word. He had never been fond of mouthy women, and most of the women in his life fell into that category. Ellen sure had. Ellen could have taken a few lessons from Princess in other departments as well.

For six months, he drove Moria to visit the clubs, bars, mobile home lots, out to the track, up to Oklahoma for cockfights, drop-off and pick-up at DFW airport or Love. Once they went to Vegas. That had been a party, and it pissed Eddy off. Moria took along two hostesses from a mobile home dealers convention. The three of them drank, screwed their way across four states while Eddy kept the Caddy on the road when they weren't stopped to fill up on ice or gas. He should have been able to bring somebody along for himself, he told Moria when he threatened to quit. Moria looked angry about the protest for a moment, then agreed that he was right. After that, Eddy was able to bring whom he wished— usually Princess, but once in a while he brought Monica—on long road trips, just so he kept the one-way glass up and the tape deck low.

Hedge rode in a center seat. Always alone. All he seemed to need or want was cigarettes and sunglasses. Never said shit.

And things went all right for nearly a year. Drive the car, be on time and sober, get laid, get paid. Not a bad gig, Eddy thought, not for a player. The only problem came when he got a call to come to Bishop's and wait, like today. Half the time, he'd just sit there all day and wait, then be told he wasn't needed, to split. He hated it. The barstool bit his ass, and he wasn't allowed to drink enough to get comfortable.

"Eddy?" Moria's voice called him from behind the curtain. That was odd. Usually Cole came out and just swept back the fabric, gestured. Moria seldom raised his voice.

He went through the opening. Moria sat behind his usual plate of oysters and bottle of beer, and Hedge was in his corner as always. Eddy wondered if he ever had to take a leak. He had never seen him leave Bishop's back room except to go to the car. Cole's chair was vacant.

"Sit down," Moria ordered. That, too, was odd.

"Where's Cole?"

"Sit down. Watch."

Eddy took Cole's chair.

Moria picked up a remote control, pointed it against the wall to their right. A TV and VCR were set up there. The snow on the screen raced for a moment, then the picture flickered, blurred, focused.

Eddy looked at the front of a restaurant. Magnolias flanked the door and he could see seated people, eating, drinking behind a glass wall. There was traffic noise from somewhere.

"Red's Steakhouse," Moria said. "Houston." Eddy kept quiet. "South Main, near the Dome. Know it?" Eddy nodded. He had driven Moria and Cole to it a couple of times. "I own it," Moria added. "Major part of it, anyway."

It was a night shot, the camera was fixed. Noise from the street was muffled. The photographer was behind a window— a van, maybe. The arc lamps from the parking lot registered gold on the tape. Some people came from off camera, went into the building. The man held the door open, two couples came out.

One man was black. He wore a white suit and red shirt open to just below his chest. Gold chains formed a thick cascade down from his neck, and he had bright rings and a large watch, Panama hat, broad band. Eddy thought: Pimp.

"That's Johnny Ribbon," Moria said. "Pure dandruff. Son of a bitch, most of the time. Heard of him?"

Eddy shook his head.

Next to Johnny the two girls danced around on silver spiked heels that launched black stockings up narrow thighs into mini-dresses with bare midriffs. Stretch fabric, no underwear, cheap permanent—good-looking. Eddy knew what they were as well. But it was the other man who caught his specific attention: Bob Cole.

Ribbon handed the parking stub to the valet. The group stood on the sidewalk in front of the glass wall, laughing, talking. Ribbon put on sunglasses with a flourish, grinned to expose gold caps on his two front teeth. One of the girls looked to her right, and then they all turned and watched a black Mercedes pull up parallel to the sidewalk. No front plates, tinted windows.

From the camera's angle, Eddy was looking head-on and at a slight angle to the Mercedes. The back curbside window rolled down. The driver wore a hood, but Eddy couldn't see who was next to him. He did see the window drop, and he identified the machine pistol that pulled up and thrust itself through the opening. From the front passenger side, another short, black barrel began to spark, and the tape's soundtrack filled with screams, gunfire, breaking glass.

Johnny Ribbon's white suit was instantly dotted with crimson spots to match his shirt, propelling him backwards into the glass wall. He left the ground before he hit the oversized window. The glass shattered, and Eddy saw the man and woman at the table behind it jump away, try to run. They were knifed down by the rapid-fire weapons. The woman stuck her hand up. It disappeared in blood. The man's head exploded. A waiter raced up, his white coat was stitched with a diagonal line of red splotches before he collapsed. The hooker on the right spun around, leaped across the pimp. Her minidress appeared to be filled with small animals trying to escape while round after round raked the fabric, made her writhe in crazy spasms.

The other girl wove an arm tightly under Cole's left elbow. His right hand was inside his coat, but he remained frozen while a hooded gunman jumped out and finished off Ribbon and the fallen prostitute with blasts of a Desert Eagle .357, one each. Cole didn't glance at him. He didn't move. His face showed no expression, but his eyes fixed on the Mercedes. When the shooter finished, he shoved Cole and the girl into the car. It peeled away sharp toward the camera as the door slammed shut. The tape cut to snow.

"Good movie," Eddy lit a cigarette. His hands were shaking, but he forced them still. "Who's the producer?"

Moria sipped his beer. "It's the director I want," he said.

"We're going to Houston?" Eddy guessed. Moria nodded. "Him, too?" Eddy jerked a thumb toward Hedge, who shifted his weight. He also was smoking, and Eddy felt a sudden unexpected kinship.

"Don't leave home without him," Moria said.

For a moment they sat still, quiet. "Why didn't he shoot back?"

Moria lifted the remote control. "Look again."

He rewound the tape, then ran it forward until the shooting started. He stopped it, advanced it one frame at a time. Eddy watched the pimp fly backwards into the glass, the dining couple fall, the whore cringe down and join the pimp. His eyes moved to the other woman. From a silver evening bag she pulled a small automatic, shoved it into Cole's side, just under his elbow. Cole's hand stopped its movement. No wonder he looked so pissed off, Eddy thought. She had him: cold. There wasn't a thing he could do.

"That's Heather," Moria said. He snapped off the TV. "Real name is Earline. From somewhere around Austin. Bitch is going to wish she'd never left."

"Find her, find Cole," Eddy concluded.

Moria stood up, pulled his coat from the back of his chair. "Find her," he said. He kicked a cardboard box out from under the table. It had Federal Express markings: Overnight Delivery Guaranteed. "Tape came in that two hours ago," he said. "Take a look."

Eddy leaned over and lifted a flap. Inside a Styrofoam liner, smoking from the dry ice that packed it, was Bob Cole's head. His eyes were open, still scanning the empty back room of Bishop's Cafe.

2
Vicki

When the doorbell in Barbara Lovell's West Los Angeles apartment buzzed, Vicki Sigel was in the precise middle of her daily bath. More than a need to be clean prompted the ritual. The near-scalding water contained French milkbath and Oriental oils guaranteed to condition her skin. She greeted the intrusion into her privacy with a frown. It was too early to be Gary: probably some salesman or some kid. The buzz didn't repeat. She settled back into her bubbles, stretched out her legs, one at a time. She admired them.

They were worth admiring. Few women in their high twenties still had legs that good. Vicki had said good-bye to her twenties, but she kept her legs.

And her feet. Her feet were her bread and butter. She had, she often bragged, the "best known tootsies in America." So far, she had made more than two dozen TV commercials for sandals, mail-order pedicure kits, skin-care creams, all modeled or demonstrated by Vicki's bare feet. They were long and slender with high arches, graceful, tapered toes, and were complemented by slim, sexy ankles. She took care of them. She only wore expensive German cross-trainers when she didn't have to dress up. Even then, she carried her heels in a tote bag and slipped them on at the last minute. She ground her heels with pumice stone, bathed them in lotions, and made damned sure that every little half-moon-shaped nail was trimmed and polished every time she walked out the door. She never knew when they would walk her into a major motion picture studio.

From the study of female perfection that were her feet, it was a pleasant march up to her narrow, perfect calves, pert, dimpled knees, slim thighs, fine, tight little ass, and a belly so taut she could bounce a quarter on it. Her boobs weren't large, but big tits were out these days, had been for a while. Her nipples were small, red and perky, slightly upturned. Her long, auburn hair, striking hazel-green eyes, turned-up nose, covered with only the shadow of a nest of freckles, still gave her potential.

She was years away from plastic. She was close to a career. Tonight was the night it could start.

She wiggled her toes and stretched her legs again, held them high above the bubbles. It was a long way from West Texas to Hollywood especially the route she took—but she was almost there. And those legs would go the distance. They launched her ten years ago, when she was a Rangerette at Kilgore Junior College, right in the middle of the Macy's Thanksgiving Day Parade. It was there Roger T. picked her out of the high-kicking lineup. He chased the Rangerettes four blocks before he got her attention, waved her over to the curb beside him. His smile stood out even in that crowd. Vicki wasn't slow to take notice that he was beckoning to her. She wasn't slow to figure out what he wanted, either.

Even now, she couldn't say what made her break ranks and run over to him. It took courage she didn't know she had. It cost her her membership in the Rangerettes, eventually cost her a college degree. But it didn't cost her her virginity. When she was sixteen, she gave that away to Bobby Bailey beneath an oil rig on the rusty banks of the Red River while her steady date, Terry Dee, stood in the parking lot, smoking, waiting for her to come back. She never did. Bobby was all-regional that year. She was homecoming queen. It was a start.

Roger T. said he picked her out because she had the best legs on the line—which was a lie, but she didn't care. They left the parade and the Rangerette chaperon screaming behind them, walked down Broadway to the Flatiron Building, turned and strolled up Fifth Avenue all the way to Grand Central Station. He told her he was an agent for acting talent, and she was the best-looking thing he'd ever seen in a parade. He was *not* the best thing Vicki had ever seen. He was Jewish, tall and skinny, weak-chinned, flat-footed. Normally, she wouldn't have given him a glance. But he was a New York agent: that sold her. This, she decided, was a chance she should take.

In a dark bar on Forty-sixth, she took off her white cowgirl hat and let him kiss her and rub her tits. She allowed him to slide a hand high up under her short skirt where his fingers kneaded her crotch through her tights. But that was it, then. Only after he promised her a part in a TV show did she consent to go home with him.

Smart move, Vicki thought. She sure as hell couldn't have gone home with the Rangerettes—they had a "Code of Conduct" a convent would be proud of—and she didn't have but twenty dollars to her name. That was sewn into her bra. Her purse was back on the bus, she never saw it again.

Ugly as he was, Roger T. was sweet and well hung. He was also half queer: swung both ways. She didn't find that out until later. His apartment was in SoHo, and once they entered, it became home. He got her the part, a bit in a syndicated sitcom—*Neighbors*—shot in a seedy studio uptown. She changed her name from Vicky Bland to Vicki Sigel—the "i" was sexier, Roger T. explained, and "Bland" had to go for obvious reasons. "Sigel might be Jewish," Roger suggested. The role was Tina Twinkle, the college-student-daughter of the neighbors, home for the weekend. Tina was an airhead who bounced around in filmy nightgowns, string bikinis, bare midriffs and crotch-hugging short shorts. She was dating the son, chasing the father, driving everyone crazy by flashing her ass and making suggestive remarks that could be taken a half-dozen ways. Vicki read the part. Major prick-tease, she thought.

She was right. She played it bigger than it was written, stretched her one-shot "guest appearance" into a longer run. Tina transferred to the local college, seduced the father, wore skimpier costumes than ever.

Roger said he always cast against type. It was a good joke. By then, she realized he was, too.

The job lasted five weeks. Roger was gone in two. She caught him in bed with two men, the show's producer and a swishy little cameraman from Chicago. She packed the four outfits Roger bought her and moved to a cheap hotel on the West Side where winos and street junkies flashed her every time she walked to the subway. She got an AIDS test: negative. She couldn't get another part, and junk food was playing hell with her complexion. Her final check barely paid her hotel bill, covered the plane ticket back to Dallas.

She missed finals, flunked out of Kilgore, but the next year she got a job at a high-tipping West End cafe in Dallas. It was a Tina Twinkle kind of place where no one minded the overcooked burgers, rubbery chicken, and wilted lettuce. They came to watch the soft-core tit-and-ass show put on by the waitresses. She took some acting courses at UT-Arlington the following year and did summer stock at Casa Mañana in Fort Worth for a couple of seasons. But she couldn't get back into the student-for-hire groove. Too many patrons kept asking her if she was on the menu. She was having too much trouble saying no to the flashing C-notes that came with the questions. Vicki Sigel: blue plate special.

She turned twenty-one, realized that good legs and a tight ass wouldn't last forever. She sold her car, took a Greyhound for Hollywood.

That was eight years ago. She had no big break, except for meeting Gary, and that wasn't a break. It was just a shot.

When she hit LA, she was broke in a town where not having money was a felony. She could type and answer the phone, so she worked as a temp and held off a horny landlord in Pasadena with Tina Twinkle remarks, short skirts, lots of thigh whenever he came around. A well-timed crotch shot was worth a week's extension. If she left her panties off, it was good for two. A blow job could get her a month's rent free.

When a flu bug knocked out a whole typing pool at Fox, she was called to retype edited TV scripts: dull work for dull people. Gary was a director there. Small-time, but he was straight. He spent most of his energy shooting commercials on subcontract. He found her, just like Roger T. did in New York. But it wasn't her legs that sold him, or her potential as a piece of ass.

"How're your feet?" he asked her one day while he looked over some finished copy.

"My what?"

"How're your feet? Do you have pretty feet? Sexy feet?"

Vicki thought: freak. "You got a thing for feet?" She had been in Hollywood too long not to know that forty-five-dollar haircuts and five-hundred-dollar suits were often worn by the worst perverts, the kind of guys who liked it hard and dangerous, the kind who hurt women for fun.

"No," he laughed. "We're shooting a spot for Dr. Scholl's sandals. I need an actress with good feet.

"There's not much acting to it, really. All you do is slip on the sandals and make them look comfortable. Walk around a little."

"I'm not union."

"That can be handled." He winked.

"I won't fuck for a part," she lied.

"Give head?" He smiled, but there was nothing mean in it.

"Not that either."

"I've been known to cast for talent."

"What makes you think I've got any?"

"Cute accent, pretty hair, great legs, nice ass, drop-dead smile, eyes that would look good over the rim of a wineglass. What'd' you say?"

"I don't think so." Vicki flashed a false smile. "Call me when you've got some lines."

"I might just call you anyway." He pulled out an address book and gold Cross pen. "I've got a great set of wineglasses. What's your number?"

"Eat shit." She smiled.

"It's for network. Two hundred above scale plus residuals. If you get it, I can probably get you more work. And a union card." He continued to hold the pen.

"Easley-eight, seventy-four forty-eight. It really is 'Eat-Shit': E-A-T-S-H-I-T." Vicki held her smile. "That's my agent's line."

He looked at her. "You have an agent?"

"Yep. And I don't fuck him either."

"You as talented as you are tough?"

"I'm not tough." She ran her tongue slowly over her teeth. "I'm just experienced."

"Stage Three. Eight o'clock." He scrawled an address on a pad. "Sharp. This is a cattle call, so come prepared to spend the day."

"Will I get it?" She looked at him steadily.

He smiled again. "Depends: How're your feet?"

Vicki got the sandals commercial. She was surprised to see how many veteran actresses young and old showed up to wiggle their toes—and their tits—for Gary and the sponsor's representative's inspection. She was more surprised to see how many stripped all the way out of their jeans and slacks when they were called up to audition, leaning over and giving Gary and everyone else a good look at braless boobs under the largest collection of loose-necked sweaters and flimsy tee-shirts she had ever seen. Some were overweight, old. They strutted around in their panties, made sure Gary and the sponsor got a full view of their crotches and asses pressed tight under skimpy briefs two sizes too small. Others were just kids, barely out of school, barely out of somebody's bed. A lot of the girls knew each other. While they waited to be called, they huddled and snorted coke. Vicki stuck to decaf and had a chat with the sponsor's rep's assistant during the first break. He was discreet when he ogled her buns as she walked away.

When her turn came, she kept her slacks on, rolled up the cuffs. Her feet were great. "Sexiest goddamned feet I've ever seen," she heard Gary say while she modeled the sandals in the audition. "Just looking at them gives me a hard-on." He invited her to lunch. She turned him down. Dinner, too. The next day, she did the shoot. Four hours' work and more money than she made in a week as a temp. They went to dinner that weekend.

Gary came through: got her into SAG. More commercials, all featuring her feet, followed. She didn't go down on him until after the third one, a month later. She still hadn't fucked him, although she had been to bed with five other guys: all actors she met around the studio, and one hopeless shortstop for San Diego. All for fun, except the shortstop. He'd been called up, played two out of five games, went 0 for 8 and made five errors. They were sending him back down to El Paso. She caught him on the fall, felt sorry for him.

She always felt sorry for losers.

But she never felt sorry for Gary. She remembered Roger T., and she wanted to get more out of Gary before she gave him what he wanted. She also wanted to make sure he was as straight as he seemed.

He seemed to be. If he dated other girls, she didn't know it, and he didn't show any signs of having a thing for boys—or men. He didn't do anything heavier than marijuana, didn't do that unless somebody handed him a joint. She accused him of faking it even then.

He smiled. "That's a funny thing for a woman to say."

She leaned forward in the tub, opened the hot water tap. Gary was a producer now. In Hollywood that didn't mean diddly. Half the busboys and parking attendants in LA were producers. But Gary was also her agent. She had lied before. The Eat-Shit number belonged to her landlord, who also put it on his license plate. Gary had promised her a four-ad deal for an Isotoner Christmas spot, followed by two Band-Aid ads and a spot for skin softener.

But promises were cheap: pussy costs. She'd had it with commercials. She wanted a role: TV or film. Didn't matter. She was past thirty, and her butt might decide any day to take a one-way trip to her thighs. Suzanne Somers might have played twenty when she was forty, but Vicki was a realist. It took two hours three times a week at the spa to keep the cellulite at bay, the tummy tight, calves toned, bottom cute. Gary could find either a role or somebody else to hustle, somebody else to fuck.

When she thought about it, though, she had to admit he had never really hustled her. There were late dinners, long lunches, two drives up the coast, a handful of overnights at each other's apartment when they both had a lot to drink. But no moves. Now and then a suggestion, especially on the overnights, but one wound up on the sofa, the other in bed. At breakfast they joked about the isometric value of enforced celibacy.

She hadn't seen anybody else in six months. But at every audition there were so many good-looking teenagers hanging all over Gary, rubbing their tits on him, wiggling their asses for him, she couldn't understand what made him stay with her. It must be more than a hope that he could sleep with her. Whatever it was, she was determined to make it work for her, to make sure that he delivered the goods before he got the payoff. If what he wanted was between her great-looking legs, then he was going to need something more than a hard-on: He was going to have to come up with a contract.

The doorbell buzzed again, and she lowered herself back into the diminishing bubbles.

"Goddamn salesmen." She growled. Or political pollsters, or some kid with a fistful of magazine coupons he honestly believed would pay his way to college. But it could be somebody for Barbara, she thought. It was Barbara's apartment.

Vicki was staying over to cut down on Gary's crosstown drive-time. They were going to a party in Hollywood. Ron Howard was supposed to be there, Robert Redford and John Malkovich, too. Maybe Tom Hanks. A handful of starlets looking to get laid were coming. But Gary said none of the gum snappers had a chance. There was talk of a new film, a western, shot on location in Montana.

"They've got Juliette Lewis for the title role. But they're looking for a second lead: older sister part," Gary told her.

"Fuck you."

"Fuck them," he grinned. "*Or* me. For once. That might work. Change your karma. You might get lucky."

She figured he was the one who hoped to get lucky. If the party was good, if the part was for real, he just might: time to give a little. She spread her hands into a diamond shape and framed her pubic area under the bubbles. He was trying, he seemed to like her. And the heavy petting and oral sex was getting to her: wasn't natural. Maybe it was getting to him, too. Maybe that's what the holdup really was. He also told her he was up for first assistant director on the production. Normally, he wouldn't take it, he told her, but working with Howard could be a break for him. Her, too. He winked when he said it. Had he meant it? Vicki couldn't tell.

The buzzer sounded again.

"Go away," she shouted. She liked to stay in the tub a good half hour as the Vietnamese woman who ran the herb-and-oils shop in Venice told her. The woman claimed to be over eighty and had the skin of a pampered child. No teeth, though. Just black gums. The milkbath was Vicki's own addition. She slid further down into it, resolved to ignore the doorbell. If it *was* somebody for Barbara, she wasn't here, anyway. If it was Gary, he could drive around a while. These blandishments cost too much to waste.

She had only known Barbara about six months. Sweet kid, well raised, but nuts. She was also a Texas girl, born in some small town Vicki had only heard of once or twice before. Their friendship was instant and mutual. They both worked out regularly, and that was all they had in common, but they got along well in spite of their age difference. Not more than nineteen, probably, Barbara claimed to be twenty-three. It was funny, Vicki thought. She spent the first twenty-one years of her life trying to be ten years older, and the rest of it trying to be ten years younger. Vicki shaved years off her resume like hair off her legs. Barbara had a variety of fake IDs to get her into nightclubs and bars. Even so, Barbara acted older than nineteen, and often Vicki acted younger than her thirty-one years herself. Early maturity and arrested emotional development: a good team.

They met at the studio. Barbara worked in the Fox commissary part-time while she took courses at UCLA. She had no ambitions to work in the movies or TV. Didn't even like movies. Wouldn't go with Vicki to see any, and Vicki went almost every night. Vicki's life was the movies.

Barbara was majoring in criminal science, said that as soon as she finished, she was going to apply for the police academy in LA. She was dating a cop, a homicide detective from Santa Barbara named Sandobal, a transplant from New York, or New Jersey. Vicki thought: Yankee.

Sandobal was in law school, working his way through as a cop, and Barbara thought that was a great plan. Vicki thought: Waste of brains and looks. And they were in love. Or in lust. So it seemed from the noises that came from the bedroom when he was there, when Vicki stayed over, slept on Barbara's sofa—couple of animals. It was insane. Laughable. He roared, she moaned. Vicki thought: Blue radio.

Barbara was well-built, not muscled up, but solid. She worked out daily and was a dead shot with the .38 Smith and Wesson she kept loaded but locked up in a battered metal briefcase next to her bed.

"It's my 'bidness,'" she claimed when she first showed it to Vicki. "A present from Eddy, my dad. He said if I was going to live out here with all the 'fruits and nuts,' I needed some protection. So I learned how to use it. He was in prison. In Texas," she added: matter-of-fact.

Vicki thought that was a lousy recommendation. She had never known anyone who knew anyone who had been in prison, and she hated guns. She had since her mother ate her father's .44. Everyone said it was an accident, but accidents like that just don't happen. Then he died—hunting accident, the same bunch of everyones said, only Vicki knew better. Hard to shoot yourself in the back of the head. She stopped thinking about that five minutes after the funeral. She sold every one of his firearms, even two air rifles and a pellet gun. She spent the rest of high school on an aunt's farm near Carney Wells. There were guns there, too. Vicki never touched them.

Barbara talked Vicki into going to a shooting range with her once. There Vicki showed off her hatred of shooting by keeping her eyes closed and missing the target every time. Barbara could group six shots in a space the size of an orange at fifty yards.

"You're just scared of guns," she told Vicki.

"Not afraid. Just don't like them."

"It's just like sex."

"Not as loud," Vicki said. Barbara blushed.

She made Barbara agree to keep her .38 locked up, refused to come over unless her friend promised her the weapon was in the briefcase, locked. Barbara thought it was funny. Vicki never laughed.

Barbara was not cop material in Vicki's opinion. She might make it on Rodeo Drive where the worst offense was some drunk or a rich cokehead driving crazy, but in LA, rookies were routinely sent to the East Side, East LA: gangbangers, junkies, hookers, wetbacks, and escaped felons. They'd eat this pretty, brown-eyed brunette alive. In Vicki's estimation, Barbara thought "hard drugs" meant regular coffee and a cigarette, that "around the world" was a yo-yo trick. She knew she had a rich aunt somewhere, rich uncle, too. Knew she had grown up used to the better things in life. Barbara could tell the difference between wines, the difference between bottled waters. The girl had taste, no question. There was a strong side to her as well, just not tough enough to be a cop.

No, Vicki told herself often, Barbara had a deep streak of softness in her that she couldn't hide under a set of starched blues, no matter how much she worked out or how tightly she shot a pattern. She had been pampered, even if she didn't want to be. She beamed money even if she didn't have any.

The doorbell buzzed once more. Then again. Longer this time. Son of a bitch was leaning on it. Vicki swore aloud, rose from the tub. She used the shower massage attachment, washed off the bubbles.

It had better not be Gary, she warned herself. He'd be two hours early, and she wasn't ready. She still had to wash her hair, put on makeup, figure out how she was going to get a size nine body into Barbara's size seven dress.

Then, she thought, it might *be* Barbara. Vicki had the only key. Barbara had a late afternoon aerobics class. Wasn't due home until five-thirty. Maybe she pulled a muscle or something, came home early. Wouldn't be the first time, Vicki thought. That girl pushes herself too hard.

She stepped out of the tub, grabbed an oversized towel. Except for the ends, her hair wasn't wet. She wrapped it anyway. She coiled the towel around herself, inspected her shape in the mirror. Her legs were as good standing barefoot as they looked in heels. Last week, Gary said Hanes was looking for someone for a series of spots to launch a new line of runproof panty hose. The idea was a bunch of bimbos playing beach volleyball in bikinis, wearing the hose, of course, showing how they wouldn't run or tear even under stress. "Feet to legs," he grinned. "It's a move up."

She frowned at the idea. Fuck ads. It was time for a real role. With lines. Gary needed to get off *his* ass if he wanted a piece of *hers*.

The buzzer sounded again, longer yet, more insistent. She stomped out of the bathroom and down the hall, leaving wet footprints on the Spanish tile.

The apartment was in an old but stable neighborhood on a wide boulevard that still had sidewalks safe enough for people to use. No urban renewal, not yet. It was constructed back when apartments were temporary addresses for tenants on their way up. They were roomy, airy, decent places to live, but not fancy, and the rent was cheap, at least for LA.

Vicki peeked through a side window and spotted two bicycles. "Bicycles?" she asked aloud. "What kind of salesmen ride bicycles?" She thought: twerps.

The spy hole revealed a distorted view of a clean-cut young man with a too-short haircut. He wore a white shirt, black tie.

"Mucking Formans," she whispered. "Screwing up people's afternoon." She recalled seeing the duet of missionaries roving the street when she pulled up. There had been an article in the *LA Times* about how many were "invading" the city a couple of weeks ago.

Resentment crept up on her again. Her good mood was ruined. She felt mean, cheated. She decided to give them a show, teach them to bother people with their holy bullshit, scare the little fuckers' nuts off.

She flung open the door and fanned the towel out like a cape.

"Well, boys, they got anything like this back at Bring 'Em Young?"

The two young men stood there agape. Their eyes enlarged. They gawked at her. One was slightly built and red-headed. His hair was cropped close to his skull, and there was a tiny hole in his earlobe. Did Mormons allow earrings? Vicki didn't know. The other was dark-haired and stockier than his companion: thick-lipped, dull. He clutched a large nylon duffle in one hand. One hand hefted his crotch.

Vicki stood still, an evil leer pasted on her face, then closed the towel and put her hand on the doorknob.

"Why don't you boys go to a titty bar?" she asked, began to move the door shut. "Get a real peek. Get laid, get drunk. Do something normal before you're too old to appreciate it. God won't care. Really."

The two exchanged a quick glance. Then, the dark-haired one grabbed his stomach, doubled over.

"Quick," the other said. "He's having a reaction."

"You can't have a reaction from *looking.*" She knotted the towel in front of her and blushed at the same time.

"He's diabetic." His companion was groaning and gasping for breath. "He's having an insulin reaction. You got some orange juice? A Coke? Just sugar will do. Anything sweet." He put his arm around the dark-haired boy, guided him toward the open door. "I got to lay him down."

Vicki instinctively backed away and allowed the redhead to escort his ailing companion past her into the apartment.

"Go get some juice or a Coke, for God's sake. I'll call an ambulance." He dumped him on the sofa, fetched the bag from the landing, shut the door behind him. "Move, please!" His voice cracked in panic.

Vicki leaped to the kitchen. Barbara had carrot, apricot, and celery juice in the sparsely stocked refrigerator: no orange juice, not even a diet soda. She rifled through the shelves.

"I found some brown sugar. Is that—"

"Pour it in a glass of water. Quick!" he called from the living room.

She did so, wondered if it mattered whether the water was warm or cold.

"Here," she said as she passed through the swinging door. "I—"

The scene that greeted her was far different from what she expected. She stopped. A chill ran up from her damp legs, made her shudder.

The dark-haired boy was now standing upright and casual, a long hunting knife in his hand. He was smiling. The redhead was next to him, also grinning. He had a long-barreled revolver aimed at Vicki's belly. A lump formed in her throat, immediately dove to her lower abdomen where it took root and grew. She looked at them with a hot awareness of her own stupidity. Now, she saw them as they really were. They were not "boys." Not "twerps."

"It's not even my—"

"Come over here and shut up," the redhead ordered. She didn't move. He cocked the revolver. "We can do this hard, or we can do this easy." She stayed where she was.

"Look." He glanced at the dark-haired man. "If you're not over here in ten seconds, I'm going to put a bullet through your kneecap. Won't kill you. But it's going to hurt like hell, and you'll never walk on that leg again."

That penetrated the fuzz surrounding her brain. She walked over to him. She bit her lip to keep from screaming. One hand stayed up at her breast, the towel knotted inside it. Her breath made wind tunnels of her ears.

"On your knees."

She lowered herself, feeling as much anger as fear. "If this is all you want, then—"

"I said for you to shut up." There was no threat, no anger in his voice. He was almost tender. "You talk too much. Now, you're going to listen."

"Well, at least use a condom. I don't need—"

He put the gun's long barrel in her mouth. "Shhh. We don't need no rubber. It's a new gun. A virgin."

Vicki's anger instantly evaporated, and a new sort of fear was born. She was shaking. The gun barrel clicked against her front teeth.

The redhead smiled. "Keep your tongue on the barrel. You blink once for yes, twice for no. Don't even try to talk. This is a .22 Magnum. It'll do the job. If I pull the trigger, you're gone, and the neighbors won't hear anything more than if you popped a pimple. Got it?"

After a second or two, she blinked.

"I'm Red, this is Blackie. That's all you need to know. Got it?"

She blinked. Blackie made a show of shaving off some hair on his forearm with the knife's blade.

"He likes to hurt people. Like to hurt you. Got it?"

She blinked.

Blackie started ransacking the apartment. He pulled out drawers and upturned them. He found a pile of envelopes—Barbara's bills and letters—glanced at them, nodded to Red, threw them down on the floor. He cut through the telephone cord. He went into the bedroom and in a few moments came back with the other telephone, dumped it on the sofa.

"Now, like I said," Red went on, "we can do this hard, or we can do this easy. If we do it easy, you're going to be fine. Nobody's going to hurt you. If we do it hard, you wind up dead. Or worse." He glanced at Blackie, who went back into the bedroom. She heard him dumping out more drawers. "Got it?"

Bile rose in her throat, but she swallowed hard and blinked. There were tears in her eyes. The knobby sight on the revolver's barrel cut the roof of her mouth. The barrel's tip touched a filling, and magnetic pain shot down her neck. She had to force herself to remain still. Her hand still held the knot of the towel in front of her. The other was clenched down at her side. She could feel her nails bite into her palms.

"We're going to take a little trip," Red said. His smile was not reassuring. Blackie came out with Barbara's metal briefcase. The pistol was inside, and Vicki felt a new surge of panic. He started banging on the combination lock with the hilt of his knife.

"Put that down," Red ordered.

Blackie looked at him for a second or two, shrugged, dropped it.

"We're not thieves, and we're not rapists," Red explained: patient. She didn't know if he was talking to her or to Blackie. "We're professionals. Stop acting like a fucking jerk and get her some clothes."

Blackie shoved the knife into his belt and moved back into the bedroom. "What you want? A dress?"

"No. Shorts. Sweats. Stuff like that. Bring them out here."

"What—" Vicki started to ask around the gun's barrel. Blackie shook his head.

"Shhh. You're doing fine. Keep quiet, and you're going to make it. I like it easy." He spied her purse on a table near him. With one hand he grabbed it, dumped it out, used a finger to sort through the contents. Then he looked at her closely. "You got a habit? We need to take your stash?"

She blinked twice, rapidly.

He looked disappointed. " 'Just say no,' huh? Good girl. That'll make things easier."

Easier for what? Vicki demanded silently. What's happening here? The fear that had grown into a large, solid rock inside her began to liquify.

Blackie returned with a mauve running suit. Barbara's. He also had a fistful of lingerie: Vicki's. Frilly stuff, too fancy to wear under sweats. She had brought it for the party, laid it out on the bed before she bathed.

"Get up and get dressed. And no talking." He withdrew the pistol. "None. I mean it."

She rose slowly and pulled on the underwear. Her mouth tasted oily from the pistol's barrel. She swallowed hard into her churning stomach. He watched her impassively as she stretched the nylon suit onto her legs, all the time trying to keep herself covered with the towel. He lowered the gun, but it stayed in a position where he could raise it, shoot her in a second. Blackie leaned against the sofa, leered at her.

She tried to swallow, almost choked. "Could I have a drink of water?" she asked in a hoarse whisper.

He looked at her sharply, shook his head.

She unwrapped her hair, pulled the top of the suit over the flimsy bra, then looked down at her bare feet.

"Get her some shoes. Find some go-fasters. We don't want her to look weird."

"We gonna get something to eat?" Blackie asked.

"Later."

"You said we could eat."

Red lifted the gun slightly. For a second, Vicki thought he

was going to shoot his companion. "We'll eat later. We're behind schedule. Now, get the goddamn shoes."

Blackie obliged, and she strapped the running shoes onto her bare feet with a wince. They were still pruny from the bath. Fungus within the hour, Vicki thought.

She followed Red's instructions, returned to her knees in front of him. He told Blackie to get her a glass of water. She sipped from it, and he put the gun back in her mouth. The water hit her stomach like acid. She gagged, then found control once more.

Blackie pulled tee shirts, jeans, and matching leather bomber jackets from the duffle. They took turns holding the pistol while they changed. They were well-muscled beneath their clothes, had worked out. But they didn't show off for her: all business. They left the "Mormon costumes" wadded on the floor. Red also put an earring in his left ear: a diamond stud. Larger and more expensive than anything Barbara owned. She thought: Punk.

"Ready?"

Blackie nodded.

"Okay. Now, we're going to walk right out of here, down the stairs, and to a brown Lincoln parked on the curb."

That was a red zone. Vicki prayed it had been towed.

"You keep your mouth shut. If somebody says something to you, you tell them we're your cousins. From Texas. You're taking us to SeaWorld. If they push it, tell them we'll spend the night and be back tomorrow. Got it?" He waited. "Got it?"

She blinked.

"Say anything else, even one word, you're dead. So are they. Got it?"

She blinked and fought back nausea once more. Her body was losing control. Her stomach was cramping. Get tough, she ordered herself.

"You're looking bad." Red's eyes narrowed. "You better have it straight."

"I feel sick as shit," she spoke around the barrel. She didn't care what happened to her. She wasn't ready to go anywhere feeling like she did: gun or no gun.

"You're well enough to get to the car. It's a short walk."
He cocked the gun again. "Or you can hang around and let
LA's Finest wipe your brains off the wall. Which do you want?
Go and live. Stay and die. Make up your mind."

She swallowed her sickness once more, blinked.

"Thought so." He stood up, thumbed down the hammer,
put the gun in his belt beneath his jacket. Blackie drew the
knife, hid his hand under his coat.

She stood, and they escorted her out of the apartment. Blackie
was on her left, and she could feel the pressure of the knife in
her side. Once out on the landing, Blackie pulled up short.

He shoved the bicycles inside the apartment. Only one went
in all the way. The other jammed between the frame and open
door. Blackie reached out to help him, but Red slammed the
door against them, forcing them inside.

"Should have took them with us," Blackie muttered.
"Didn't even wipe them down."

"You didn't do that?"

"You didn't tell me to."

"You're a dumb motherfucker, you know that?" Red asked
him.

Blackie looked puzzled, then nudged Vicki. "Give me the
key."

"I don't have the key," she said softly. "I don't even
have—"

"Fuck it. Let's go," Red barked and shoved her along.
Blackie fell in behind her.

They saw no one on the landing, stairs, or in the courtyard.
When they reached the sidewalk, she saw to her disappointment
that even though the Lincoln sat in a well-marked No Parking
Zone, it was still there. She had been towed away twice when
she couldn't find one of the visitors' spaces empty.

It was after five, people were home. Several were out water-
ing their yards, a half-dozen joggers were in evidence. No one
here knew her. No one could help her if they did. She wanted
to run, but the boulevard stretched away straight on both sides:
no chance.

No breath either. She thought she was in good shape, but

every intake of air seemed shorter than the last. Her heart was thumping hard beneath the running suit.

They were almost to the Lincoln when Barbara's black '67 Mustang wheeled up into a numbered parking slot. Vicki felt her whole body tense, ready to leap. Red and Blackie paid Barbara no attention, but she opened the door and jogged over to them with a curious smile on her face. They pulled up, surprised, edgy. Vicki felt Blackie's knife prod her.

"Hi," Vicki said before Barbara could speak. "I knew you were going to drop by, but my cousins. . .uh, from Texas came in and surprised me. Hope you won't be disappointed." She rolled her eyes, flicked from left to right, hoped Barbara could read her.

Red and Blackie pasted grins on their faces. Barbara's dark eyes were confused. She looked at the running suit: hers. "Nice fit," she said.

"Been meaning to diet," Vicki said.

"What's going—"

"This is Red, this is Blackie," Vicki almost shouted and nodded at her two companions. Blackie's grip on her forearm tightened. She could feel the knife's point piercing the fabric of his jacket. She forced her tone down to normal. "Guys, this is—uh, a friend of mine."

The two men muttered something. Barbara continued to stare open-mouthed.

"Cousins," Vicki went on hurriedly. She waved her hand in a general eastern direction. "From Texas! We're going to SeaWorld! Won't be back till late. Maybe tomorrow! Hey, water my plants and take care of my mail, okay?"

She sounded so fake, so phony, surely Barbara saw something was wrong.

Blackie pinched the flesh of her arm. Red turned toward her, thrust his hand inside his jacket, took her other arm hard. Vicki thought: Bruises.

"Listen, we got to go," she chirped. She looked toward the Lincoln. Down the street, the LAPD turned the corner. Fear shifted out of the way, hope swelled inside her: About fucking time.

"Yeah, pleased to meet you," Red muttered, his eyes flickering between the two women and the approaching patrol car.

"Yeah," Blackie grumbled. "See ya." He turned Vicki around, steered her toward the Lincoln. The black-and-white slowed down when they spotted the illegally parked vehicle.

"See ya." Vicki repeated—dumb. She turned her head. Both men were keeping their heads down, eyes on the cops. "Help me," she mouthed silently to Barbara, who chose that moment to look at the apartment building, as if checking to make sure that she was in the right place. Barbara's hands were on her hips. Her mouth still hung open. She didn't move.

Vicki looked around, saw the prowl car cruise on by. Hope rushed out, chased it, waving and shouting. Vicki stood still, held her breath. They turned the corner. Red opened the back door. Shit, Vicki thought. Fear returned, twisted her stomach again. She felt herself sinking into a black hole as Blackie guided her toward the Lincoln.

The car was new and had dark-tinted windows. Red stood back from the open door. Blackie gave her a sharp nudge, and she scooted into the vehicle: leather interior. The inside door handles had been removed. Blackie followed her, Red went around, entered the driver's seat, they pulled away.

"The thing about the plants was a nice touch," Red complimented her.

"The mail, too," Blackie said.

She looked over her shoulder and saw the cops returning from the opposite direction. Hope still chased them, but it was losing ground. Barbara had disappeared.

Blackie reached down into the floorboard, pulled up a bright set of handcuffs.

Vicki recoiled, but he grabbed her wrist, pulled it behind her.

"Case you get any ideas." He pulled her other arm around, snapped the bracelets over her wrists. He squeezed her breast when he pushed her back

"Watch it, buster," she shot automatically.

He flicked out his hand, slapped her solidly across the face.

"Cut it out, man! And you: Shut the fuck up," Red ordered.

Vicki's sickness surged up. Her cheek stung. Her insides roared. When the car entered the boulevard lane, she leaned over and vomited. What was left of a fairly expensive lobster salad Gary bought her for lunch spilled out between her legs, splashed up onto the trousers of the running suit.

"Godfuckingdamn!" Blackie shouted. He gagged loudly in sympathetic reaction. "She's blowing beets back here!"

"Get hold of yourself!" Red yelled.

"I need water," Vicki gasped. She heaved again: gagged, choked. "I need—"

"Shut the fuck *up!*" Red shouted. "I ain't going to tell you again."

He wheeled the Lincoln around a corner, lowered all the windows.

"There's a gas station," Blackie spoke through a tight throat, gasped, breathed through his mouth.

Red turned into the parking area and jumped out. Blackie hung his head out a window, gulped air.

Vicki was shivering, too weak to move. The handcuffs bit into her wrists.

Red returned and flung in a wad of wet paper towels.

"Wipe it up, clean her up," he said.

He went inside the station and returned in a moment with a can of 7-Up. He opened the door, got in, handed it to Blackie.

"Here," he said. "Let her drink this slow. Clean her up."

Vicki forced herself to stop heaving, hyperventilating. She took a sip of the drink, then another, tried to will her stomach to be still. Red pulled the car back out into traffic, and Blackie mopped her with the towels. His hands were careful, almost gentle on her legs.

She leaned back when he finished, allowed him to hold up the can so she could sip the soda, then tried to make herself comfortable. Her hands were in the way. She squirmed.

"Pull another stunt like that, and you're going to be more trouble than you're worth," Red warned. "So get your shit together, and I mean now!"

"What do you want with me?" Vicki asked finally. "Where're we going? Tell me that at least."

Red looked at her in the rearview mirror. "Texas," he said. "That's all you need to know. Be a good girl, and you'll get there alive."

"Who are you?"

"That's none of your business. So shut up," Blackie growled. He had the wet, wadded towels in his hand. "I need to stop. My hands smell like shit."

"Why didn't you wash them back there?" Red asked.

"They didn't stink then. I—"

"We'll stop in a while." Red pulled up onto the freeway and pushed into rush-hour traffic.

Vicki squirmed, sought a comfortable position. She looked out the rear window. Barbara would go upstairs, see the mess, call the cops. This would all be over soon. She leaned back, kicked off her shoes, put her soiled, wet legs up on the seat in front of her. Her feet were damp, but they would dry. No real damage done. Not yet. The dress she was borrowing from Barbara had long sleeves, would cover any bruises. She mentally checked her face: number two pancake, she thought. She looked out the window. Any minute now a black-and-white would be pulling in behind them, lights going, siren blaring. They wouldn't get out of the county.

Another thought struck her. There would be cops, so there would be reporters. That meant publicity. Eleven o'clock news for sure. She couldn't buy this kind of coverage! If they had trouble finding them, chased them long enough, she could make the *Morning Report*. "Starlet Kidnapped," she read a headline in her mind's eye. Gary would be thrilled! She wished she had washed her hair.

Now empty of fear, she sensed a kind of excitement growing inside her. She glanced at Blackie, who stared out at the bumper-to-bumper traffic around them. A resolve stiffened inside her.

"Listen, I want some clean clothes. These don't fit for shit. And while you're at it, I'm going to need some socks. And I want a bath. I need to wash my hair."

"You can make do," Blackie grunted. "Or you can fucking die."

''You boys talk tough,'' she shot at him. ''But have you got a lot to learn about women.'' They had a lot to learn about everything, she thought, then, with a long look at the back of Red's cropped head, she felt the fear once more creeping around her insides. She closed her eyes. So do I, she said to herself, so do I.

3

Houston

It was hard for Eddy to tell if it had rained in Houston. "In Houston it never really rains," his brother, Quince, once said. "It just pisses on you. God doesn't like Houston." Eddy wondered why Quince stayed there if he hated it so much. But then, Eddy never understood Quince. He never much liked him, either. Piss on him, Eddy thought.

A fine mist covered the glass. He flipped on the windshield wipers, but the only effect was to spread bug goo in a white smear. He hit the washer. The mess liquified, got worse, mist continued. He thumbed down the window, looked out that way.

It really wasn't even piss, Eddy thought. Mostly it was just peter dribble. Houston stank like a toilet in a cheap bar.

When the big Buick skimmed around the interchange from I-45 to 610-East, wisps of steam rose from the blacktop beneath the onrush of five o'clock traffic. In Dallas, people got out on the freeways and hauled ass: in a hurry, going someplace. In Houston people just drove fast, like it was required to keep the car. Then they all just stopped. Sat. No reason. No construction, no wreck, no nothing. They all just stopped.

The trip down the interstate had been quiet but strained. Moria planted himself in a deep sulk on the passenger side.

Hedge was a silent lump against the back door, right behind Eddy. Except for a Cowboys windbreaker thrown over his huge shoulders and a pair of sunglasses, he looked the same as he always did: a small mountain with hair. He cracked his black-tinted window, chain-smoked. Eddy thought: smoldering piece of luggage. Except this particular baggage had fish-green eyes behind dark shades focused on the back of Eddy's head. He also kept a 12-gauge Winchester pump on the floorboard between his feet.

Eddy also lit one cigarette after another. He had burned the better part of two packs of Camels before they hit Conroe and the Houston outskirts. He was nervous. This whole thing felt bad. So did his throat.

When they left Dallas, Bishop provided them with a cooler full of Bud, sandwiches, and several packages of Fritos. Moria drank one beer right away, then he nursed the second, ate nothing. Eddy didn't eat or drink. If Hedge helped himself, he never saw it. Eddy put the Buick on the blacktop and kept it there. Excepting a pit stop for gas and a john north of Huntsville, they hadn't left the car. Even then, Hedge stayed inside, his door slightly open. Eddy thought: Hollow leg.

Moria was in a blue funk. Eddy figured he was pissed off about Cole—or maybe grieving. He wanted to be sympathetic, but he couldn't work it up. Cole was a hard guy to miss.

After an hour of silence, Eddy felt the need to talk, break the silence. It ate at him. If somebody didn't say something, he would. "Guess you and Bob were together a long time."

Moria sipped his beer. "Yeah. Since 'Nam."

"Too goddamn bad."

"Yeah. I figured we humped about six hundred miles of shitty trails. Booby traps, ambushes, snakes, spiders, sappers, screwed-up maps, friendly fire, nape and Agent Orange. Came out without a scratch. Cole had this great sense of danger. He could see through the fucking trees."

"So what happened last night?"

"Even the best get stupid," Moria said. "You can't trust nobody. Nothing. This goddamn city's worse than 'Nam." He sighed deeply, shook his head. "Worse than anywhere. Got to watch your ass every second. Thought Cole knew that."

He looked hard at Eddy. "Don't get the wrong idea. We were partners, not lovers. I run the show. This ain't no sentimental journey. Cole got whacked. That's it. I need to know who, and I need to know why. And I need to know what Cole—" He bit off the sentence, rubbed his chin quickly. "What he was into."

"I thought you were partners. You don't know what he was into?"

"Like I said, we weren't lovers. He had his own piece here and there."

"Sort of a profit-sharing program. Fringe benefits," Eddy said. He regretted it. Moria's face hardened.

"It ain't funny," he said.

Eddy shook his head. Moria had that right. "So, what next?"

"We'll look for the twist. Heather Whatshername. Maybe the hit was on Johnny, and Bob just got in the way."

"Pimps don't get hit like that," Eddy said. "People 'in the way' don't either." People "in the way" didn't get their heads FedExed, he added to himself.

"Maybe," Moria said. "Maybe he got hit on his own. Maybe he got hit because of me. But now, either way, I got business in Houston. We got business in Houston."

"Does that mean I'm a partner?" Eddy asked.

"It means you're a dickhead," Moria said. "And if you don't keep your mouth shut, your eyes open, you'll be a dead dickhead."

"What if I don't want—"

"You're part of it," Moria said, "because you're part of me. Of us. He is, too." He nodded toward the back seat. "It's business. Just business, no matter what. You cover my ass. Make goddamn sure you keep your eyes open."

Eddy doubted he could keep his eyes open the way Cole had. The man's eyes were like search lights, never blinked.

Moria said nothing else about Cole. Instead he pulled the phone off its mount and made some calls. He punched in the numbers and spoke into the handset quietly. The calls pissed him off. Twice he juiced up the radio to cover his words and kept his eyes on Eddy.

Eddy had wondered before just how much Moria trusted him. Now, he guessed he knew.

After a bit, Moria slammed the phone back onto its rack. "Like I figured," he growled mostly to himself. "Nobody knows shit. Or nobody's talking. I've talked to everybody in Dallas. Whatever went down came out of Houston. No question."

Eddy liked driving the Buick. It looked like a standard '79 sedan. Once red, it had faded to pink. The bumpers were rippled, the front fender bright-blue. Sanding marks stood out all over it, there was a crack in the windshield. No two tires matched, but they were all new, high quality, deep tread blackwalls. No wheel covers.

"You can't tell by looking. You can park it anywhere," Cole told him when Eddy asked why they kept such a piece of shit around. "Nobody steals a junker like this. We use it for special."

Special was right. Eddy knew that the first time he started it. Cole told him there was a 442 under the hood, bored, stroked, and supercharged. The scoop was hidden in the grillwork. Eddy thought: Bitch on wheels.

"Zero to sixty in six seconds," Cole confirmed. "Top end's one-sixty on the straightaway, maybe more if you punch it right. Rebuilt, light-weight chassis. Custom-designed transmission— shifts slick and quiet—tight rear end, corners like a hooker, purrs like a cat, but it'll wind out when you put the juice to it."

"It's givin' me a hard-on," Eddy grunted.

"Don't fuck it," he replied. "It won't fuck you."

Eddy hadn't. He barely got to drive it. Cole took it when anyone did, would have had it this week, but he flew instead. Eddy was glad.

When they passed Buffalo, Moria told him he wanted to make a stop out on the loop: check one of his lots. Eddy spotted it coming up on the left: big sign, like the other lots Eddy had seen—Life on Wheels—RVs, mobile homes. Off in the distance, downtown's glass and steel steamed. Traffic was heavy.

He took the ramp at fifty, made a U-turn under the overpass. The lot was crowded with motor homes, double-wides, and run-of-the-mill fourteen-bys. There were also old pickups, a couple of rusty vendor vans, a boat or two, and a half-disassembled tractor parked in the mud. They pulled up, parked.

"Look," Moria said. "I don't know what's going down. I don't know where I stand. Where you stand. The only person I'm sure of is him." He jerked his head back again: Hedge. Eddy checked the mirror. No reaction. "Anything might happen. Be alert."

Eddy nodded and Moria jumped out, looked around, then turned. Eddy slid the window down.

"You stay in the car. Answer the phone. Take a message. Get it right." Moria glanced at Hedge. "Anybody drives up, he'll send them away."

Eddy heard the back door handle working. Moria turned and waddled—that was the right word—up the wooden steps to the fake redwood porch in front of the office. There was a red SORRY WE'RE CLOSED sign on the window. Moria walked right in.

The phone buzzed, and Eddy picked it up and punched the TALK button.

"Yeah?"

There was a pause: static, crackle.

"Where is he?" A woman's voice, he thought. Wasn't sure. Rough, scratchy.

"Who you want?"

Hesitation. "Cole."

Eddy felt a chill run up his back. "Not here. Got a message?"

"Who's this?"

Eddy hesitated. "Who's *this?*"

The voice also hesitated. "This is the call he wanted."

"So, you got a message or not?"

"Yeah." A pause. "Tell him 'Disney will deliver.' " More static, breakup. Cellular, Eddy thought, way out. There was some swearing. Eddy frowned. Asshole, he thought, woman or not. "Anything else."

"Tell him the deal is two hundred grand *each* for clean and dressed. Less for damaged goods. Tell him Balmorhea, Friday, late P.M. Got it?

"Got it."

"Say it back."

" 'Disney can deliver. Two hundred grand each for clean. Less for dam—' "

"Clean *and* dressed," the voice corrected. Eddy squirmed slightly.

"Clean *and* dressed. Bal. . .' What was that?"

"Balmorhea, goddamnit! You got it or you need to write it down? Who the fuck is this, anyway?" Eddy could almost see the speaker looking around, checking her back—the nervous type. Eddy didn't like this spy-movie bullshit.

"Say it again. Spell it."

"Balmorhea: B-A-L-M-O-R-H-E-A: Balmorhea. Friday late P.M. Say it back."

" 'Balmorhea, Friday late P.M.' Got it," Eddy finished before the voice could interrupt again.

"Okay. One more thing. Tell him, 'long and green.' No bullshit."

"Got it."

There was a click at the other end, and Eddy replaced the phone. He looked in the rearview at Hedge. The shades were off as light faded into late afternoon. The man's green eyes were blank, impassive. Eddy might be invisible. "You get that, too?"

No answer. Hedge lit another cigarette. He had one foot on the ground outside.

Eddy sat back, mentally repeated the message. Things were getting complicated. The videotape still bothered him, made him jumpy. He kept replaying it in his head: professional hit, no question. But sloppy—civilians in the way. Sending the head was a nice touch. Kind of thing only somebody who knew what would scare the shit out of Moria when he opened it would do. This didn't have to do much with the mobile homes and Winnebagos or the fuck-and-suck business Moria ran out of the back rooms of his joints in Dallas. It smelled like dope.

People didn't kill people like that for anything less than a certain amount of money. And dope was all Eddy could think of that brought in that kind of money. But Moria didn't deal dope. That was what Cole said. Maybe Cole was wrong. He sure as hell was dead.

Moria was playing this too close. Everything told Eddy that this was bad, going to get worse. It made him nervous, like a mistake in the making. This was not his kind of gig. He wanted out. It wasn't just Cole. Shit like that happened. Nobody got used to it, but everybody came to expect it. Hardball was like that. But all this bullshit code-talk. "Disney can deliver." What did that mean? That wasn't part of any player's game. A guy didn't have to grow up on the streets to know that. Players were straight. They told you what they wanted, what they would do right up front. No fucking around. When a guy worked with a player, he dealt straight: business. That way, he survived.

Eddy played straight. He expected Moria to do the same.

He wanted to get out of the car, walk out on the interstate, find a phone. He had a couple hundred in cash on him: cab to Hobby, Southwest to Love. He could be home in bed before Moria figured it out. He looked through the back glass at the rush of traffic on the access road. Take a walk, he said to himself, there's the money from the gun deal. He hadn't touched it, and Tommy Bodine was still driving a tractor at Sugar Land.

He could grab Princess or Monica or both. Split to Mexico. Drop out while this cooled off.

Suddenly, he thought of Raul. Mexico equals Raul. Maybe. Made sense. Nothing else should have brought the squirrelly little prick to Eddy's mind, but he popped up all the same. He wondered if he was in Mexico. Their last meeting worried Eddy like a swelling boil. But if he was in Mexico, that meant Mexico was probably out. Where Raul was, there usually was trouble of some kind: fuckup, Eddy thought. He worried about Raul when he thought about it, but the truth was, he didn't think about it too much. Raul would turn up when he needed something, if not in Mexico, then somewhere else. Things would turn around.

But this was stupid. Eddy was Moria's driver. That was it. He didn't want to get in deeper, to be part of anything.

Eddy shook his head slightly. No. Moria was right. This was just business. Sentimentality was for suckers. Cole got hit, sooner or later Moria would hit back. If he could, if he thought it was justified. He was a fat, slimy little click with ears, but he had business sense. And he was tough. He wouldn't do anything to fuck himself up because of a broken heart or anything else.

But if he hit back, someone would probably hit Moria. Sooner or later, Eddy thought, someone would probably hit him.

"Mistake," Eddy mouthed the word but didn't speak it. He didn't move, either. Instead, he lit a Camel and pushed the window button. Humidity rushed in on him.

Houston, Eddy thought: Piss.

Eddy had made two big mistakes in his life. Both had turned out better than they should have for a jock with little talent and less future. The first gave him Barbara. The second made him a player. In a way, they were connected.

He came back from Canada, his knee in a plaster cast, his hopes for pro ball over. Any chance he had was snapped away with a resounding pop on his own forty-yard line by a big lineman from Ontario. Except for the knee, he was in good shape, but he didn't know what he was going to do. The Army wouldn't take him. His old man wouldn't talk to him. He had four grand in cash and pain in his leg. He also had a lot of anger.

Then he found Ellen. He knew her when she was a cheerleader, he was a defensive back for SMU. They dated once or twice, but it didn't go anywhere. After college, she worked as one of the bimbos on the Cowboy's pep squad for two seasons, but she was caught in bed, going up on grass and down on Tom Landry's defensive backfield. That pushed her off the sidelines forever. She stewed for Southwest for a couple of months, found pills lasted longer than grass, got knocked up by one of three pilots, fired after the abortion. They cut cards to see who would pay for it.

She hit the cocktail waitress circuit, started working her way down. That's when Eddy ran into her again.

She looked like she always did: short, dark-skinned, black-eyed, compact little body with legs to her chin, saucy little tits, and a go-to-hell expression that made a guy hornier than a three-clicked dog. That was fine with her. She loved to fuck, loved to speed. Those were the two things she knew how to do best.

She remembered Eddy. Or she said she did when they ran into each other in Adam's Apple, a motel lounge in Arlington where a lot of washed-up players hung out, talked about the game they couldn't play anymore. He remembered her, clearly. He also remembered a trip to Mardi Gras their freshman year. Mostly he remembered their motel room. And he remembered being inside her, a lot.

Adam's Apple was connected to a Ramada Inn. They took a room two hours after he bought her a drink. They spent all of a week and most of his cash drinking, speeding, smoking dope, bed-hopping their way from motel to motel across the Metroplex. She said she liked a constant change of scenery. She was as good as he remembered. Better even, when she was high. So was he. He liked it that she didn't try to hide her past, her appetite for sex. And he bought her story that she was tired of it all, that she wanted to settle down, go straight, have kids. She told him about her abortion. She cried. They flushed two hundred pills and hugged each other all night long.

The marijuana she kept.

She was dependent on weed then: a joint every hour at least, and good stuff, Colombia Lace and Panama Black, not the dill-cut shit the kids were peddling on the street. But Eddy kept the vow. He liked being clean more than he liked being scared. He got off drugs and stayed off, but he kept drinking. It was for the pain, he said.

But it wasn't his knee that hurt, and tequila wouldn't help it anyway. His old man, wealthy as he was, had thrown him out: called him a dumb jock, a bum and a waste, white trash, never amount to anything. Eddy wanted to find something solid to prove the rich old bastard wrong. Mostly, he told Ellen, he wanted his cut when the son of a bitch croaked.

He found a gym and spent his days pumping weights, his nights pumping Ellen. She couldn't get enough of him. It was like she was addicted to his cock, like she worshipped it.

Eddy rolled with it: drinking, fucking, watching her get high, talking about the future, about what he was going to do. It took a while, but he finally admitted two things: She was headed into a grass-lined toilet. And his old man was right: he wasn't going to do shit.

Winter passed, then spring. Eddy tried to sober up. He told her he didn't know anything. Couldn't do anything. Since his freshman year at Highland Park, his talent was in his shoulders and legs. He made All-State his senior year. College scouts spotted him in a game against Fort Worth Pascal. He picked up the center and the guard and dropped them on the quarterback. There were broken bones on the play, none of them Eddy's. Eddy drew a flag, but two guys were carried out on stretchers. Then a third-and-ten—a screen pass. Eddy hit through the receiver, lifted him up, bounced him into the band, lined up for halftime. The ref threw him out of the game, but he got a scholarship offer from four schools. He picked SMU. There was a car, a couple of girls a week, a bank account. He thought it would please the old man, but he couldn't have cared less.

"Football's for morons," he said. "The smart guys own teams. The uniforms get bought and sold: cattle."

College was a bitch. Eddy was smart enough, but there was no time to study. He was a psychology major: the non-major for jocks who didn't want to take business. He spent his time losing at poker to the rich kids, working out, shooting steroids, smoking dope, drinking, screwing beautiful, wealthy, stupid co-eds. He kept a C average but never made class, made all the practices but didn't play much. SMU wasn't into power in those days. It wasn't into winning either. The coaches wanted a "finesse" game. Lots of passes, lots of razzle-dazzle, lots of turnovers. When he went in, they were usually down four TDs and the clock was gone. In four years, he played in only three winning games.

Two of those were against Rice. Nobody watched games against Rice. The alums didn't even show up for games against Rice. Hell, Rice didn't show up half the time, some said.

He didn't get drafted. He went free agent, but nobody wanted him. He tried to walk on with the Cowboys and the Oilers. He thought he had a chance with Houston. They had a shot that year, and they ran a power defense. Eddy was big. His older brother, Quince, a hot-shot lawyer in Houston, had a client with a small piece of the team and put the word in for him. But no dice. Bum Phillips was going through rookies like the city went through clean air. Eddy never got a tryout.

His parents died the same year. The old man took on a Mayflower van on Central Expressway: killed both of them instantly and fucked up a pretty nice Rolls, Eddy told Quince when he phoned him with the news. Quince told him that ten grand and a three-year-old Caddy was his cut of the family fortune: he was lucky to get it. The old man had run the business into the ground, spent what he didn't piss away on booze and European vacations on a twenty-year-old blonde. If he hadn't died, he probably would have wound up with a room at Big Spring Federal and a paternity suit, Quince said. She was suing anyhow. Filed papers on her birthday. If the truck hadn't taken the old man's head off, then the old lady would have after she found out that he had two more kids than she knew about. Now, though, she'd never find out.

When the old man died, he owed the world. All Quince could do was save the car, some cash. He handled the bimbo, bought her off. Sent the kids to college. Sent Eddy on his way.

"Take the money and run," he advised Eddy.

Eddy ran.

Quince didn't give a shit. He was already set: big-deal lawyer in a big-deal city. Hillary, their sister, was married to an Arab she met at a college party: sheik's son, oil money, and four ugly wives and a dozen kids back in Sandniggerland. He owned a string of hotels and discos on the East Coast, got in on the ground floor when gambling went legal in Atlantic City. He gave her everything she wanted, she said. She didn't want family. She didn't come home for the funeral, didn't even return Eddy's calls.

But Eddy didn't call much. He had good reason to hate Hillary.

Eddy tried to walk on in Green Bay, Detroit, Minnesota, Chicago. When he didn't get past the gate guard in Cleveland, he was broke. He sold the Caddy for two grand to an up-and-coming pimp, shipped out as a general deckhand on a scrap metal barge bound for Canada. When he got there, he had spent three days hanging off the rail, vomiting into the lake. He took his pay, drifted up to Toronto. He bummed around a gym long enough to meet some guys, then found a home with the Toronto Towers, a semipro team looking for a franchise. That lasted two years, and then his knee went, the team folded, and he came back to Dallas, no better off than when he left.

He married Ellen.

It seemed like the right thing to do. She liked him, liked their sex, and her daddy owned a farm near Windthorst, a town so small people passing a big truck would miss the whole damned place. Eddy didn't know thing one about farming. It turned out not to matter. He got on as assistant coach at Windthorst High, and he and Ellen moved into a mobile home on her daddy's farm, way on the north side, way out of sight.

Ellen's mother had died when she was in junior high, and Ellen left for college when she was seventeen. Now, when the old farmer looked at his only child, he saw a drugged-out whore who brought her latest, biggest trick home to live. "Bet you could eat your way out of a cow," was the nicest thing her father ever said to Eddy.

The old man gave them the lot, co-signed for the mobile home, a used pickup, but that was as far as he would go. He told Eddy he could have his daughter and the "shit-load of heartache" that went with her, but to "stay the hell out of his life." He then fenced up two mean dogs around his house to make sure they did. Eddy might not be the cause of her condition, he told everybody in Windthorst, but he was the result. "Hell of a note," he said to the boys at the Dairy Queen.

The Windthorst Dragoons didn't win a game the first season. Eddy was fired in the middle of the second. The band's drum majorette publicly accused him of seducing her, knocking her up.

She was partly right. He had screwed her, once. But the baby wasn't his. That honor belonged either to the head coach—who set Eddy up with her in the first place when he started banging her older sister—or to the principal, who had pawned her off on the head coach and also taken his turn with big sis. The rumor was that the two girls had slept with every male teacher in the high school. It was hard to tell, but not hard to sell. Two years apart, they looked like twins. Six-one in their bare feet with a pair of tight-rippled thirty-eights and legs like colts, they were impossible not to want. Had been since they turned fourteen. The drum majorette was already pregnant when Eddy hooked her.

"Chip off the fucking block," Quince growled when Eddy called him for advice. "All I can tell you is to put a bell on it and tie it down."

Eddy took the fall on the job to avoid going to jail for stat rape. The principal ran off to Reno with the drum majorette on her eighteenth birthday. The head coach slid into the principal's office and out of his wife's bed. Eddy came out clean but unemployed.

In the middle of everything, Ellen turned up pregnant, and in the spring, Barbara was born.

Eddy cashed in his retirement, went to truck-driving school in Mineral Wells, took a job for a meat-packing company out of Weatherford. He was gone for two, four days at a time delivering to restaurants and small grocery chains all over North Texas. Ellen quit grass when she was pregnant, but every week when Eddy came home, he saw more and more tequila bottles in the garbage. Eddy told her booze was worse than grass for a pregnant woman. Ellen told him to fuck off. Barbara came out fine, but Ellen was going down the shitter once and for all: Eddy knew it.

What he didn't know was what to do about it. His salary barely covered the mobile home payments, groceries, or the rusty second-hand Chevy pickup he drove back and forth to Weatherford. Ellen had her own car, a newish Volvo—said it was a present from her daddy—but it was always breaking down, something that amazed Eddy, since she claimed that she never went any place. The odometer was disconnected: he had no way to check on her. They were broke, she was drinking herself to death, and if Eddy sold everything they had, he couldn't raise the price of a divorce. The future was dark. The only light was Barbara.

Things rocked along for more than ten years that way. Ellen would sober up for a while, then fall back into the bottle. They had mean, ugly fights. He never hit her, but she got in her share of good licks between steady indictments of him as a worthless son of a bitch. She often split his lip and once gave him a concussion with a baseball bat. He wanted to hit her back, but he never did. He just took it. Hoped she would change. Nothing made her happy. She hated the farm, living in a mobile home. That was all they agreed on. She hated Eddy, too. But she was good to Barbara, at least at first.

When he parked his fridge-rig and came home on Thursday or Friday, she was usually in a good mood. But she talked too much. He guessed she was sleeping with somebody, but he couldn't figure out who or how. Windthorst was too small to keep that kind of secret. It usually took him until Sunday to get pissed off enough to accuse her, then she threw him out. He slept in the truck for the week, then he came back on payday. He always came back on payday and handed her his check— for Barbara. Then they started over.

She quit drinking—cold turkey—when Barbara turned twelve, and he thought that things would get better. Then he found her stash of needles and a collection of matchbooks from half the motels in Wichita Falls. He also discovered that Barbara was failing most of her classes. He went to the principal, bulled his way past the cynical answers about a lousy father and a rotten home life. She had missed half the days in the fall term. He questioned Ellen and discovered that she left Barbara alone two, three days at a time. No clean laundry, no food, no supervision. "I need a change of scenery," was her only excuse. He hit her then. Knocked her through a door, grabbed Barbara, took off for Wichita Falls.

He wanted to find the dealer who was supplying Ellen, maybe kill him. Instead, he drove around the city until Barbara fell asleep, stopped and gassed up and went to Houston, to Quince, begged for help. A bachelor, Quince fell in love with Barbara. She charmed him completely. He couldn't do enough to help. He staked Eddy for a house in Fort Worth, then filed papers. That got her away from her mother, forever. Ellen went to Colorado with her dealer.

Before she left, she set fire to the mobile home, burned it to the ground. That was the only thing she ever did that was completely all right with Eddy.

* * *

Eddy surveyed the mobile homes on Moria's sales lot. Many had rusty whiskers and sat like beached ships where the truckers parked them. Repos, Eddy thought. He hated living in one. Tin cans: hot in the summer, cold in the winter, leaked when it rained, fucked-up miserable the rest of the time. Grass wouldn't grow near one. Snakes nested beneath them. Death traps in a high wind. Low-rent housing for losers.

And Moria owned ten, twelve lots in Texas, a couple more in Oklahoma, some in Louisiana. Cole hated them, too. Always called them "people boxes." Eddy thought: Coffins.

Moria and a guy in a loud sports jacket came out of the office and looked around quickly, checking the lot. Somehow, he seemed shorter, fatter away from the back room at Bishop's. He was wearing his Miami Gangster outfit: white suit, no tie, no socks, shirt sleeves rolled over the jacket's pushed-up arms. He liked that look. Wore it all the time. Must have a dozen of those suits, Eddy thought. The guy next to him was two feet taller than Moria. But he was nervous. He pulled at his cuffs, looked around, smiled, smoothed back his hair over his bald spot. He looked scared, but he was bluffing confidence. Eddy thought: High roller. Moria hired nothing else to run his lots.

Moria had on shades, and he slid them down his nose and inspected the homes on the lot in the dusk. They came down the steps and walked into the metal forest of repos. Moria walked funny, tried not to step in the mud. He kept looking behind him. The high roller talked too much, used his hands.

Eddy checked the rearview. Hedge had his door open a bit wider. When they had been gone a moment, he relaxed, lit another cigarette, and Eddy snapped on the radio. The silence was getting to him again, and the car was steamy. Country music flooded in, and he punched the buttons until he found an R&B station. "Outskirts of Town" blasted through the speakers. He lit a Camel.

After a couple of minutes, Moria appeared between the people boxes, glanced around before moving, then made his way back to the car. He was in a hurry now, slammed the door when he got in: "Drive."

Hedge pulled his door to. Eddy turned the Buick over. The engine made a low rumble under the faded hood. He backed away from the office, guided it out of the lot and onto the access road. The high roller didn't appear. Moria let out a long breath, pulled out a handkerchief and wiped his face.

"Messages?"

Eddy nodded. "One. For Cole."

"Well?" Moria was sweating lightly: impatient.

Eddy repeated what he memorized. He watched the mirror to see if Hedge was checking his accuracy, but his dark lump was settled, eyes half closed. Drugged or dead, he wouldn't look any different. Eddy checked the lot as it faded around a curve in the freeway's access road: no high roller.

"Two hundred!" Moria laughed.

" 'Long and green,' " Eddy repeated. "Each."

"And they asked for Cole?"

Eddy nodded.

"Long and green, my ass! Where'd he think he'd get that kind of money? That dumb fuck never made that much at one time: long and green or short and blue. Not without me knowing it." He made a pumping motion over his lap. "Son of a bitch was jerking me off. Swear to God. Say it again." Eddy repeated the message. "Where the hell is that?" Moria opened the glove box and pulled out a map. "Is it a town or what?"

Eddy shrugged. He guided the Buick up the ramp and into heavy traffic. Rush hour was over. He could tell because nobody was stopped.

"It's a town all right. Middle of Bumfuck, Nowhere," Moria groaned. "Halfway to goddamn New Mexico. More than half. Friday. What's today?"

"Wednesday," Eddy reminded him. Cole was killed on Monday, he calculated: Monday night or early Tuesday.

"What's this 'Disney' shit?" Moria wondered aloud. "Cleaned and dressed? Does any of this make sense to you?"

The question required no response. Eddy punched the Buick to get around a slow-moving concrete truck, the only vehicle in sight not making more than seventy. A motorcycle cop passed them on the opposite freeway lane, slowed, gave them a long look over his shoulder. Eddy braked, brought the needle down to sixty-five.

"Watch it," Moria said, shifted his weight around and eyed the cop. He reached behind his coat, pulled out a Colt .357. Outside light caught the blue of the barrel, made it shine.

Eddy studied the gun. It was huge in Moria's hand, ugly. He looked away and flicked his butt into the airstream. He couldn't believe a man as round and short as Moria could conceal such a large weapon. He mentally fingered the automatic behind his own back.

"Expecting trouble?"

"Not now. Trouble's behind us."

Eddy checked the rearview.

Moria chuckled: dark. "Had to fire a guy." He dropped the pistol between his knees, gave Eddy a look over his sunglasses.

Eddy's heart jumped. He shoved a Camel in his mouth. "Matter of trust?"

Moria smiled. "Nothing to do with you. Let's get to the hotel. It's getting dark. I'm hungry, and I'm horny."

4
Arizona

It took Vicki exactly four hours to come to terms with the fact that she had been kidnapped by a couple of jerks. They were a long way from being the professionals Red had insisted they were. They bickered constantly, weren't close to having their shit together. She also decided that they were almost as scared as she was. The difference was that they had the gun—and the knife—and she wasn't so dense that she couldn't figure out that even a couple of dimwits could be more dangerous than professionally hardened criminals.

Even so, she gained confidence with each mile that passed. She decided to make herself as troublesome as possible, hoped they'd just let her go. *The Ransom of Red Chief,* she thought. Who was in that? Lon Chaney? Then there was that thing with Bette Midler. Lost all that weight. Lousy movie.

Vicki raised enough hell about her soiled clothing and need to pee that they finally stopped. A Kmart in Loma Linda provided socks, a replacement set of sweats: cheap fleece. Vicki complained about the quality. They'll look like shit on TV, she thought, when she pulled on the sky-blue polyester and cotton trousers. Added ten pounds to her hips, she thought. Red forbade her to go inside to use the restroom in the Kmart, but after she

bitched for fifteen minutes, they wheeled off and into a closed
filling station near Banning, broke the padlock off the women's
room. Blackie stood guard outside the door, opened it up to
check after she came out. The handcuffs stayed on.

Jerks or not, they were careful: Red pegged the speedometer's
needle on sixty, even when they could legally go faster. They
all wore seat belts. Blackie even buckled Vicki's loosely around
her. Red was conscientious: signaled when he changed lanes,
kept his distance from cars in front of them. Several police
cruisers passed them on both sides of the freeway, but she had
no chance to signal. There was heavy metal on the radio, the
black windows stayed up. The two thugs chain-smoked until
they ran out. Then they sulked. Vicki wanted a cigarette, too.
That was a measure of how bad things were going: she hadn't
smoked in five years.

They were apparently short on cash, hadn't counted on having to buy clothes. Blackie's demands to eat forced Red to
make another stop in Palm Springs. He pulled into a McDonald's drive-in window, ordered for all of them. Sick as she had
been, Vicki couldn't imagine eating. But she surprised herself,
gobbled a cheeseburger, fries in huge bites after Blackie
unlocked her cuffs. It was the most fat she had ingested at one
time in three years. The cuffs went back on before she got a
chance to burp.

They had to count pocket change to fill up the Lincoln after
they ate.

Once out in the desert, Red and Blackie visibly relaxed.
There was a phone mounted in the front seat, but neither could
figure out how to use it. They'd tried off and on since leaving
LA. Vicki knew how. She had used Gary's often enough, but
she wasn't going to give them any lessons. She wanted them
to have all the trouble they asked for. They punched buttons,
then argued about how to do it right, but all they could get was
static, funny tones, beeps. She gave them a smile when they
asked her what was so damned funny.

Vicki actually couldn't see anything funny. She was now
worried that maybe nobody was coming to rescue her after all.
What the hell was Barbara doing? She'd gone upstairs, surely.
Must have seen the goddamn bicycles, the wrecked apartment,

the discarded ''Mormon suits.'' Why didn't she call the cops?
Vicki couldn't figure it out. Her eye caught the quartz time on
the dash. Seven forty-five. Shit, she thought: Gary.

Howard's party started in an hour. She was going to miss
it. Gary was going to be pissed off. She wondered how pissed
off he would be if she turned up dead. But then, as each mile
passed between them and LA, the less sure she was that she
was in any danger at all. She didn't know what these two idiots
were after, and she didn't like it taking so long to find out.

Finally, they gave up on the car phone, found a pay telephone
at a truck stop. Blackie got out to make the call. He wasn't
gone but a minute.

''You get her?''

''Got her fucking voice mail.''

''What?''

''I got her voice mail. A recording.'' He got in, slammed
the door. ''So?''

''So I left a message.''

For a moment Red looked stunned. ''You did what?''

''I left a fucking message.''

''What did you say?''

''I told her we kidnapped the babe and were on the run from
the cops.''

''What!''

Blackie laughed: Idiot. ''I left a message that the Boys from
Disneyland had their souvenir''—he jerked a thumb toward
Vicki—''and everything was okay. I'm not stupid.''

''That remains to be seen,'' Vicki muttered.

''What?''

''Nothing.''

Red relaxed, Blackie drove off toward a darkening eastern
horizon.

It was well after dark before Vicki gave up on seeing the
flashing lights of California Highway Patrol. The closer they
got to Arizona, the less hope she pinned on being rescued right
away. It was night in the desert, her hopes of aborting this
fiasco set with the sun.

She sure as shit didn't know what Barbara was doing. That pissed her off worse than anything.

She couldn't have been *that* convincing with all that bullshit about cousins from Texas. *Nobody* went to SeaWorld this time of year. Barbara knew that. And what about the tip-off with the mail, the plants? Barbara wasn't dense. Hell, Vicki practically gave her a map to follow her. Why hadn't she just waved down those two cops and told them to pull the Lincoln over, yank these two clowns out, end it all right there? That way, she would be at the party now, showing off her smile, flashing some thigh, telling her story to Malkovich or somebody. Gary could be getting into residual negotiations. She might be getting into his bed tonight, not riding across the goddamn desert with Pancho and Cisco.

They were well across the Arizona line when Red pulled into a rest stop. There were a handful of tourists and truckers moving around under the arc lights. He parked, let the engine idle.

"You need to go?" Red asked. "Last stop for a while."

"Yeah, I need to go," Vicki snapped at him. She saw no reason to be afraid anymore at all. Whatever bad was going to happen already had: missed the party. Even her chance at a major PR coup was fading. They couldn't do a thing to her worse than what they had already done. Blackie had already hit her. In the face: bruises for sure. There was no mirror in the restroom in Banning. There wasn't much to lose. She leaned forward. "Unlock me."

Blackie looked at Red, and he nodded.

"Wait till the Women's is empty," he said. "Then you go with her."

"Look, boys, I go potty by myself. Been doing that longer than you."

"Go with her," Red repeated. "I'll let you out in a minute."

"I went by myself before," she protested. "And I need to go now."

"This one's open for business," Red muttered. "Hold it a minute."

She sat back, rubbed her wrists. There was an ugly, purple

bracelet of bruises around each. Gary told her her hands were almost as good as her feet. She felt a new flush of anger. "You guys are fucking up my career."

"Shut up," Red whispered. He turned around and kept his eye on the restrooms. "In a second. Get ready."

She came out steaming. Blackie followed her inside, but instead of standing in the doorway, he positioned himself so he could watch her the whole time. There were no doors on the stalls. She never felt more exposed, not even when she'd flashed them in the apartment doorway. She intended to give standing orders about this sort of thing: it was one thing to watch her get dressed, cop a feel. It was another to watch her pee, move her bowels.

Red was in the back seat. He motioned her in, and she hesitated. Blackie gave her a not-so-gentle jab in the ribs, then pushed her inside. He slammed the door behind her.

When she hit the seat, her anger exploded. "I've had it with you two bozos. You can either tell me what's going on, or I quit."

Blackie opened the front door, slid behind the wheel.

"You quit?" Red looked confused. His pistol was in his waistband.

"Yeah! I quit. Scene's over. Cut, print. What I see here is a couple of perverts, freaks. One's a nut for oral dildos, and the other guy's got a scatology fixation. You want to watch girls pee, why don't you go to Tijuana? Go to a movie. This show's over. I've had it."

"Shhh." Red shook his head, put a finger to his lips. Outside two fat women in shorts and floppy hats stared at the Lincoln. One was walking a large poodle. Vicki's voice carried. Gary ought to hear this, she thought: Bette Davis was never this good. Joan Crawford either.

"Fuck you!" she yelled. "Fuck both of you. The party's over. I'm getting out. Here!"

She turned to put her hand on the door handle. It wasn't there. She forgot: removed. When she turned around to yell at Red again, his half-open hand caught her flat on the mouth. Her neck snapped, the back of her head bounced off the window. She tasted blood, stars shot across her eyes.

"Shit*fuck*!" she gasped. "That hurt!"

"Lean forward," he said. When she didn't move, he grabbed a knot of her hair and pulled her across his lap. "I said, lean the fuck forward!" His hands bunched her hair tightly, yanked it back from her scalp. She started to scream, but he shoved her face hard into his crotch. Her mouth jammed against the bulge of the revolver in his pants. He jerked her arms behind her. Pain spliced her shoulders, she heard the click of the handcuffs. He pulled her upright, pushed her over against the door.

"You got a mouth on you. That's for sure. Let's go," he said. Blackie pulled out into the night. Vicki licked her cut lip, wept silently. They might be kids, she thought, but they played rough. She was sure she'd broken a tooth.

"I need to sleep," she said half an hour later. Red was dozing in the other corner. Her head throbbed. That tooth also hurt. She couldn't stand the touch of her tongue on it. If they'd cracked it, broken it, that was all she wrote. Caps—good caps—cost big money, and they never matched right. The dashboard clock said eleven-thirty.

"So, sleep," Blackie ordered. Red roused himself.

"I can't with these on." She leaned forward and offered her manacled wrists to Red. For a moment, he did nothing, then he unlocked them.

"Let's get one thing straight, Barbara," he said in the same, calm "all-pro" voice he had used back in the apartment. "You weren't *invited* along on this trip. You've been goddamn kidnapped, abducted, whatever. This ain't no game. This is a federal beef. We know it. You better know it. We've crossed a state line now. We get caught, it's twenty-to-life if it's a dime. I won't make that. Blackie won't neither." He paused. "We've been away before. And we ain't going to get in any shootouts with no cops. This goes down easy or it goes down hard. Hard on you. Got it? Cops show up, you're the first to fall. That's the way it is. Murder's no harder than kidnapping, and the food's better on death row. You're going to Texas, and you're going with us, quiet and easy. You're bought and paid for. Or will be. But you give us trouble, we'll hurt you. Like I said, easy or hard: up to you."

He sat back and eased the pistol out, then leaned forward and dropped it into the front seat. "You're pretty. Let's just hope you stay that way. This ain't no sex crime, and we ain't no freaks. We're professionals." His voice was ice. "You got a mouth, and it's going to fuck you up, you're not careful. You keep it shut, do what you're told, in a day or two you can go back to fucking whoever you were fucking when we showed up."

He called her Barbara! Vicki almost missed it. They thought she was Barbara. She laughed.

"Boy, you guys get the Wurlitzer Prize! You really fucked up this whole deal. You got the wrong girl. I'm not—"

The car phone buzzed, and Red leaped over the front seat and picked it up. "Quiet," he ordered. He hesitated, then pushed a button on the handset, put it to his ear.

"It's about goddamn time," he yelled into the receiver. "I didn't know if this thing worked. What? There's static out here. I can't hear you." He turned to Blackie: "Al."

He listened.

"Yeah, well. That was his idea. Yeah, real cute." He lowered the instrument. "She really liked that Disney shit." Back to the phone. "What? So what? So, where is he?" He listened. More silence, and his eyebrows shot up. "Yeah, like he said, we got her. Box of rocks. Fell right into it. Easy as hell, just like you said. The Mormon thing worked smooth: shit under water. She's a mouthy little bitch, but she's learning." He glanced at her. "Got it. Blue van. Tono-what? Yeah, yeah, we'll find it if it's on the highway. No, she's okay. Clean and dressed. Like the man said. Hey, you want to talk to her?" He listened and looked at Vicki again. "She's in one piece. Not a bad piece, either. Okay, okay. I got you. Not unless we have to. Okay, okay. Don't worry. There's no way we can fuck this up now. Not on *our* end."

He talked on, but Vicki stopped listening. Her mind raced. This was no random kidnapping. It wasn't some spur-of-the moment thing: pick a name off a mailbox, snatch a girl out of an apartment, hope her folks have money. They wanted Barbara, thought they had her. But they didn't, weren't even close.

But that didn't make sense, either. Barbara didn't have any money. She had *had* money—not now. She schlepped dishes in a commissary, for Christ's sake. Her father was in prison half the time. She had an uncle somewhere—Houston?—some kind of lawyer. But she hated him, didn't speak to him. Same with the New York aunt. That's where the money was. If anything, Barbara was a bigger nobody than Vicki. Shit, she thought, they probably didn't even have the right fucking Barbara.

A smile creased her lips and made the split hurt. She started to tell them that they had left Barbara way behind, walked right past her and didn't even know it, when the thought struck her that maybe that wasn't a good idea. They weren't so far away that they couldn't dump her out, maybe with Blackie's knife in her, go back for the right woman—even for the wrong Barbara—if that was the deal.

"Right," Red said into the phone. "We need a stop. We been up two days already. I don't know. Okay, okay. We'll make it." His expression grew angry. "Oh yeah! Well, listen Al, baby, maybe you ought to try it."

Who was Al? Who were they talking to? What the hell was going on? Oh Barbara, Vicki thought. What have you gotten yourself into? She bit her cut lip hard, thought better of it, and relaxed. What have you gotten *me* into?

"Friday. Right. Heard you the first five times. Look, I don't give a shit about that. Okay, where then? What?" He leaned way across the front seat and opened the glove box. "Bal-mo-what? Balmorhea? What the fuck is that: town or what? Yeah, okay. Hey, you got a pen or something?" he asked Blackie.

"What do I look like, a secretary?"

Red leaned over and found a stubby pencil in the glove box. He pulled it out, sat back, and spread a McDonald's napkin over his knee, tried to see by moonlight. "Okay, shoot." He scribbled down a series of letters saying each one, then relaxed. "Say," Red lowered his voice. "Nothing's changed, right?" He waited. "How much?" He whistled through his teeth and punched Blackie on the shoulder. "No shit?!" He put his hand over the mouthpiece. "Two hundred fucking grand! Each?"

Blackie lifted his hands off the wheel, danced in the front seat.

"Right. Right. Right. Yeah, I got it wrote down. But you'll be there. What the fuck difference—okay. I said 'okay,' goddamnit." Red hung the phone up on its bracket, fell back into the seat.

"Two hundred fucking grand! Each? South America, here I come!" He whooped. "They got some crazy little *chicas* there, an' I'm gonna get me some!"

In a quick move, he put his arms around Vicki and kissed her hard on the same spot where he had hit her before. Her lip was pulsing, sore, she pushed him away. Her face was going to be black and blue, she thought. She was now sure she had chipped a tooth.

"You are a fucking gold mine, sweet-meat! A fucking gold mine!"

"Yeah, well, bully for me."

"How?" Blackie asked.

"How what?" Red responded.

"She said we really fucked up. I want to know how?"

Red looked at her. "Yeah, that's what you said. How? How'd we fuck up?"

Vicki's mind sprinted back to her statement.

" 'You got the wrong girl,' " Blackie quoted. "That's what she said."

Red stiffened. His hand turned into a fist. "Yeah, right. Like hell."

"Yeah, like hell," Vicki said, and she started to tell them. Fuck the knife, she thought. These guys weren't killers. Then she saw Barbara's face in her mind, imagined her calling the cops, gathering the posse to come rescue her. TV. Publicity. Maybe she was being overanxious. She shifted her tone. "My old man hears about this, he's going to have you guys for lunch."

Red relaxed, sat back, and laced his hands behind his head. "Oh, sweet-meat," he smiled. "Your old man's the number one cause of this shit."

* * *

Vicki was sound asleep when she realized they had stopped. She blinked awake. The dashboard clock said two twenty-five. It was dark through the smoked windows, but she could see they were sitting in a picnic area somewhere in the desert: no johns, no water fountains, just a row of concrete tables, benches under wind-stripped metal awnings. The moon declined in the west, not quite full; she spotted four or five semitrailers lined up, parking lights on. Otherwise, they were alone.

"Where are we?" she asked Red, who was slumped against the window. He scanned the highway about seventy-five yards away.

"None of your business. Go back to sleep."

She noticed that the driver's seat was empty. Blackie's form lumbered up from behind one of the picnic tables. From his limping, hunching motion, she could tell he was zipping up. Reminded her of her own needs.

"I need to go."

"Now?" Red glanced at her. "There's no johns here."

"Tell it to my bladder," she said. "I need to go."

Blackie got in, slammed the door, shuddered. "It's colder'n fuck out there. I thought the desert was hot."

"She needs to go, too."

Blackie turned slightly. "Where?"

"Just open the goddamn door," Vicki said. "Either let me out or grow gills."

Red pulled the handcuffs up. "Lean forward."

"Fuck you. If I'm going to have to squat, I'll be damned if I'm going to fall back in it. Send Butch, there." She jerked a thumb toward Blackie. "He likes to watch."

"Let her out."

"Gee, thanks, guys." She grabbed a fistful of napkins.

Blackie came around and opened her door. She stepped out and gasped. He was right: the autumnal desert night was freezing. Her breath vaporized in the dry air.

"Y'all take me to the *nicest* places."

"Cut the shit," Blackie said. He held up something and the

moonlight caught it. "And don't get stupid," he said. "I can peg this in your back at twenty-five yards. Even if you're moving." He grinned widely in the blue-gray. "I practice!

"I thought I was worth big bucks to you."

"I can hit a leg, too."

She moved off between the picnic tables.

This time he didn't watch her. He sat on a table where he could keep an eye on the car, the highway. She moved off thirty paces into some sandy weeds, completed her chore.

When she finished, she adjusted her clothing, stood up, and stretched. The air was crisp and frosty. Her head and face were sore, so were her wrists. Even her legs were stiff, and her butt hurt. Off to the south she could see the silverlit desert. The word "moonscape" came to her mind. It would be so easy just to walk off. She was sure she could outrun both of them. A hundred yards out in all that cactus and sand dunes, they'd never find her. A mile, though, and she'd be lost, she counter-argued. Snakes, Gila monsters, scorpions, God knew what else was out there. Such varmints didn't frighten her. She was a farm girl. But the idea of running off into the desert in the middle of the night didn't seem logical.

She glanced over to the row of parked truckers. Fifty yards, maybe, she calculated. Red had his pistol, but he was in the back seat. No door handles. He'd have to scramble over the front, then get out. Couldn't even roll down a window until he turned the key on. Blackie wasn't paying attention to her. Her little outburst had done her some good there. She could get a jump. Maybe be at one of the trucks before he even realized she was gone.

Then, maybe not.

Maybe the trucker was sound asleep. Maybe he wouldn't open the door at all for an hysterical woman being chased by a two-bit thug with a knife.

It was like the first time she ever stood at the end of the high dive, just a kid, scared to death, but confident that it wouldn't hurt. Her old man yelling at her from the ground. She argued, weighed possibilities, then decided not to decide. She would just do it. That's the way she went off the high dive. That worked out all right. Focused on the memory, her legs tensed, ready to spring into a run.

"You 'bout done?" Blackie's voice cut through the moonlight, froze her. He had his back to her. "Jesus! Hurry up. It's cold." She sighed, then turned, trudged through the sand back to the table. Nothing else to do.

"I didn't watch you," he grumbled. She let him take her arm, guide her back to the car. "I could've, but I didn't. I ain't no freak."

"I'm sorry," she said, made it sound like she meant it.

"We was away. San Quentin. Lots of freaks there, but we stayed clean. Looked out for each other."

"Couple of sweethearts."

"It wasn't like that." His voice took on a flat tone. "We was straight. Cell mates. Three years. Went in together, come out together. If we go back, though, it could be bad. It's bad for lots of guys. We don't want to go back."

"You have a hell of a way of showing it."

There was still a chance, she thought when they reached the sidewalk. He had a loose hold on her. She could shove him down, grab the knife, run for it. Before the debate in her mind could start again, headlights flooded the driveway up to the parking area.

"Al," Blackie breathed out. "About goddamn time."

The lights guided a Dodge van into the parking slot next to the Lincoln. Blackie hurried her up to the side of the car, opened the door to let Red out.

"You're late," he called to the driver's side.

"You're in the wrong fucking place," a woman's voice yelled back. "You're supposed to be at the *rest* stop fifty miles from here. This is a goddamn *picnic* area. Can't you fucking read? Didn't I say, 'Tonopah'?"

Red didn't answer. He came over to Vicki, spun her around, grabbed her arms, cuffed her once more. Rougher than usual, she thought. She was shivering, her teeth chattered. She couldn't tell if it was fright or the cold. Blackie opened the trunk and pulled out a nylon duffle bag. He put it on the hood of the Lincoln. Red took something out, then went around to the back, crawled underneath the car.

"You got everything?" the van's driver called.

"Nothing to get," Blackie said. He took a screwdriver from the bag, went to work removing the Lincoln's license plates.

"C'mon," the woman's voice whined. "We're running way behind. Let's go."

"He's rigging the car," Blackie said. He finished with the front plate, then went around to the back.

"You already should have done that. Jesus, what's wrong with you guys?"

Blackie brought the pair of plates to the front, dumped them into the duffle. Red scrambled out and stood up. "Three minutes," he said.

The pair flanked Vicki, escorted her to the opposite side of the van. They slid the door open, shoved her into the rear seat. It was fancy inside: carpet, miniblinds, even a small sink and counter mounted in place of one of the seats. Red pushed her through. On the floor, she saw a pistol-gripped shotgun, sawed off.

The rear seat was folded down like a bed, and she flounced down and then sat up. Her arm ached like she'd sprained it when she hit the cushion. It was dark inside the vehicle. She couldn't see the driver clearly.

Blackie pulled the door shut, took the front captain's chair. Red took the middle seat. "Colder'n hell out here," he said.

"Yeah, well, it's about to get a lot hotter," the woman's voice responded. "Got time for a toke?"

Blackie snapped on a reading light, consulted his wristwatch. "Two minutes, less."

"Let's go," Red ordered. "We can fix one on the road." He looked around. "This is cool."

"Yeah, well, courtesy of yours truly." The driver pulled out. "All the accessories." Red picked up the gun. "My idea, too," the driver said. "Don't like to travel naked. Soda's in the cabinet under the sink," she added.

They drove to the end of the parking area, stopped. While the van idled, they all turned around, looked through the side windows. Vicki stared along with them. The Lincoln was now a hundred yards behind them, dark behind the parked trucks.

"Any second now," Blackie said, his eyes glancing down at his watch.

''Kill that light,'' Red ordered.

At once, the desert night was lit by a yellow fireball. The Lincoln erupted in flames and smoke as multiple explosions rocked the picnic area, illuminated the tractor-trailer rigs with high-noon brilliance. The concussion of the blast rocked the van slightly. Vicki fell backwards onto the folded seat.

''What the shit!'' Her arm twisted beneath her, sprained for sure now. Tears filled her eyes.

The driver turned and floor-boarded the van out onto the interstate. Vicki bounced on the rear seat. Behind them a bright tower of fire lit the night. Another explosion shuddered through the van: A tractor rig went up.

''What the hell did you do that for?'' Vicki yelled.

''No evidence,'' Red said, leaning out of his chair. ''They're looking for a brown Lincoln—if they're looking: two guys, pretty girl, California plates. This way, just an accident. No prints, no evidence. Parked car went up: big deal. They'll be a week trying to figure out if anybody was inside.''

The driver laughed a dry, high laugh. ''These boys are on parole,'' she said. ''Can't leave the state. Don't want some nosy cop sniffing around an abandoned car, finding their scent, spreading their yearbook shots around. Now, are you going to fix me some toot or not. We got a long day ahead—lots to do—and we got to make up some time.''

Red pulled out makings, fussed over the tiny counter.

''Hold it steady,'' he ordered. He razored the solid cake, scraped it into a narrow glass vial, passed it up to Blackie, who handed it to the driver.

Vicki heard a loud sniffing sound, and the vial came back. Red made another portion, refilled the vial, handed it to Blackie. While he sniffed it, Red cut a third quantity, used a straw to pull it into his own nostril. The rear dome light came on. Vicki squinted into its white curtain.

''Quite a little package,'' the driver said in a choked voice. She sounded as if she needed to sneeze. ''Pretty, too.'' Vicki saw two small black eyes peering into an oversized rearview mirror. ''Ain't you going to introduce us?''

Red looked at Vicki, shrugged. ''Oh yeah. Barbara Lovell, this is Al.''

5
Hillary

Eddy Lovell's second big mistake in life came only a year after he and Quince finished the legal maneuvering to make sure Ellen would never see Barbara again. Quince's cooperation surprised Eddy. Another surprise came when Quince suggested that Barbara should go to New York, live with their sister Hillary for a while.

"How're the Rockets supposed to do this year?" was Eddy's reply. Quince got the message.

He then suggested that Barbara come to Houston, live with him for a while. Eddy nixed that idea as well, but with more tact. The only thing he had to hang on to was his daughter. He wasn't about to let go of her.

Eddy moved into a duplex in Fort Worth, just off Rosedale, continued to work for the Weatherford Packing Company. It was good, steady work, kept him in shape. When he wasn't hauling boxes of frozen cut meat, he was slamming whole sides and halves around. Sometimes he carried a hundred beeves over his shoulders in the course of the day. The Metroplex was booming in those years. Steak and oil: Breakfast of Texans.

They weren't worried about cholesterol and bank failures. Not yet.

He was pulling down two-fifty a week, net, but it wasn't enough. Barbara was growing, ready for high school. The housekeeper he hired—Ramona Castillo—loved the little girl, but she nagged Eddy worse than Ellen did. Eddy didn't mind: kept him on track, ordered his life. The neighborhood he lived in was changing fast. Respectable whites and Hispanics were moving out, made room for black buyers who usually couldn't qualify, settled for a lease. "Porch monkeys," as Ramona called them, were everywhere. Every other house was vacant, grass overgrown, broken-down cars in the yard. The street was full of wings after sundown. Gangs formed on every corner, crack houses on every block: no place to raise a kid.

Eddy didn't have much chance to make more money. He could have signed on with a long-haul outfit, made good pay, but that meant leaving Barbara for weeks at a stretch. He wanted to stay local, keep an eye on her. But truck drivers were easy to find in a town where washed-out football players were more common than cowboys. Every bar was loaded with muscle-bound has-beens looking for an honest hook or a clean hooker, or both. Most were younger than he, some in better shape, a few had learned something in college. Eddy held on to his job like a life preserver. He didn't know what else to do.

He made the error of telling that to Quince, and his brother again responded. Not in the way Eddy hoped: handing him a couple of grand to set him up in a better area, maybe let him buy a decent car, get in with a good crowd, make contacts for a better job. Instead, Quince called Hillary. The sister who couldn't find time to come home to bury their folks, took her private Lear out of Kennedy, was in Fort Worth before AT&T figured the cost of Quince's call.

One Friday, Eddy phoned in to check for any last-minute orders before hauling from Arlington back to Weatherford: habit. If everything was cool, he liked to hit the gym, work on the machines, push himself until he hurt. It was his only release, his only pleasure. The dispatcher told him some "Mescan broad name of Ramona" had been calling every fifteen minutes all day. "Said to haul your ass home. Listen, man, boss don't like no personal calls here. Don't like Mescan broads callin' in neither. Who you screw is your beeswax, but don't have them trying to run you to ground at work.''

Eddy never heard him finish. He pushed the meat truck hard up I-30 and down I-35 to the Rosedale exit, hit the porch at a run. He paid no attention to the red 'Vette parked in front.

"What's wrong?" he demanded of the housekeeper when he slammed through the door. But his eyes told him that whatever he had been imagining was no match for the hell he was about to face.

Eddy hadn't seen Hillary since he was in college, but he recognized her the second his eyes focused. Five years older than he, three younger than Quince, she could pass for early thirties in the light, maybe twenties in the dark: plastic, and lots of it. She always hated Eddy, never failed to let him know it. When she had to babysit him, her favorite game was to hold him by his ankles over the toilet, threaten to flush him down it. "You're just a piece of shit," she sang while he cried. "A little turd who came along to screw up my life. You're nothing but an *accident*, you know that?" She laughed. He screamed. Eddy thought: Great kidder, Hillary.

Now, she perched on the vinyl-covered divan like it was upholstered with human skin. No more than a quarter-inch of cheek held her well-sculpted butt in place. Red lace stockings jutted out of spiked heels, folded over perfect knees, then dove under the supershort hem of a red leather minidress. Her eyes were mint green: Contacts, Eddy thought. Her skin was pale, paper-white, her hair straight and blonde. Everything else was red. Her lips looked like blood, her nails like crimson scimitars.

"Hi, Eddy," she said. "Thought I would drop in to see my niece."

Her voice would chill ice. It matched her attitude. She might have come across town, Eddy thought.

She jollied a nervous Ramona and bubbling Barbara out of the room with saccharin promises of a trip to Neiman's, dinner in the West End. They left, and Hillary scooted another fraction of high-maintenance, cosmetically enhanced rear end onto the ripped, cream-colored vinyl. She put on large-framed, red-rimmed shades, studied Eddy and his abode.

"Want a drink?" he asked. His hands and white uniform

were blood-stained from handling raw meat. He needed a shave, was clumsy standing in his own living room and feeling apologetic. He itched all over, wouldn't scratch.

As if she heard him, Ramona appeared with a tray. Eddy couldn't imagine where she came up with it, then he saw it had a scratched Schlitz Beer logo on the surface. There was a can of Old Milwaukee and a steaming mug of coffee on top of it. She served them like they were customers: VIPs. Almost bowed when she backed out of the room.

"Eddy." Hillary pulled out a pink cigarette, tapped it once, and then lit it with a gold lighter. She might have been talking to a hired hand, Eddy thought. "I'll come directly to the point: Is this your idea of a place to bring up a daughter? Especially one as beautiful as our little Barbara."

Eddy felt himself flush. "Didn't know she was yours." He pulled a Camel out, lit it with a match: crude. "Missed you at her delivery." She smiled. "Missed your gift at the shower. Birthdays, too." Eddy blew a smoke ring, sat back. "Fact is, about the only thing we *haven't* missed is you. You got a hell of a nerve, you know that? More balls than any guy I know. More than any fucking *team* of guys."

She sighed. "Football always was a big thing to you. I'd hoped you'd outgrown it by now. But I can see you're still a jock."

"As I remember, you had a yen for a couple of jocks yourself."

She gave him a whimsical expression. "Oh well, tennis, golf, one or two baseball players," she said. "But never football." She sipped her coffee, frowned. It was instant. Cheap instant. Bitter as gall. Ramona claimed there was less waste with instant. "You poor thing." Hillary scowled at the cup. "I've really missed seeing you, Eddy."

The conversation felt too friendly all at once. Need to keep it on track, he thought. "Been to any good funerals lately? We had a great one about thirteen, fourteen years ago. Nice folks. You knew them, I think."

She smiled again, sipped the bitter coffee, puffed her cigarette. Lipstick stayed on the filtertip. "I was in Monte Carlo.

I didn't get the wire from Quince until two weeks later. What could I do?''

Hillary had always been a bitch: gold-plated, like her lighter, Eddy thought. She made her reputation as a prick-teasing little rich girl at Hockaday. Then at Trinity University in San Antonio, she dropped her amateur status and her pants. Majored in cock and balls: big time. Minored in booze and drugs. She reminded him of Ellen in uncomfortable ways. But Ellen was bush league compared to Hillary. Hillary played to win.

After three pregnancies, three trips to Europe, three abortions, two high-dollar detox clinics, the old man moved her back to Dallas, stuck her in SMU, told her he would cut her off if she came home knocked up again and without a diploma. She got the degree—home economics—she didn't get pregnant. But she ran off with Karem Moumhad on Commencement Day—left the old man with keys to a new convertible in his pocket, Eddy remembered. Except for a couple of weekend trips home—"layovers" at DFW, Eddy thought, or just lays, since she kept up with all her old stud-buddies in Highland Park—she stayed in New York ever since. She didn't keep in touch with Eddy. Or with Quince. Or so he said. Eddy thought different. She and Quince had always been close. Quince would do anything she told him to.

"Thought you were on your way to the Sahara," Eddy said. "Mecca or Cairo. Aren't you number one harem girl or something? Or have you slipped on the hit parade? Can the sultan still get it up that many times a night? Jesus, what does he do? Use roller skates between beds, or does he do you all at one time? Maybe you have to take a number?" He leaned back in his recliner, embarrassed. The stuffing was coming out of the chair like the acid was coming out of him. He drank off the beer, chain-lit another cigarette, and was pleased to see that the ashtrays had been washed. Ramona was a good woman: the place was clean, but shabby. Eddy felt shabby, and he wasn't clean.

He could feel Hillary's looking around, checking, evaluating, and deciding that it was just the right house for an accident to live in. Her eyes came back to him. He could see what she saw. It stared back at him from the mirror every morning.

"Daddy had such high hopes for you."

"Yeah, well, you didn't exactly turn out to be the Junior Miss, did you? You still haven't said: How's old Abdul doing?"

"Bigotry never becomes, Eddy," she said. She crushed out her cigarette. "You remind me of all the reasons I wanted to leave this part of the country. You really do need to come up to New York. I could show you around."

"Been there. Exhibition game. Semipro team out of Newark. Sent you a couple of fifty-yard-line seats. You make it?"

"I don't go to sports events." She looked away. "At least not football."

"Crude game, right? Least, that's what you said. Crude fucking game for crude fucking people."

"I doubt I chose those words."

"I doubt you did."

For a full minute neither spoke. Dust hung in the room like shredded curtains. Eddy put out his cigarette. Mexican sweat, he thought.

"So, what brings you here? You still married to this camel jockey or not? What's the price of oil these days? Two blow jobs a week?"

She stiffened, then relaxed. "You're hard to take."

He shrugged. "I'm sort of 'take us as you find us kind of folks.' I heard that on TV. You watch TV? Or is it too crude, too?"

She stared, then sighed, as if speaking to him was a burden, then brought him up to date. Her sheik's-son-husband had already married another one of his other wives in the U.S. That made their union bigamous. To avoid prosecution, he fled the country. She sued. Quince worked with her—that accounted for the family interest, Eddy calculated—and she managed to get control of most of his state-side assets, including three hotels—two in Manhattan, one in Atlantic City.

"I've four cars and a Lear Jet," she said. "Not bad for a country girl."

"Pretty sharp," Eddy admitted. Might be good for a loan, he thought, flashed regret at what a prick he was being. "So, what do you want?"

"I thought that would be obvious. Personally, I don't care if you fall into a hole and die."

"Or a toilet."

She fixed a blank expression, then went on. "I'm here to see after Barbara's needs."

She then explained about Quince's phone call. She came to offer Eddy an "opportunity." Barbara was a teenager, now. It was time she had a future and a role model—"preferably female," she added. She'd take her back to New York, "put her into a good school, bring her out."

"Bring her out?" Eddy felt the room falling away from him. He struggled to keep from racing out, grabbing Barbara, running away. He lit another Camel and studied his blood-stained hands.

"Quince has made all the arrangements," she said.

"Yeah," Eddy admitted, bitter. "He's a great arranger." He breathed. It hurt. "What's in it for me?"

"For you?" Hillary's well-plucked eyebrows shot up. She was still beautiful, rich, spoiled as ever, Eddy thought. "You don't change, do you? What do you want? Money? We're talking Smith, maybe Harvard or Yale, Eddy. I can do that through the people I see daily."

"I'll bet they 'see' more of you than you do of them."

She ignored the remark. "Ten years from now, she'll be an MBA on Wall Street making more an hour than you do a year. You ought to be asking what's in it for Barbara."

"You said money. How much?"

"How much? Are you serious?" She stood, paced. "A thousand. Ten?"

"How about a million?"

"A million! You're insane."

"Then give me a hotel. You seem to have a couple you're not using."

"You *are* insane! Stark-raving mad." She lit another cigarette, sat down. "All right. Fifty thousand. That's it. You cretin. I have my plane waiting. We can leave tonight. She will *not* need to pack. I've seen how you dress her."

"No thanks."

"No thanks? What the hell is that? An answer? This isn't an offer. If I have to, I'll take her."

"How?"

Hillary took a beat, then dove in: loved it. "She has a junkie prostitute for a mother, a broken-down truck driver for a father, who's living with an illegal alien whore."

Eddy sat up, bewildered. A whore? "Who? Ramona?" He looked at the door. "She was born in Chicago. And she's not—"

Hillary ignored him. "You still drink a lot, Eddy?" She smiled: sinister. "I saw the way you guzzled that swill. I'll take her. Quince says it's easy in Texas. You're damned near bankrupt. We'll file a few papers. You're better off without her, anyway."

Eddy almost threw her out the door. As it was, she broke a heel when he escorted her roughly down the concrete steps, stood her next to her rented car. She forgot her language standards and called him a "fucking redneck," a "goddamn son of a bitch" when he flung her behind the wheel, slammed the door.

That was that. He thought.

The next day, they fired him at the packing plant. He had no idea how Hillary—or Quince—*arranged* that, but he was sure one or both of them had. He was also sure they were far from finished with him, or with Barbara.

It took a month, but he got another job. Driving again, this time cross-town deliveries for a wholesale liquor company in Grapevine. His route brought him to the bars and back alleys of Dallas and Fort Worth, didn't pay as much as he was making before. Still, it was a good job: hard work, not much concentration required. He filled orders, hefted boxes full of heavy bottles, collected on overdue accounts. They got along.

When Barbara entered high school, she didn't need or want him around so much. She spent evenings with friends—good kids for the most part, squeaky clean, low-rent Young Republicans who didn't mind visiting their shabby house on Rosedale. But it didn't take a genius to figure out that her thick-necked, truck-driving father's presence was an embarrassment. Ramona told him he needed to "get out more" at night, find a woman, have some fun. She glanced quickly toward Barbara when she said it. Eddy took the hint.

He began spending time with Ramona's brother, Raul, a short, nervous semi-idiot who had to keep reminding himself that he was Hispanic. A part-time mechanic, Raul also came from Chicago and only barely spoke Spanish, though he had the street gang lingo down pat. They both had a taste for the hot R&B Deep Ellum offered, spent a lot of time sipping suds, listening to music, hitting the low-rent titty bars and scouting for what Raul called *putas* when he thought about it, "wimmin" when he didn't.

Raul had two ambitions in life: owning a hot Camaro and making a big score. The order didn't matter. Eddy doubted he would realize either.

It was in one of the lounges that Eddy met Monica—sometimes singer, sometimes dancer, sometimes cocktail waitress, sometimes call girl, depending on what came her way—and they developed a stand-off, sometimes-when-they-felt-like-it relationship. She had a four-year-old daughter to support along with a two-hundred-dollar-a-week nose habit. But she could be sweet, could act the part of the responsible mother even with her penchant for bare midriffs, navel rings, sexy tattoos.

And she was jealous as hell, though she made no overt claims on Eddy, pretended not to care who else he might be banging. But Eddy saw through that: Monica cared. They turned soon into friends more than lovers.

Hillary would shit, Eddy thought: him hanging around with a loser spick and a junkie whore.

Raul and Monica. They kept him out of Barbara's way. But it was Raul who put his ass in the crack for good. And it was Raul who made him a player.

Raul also kept Eddy's pickup going long after it should have been mercy-killed. He couldn't afford a new car. He couldn't even afford to take the old six-banger to a regular garage for the work it constantly needed. Barbara's growing teenage demands ate up everything he didn't hold back for a couple of beers and Monica.

Then, without warning, Hillary was on his ass again. She took a different approach: diplomacy. She wrote to him, almost weekly. Chatty little letters, sisterly, heavy with perfume, asking about him, about Barbara, always a concluding suggestion that he send Barbara up to New York "for a visit." Eddy didn't write back. He intercepted letters she sent directly to Barbara, tore up the checks she enclosed. He wanted no part of her. He wanted Barbara to forget she existed.

Money was his constant enemy: always hunting it, never finding it. He felt like a junkie or a wino. All he thought about was how to make a couple of bucks. The pickup needed work, didn't get it, Barbara needed braces, clothes, spending money, got them. Eddy took an all night shift at a gas station until he started falling asleep behind the wheel of the truck. Ramona bought groceries out of her own pocket. Eddy talked about money all the time. It bored Raul and everyone else who heard about it. It bored Eddy.

One afternoon, Raul asked Eddy if he'd like to make some quick, easy cash.

Hard up as he was, Eddy was suspicious. Raul was a near-moron who always was fantasizing about "eezee dingus" and ways of getting it. Few were even marginally legal, all involved a con of some sort. Eddy put him off for a couple of days, then said he'd listen. Raul introduced him to two guys: Dodd and Henderson.

They met in a cafe not far from Bishop's, a place then unknown to Eddy. Eddy drank coffee. They drank tea. Sat close together: one looked left, the other looked right. Siamese twins, Eddy thought: don't look alike, but sewn together.

Dodd was tall, thin, almost emaciated. He dressed well, had a pencil-thin mustache, spoke with an accent. Maybe French, Eddy thought. Henderson was also a sharp dresser, but he was heavier, running to fat. His hands were hammy, hairless, like his face. Made Eddy think of a Cabbage Patch doll. The two sat next to each other in a booth, shoulders touching: no intimacy, just a need to know the other was there, what he was feeling. They heard every word said to them, ate them, digested them, retained them.

Eddy sat down and saw the diamond ring each wore on his pinky: Armani suits, Rolex watches, French cuffs, expensive shades, even in the cafe's gloom. There was something strange about them, something phony: like they were acting all the time, playing like gangsters in the movies. They weren't cool, but they were there, and they had action for Eddy.

"We got some clients who. . .uh, owe us money," Dodd said, looking around behind them. Henderson did the same. "They're sort of. . .uh, reluctant to pay."

"So, go to a collection agency."

"That takes time. They take forty percent," Henderson noted. "And there are questions. Paperwork."

"There's not always. . .uh, paper on our loans," Dodd concluded. "The contracts are. . .uh, personal. Some of our clients are reluctant to. . .uh, meet their obligations. Some persuasion is required. Incentive, you know?"

Eddy knew: shylocks. He took the job.

The first collections were easy. Eddy was big enough to intimidate the suckers without so much as a spoken threat. He reminded them of what they owed, gave them twenty-four hours to come up with it, and they did. Or they skipped. There wasn't much to do about that. He got ten percent for a partial collection, twenty if he came up with it all. In a month, he learned to keep an eye on the suckers, made sure they saw him watching them. Fewer skipped. Mostly, he came up with it all.

Dodd and Henderson were pleased. Raul was thrilled. He got a half-point commission on every collection: finder's fee for bringing them Eddy.

Eddy wasn't proud of the work. But it added to his delivery man's salary, kept him going to the gym on Lower Greenville Avenue to work out, kept him sharp. They moved from the Rosedale dump to a place near TCU. It was pricey as hell, but offered a decent school for Barbara.

For more than a year he made calls for Dodd and Henderson, sometimes two, three a night, never hurt anybody. They told him they liked his work, might have something bigger for him later. Eddy wasn't interested. He could feel the edge with his toe, didn't want to step over.

Then things went sour. A mousy little guy lost big to his bookie on money borrowed from the two shylocks. He had a nose habit to boot, was trying to deal his way out. He was in for fifty grand to the twin sharks, probably more to the bookie. He was scared. Eddy found him in a bar on Harry Hines. Eddy barely got out who he was and what he wanted, when the little clown panicked, threw a punch.

It was a wide roundhouse. Eddy caught it in his fist: pissed him off. The little fart didn't weigh one-thirty, drunk and dripping, couldn't have hurt him if he'd connected with both hands and a barstool. Eddy should have just stood there, taken it. But he didn't think about that until later. He held the punk's fist in his hand, crushed it: pulped it.

He never forgot what it sounded like, felt like when the bones cracked, folded in his big palm.

That should have been the end of it, he should have quit: it wasn't, he didn't. The punk filed charges. He had a bar full of witnesses: Gold-Card Yuppies sucking after-dinner drinks, ecstatic over the tale they could tell at the office. The cops picked him up after work on Friday, and Eddy was introduced to the Dallas County penal system for the first time. Two days: queers and drunks, seatless toilets, stale bread, greasy chicken and watery soup. Eddy worried himself sick about Barbara.

Raul sent word that Ramona had things under control. Eddy relaxed.

Dodd and Henderson bailed him out Sunday night, took him to a hotel room in the Anatole where they sat on a sofa in the dark, lectured him. They warned him against such public rough stuff, told him they couldn't afford the exposure. They liked him, liked his work and again told him that bigger things might be coming.

He had to stay clean, they told him, out of the can, and especially out of the news. "No uh, publicity," Dodd said. "No exposure." Then they sent him on another series of jobs. They wrote off the punk's debt, he dropped the charges, but Eddy had been arraigned: DPD had his picture, his prints, his number. He wasn't a player. Not yet. But he had a sheet.

And he had a feeling they were watching.

The next time wasn't so clean. The mark was a cooker. He ran a PCP lab behind his video rental store. It was a sex film shop, legit but catering to the sicko element. Mostly, it was a front for dealing the hard drugs he made in the back room. Eddy came in just after closing, just ahead of the poppers and mainliners waiting across the street. The guy was only in for ten grand, but he was six months late. He begged Eddy to give him a week, maybe two, and he'd come up with it. Offered him "stuff:" meths, ludes, even crack. Eddy said no, but he was sympathetic. For an operation like this, ten grand wasn't worth much of a sweat. The guy was piecrust, but he was good for payoff. Eddy was thinking it over when the sucker went to the front of his store, locked the glass door, then took a steel chair and smashed it.

Bells and sirens went off everywhere. The guy yelled, "Stop thief!" Screamed robbery. Before Eddy could split, he was grabbed by the mob outside—all junkies—who beat the shit out of him, held him for the cops.

Assault again. This time with attempted robbery. Bail was high. The shylocks stayed out of it, wouldn't return Eddy's calls. Eddy had shirts older than the PD who defended him. He tried to call Quince, but Quince ducked him, sent a message asking Eddy if he wanted him to call Hillary: "for Barbara's sake." Eddy tore it up, threw it in the toilet.

He copped to B&E, did ninety days in county. The only good thing was that he kept his job. And he kept Barbara.

Dodd and Henderson called—through Raul, always through Raul—a week after he got out. They couldn't risk using him anymore for collections, they said. Besides, they were quitting the loan business. Too many small-time bankers rolling small-time dealers in the area, they said. Dope complicated things: made loans risky, suckers desperate. Gamblers were safe. So were drunks, skippers: like that. But dope dealers wanted to roll high and often. Never could handle the freight. They said.

Eddy didn't buy it. But he listened. He didn't really see he had a choice. He had been fired before.

Then, they told him there might be some other sort of work: the "bigger thing" at last. Riskier for him, he figured, sure thing for them, if he was interested. At the time, he wasn't. He said no. He was going straight. He couldn't afford to risk losing Barbara. Quince's message haunted him at night.

They were offended. He could tell. Said they would be in touch. About then, Hillary turned up the heat. She started phoning Barbara. The checks got bigger, harder to tear up. Barbara began asking questions about why she couldn't go visit her aunt if she wanted to. Hillary even started calling Ramona, asking her why Eddy was being so pigheaded.

Then Quince came back into the picture: again. He sent him notes asking the same thing. Eddy ignored them, but he couldn't ignore the bills that mounted up. His pickup finally quit. Raul even gave up on it.

"It's got more'n a hundred-fifty thou on it, bro," he said. "There's nothing in there worth fixing. You need new wheels."

Barbara needed things, too. A good-looking, olive-skinned sophomore, she wanted to be on the Pascal pep squad, maybe cheerleader. She reminded Eddy a lot of Ellen—in a good way—but he buried the thought. She also wanted a car, though she never really asked him for one. She never asked for anything. Eddy just felt her needs, her wants. He ached inside.

He worried what she thought about his being busted, but she told him she thought it was "cool." Eddy thought it was shit. And his income dropped. They were eating, but Ramona was working for free, had been for months. Eddy figured she only stayed because of Barbara. His rent went up, and he wasn't clearing more than a hundred and a half a week after taxes. He looked for other work, nothing turned up. The boom was busting, and everybody wanted to drive a truck, especially former S&L officers.

He called Quince. It hurt: no choice.

"I understand Hillary made you an offer," he said.

"I don't think I heard that," Eddy replied.

"I also heard you had another offer. From your former employers."

Eddy was confused. "Who? The meat packers?"

"No," Quince said quietly. "The other guys."

Eddy thought: Dodd and Henderson. "How the fuck you know them? They're a couple of small-time players. Not your class, big brother."

"I'm a lawyer," Quince said. "I keep up. I know what you're doing. You really think that's the way to keep Barbara. With you in jail?"

"So why should I call them?"

"You're going to have to do something," Quince said. "I can't help you. Not anymore. Call them." He hung up.

A month went by, and he cratered. He told Raul to find Dodd and Henderson, ask for a sit-down. They agreed too fast, as if they were waiting for him to come around.

It was a simple job. Not much to it. They needed a wheel man: Raul, Eddy suggested. They agreed. But Eddy had the key: the liquor delivery truck.

It was a Mercedes bobtail, wide and heavy, clumsy on the front end, hard to handle in high-speed traffic. The gear ratio was tight. Downshifting too fast would cause it to fishtail, maybe turn over. Eddy had bitched about that since he started driving it.

He was to be on I-30, just east of Mesquite at ten o'clock on a Tuesday morning: part of his regular route. He was to watch for a Purolator Security van. Part of their regular route, too, he was told. When he spotted the van, all Eddy had to do was get near it, make a tight lane change, swerve a bit, clip the armored vehicle, force them off to one side. When everybody got out to look at the damage, Dodd and Henderson would show up, tie up the guards, take the haul. That was it: quick and clean. Eddy would look like an innocent bystander. To make it look good, they'd tie him up with the guards, take his wallet, couple of cases of liquor for show.

He went over the plan for two days, looked for flaws, looked for ways around doing it. He couldn't find any. They met at eight that morning in the parking lot of a big baptist church about halfway between Dallas and Greenville. Raul was there, so was Dodd and Henderson: stapled together, Eddy thought: couple of bookends.

They were well dressed: expensively tailored suits, snap-brim hats and gloves, shades. They showed him a map, described the Purolator van again, went over the time table, covered the particulars like it was the first time they'd been over it.

"There'll be two. . .uh, guards," Dodd said, lighting a cigar. "Armed. But they're private cops, not pros, not looking for trouble. This is a private contract. They've been making this run for. . .uh, two years. Every Tuesday."

"Regular as Serutan," Raul added, eager.

"The guards have no idea this one is any different from any other."

"So, is it?" Eddy asked.

Dodd and Henderson exchanged looks, nodded.

"What's our cut?" Eddy asked, nodding at Raul, who leaned against the getaway car: a blue Mercury Sable sedan, nondescript, blackwalls. Cop car, Eddy thought.

"Hundred thousand," Dodd said.

"Maybe two hundred, if things go smooth," Henderson added.

"Jesus, what're they hauling?" Eddy asked. "Gold bricks?" Eddy assumed they were stealing cash. He looked at Raul. His dark eyes were sleepy, disinterested, hid his glee. Eddy admired his reserve, then envied his stupidity.

"Just follow instructions," Dodd said. "Don't foul up."

They went to the sedan, got into the back. Raul walked over and handed Eddy a .45 automatic: GI, rusty.

"Don't need a gun." He shoved it back at him. "Not for my part."

"Better take it, bro. Sometimes things don't go smooth. You know?" He turned and spoke out of the side of his mouth, pretended to bend over and tie his shoe. Eddy noticed he was wearing boots: no laces. Stupid little shit, Eddy thought. "What you think they're getting? Dope?" Eddy shook his head: No idea.

"Whatever it is, it's worth a shit-load," Eddy said.

"So take the piece," Raul thrust the weapon out again. "This kind of deal, things could get hinky." He winked.

Eddy looked at the gun, accepted it, shoved it into his waistband, pulled his windbreaker over it. It was heavy and uncomfortable, but he decided to keep it. Whatever these guys were hauling was worth more than just money. It might be worth a life.

He side-swiped the Purolator van just as planned. The Mercedes careened when the back bumper caught the front of the blue-and-white security truck. The van also weaved dangerously, but in less than a quarter mile, both were pulled off on a vacant frontage road.

"You drinkin' that shit or what?" A burly guard yelled at Eddy. He stormed out of the van and raced toward the Mercedes cab, yanked the door open. "You ever hear of a turn signal?"

Eddy was a head taller than the guard. They stood there, looked at each other. The guard seemed surprised that Eddy was so big. The driver saw him, stepped out, hand on his holster. But he stayed near the van. Professional, careful, Eddy thought.

"Hey, I thought I'd cleared you." Eddy looked around. He opened both palms. "You're okay. No harm done. We're insured. Let's just get information and—"

The blue Mercury wheeled off the exit ramp, nearly ran into the van. The tires screamed as it swerved to a halt, gravel flew. It hadn't stopped completely when Dodd and Henderson threw open the doors and leaped out. They were wearing green coveralls over their dress suits. Raul wheeled the car around, crossed the narrow median, parked nose out on the shoulder of the interstate, twenty-five yards away.

The guards watched, frozen when the two men pulled sawed-off shotguns up and pointed them in their direction. Eddy couldn't help but grin at them. It was slick: clockwork. Like TV. He was wrong about the odd couple. They were definitely players.

The driver came to, drew his pistol, but Dodd pulled the trigger on his shotgun and blew a hole big enough to read through into his midsection. He flew against the open door of the van, rolled into the ditch. The other guard spun around, gave Eddy one terrified look.

"Son of a bitch," he said before he was cut down by Henderson. The side of the van—Eddy's legs, too—were splattered with blood.

It all happened so fast, Eddy didn't have time to blink.

"Get it," Dodd ordered. Henderson leaped into the van.

Eddy stood motionless, stared at the fallen guards. Dead, he thought, deader than rocks. It was chilly, but sweat dropped into his eyes. He felt moisture under his arms. His left knee was stained with fresh gore. He'd never seen dead men before.

"Locked," Henderson yelled. Dodd went to the driver and

rolled him over. He ripped a bunch of keys from his belt, flung them inside.

"Hurry the fuck up, for Chrissake!" It was the first time Eddy had ever heard either man swear or raise his voice.

"You didn't say anything about this," Eddy yelled. The roar of passing traffic swallowed his words. Dodd looked at him, smiled. Eddy thought: Snake.

"Got it!" Henderson yelled. He dropped to the pavement with a silver-metal briefcase in his hands. Repeated: "Got it." Then he scrambled through the grass over to the car, tossed it into the back seat of the Mercury: grinned a wide, fat grin, then started back.

"You stay here. Wait for the cops," Dodd said. He held the shotgun loose in the crook of his arm. "Just like we planned." He smiled, too.

Eddy glanced at Raul hunched behind the wheel. He gave Eddy a sick, apologetic look.

"Shouldn't I *go* for the cops? I mean, won't it look bad if I just hang around here and wait? This was *not* part of the plan, goddamnit! These guys are dead! You were supposed to tie them up." He looked down at the two corpses.

Dodd shrugged. "You're right." He transferred the shotgun to his left hand, reached inside his coveralls. "Here. . .uh, this'll help." He pulled out a small automatic and shot Eddy point-blank. His knees buckled and he felt himself fall, hit the blacktop, his head bounce on the ground. At the same time, he saw the Mercury pull away fast, gravel sprayed behind it, left Henderson standing, gaping, then running behind it, yelling.

Then the interstate swept away, the world went black.

The feeling Eddy had when he saw Dodd pull out the pistol and shoot him was much like the feeling he had when he pulled off I-45 and made his way across downtown Houston to Main Street with a well-armed Moria Mendle sitting complacently next to him. Smoking gun, Eddy thought. They passed through the late rush-hour traffic, headed for the medical center.

Eddy could sometimes feel the slug tearing through his side, eating up a kidney, pushing its way out the back of his jacket. Like a shit pain, Eddy thought, a bad one.

Even though he was down, out, badly hurt when a highway patrol car finally stopped by to investigate the apparently abandoned vehicles, he was a prime suspect in the robbery-murder, mostly because of the .45 he had on him. And his record. It wasn't much of a rap, the leggy, pouty-mouthed PD he drew this time kept telling him, but it was enough.

Her name, typically, was Zelda: hardline ball buster—white stockings, black dress, stringy hair, no makeup, no tits, big ass, bigger grudge. She told Eddy she only worked as a PD so she could establish herself as a legal advocate for battered women. Eddy knew she hated him on sight, had him pegged: male, guilty.

"This time you're going away," she said. "Only question is how long."

She was disappointed. They couldn't prove a thing, and Eddy wasn't talking. Being that badly hurt helps keep a guy quiet while he waits things out. Ramona came to visit him when he got out of surgery. She was frantic. Raul, she told Eddy, had disappeared. He called her twice, wouldn't say where he was, what he was going to do. For once in his life, he sounded scared. He told her he was "outta sight" and staying that way. "Tell Eddy this was heavier shit than we knew," he said. "Heavy, heavy shit." The cops weren't looking for him, but somebody was, somebody bad.

Eddy knew who. He knew why. The what, though, remained hidden with Raul.

The next week, Eddy got a get-well card: "Don't worry about nothing," it read. "I'm cool. Our score is cool." He mailed it to Ramona. She delivered it to Eddy. It was typed, wasn't signed. Inside was a photo of a 1968 Camaro clipped from some car magazine: "Classic Hot Wheels," the caption said. A red circle was drawn around it. "Mine," was written in the margin.

Dodd and Henderson disappeared. Their phone was disconnected. No forwarding address: there never were.

Eddy called Quince. The conversation was less than satisfying.

"You fucked up. I don't want to hear from you," Quince said. "Ever again."

"You set me up," Eddy said. "You knew about it. Knew about Dodd and Henderson."

"Who?" Quince asked, flat. "I don't know what you're talking about," Quince said. "You're a criminal, Eddy. And you're stupid."

That much, Eddy thought, was right. He hung up.

Eddy kept his mouth shut, let Zelda do the talking. She didn't say much. Not to help him, anyway. Dallas detectives came to see him on the hour, DPS and Texas Rangers on the half hour. Sheriff's department even sent an investigator. Some federal suits dropped in "for a chat," asked him about Raul, but he faked sleep, and finally the feds left. The ADA came twice. The second time, he just stood there and looked at him. Eddy opened his eyes.

"Piece of shit," he said. Eddy stared. "You're going away."

And he did. But they couldn't tie him to the killings. The shotguns disappeared with Dodd and Henderson. His role in the robbery was in question, too, since there were no witnesses, and the .45 was cold. Didn't even work. No one knew what was taken from the van. Or no one would say. The manifest disappeared. The Purolator people claimed they didn't know a thing, that the guards didn't work for them, that it wasn't their van. Eddy figured: lawsuit.

Things got more confused after that. Nobody knew shit. Nobody was talking. Eddy refused to say anything to anybody, Zelda pleaded the charge down to Carrying a Concealed Weapon to get him out of it and off her case load. Everyone seemed happy about that, especially and surprisingly, the ADA. Too happy. They asked, he said okay, said the judge was sick of the whole goddamned thing. So was Eddy. He wasn't a player—not yet—he was just a patsy. He knew the whole thing smelled. He didn't care. Two-to-five was better than Murder-One and a needle.

That was Eddy's first time in the TDC. He started the full nickel in Huntsville as soon as he could move around. Raul stayed out of sight, but sent short, meaningless notes to Eddy through Ramona. Said not to worry, the "Big Score" was safe. He kept sending pictures of "hot cars," all Camaros, all labeled "Mine."

That clued him that Raul still had the briefcase, for what that was worth. Eddy decided that it was worth a lot. But he wasn't sure it was worth it to him.

Dodd and Henderson went to the moon.

Eddy scanned the papers, kept wondering what was worth so much blood, so much risk. He never found out. As soon as he was sentenced, everybody forgot about it. Not even the cons knew, and the cons knew everything.

Except for the pain in his side, it was like it never happened.

Huntsville happened. Eddy never forgot it. He called it "graduate school." When he came out, he had an education: He was on his way to becoming a player.

Before Eddy knew about it, Barbara was gone. Quince came up in person, shipped her to New York to finish school under Hillary's supervision, with Hillary's money. She didn't even come see him. That hurt Eddy worse than Dodd's bullet.

"She's the daughter I never had," Hillary wrote to Eddy. Then, underlined, *"Stay away from her, or else."* She signed it, "Love Always, you little turd." Sweet sister, Eddy thought.

Eddy wrote to Barbara every week. No reply. He wasn't stupid, knew that Hillary was doing to his letters exactly what he had done to hers. He tried to contact Ramona, see what she knew. She was gone, too. Quince refused his phone calls. Raul stayed disappeared. Only his notes showed up. Finally, they stopped, too.

Only Eddy remained. He tried telephoning Barbara at the last address he had for Hillary, but the number was unlisted.

For nearly a year after he got out, he tried to get in touch with Barbara, talk to her, let her know he was safe, well. He started to go to New York a dozen times, chickened out. Didn't know where they were, anyway. He wrote her every week: no answer. Letters came back: "Address unknown," or "No forwarding address." Each rejection penned in Hillary's flowery hand. He called Quince, even begged, offered money—

that was a laugh—finally threatened Quince that if he didn't come across with a phone number, he would come to Houston and beat it out of him. Quince told him to come on: flat refused. But Eddy heard the fear in his voice. So he sat down and wrote again, but to Hillary this time. If he didn't hear from her, he was coming up there, turn the city upside down. He was taking Barbara back.

One spring afternoon, two days later, Quince called him at Monica's, where he had been staying since getting out. His lawyer brother gave Eddy the phone number. "This is it, Eddy," Quince told him. "I've fixed it so you can talk to her. But we're quits, you and I. I have no brother. I don't need a liability. Don't try to contact me, ever again."

"Just put me back with Barbara," Eddy said. "It'll be like I never was."

And he wasn't. Not as far as Quince was concerned.

He called right away, but there was no answer. He dialed the number every hour all night, but no one picked up. Then, the next morning, after more than two years, he heard Barbara's voice.

The conversation was strained at first, awkward. Like asking for a loan, only the collateral here was something too tender to measure. They both probed with small talk, like a surgeon searching for a bullet.

She sounded the same as ever, except older, more sure of herself. She assured him that she held no grudge for his screwing up, leaving her in her aunt's hands. She said she was happy— he could hear the lie—then she broke down, said she had had enough. Hillary was a pain in the ass, she said. "She's always trying to get me to fuck some preppy."

Eddy was shocked at her language. Said so.

Barbara laughed. "Don't worry. I'm just learning to be a New Yorker. Besides, that kind of talk keeps Auntie Bitchie's friends away from me."

"Auntie Bitchie?"

"My little name for her."

"It fits."

Barbara laughed. Having an ex-con for an old man gave her

something to talk about, she said. That kept the society boys away from her, too.

"Whenever a guy, you know, wants to go too far, I just tell him about you."

"What do you tell him?"

"That you're a Texas Mafia boss who'll feed him to the fishes as soon as you get out of the slammer."

"You see too many movies."

"I get straight A's."

"So what are you going to do with all that,"

"Don't tell Aunt Hillary"—she said "Haunt Hallaray"—"Auntie Bitchie, that is, but I think I want to be a gangster, too." She laughed. He winced. "Or a lawyer."

"It's about the same thing." Eddy tried to laugh into the phone. Then he coughed and said in a serious tone, "The world needs more lawyers."

"With guys like you around, you're telling me! Hey, maybe I'll be a cop."

They laughed about that. She was grown, he thought. His girl was a woman. She would never come home. It made him happy and sad all at once. He looked around Monica's cheap one-bedroom apartment: saw the dirty clothes, the sink full of dishes, the blaring TV, the ratty furniture, broken toys, broken dreams. Her daughter was taken by Social Services two months before. What home? he thought.

When they hung up, Eddy felt lost. The girl he had held in his memory for so long had disappeared. He lost her on the frontage road of an interstate. He blamed Raul. But he mostly blamed Quince. When he thought about it longer, he blamed himself. Hillary was right. So was Quince. He was an accident. He never was anything else.

All that kept him alive in prison was the thought of finding Barbara, of talking to her. Instead, he had found a different person: street-smart and sharp-tongued. She reminded him of himself: a wiseguy, a smart-ass. He wasn't sure how to feel about that. But he knew he had lost something. The question was what was there to replace it?

He sat down on Monica's bed and wept. It was the first time he cried since he was a kid. He then made a promise to himself, to her. He wasn't going to be a loser anymore. He was going to use what he knew. He didn't know how, but he sure knew why.

Barbara gave him an address in Brooklyn where he could write to her. Eddy admired her guts. They wrote every week, talked on the phone every month. She called him every time, said it was too risky for him to call her, that Hillary was a total bitch. It was best if she stayed in the dark. Eddy didn't care. If it pissed Hillary off, he never heard about it. There wasn't much she could do anyway. Barbara was eighteen now.

Barbara told him Hillary had made big plans for her. College, even marriage was on the menu, she said. But she had other ideas. Hillary could go piss up a rope. Eddy laughed. In late July, she told Eddy she was heading to California.

"What're you going to go on?"

"Are you kidding? I've got money I'll never spend. She gives me an allowance. I've been banking it. You want some?"

Eddy winced. "So you're just going, huh? You think she'll let you? She'll just come get you."

"Naw. She's getting bored with me. I still won't screw around with any of her friends' sons, so she spends half the time pouting. And taking me shopping. You would not believe how much she blows on clothes. I'm leaving in a week, driving out with a friend. A guy," she added.

"One of the preppies?"

"Naw, he's a cop. From Jersey."

"A cop?"

"Yeah. He got on with a force out there near LA. He's going to go to law school."

"A cop."

"Don't sweat it. He's cool, and we're not heavy. I may need him if she decides she wants me back."

"What's his name?"

"Louis Sandobal."

"A dago?" Eddy asked. "You're going to California with a dago cop?"

* * *

"He's not a 'dago.' " Barbara laughed. "He's from Newark. Newark, New Jersey." She laughed again. "They all look alike, you know."

"Jesus," Eddy said. "Have you really thought—"

"I'll call when I get set up." Barbara cut him off. He knew she wasn't telling him all the truth, that she was hiding something. The feeling hardened him, reminded him of Ellen. He realized he felt it in every conversation they had. He couldn't decide if she didn't trust him, or if she was protecting him. "Give me two weeks." She paused. "Do Auntie Bitchie and Uncle Quince have to know where I am?"

"They can find out."

"They're always plotting."

"About what?"

"This and that." She paused. "You mostly. Don't tell them where I am, exactly. Let them figure it out. I'm old enough. Screw 'em."

"You going to live with this dago cop from New Jersey?"

"No. I told you we're not heavy."

"California's heavy. And it's crazy."

"So are you, ex-con. But I love you. He's just a friend."

"People get killed out there."

She took a moment to answer. "People get killed in Texas, Eddy."

She had a point, and he knew what the point was. "What's with this 'Eddy.' What happened to 'Daddy'?"

"Just practicing. I told you, I'm going to California."

"Yeah, well. Be careful. I mean it."

"I don't have to be careful. I'm smart."

That's what you think, Eddy said to himself.

Eddy violated parole within two hours after he hung up: bought a nearly new .38 Smith and Wesson from a pawn shop, thought he would UPS it to Barbara as soon as she had an address. He didn't, not then.

Neither Hillary nor Quince tried to contact him. Or Barbara, so far as he knew. She stayed in touch with him, though. She was going to school in California, dating a cop, an Italian cop, from New Jersey. Life was funny, he thought. He fell into Deep Ellum and picked up where he left off. There was a difference now, though: he was going to use his education. He was a player.

6
Raul

In New York or other major cities, the Medical Arms Pavilion would be called a "residential hotel." In Houston, it was just an odd place to live. Constructed in the fifties in the middle of what real-estate high rollers hoped would become one of the nation's major medical centers, it was designed for long-term tenants: out-of-town family members hanging around waiting for some seriously ill and seriously rich relative to die. It thrived then. Soon, its neo-art-deco furnishings, tall ceilings, classical lines went out of fashion. Newer hotels and motels were built, some with modern luxuries: in-room saunas, tennis courts, call girls, cocaine on demand.

The Medical Arms Pavilion declined, became a stopover for wanna-be high rollers: wildcatters looking for a grubstake, land developers looking for a bankroll, middle-aged lovers looking for a place to hide.

In the mid-eighties, the loose money that kept it afloat dried up. The owners went Chapter Eleven, started looking for a buyer. Four Japanese surgeons snapped it up, refurbished it, combined rooms into suites, sold them as swanky condos to rich physicians: guys who needed a tax dodge and a convenient place to boff nurses and wealthy patients' wives—or husbands.

Around the medical center, for a while, it was called "Pussy and Proctology Arms," for short, "the P&P." In more recent years, it took on the name of the "AIDS Inn," when two prominent orthopods confessed that they were HIV positive and wanted to live out their final years—or months—in homo-marital bliss. They got a full page spread in the *Houston Post*. That drove most of the doctors out. Some said it drove the *Post* out of business, too.

Rich medico sellers found plenty of buyers, recession or no—in Houston, hard times meant trading the Ferrari for a Cadillac. By the late eighties, some of the rooms were owned by crooked lawyers, disreputable businessmen, dirty politicians. They called themselves "Bush Dodgers" and had neat little money laundering schemes mixed in with pork barrel rake-off and foreign arms deals. Cops estimated that on any given night, there was more cash in the Medical Arms Pavilion than in the National Mint.

There was a chef on staff, an exercise room with a full-time trainer, and an executive's club on the tenth floor. Hot tubs were installed on the balconies, and fully equipped wetbars were standard equipment. Hookers, nose flake now all came from private stock. Moria bought in early, used a three-bedroom luxury suite as headquarters when he was in town. He allowed no one else to occupy it, not even Cole, not unless he was there as well.

Cole didn't care. He had his own connections in Houston.

"It's his getaway," Cole told Eddy once when they dropped Moria off and then drove out to the Marriott just off Main where Eddy hung out. "He doesn't stay there all the time. Likes to work out of the restaurant when he's in town. Mostly. But he likes this place. It fits him, he says. It's classy."

Eddy didn't feel classy when they pulled into the driveway, parked under the canopy. His gut hurt. The grim acknowledgment that Moria had killed the guy in the loud sports jacket took some time to set in. The old, sick pain of a bullet ripping through him returned. The idea that now he was Accessory to Murder-One didn't help. He didn't sign on for this shit. It wasn't part of his deal. Twenty-to-life was a guarantee, and they didn't parole three-time losers.

The urge to get out swarmed around his head. He checked Hedge in the rearview, but the dark man had his shades on again. He smoked and stayed as he was, while a doorman rushed around opening doors on the battered Buick.

Eddy was anxious to drop Moria, get to a motel, think this through, maybe split. Whatever was going on was not in his job description. all he was supposed to do was to drive this fat little prick around. In the past eight hours, he had been a sideline witness to a half-dozen murders. Driving, backing up action for money: that was straight business, straight payoff. Murder was something more. Too much, Eddy thought.

He decided on the Holiday Inn over by Hobby. Close to the airport, close to a getaway. He needed to think.

He didn't get the motel. Moria grew sullen again on the drive across town. He spoke only to tell Eddy to ignore the valet, park the car himself, follow him inside. Hedge got out silently, grabbed Moria's two suitcases, Eddy's shoulder bag, the portable phone, trudged after Moria past the doorman.

Eddy slammed the Buick into an open space, got out, locked it, found Moria and his man waiting for him in the lobby. Moria nodded once, turned and started toward the security desk.

"Mendle," Moria said when he passed the uniformed guard. "Check your list." The guard frowned, consulted a pad in front of him, then Moria pulled out a wad of bills. This brought a snappy salute, broad smile. Old coot, carrying a rusty .38. Eddy thought: Retired cop.

"No need, Mr. Mendle," the guard said through a grin. "Good to see you again." Moria gave him a sawbuck.

"Asshole," Moria muttered to Eddy when they got on the elevator. "The world is full of assholes."

The suite was on the fifth floor and was large, gaudy, overdone. Eddy thought: Ersatz Vegas. The most recent remodeling had restored the old-fashioned decor, but subtle modernization was evident. The entryway led to a landing, overlooked a sunken living room. A bank of lights recessed into the ceiling. Two sofa-chair arrangements, fake fireplace, full bar, mini kitchen off to one side. Dark brown carpeting gave way to blood-red tile. The opposite wall was made up of glass doors that opened to a patio. The rim of a hot tub was visible. It was covered, but Hedge dropped his burden in the middle of the room, walked straight through, began opening it for business. He read Moria's needs like they were printed in neon.

Three bedrooms, each with its own bath, fed off the living area. One wall had blond cabinets: stereo equipment, TV, VCR, more liquor than would fit on the glass shelves behind the bar. A small dinette was in the corner.

"Call up some food," Moria said. He picked up his bag, the phone, went toward the bedroom on the left. "You take the front room. Let Hedge have the back. He likes the view."

Eddy stood where he was, looking after Moria's disappearance. This was the best chance he had to check out of the deal: turn and go. He reached around behind him, adjusted the pistol. Part of him wanted to run. Part of him said stay, or he'd regret it. He didn't know how long Moria's arm was. He did know that he put a heavy price on loyalty. It was his best—maybe his only—quality. Eddy wasn't an idiot. He knew Moria was a player, but this game was growing too large. Eddy had doubts that Moria could handle it.

A full minute passed. Hedge pulled the tarpaulin off the hot tub, snapped the pump switches. Eddy hadn't moved.

"What's the matter with you?" Moria came out. He had shed his white suit, now had on a baby-blue, floor-length terrycloth robe. He kept the dark glasses. The bulge in a side pocket told Eddy that he retained his piece as well. "Order up something to eat. You deaf?"

"Why'd you ice that guy?"

"What?" Moria came in, sat down on the sofa next to the phone. Eddy saw that it had a row of buttons. Five, six lines coming in. "Oh," he said. "Ralph the Mouth? Old business. He'd had it coming a long time." He shook his head. " 'Ice him,' " he chuckled. "You watch too much TV."

"So, why?"

"We had a talk," Moria said. "Couldn't come to an understanding."

"What the fuck's going on?"

"What the hell is this? Quiz show? You're being paid to drive, not to think. Quit bitching and do as you're told."

Eddy stood still and looked at his boss. "Did. . .this guy have anything to do with Cole? I thought we were here to find the hooker."

"We are. And we will. And yeah, he did. Sort of. Cole was down here to handle him. Didn't do it. I have no idea why." He nodded toward the VCR. "Ralph had nothing to do with the other business. We'll find out who nabbed Cole, who 'iced' him. Have to. That's why we're here. The other business. That's why he was down here: take care of old Ralph. It was an in-and-out. Maybe he didn't have time. Ralph said Cole called, never showed up. We know why."

Eddy moved over and sat down. "I didn't think. . .I thought—"

"Sometimes it pays to take care of business quick," Moria sighed. "If Cole had done that, we'd be at the Rib Hut on Greenville right now. I got no idea what he was doing with Johnny Ribbon: dipshit." Eddy couldn't decide if Moria was talking about Cole or Johnny. "Cole had his own thing. I told you that. Thought he had better sense than to hook up with Ribbon."

Moria picked up the phone, punched a button, stopped, looked at Eddy hard. "Ralph's been skimming for a couple months. We warned him. He liked the Oilers. And the Astros. Played them once too often. Guess his luck went sour. Sure as hell did today. He was into his bookie for a good hundred grand, maybe more. Hard to tell, way he kept the books. He was getting to be a liability. Had a mouth. And if he shot it off to the wrong people, then we'd all be in the toilet.

"You don't need a college degree to figure this out. He needed cash. His lease was up. Bob came down here to take care of him. You got to do that sometimes, or you lose loyalty."

He gave Eddy a narrow, pained look. "I didn't kill him, if that's what you're thinking. But he won't be walking for a while. Not for a goddamn long while. I pick up his markers, he goes on welfare. If he keeps his mouth shut, he keeps breathing. That's the way this game works. You know that. You didn't just fall off a fruit truck.

"The point is that none of my people screw me. Not for money. And a blown kneecap or two is nothing to what the shylocks down here would do to him." He smiled, wistful. "Cole might have iced him. I don't ask how Bob takes care of business, and I don't worry about a walking piece of shit like Ralph. Bob is—was—a coldblooded son of a bitch. But taking care of this sort of thing was his end of the business. You know that, too. Or you should."

"What's your end?"

Moria stared at Eddy, hard. "I don't know why I'm telling you any of this. You're either with me or you're not. I decide to take a guy off, any way I choose to, you're in or you're not. I don't owe you anything. Not anymore. You're well paid."

"When you tie me to murder, you owe me." Eddy folded his arms. "Money doesn't buy that."

"Murder? I don't do murder. I do business. Murder is personal."

"Dead is dead."

Moria shrugged. "Maybe."

Eddy felt himself start to relax. He wasn't sure he believed Moria. He was only sure that he wasn't going to take the rap for murder. He also felt justified: Moria was warned.

"What I need to know, need to know now, is if you're in or you're out."

Eddy stiffened. He noticed that Moria's hand was now in the pocket of the robe. "I can't afford to have some pussy watching my back who might rabbit on me, sell me out."

"If I was going to sell you out, I'd have done that in Huntsville."

"Maybe the price wasn't right."

Eddy smiled slightly. "In prison, the price is always right."

Moria looked at him, nodded. "That's what I thought." Moria picked up the phone again, punched numbers. "Now, go in there and use the other line. Call up some food. I feel like a steak: burn it. Get what you want."

"What about him?" Hedge was pouring chemicals into the hot tub.

"Get him *two* steaks. Rare. Raw: hot, pink on the inside. He'll be hungry. Man eats more than he makes."

Eddy picked up his bag and moved into the bedroom.
In spite of everything, he realized that he was hungry.

When Eddy got out of the joint on the CCW and back to
action in Dallas, everything was different. The street action
had changed, gotten leaner, less predictable. Gangbangers were
taking over: street-stupid punks with big guns and tiny pricks,
looking to use one to make the other grow. They killed for
fun, status. It was crazy, and it was no place for a guy who
had bottomed out. He had the stuff to be a serious player, but
he needed a connection.

He first met Tommy Bodine in Dallas County. Bodine was
a coon-ass from Port Arthur who was serving out a short ride
for reckless driving. He had been in Huntsville four times,
Sugar Land twice, but always on nickel-and-dime beefs that
didn't amount to much. Three two-to-fives, a parole violation,
couple of short boxcars he never served out: small-timer. Everyone from the Dallas DA to the Parole Board knew it. Tommy
knew it, too.

Eddy stayed in touch. Bodine called him once a month,
brought him up to date on the inside news. It was always a
good idea to know what was happening inside.

"Lots of bad motherfuckers in here these days," Tommy
said. "Violent motherfuckers! Don't do violence. Hurt people,
they put you away, cher. They don't give a shit for a light-
weight rip-off man. I need to get out of here. Hell, they *need*
my ass on the street. Who gonna do their shit for them?"

Before the gun bust, Tommy had dealt drugs for a while,
but cocaine dropped from twenty grand a key to just over ten.
Everybody was selling it, especially the gangbangers. Grass
was up to a grand a pound. Nobody but Yuppies and college
kids wanted it. Crack was the ticket, then: easy to package,
easy to sell, easy to hide. But it could buy a hard ten-to-twenty
with the feds, especially if the dealer had a sheet. Tommy had
a sheet, so he quit dope. He ran cars over the border for a
while, then he quit that, too.

"Got tired of clicking around with greasers," he said. "You
boost something cool, run it down there thinking you're going

to get four, five grand, they say they don't have it when you get there. What'd'ya do? You can't take it back, you don't want it yourself, so you take a dime on the dollar and leave 'em laughing at you.'' He turned to burglary and a little gun-running. "I may be small-time," he said, "and I may be in the joint, but I'm a player. You bet your ass. They can't take that away.

"That's why you went away on a bum wrap, cher. You got ripped off, suckered. I guarantee! Them guys let you take the fall. Lots of guys work like that. Spend half their time looking for somebody too stupid to know fuck from fart.''

Eddy mulled that over. He had been stupid. Raul took off on him, left him to fall, left him bleeding, set up. Eddy did a package, learned to sleep with one eye open, one hand on his cock. He still wondered what was in the briefcase. But then he stopped hearing from the little jerk Raul. Eddy figured whatever it was, Raul had sold for a tenth of its value, bought a car, split.

"I'm not done with those guys," Eddy told Bodine. "They owe me."

"Shit, cher, let it go," Tommy advised. "Them guys is gone. Even if you catch them, what you gonna do? Kill them?''

"Something like that."

"Cher, that ain't no good at all. Revenge is for crazies. Losers. Pissed off 'groids with a rag on their head, boom box in their ear. You got to figure a way to use it, not lose it. You got to be a player to stay in the game."

When Eddy got out, Raul was gone. Fell off the planet. Nobody heard from him. Nobody knew him. That told Eddy he was still around. When you're really gone, everybody knew you. He didn't worry. Raul would turn up, and when he did, Eddy intended to get some answers. He remembered Bodine's advice, though: no revenge. For the time being, things were sweet, Barbara was okay, Eddy felt good.

Nothing went sour until the gun deal. Bodine set him up for that. Eddy remembered Bodine's lessons, even if Bodine didn't. He took the fall for the convenience store robbery, went back inside. Then he met Moria, then he got out. The cash stayed stashed: rainy day, Eddy thought.

But in Houston, it was always a rainy day. Today, Eddy reminded himself, he was in Houston.

Hedge was hungry. He went through both his steaks, what was left of Moria's. He was sulking again. Eddy's appetite disappeared when the food arrived. He only picked at his meal, then lit a cigarette, watched the large, quiet bodyguard fork hunks of meat into his mouth; each bite got twenty good chews. He ignored the fried potatoes, drank bottled water, looked at no one, said nothing. When he was eating, he showed more animation than Eddy had seen before. At full height, he was just under six feet. Big muscles, bandy legs, no gut. His hair was wiry, graying in places, even on his shoulders. A tattoo— diamond pierced by a woman's leg—was on his left arm. Little fingers on both hands were missing; hacked off. He wasn't a player, but he was a hell of a backup man, Eddy thought— better than Eddy had ever been in the looks-alone department. Nobody would fuck with anybody if Hedge was standing there.

"Want something else?" Moria asked.

Hedge looked at him: lids half closed over flat and unexpressive greenish-gray eyes. "Burger, maybe," he said. His accent was foreign: Caribbean, Jamaican, maybe. Hands were heavy, short stubby fingers. Nails bit to the quick. Cauliflower ears. Eddy thought: Boxer.

"Make the call, order it for him," Moria waved at Eddy. "He don't like the phone."

Moria did. He left the table, picked up the other phone, dialed, and started talking in low tones, getting angry, cajoling, but never pleading or requesting. Sometimes, his tone said he was giving orders. But sometimes he listened, his eyes tight on Eddy. When he saw Eddy was listening, he glanced at the cabinet. "Put some music on, or TV. Turn it up."

The girls arrived ten minutes later. Eddy answered the door, stood back in surprise. They filed past: giggles and swish. There were four: names like Traci and Kari, Buffi and Wendi. All eyes. They carried small bags along with purses. Whores, Eddy thought. Moria didn't bother with introductions. They already knew Moria. Loved his short, fat ass, Eddy thought.

They barely glanced at Hedge, who now squatted in one of the chairs in the corner of the room and waited on his hamburger: just like the back room of Bishop's. He was there, but he wasn't. He kept on dark glasses to cover his eyes. Eddy figured he probably missed the darkness.

The girls did look at Eddy, but he ignored them and went to his bedroom, ordered up Hedge's burger, and lay on the bed, stared at the ceiling. He heard water splashing outside his window: they were all in the hot tub.

He thought of Barbara—bit it off, then of Princess, who was waiting for him to come home tonight. He guessed. He wondered if he should call her, wondered if she cared when he didn't call or come home. Home, he thought: a suite at the Sheraton. Room service, sauna, workout room, and she didn't have to dance or trick for Moria so long as Eddy stayed happy with her. To her, Eddy was a bankroll. The woman spent fifties the way other people spent ones. She'd tip twenty bucks for a two-dollar tab. Then laugh.

She was devoted to her body. It was something that commanded devotion: hips like a teenager, tits like a foldout, and legs that never seemed to end. Manicures, pedicures, massages, exercise, leg treatments, facials, she did it herself, or paid somebody to do it. She fooled with herself more than a con on a twenty-year stretch in solitary. But not in the same way. She required a steady diet of cock: his or somebody's. He was no fool. More than once he'd called down for clean sheets. He didn't care who she balled when he wasn't home, but he was damned if he'd sleep on some other guy's peter tracks.

And she went through his stuff regularly. Moria didn't like secrets.

He learned to keep anything personal at Monica's. Princess learned that, too. She hated Monica the way a fat woman hates high heels. She put up with her, but she didn't like her, never failed to bitch about her, either. But she didn't complain loud. Moria kept her too well for her to bitch about much.

He wondered what her real name was. Heather was Earline. That was nearly funny. Princess was probably named Hilda or something. Parents could be stupid.

But the woman could fuck. That she could do. She was a

wildcat in bed. Came quick, then again and again, knew how to make him wait, keep him hard. She didn't say shit, which was good. She knew better ways to use her mouth.

Monica, though, got mouthier as she got older. Got nosier, too. One of these days, he'd have to move on.

He picked up the phone to call Princess, then maybe Monica, then put it down. What could he say? He was in Houston, with Moria. Doing what? Well, maiming guys, he thought, but he wasn't sure. Maybe killing guys. Looking for a whore, but he wasn't sure of that, either. Looking for a killer. Maybe. All he knew was that the ceiling overhead needed painting. That seemed to sum up his life in some way. It was enough.

The doorbell rang: Hedge's burger. Eddy stayed where he was. Let him get it. The gun hurt his back. He pulled it out and dropped it into a nightstand drawer, pulled off his shirt, lay back. Around his neck on a chain he kept the key to the locker at Love where the twenty-five large was stashed. It trailed across his right nipple. He held it up, looked at it: a way out.

It reminded him of his old dreams, of days when he thought he could get ahead, make a life for himself, pushing that old pickup around. The hours he'd logged in that pickup sagged in his memory. The hours he and Raul spent bent over the engine, trying to figure out what was wrong, now pulled his thoughts lower, brought an ironic smile.

He wondered where the little son of a bitch was now. Mexico, probably.

After nearly two years of silence, Raul finally turned up. He came knocking at the door of Eddy's suite at the Sheraton. It was one of those miserable, hot summer days Dallas seemed to have a patent on: a Sunday—too hot to swim, too hot to do any goddamn thing but lay around and sweat. Eddy and Princess were still in bed, though it was after two. She was painting her toenails, reading the funny papers. He was watching TV. The Rangers were playing a matinee in Chicago, losing as usual. Princess had ordered pizza. Eddy was bored, thinking of calling Monica, seeing if she wanted to catch a movie. He knew Princess wouldn't. All she ever wanted to do was fuck, take baths, paint her toenails.

Lately, Monica didn't want to fuck much at all. In an odd sort of way, that pleased Eddy. He discovered a curious comfort just sitting next to her in a movie, watching TV in her dingy apartment, eating Chinese takeout, and talking about her daughter. She'd been gone two years. She missed her. It gave her and Eddy something in common, but it shut down the sex factory.

He looked over at Princess, lounging like a cat, on her stomach, reading, her long legs crossed over her perfect, naked ass, tits pressed flat beneath her, cotton-spaced toes waving in the air, drying. There was a lot to be said for just fucking, Eddy thought.

There was a knock at the door: pizza. Eddy waited, Princess ignored it. He got up, pulled on his pants, answered it: Raul.

The last time Eddy saw Raul, he was behind the wheel of the plain blue Mercury, spinning out, Dodd and Henderson running after him, waving their arms, yelling, leaving Eddy on the ground, bleeding. Now, there he stood: weight shifting, eyes darting around, trying to see past Eddy's bulk, a small, sick smile on his face.

"What's happening, bro?"

Eddy felt like grabbing the little shit, slamming him up against the wall. But he didn't. Raul seemed too pitiful, too scared. He had always been herky-jerky, jumpy and hard to settle down. There, standing in the doorway, he was so hyped he could barely stand still: eyes bloodshot, bulged. Sweat ran rivers down his forehead, though it was cool in the corridor.

Eddy stood watching him for nearly a full minute. Neither spoke. Then Eddy remembered Tommy Bodine's words. He smiled. The gesture surprised him. It made him feel glad to see Raul. The feeling didn't last long. Raul was filthy, stank. Eddy almost gagged when he smelled him: sweat and fear. He noticed that Raul twitched, nearly danced. Fried, Eddy thought.

"You gonna hit me, man?" Raul asked: a smile. "You can hit me if you want. I got it coming."

Eddy thought about it. It might make him feel better, might make them both feel better. But he didn't. Instead, he moved aside, allowed Raul into the living area of the suite.

Princess, wrapped in a sheet, came out to get the food. "Who is this?'' was all she said when she noticed he wasn't carrying a Domino's box. She wrinkled her nose. Raul's body odor filled the room.

"Old friend," Eddy said.

"Get rid of him. I'm thinking of waxing my legs," she said, wrinkled her nose. "He stinks."

Raul looked like roadkill. He hadn't shaved in days and was flying higher than the hotel. Eddy could almost see the stench coming off him: waves.

"Hey, man," he said. He blinked, as if he just awoke, realized where he was, who Eddy was. "What's happening, bro?"

Princess turned and rolled back into the bedroom. "Call me when the pizza gets here." She dropped the sheet just before she shut the door, flashing them with her butt. Raul rolled his eyes, breathed out. His teeth were black with rot. "Nice setup, man. Piece of ass, everything."

His voice was shaky, strained, high-pitched. He could hardly hold his hands steady to light the cigarette he bummed off Eddy. "How's Monica?"

Eddy winced, cast his eyes toward the bedroom. "How'd you find me?"

"I still got connections," Raul said. His eyes darted away: a lie, Eddy thought.

Raul's concentration drifted, flitted around the room. He rose, paced, kept looking at the bedroom door. Walked over to the window, checked the outdoor parking lot, four stories below. Eddy wanted to ask him about the briefcase, about the "score," but he didn't. He was waiting.

"Hey, you want to come down, see my wheels? I got me some hot wheels." He shot a telling look at the bedroom door. Eddy nodded. He pulled on tee-shirt, a pair of sneakers, followed him to the elevator.

"Listen, bro," Raul said in a whisper when the door closed. "I know you think I fucked you over. But I'm going to make it up to you. Swear to God. I'll do it, man. No shit."

Eddy said nothing. Standing in the elevator next to him was hard. Eddy held his breath. When they arrived at the lobby, Raul rushed out ahead of him. Eddy followed to the indoor parking garage. Raul walked over to an old Camaro. It was black, heavy with bondo beneath a cheap paint job. The windows were tinted dark, interior was ragged, trashed. Raul looked inside, unlocked the door. Eddy spied the metal briefcase on the seat.

"Last of the three-twenty-sevens, bro. Bored and stroked. Dual cartes. I'm going to fix her up," Raul said proudly. He was sweating rivers, always checking behind Eddy, turning, keeping an eye on every corner of the garage. "She runs like a bat outta hell. Zero to seventy in the quarter, rubber in all four. Top end at one-forty. Shifts like a motherfucker. Only problem is finding good gas, you know? That unleaded shit makes her knock like an old broad's titties."

Eddy shrugged.

Raul stepped forward. His body odor seemed to increase, and Eddy recoiled slightly. He spoke in a low tone. "Listen, bro. Can you slip me a yard or two? I gotta get out of town. Out the fucking country."

Eddy studied him. "What about—" He stopped himself. He was suddenly too angry to be cool. "What about our 'big score'? You said—"

Raul's eyes widened, he grabbed Eddy's arm. His grip was strong. "Shush, bro. Quiet!" he ordered. Then he whispered. "It was a bust, bro. Total fuckup."

"I thought—"

"Shush, bro. I'm not shifting you. Keep quiet." Eddy's eyes fell to Raul's hands. He relaxed his grip, smiled.

"What was in the briefcase?" There, it was out.

Raul shrugged, cast his eyes around. "Nothing, bro."

"Two guys don't go down for nothing," Eddy said. "Not like that. I don't go down for nothing."

"I'm not shitting you, bro. There wasn't nothing worth nothing in there."

"Nothing."

"Just two CDs."

Eddy's mind raced. "CDs? You mean like stocks or something?"

"No, man. Like music. CDs. Compact discs."

"That's it?"

"Yeah, CDs. Like *music*. Two of them. Nothing on them.

I know, I played them a couple times. Just a lot of hiss and noise and shit. No music, no talk, no nothing. Blank CDs.''

"CDs.''

"That's it, bro. No shit. Them two was crazy. You knew that. Or you found it out.'' Raul turned, leaned into the Camaro, pulled out the briefcase. "Here, bro,'' he said. "You can have them. Play them yourself. You're welcome to them. I come by just to show you. Give them to you. So you'd believe me.''

Eddy accepted the case. There was a combination lock dead center.

"It's a fancy security lock,'' Raul said. "Beats the shit outta me why. Nothing in there. Somebody sure ripped off somebody.'' He put the briefcase on the hood of the car, spun it around. "Combo's 3006, man. Like a rifle. Ain't that some shit? Took my friend two minutes to figure *that* out.''

Eddy wheeled the numbers, snapped the case open. Inside, there was red velvet. The whole thing was heavy, as if it was lined with metal. In two corners, one high, one low, a specially cut space held a compact disc. Each was nondescript, unlabeled except for a red number one on the left, a two on the right.

Raul picked one of them out, held it up to the light filtered from the garage's opening.

"Ain't nothing on it,'' Raul said. He shook his head. "Nothing. Not on neither one.''

Eddy lit a cigarette. He couldn't accept it: wouldn't. He took a bullet, lost a kidney, went to prison for empty CDs.

"Listen, bro. I'm sorry. I hung on to them for a long time. Thought maybe them two fucks would try to find me, try to buy it off me. Thought maybe they didn't know they got stiffed, too.'' Raul was talking fast-casual: Lying, Eddy thought.

"I was the one who was set up,'' Eddy said.

"Hey,'' Raul put up his hand. "You got to put yourself in my place, bro. I seen how it was going down. They whacked them two guards. That wasn't part of the deal. So I cut out. I figured your ass was gone. Should've been, too. Figured I was next.''

Eddy nodded, swallowed his anger.

"So, I seen them dump that case in the back seat, and I split. That's it, man. That's all there ever was. Swear to God. Hey, if you hadn't been in the joint, I'd showed you. Them two fucks was crazy.''

Eddy stood and smoked quietly, absorbing it. Raul danced.

"I got to have a couple yards, bro, if you got it. There's these cocksuckers after me."

"Who?"

"Don't know, man. I ain't done nothing to nobody. I been chilling out over in Fort Worth, you know. But these guys, they found me, been following me."

"What do they want?"

"Shit if I know, man. I just know they're always there, always following me. Different cars all the time. Different dudes, sometimes."

"Gangbangers?"

"No way, man. These are heavy dudes. Suits."

"Feds?"

Raul shook his head. "Not cops. I could smell them if they was cops."

Eddy caught another whiff of Raul, doubted it. "So, who?"

"Shit, I don't know. Never seen them before. Never know when they're there, when they're not, you know what I'm talking about? These are some bad-ass motherfuckers. I dropped out a couple days, they really messed up this chick I know. Said they wanted to talk to me. I need to get out of town. Now."

"I thought you *were* out of town," Eddy said. "Nobody knows where you—"

"Look, bro. I know you got the red-ass. I don't blame you. I owe you. I never meant for you to get burned. I swear, man. I'll make it up to you. Trust me. I'm going to make a deal, cut you in. Swear to God. But I need a couple yards, and I need it now. I gotta blow the country. These guys ain't fucking around."

"What do they want?" Eddy asked. Raul's eyes shot to the briefcase.

"That."

"So?" Eddy said. "Give it to them."

"You think I'm nuts? They open this, see couple of empty

CDs, they're gonna just say *muchas gracias,* maybe hand me a couple grand for my trouble?''

He put the CD back in place, slammed the briefcase's top shut as if hit by a sharp pain. "First thing they're gonna do is think *I* ripped them off. Then they're gonna hang my ass out to dry. You know what I'm talking about?''

Eddy nodded. He knew.

Raul wiped his mouth with the back of his hand. Took a breath. "These ain't the kind of guys you have a long conversation with, bro. They're crazier than Dodd and Henderson.'' He glanced around again, nervously. "Look, man, I think maybe they done something to Ramona.''

"What?'' Eddy felt something drop inside him.

"Well, like I say, I was chilled out. You know. Only person I talked to was Ramona.''

"Where is she?''

"In Chi. She was in Chi. Went up there when you went down. Back to the folks. Went to work for these people up there. A while back, I call Ramona where she's working, and they say she don't come in. I call the folks. They say she went to work yesterday, don't come home. They're worried as shit. That was two weeks ago. No word since.''

"And you think they got her?''

"I don't know, man. They're—'' He broke off, moved quickly to shift the briefcase to the ground next to the Camaro: out of sight. A Volkswagen Golf drove into the garage, parked. Raul held his breath. One hand drifted under his shirt. Eddy spotted the butt of a large revolver. A tall, well-dressed black man got out of the car, gave them a short, quick look. He stopped, extracted a long cigar, lit it, took his time, then walked quickly toward the elevator, paid them no more attention. Citizen, Eddy thought.

"I need to *go,* man. Now. You gonna help me out or not? I got this friend down south. Mexico. He'll put me up, get me some action, but I got to get there, bro.''

Eddy was confused. He reached in his pocket, found a wad of bills. Three, maybe four hundred in fifties, twenties. He peeled off a couple, saw the look in Raul's eyes: Dead man, he thought. He gave it all to him.

"Thanks, bro," Raul stuffed the money into his dirty jeans. Opened the door to the Camaro. "Knew I could count on you." He looked at the briefcase, still on the ground.

"May as well keep that," he said. "Maybe get rid of it. I was gonna throw it in the lake, you know? Maybe dump it someplace. You can do that, okay? It's bad news, man."

Eddy nodded, hefted the case. It was surprisingly heavy. Scars and dents marked the metal.

"Hey," Raul stuck out a greasy hand. "Thanks again, bro. No shit."

He started to enter the Camaro, then stopped, wiped his mouth. "Hey, how's Barbara?"

Eddy stepped back, off guard. "Fine."

"That's good, man," he said. "That's real good. She still in LA?"

"Yeah."

"Lots of action in LA. You tell her I asked on her, okay?" Eddy stared at him. "Tell her I said to watch her ass." He rubbed his face. His hands came away wet. He wiped them on his shirt. "Look, I got to tell you. Them dudes, they come 'round to where I live yesterday. They fucked up this chick I know pretty damn bad. You remember her? Audra? I don't think she's gonna make it. That's when I thought maybe I'd come see you. Let you know."

He looked up through the roof of the garage. "You got it made, bro: fancy place, fancy pussy. Maybe you didn't get burned so bad after all. Maybe I'm the one who got screwed."

He fired the Camaro. The engine leaped, purred, eager to go. "Told you she runs good," he said. Then he leaned out, motioned Eddy over. He looked deep into his eyes. "I gotta trust you, bro. I know you don't gotta trust me, but I gotta trust you. You ain't seen me, don't know nothing about me. Man, you never *heard* of me."

Eddy nodded.

"You're the only bro I got," Raul gave him a black grin. "I let you down. But I won't do that again. I'll stand up."

"Who's chasing you?"

"Man, I wish I knew. All I know is that these're some hard-headed cocksuckers." He looked in the rearview, checked both

directions, then took a deep breath, let it out slow. "I gotta go.
I don't need no more of this shit. Wish I'd never seen that
fucking case, man."

He gunned the engine once, Eddy stepped back, and Raul
left a strip of rubber six feet long when he raced out of the
parking garage.

He hadn't heard from him since.

He took the case upstairs, loaded one of the CDs into Princess's player, listened. Raul was right: hiss and static.

He replaced the disc, put the case in a closet. Raul was too
much of a liar for anyone to worry about. He'd take it out to
the lake tomorrow, throw it off a bridge. It was heavy enough
to sink. Bodine was right. Revenge was for losers. Better to
bury the past, put it behind him.

Raul was right, too, Eddy thought with a glance at Princess
who sat on the sofa, naked, her long legs folded up while she
watched TV, painted her fingernails. He had it made.

But later, in the middle of the night, he awoke. Princess lay
beside him, soughing softly, sated by one of her more extreme
sexual performances. Raul's appearance had repulsed her, but
she was turned on by the chance to flash him, Eddy supposed.
His cock throbbed from the ordeal. He felt raw.

But what woke him was not pain. What awoke him was the
sudden memory or Raul's voice. "How's Barbara?. . .She still
in LA?"

What was the slimy little spick *trying* to tell him? How did
he know Barbara was in California?

He got up, lit a smoke, went to the living room. He calculated
the difference in time, picked up the telephone, dialed. He got
her recorder, hung up. He looked at the clock. It wasn't but
midnight there. Sunday midnight. She could be out: movie,
something.

She was okay. He'd have heard if anybody was bothering
her. Her boyfriend was a cop. Why would anyone bother her
anyway? Maybe Raul was just being friendly, nosy. Maybe he
called Monica.

A stack of newspapers spilled out of the corner. Eddy gathered up the last weeks' Metro sections, scanned them. He found
it, dated two days before.

A young woman, Audra Manitole, age twenty-four, was found badly beaten in her apartment. He checked the address: Randol Mill, East Fort Worth, near Arc Park. She suffered multiple broken bones, a fractured skull. There were no witnesses, no suspects, but police believed the incident was probably drug related, as the woman had prior convictions for possession. She was in critical condition at Baptist Hospital.

He found the previous day's section. It was now a tiny item, across from the obits, moving her closer to the grave. No change in her condition. Still critical. No leads in the case, either, according to the five lines they gave her. Police were seeking her boyfriend, José Cuervo, for questioning.

José Cuervo, Eddy grinned. Aka Raul Castillo. Little spick never did have any imagination. Then, neither did Fort Worth cops.

He read the piece again, figured tomorrow they'd move Audra over a page.

Audra. Eddy conjured her. A somewhat overweight, fairly ugly half-black girl Raul had been on-again-off-again with for years. She came by the house when they lived on Rosedale a couple of times. Knew Barbara. Knew Monica. Knew Eddy. A chill came into the room, settled. Again, he reached for the telephone. Again, he resisted, lit another Camel, turned out the lamp, paced.

He went to the window, looked down into the outdoor parking lot. Cars were sparse under the arc lights. Most of the tenants parked in the covered garage. Nice night.

He started to move away, then he spotted something. A small, green car—VW Golf, just like the one that came in that afternoon—parked in a space off by itself, close to the covered parking exit. The window was down, and a man's suit-coated arm rested on the door, something in his fingers.

Eddy squinted, focused. The fingers held a long, fat cigar. It's coal tipped red even under the orange light. The citizen? Eddy thought: Coincidence.

But he wasn't convinced. He stood for nearly a half hour, watched the man, sitting, smoking, going nowhere. Same guy? Looking for Raul? Or looking for Eddy?

Or something else? "How's Barbara? She still in LA?" If

Raul knew she was in LA, who else knew? What difference did it make?

He went to the bedroom, rifled through the bureau, caused Princess to groan, turn over in protest. Then he found it. The S&W .38 he bought for Barbara months before, never sent. Afterwards it seemed stupid, silly. He took it to the living room, held it to the reflected light from the outdoors.

It was a nice piece. Heavy, well blued. The action was oiled, smooth. The hammer fell with a satisfying click when he worked it. He had never much liked handling guns, never found them fascinating. The automatic Moria wanted him to carry was uncomfortable. The truth was Eddy didn't trust it. It also reminded him of another small, black, ugly pistol that was used on him.

But the S&W was firm, challenging, attractive. He rolled the empty cylinders.

Calling her, telling her to be careful: useless. She was too sure of herself, now, too convinced he worried about her too much.

He wrapped the pistol in a pair of clean socks, then looked for packaging: nothing. Mail was not much of a priority in his life, not anymore. He didn't even have a stamp. But the hotel's concierge provided a twenty-four-hour overnight pickup service. He couldn't just hand them over a sock-wrapped pistol, though. He needed something heavy to ship it in, something sturdy and concealing. It wouldn't wait until morning. He felt desperate to get the pistol, the protection to his daughter. It wasn't much, but it was something.

He went to the closet, retrieved the briefcase, opened it. The CDs were in place. Between them was a space, velvet-lined, soft and cushy. The pistol fit there perfectly. He stuffed a box of shells in with it, then packed the whole thing tight with another pair of socks, closed it, spun the combination lock.

A sullen bellhop responded to his call, appeared at the door with an overnight box under his arm. Eddy made him wait while he shoved the briefcase inside, sealed the flap, scrawled Barbara's address on the label. "I want this to go out overnight," he said, handing the surprised boy a C-note. "The change is for you. Don't fuck it up."

The boy nodded, tucked the mailer under his arm, retreated.

It was now nearly one in LA. Eddy went to the phone and placed his call. Barbara's machine picked up again. "I'm sending you a present," he said. "The number you need is 3006. Learn to use it. Business only. Be smart, be careful."

When he hung up, he relaxed, lit a cigarette, strolled over to the window. The VW was still there, still in the same place, and the guy was working on a fresh cigar.

It wasn't until he lay down that he remembered: Tomorrow was Barbara's birthday.

7
Cops

Eddy rolled over, thought of sleep. The room was comfortable but plain. The money went into the living area. The bed was good, but the furniture was stiff: fifties junk. Another ring.

"You gonna get that, or what?" Moria yelled.

Eddy waited for Hedge to rise, go for his extra feeding. Another ring. This time a heavy knock followed.

"Goddamnit, Eddy!" Moria yelled. "Get the fucking door. What're you doing in there, jerking off?" The girls squealed laughter.

"C'mon out here, big guy," one of them yelled. "We'll help."

Eddy pulled himself off the bed, walked into the living room. Hedge was exactly where he left him, a lit cigarette in his paw the only indication he was alive. Moria's bathrobe pooled in the middle of the room.

He went to the patio door. Moria and all four girls, naked, were in the tub: clothes spread around on plastic furniture. They bobbed in the bubbles, tried to keep their hair and cigarettes dry, failed: a tub filled with tits. All eyes turned to Eddy when he emerged from the apartment. He knew how women felt when men leered at them.

"Is that the key to your heart, lover?" one of them asked, pointed at his chest, licked her lips.

Moria sat with a drink and a smoke up against one wall. His skin looked like cheap typing paper: white and limp. His breasts pooched out, fat rolled under the hairy nipples. He playfully dunked one of the girls over his crotch.

"Bobbing for sausage," he said, smiled. "C'mon in."

The doorbell rang again. More knocking.

Moria's face clouded. "Are you going to get the goddamn door or what? What am I paying you for?"

"Not to be your house nigger."

"Look, you don't want Hedge answering the door." Moria's eyes glassed over. He stroked the submerged head of the girl, closed his eyes. "Sweet baby!" he cooed. Then he turned his gaze on Eddy. "Just answer the door. Get him his burger, then strip down, get in." The girls giggled, looked seductive. One cupped her tits together in her hands, made kissing noises. "Relax. Enjoy. This is a fucking perk." He laughed at the pun. Dry. Matched his skin. "Don't be an asshole. I never even did this for Cole."

Eddy pictured Cole's head in the FedEx mailer. He wondered what Bishop had done with it. He also wondered exactly what Moria *did* do for Cole. The doorbell sounded again. Eddy went to the bedroom, put on his shirt, then padded across the living room to the door.

Instead of the pimply room service kid, two men stood in the threshold. One was tall, fat, red-faced: heart-attack candidate. He held a napkin-covered plate. Eddy smelled onions: Hedge's burger. The other was short, slight. He had a permanent, sad smile on his face, a broken tooth, bad complexion. One eye was slightly off center. Both stood heavy, bulged under their coats: prominent, meant to advertise, Eddy thought.

Eddy stepped back. Hair prickled on his scalp. His hand started to reach behind him, but the automatic was not there. The guys stiffened. He made a motion to turn, then stopped himself, thought. His eyes ran up and down the pair: five-dollar haircuts, drip-dry slacks, off-the-rack coats, 70-30% shirts, stained ties, neorubber-soled shoes. A guy dressed in a loud sports jacket raced across his mind. Eddy thought: Cops.

"Hello, Eddy," the big one said. "Thought you were on a little vacation up I-45."

The short one pulled out a wallet and dropped a badge out in front of him. "Houston PD," he said. "DaCara. Mendle at home?"

Eddy stayed tense, searched the big one's face. No recognition. Who the hell was he? He started to shut the door. "I'll see."

DaCara smiled again. It was a strange look, sideways, like he was playing some kind of joke. "Mind if we wait inside?"

The big man didn't wait for an answer. He shoved a size-thirteen wingtip across the threshold and thrust the small tray out toward Eddy. Eddy ignored it, walked through the living room. He reached down and scooped up Moria's bathrobe, hefted it to make sure the pistol was still in the pocket. Hedge didn't move except to light another cigarette.

"Cops," Eddy said. He was relieved in a way to see Moria's eyes widen then settle back to the all-business attitude he usually affected back in Bishop's. The girl had finished her work on him, sat off to one side, waterlogged, sipping a chaser. The other three didn't react to the news at all. One yawned.

"You see badges?" Moria asked.

"One: DaCara. Other guy didn't ID." Another prickle of fear. What if they weren't cops? He didn't know any Houston cops. He straightened the wadded bathrobe, felt for the pistol.

"Oh," Moria said. "DaCara already. Must be on overtime. Where are they?"

"In there," Eddy gestured. Moria rose from the water. Eddy looked at the shriveled skin dripping into the tub. The girls followed his eyes, giggled.

"I'll be back," Moria said, toweled off, climbed into the robe. "Don't let your pussy get wrinkly." He tied the robe around him, removed the pistol, shielded it with his body, dropped it into the hot tub. "Let's go."

Hedge sat exactly where he had been. The two cops were in the living area, the big one poked into the cabinets. Hedge's head was turned slightly to watch him. DaCara sat on the edge of a chair when they came in. It was now dark outside. The room was dim.

"How'ya doing, Mendle?" DaCara asked.

"Good enough. What can I do for the Houston Blues? You got a warrant?"

"Aw, it's just a social call. Nothing much. Hate for you to hit town, think we didn't notice."

"You noticed goddamn fast." Moria went to a coffee table, opened a silver cigarette box. He pulled out a smoke, lit it with a table lighter, sat down on the sofa. Eddy counter-crossed to the bar. The big cop glanced at him, then returned to his poking, prying. "Who's the dickhead ain't read Miranda?" Moria asked. "You know you need a warrant to go looking around like that?"

"Name's Billings." The cop turned and put his hands on his hips. He wore both belt and suspenders. Eddy thought: Insecure as shit. "Got something to hide?" The name meant nothing to Eddy. Who was he, how did he know him? Anxiety still worried the back of his neck. "Honest citizens don't got nothing to hide. Don't care if peace officers look around a little. You got some dope, maybe? Little nose candy?" He opened a drawer, pushed a fat index finger in among some cloth napkins.

Moria looked at him as if he were a stray dog, then shifted his gaze to DaCara. "He read a lot of magazines? True crime stuff, like that?"

"United States Marshal Theodore Billings," DaCara nodded as if to say, "Believe it or not." Billings ignored the introduction. "We call him 'Teddy,' " DaCara said. "Teddy, meet Mr. Moria Mendle. He does not traffic in drugs."

"You got that straight," Moria said: casual.

"You never know what you can find," Billings muttered, continued to open drawers, cabinets. "Betting slips, maybe? Heard you lost a bundle on the Cowboys the other night."

"I only bet the horses," Moria said. "Check it out."

"Pussy and ponies," Billings replied. "That's the book on you, Mendle. I know. The only question I got is which one you bet on, which one you fuck? My money's on the horses. You're too short and ugly to get much action out of a broad. So, I figure drugs are around someplace. Got to get them stoned first."

"Marshal Billings is on special assignment," DaCara put

in, like an apology. "He normally works out of Dallas. I'm surprised you haven't run into one another."

Eddy's mind clicked. The Purolator job: Billings. He had a mustache then, thinner, younger. It was Billings who convinced the ADA that Eddy had more to do with the robbery-murder than was apparent. He was at the scene, one of the first to arrive. Billings insisted on cuffing Eddy, even though he was only semiconscious and had more tubes in him than a bicycle shop. It was Billings who found the .45. Read him his rights while he lay on an ambulance gurney and paramedics hooked him up to more machines, shot him full of plasma.

Later, Eddy remembered, Billings camped out in the hospital room, spent hours there, waited for Eddy to wake up. Eddy kept his eyes closed, slept right through him. He knew a prick when he saw one, but he also knew a bulldog. Billings was both.

"Mr. Mendle here deals in stolen property, prostitution, money laundering, extortion, loan sharking, and maybe a little jury tampering, but he does *not* deal drugs," DaCara recited. "That's right, ain't it Moria?"

"How about murder?" Moria asked.

"Yeah, that, too," DaCara nodded, his sad smile broadening.

"You got something on me, put the cuffs on," Moria said. He rested the cigarette on an ashtray, stuck out his hands. "I'm a respectable mobile home dealer, own a few clubs. Got a few investments, got a lot of friends. Ask around." He turned his hands toward Billings's glare, then dropped them, resumed his smoke.

Billings nodded and smiled. "Yeah. I know. I know all about old Moria. And I know about Eddy, too. Don't I, Eddy?"

Eddy felt himself go tense again. He hadn't seen Billings since his arraignment. The marshal had moved up, gotten fat. But he'd obviously kept up with Eddy. He sent word that he would when Eddy bargained his way down to the CCW. At the time, Eddy ignored the threat, forgot it. Lots of cops— especially feds—said that when they saw beefy arrests gypped down to hash. But Billings was just a U.S. Marshal, a glorified process server: not worth remembering. Not till now.

"Yeah, well," Moria laughed, smoked. "You know as well

as anybody that I'm just a poor schmuck trying to make a living out of mobile homes and a few skinny investments.''

"I read that in the papers," Billings said. "But those morons never get anything right."

When did you learn to read? Eddy wanted to ask. He didn't. He shifted his weight. He was barefoot, felt insecure.

"You got a warrant, serve it," Moria said. "Otherwise, I got guests."

"Yeah, we saw them when they come in," Billings said. "Ain't you read about how dangerous that sort of thing is? What'd'ya got? Rubber machine in every room?"

Moria shot Billings a look. Bad taste, it said: crude. "Let's cut the shit, DaCara. What can I do for you?"

DaCara gave Moria an even look. He fished a smoke out of his pocket, jammed it into his crooked smile, lit it slow. "Well, like I said. We heard you were in town. . ."

"How?" Moria asked. "We got here two hours ago. Maybe. Came straight here." He looked at Eddy for confirmation. Eddy nodded. A trickle of sweat ran from his underarms down his side. "You guys ain't that good."

DaCara smiled again, blew smoke. "One of our cycle jockeys picked you up out on 610. Eighty in a fifty-five. Called in the plates." His eyes left Moria's, stared at the patio.

One of the girls with her hair still dry, nude, pale as a peeled banana, strolled in from the patio. "Dark as hell in here," she said, snapped on a lamp near the doorway, struck a pose. She held all eyes for a beat, then pushed off, swung her narrow hips in a sassy manner, crossed through the circle of men, gave each a sideways look. Her breasts floated, nipples tight. Eddy thought: natural blonde.

"Wendi wants a beer," she announced to the room. "Me, too."

She went over to the small refrigerator, opened it, spread her legs into an inverse V, and bent over, offering a full view. Her breasts didn't sway an inch. Billings's mouth dropped open. His eyes bulged. She pulled out several bottles of Löwenbräu, turned, cocked a hip, ran a long nail into her pubic hair, pretended to scratch lightly, then put her hand on her waist, faced

Moria. "We're hungry," she pouted. "Are you going to send down for something? We want pizza. No anchovies."

"In a minute," Moria smiled.

She frowned, shifted hips, twisted the top off one of the beers and sipped from it. Her tongue played with the long-necked bottle. "Frothy," she said, giggled. She winked at Moria before she moved back out to the patio.

"Stay outside," Moria said. "I'll be there in a minute."

"Don't forget the pizza."

"Just stay outside."

"Don't take too long. All right?"

"All right."

The way he talked to her, she might have been his daughter, Eddy thought. Without warning, his mind shot two thousand miles to Barbara, boomeranged back. He hadn't thought of her in weeks, now twice in an hour.

"Maybe you ain't heard prostitution's illegal," Billings said. He turned slightly sideways, leaned on the bar.

"What's that got to do with the price of crooked cop?" Moria asked.

"I'm sure Mendle's aware of the vice statutes in this state," DaCara interrupted. Then, after a beat, "Shut up, Billings." Billings's face went red. DaCara smoked, looked apologetic.

"So, you come to give me a ticket, or what?" Moria asked. "Looks to me like you got the talent for it."

"Well, the motor cop who spotted called in the plates. We just happened to catch it."

"Got nothing better to do? Should think there was some crime going on around here for you to ignore."

"With slime like you in town, we got our hands full," Billings said.

"I don't think I like your friend's tone," Moria said.

"Ain't that too bad," Billings muttered. "You—"

"Would you like to wait outside, Teddy?" DaCara asked: cold, polite. He ground his smoke out. Billings stood, glowered at Moria, then at DaCara. "All right, then," the slighter man continued, talked to the marshal as he would to a petulant child, "sit down and shut the fuck up." Billings didn't move.

"Where were we?" DaCara asked. "Oh yes. Well, the cycle

jockey going to pull you over. Write you up. But we intercepted the plate report—coincidence, really. I just happened to be in dispatch when it came in. Only place in the whole damn building you can still smoke. Anyway, I told him to cool it. I'd see to it myself.''

"So, you *did* come to give me a ticket. Jesus, you guys must be having a slow week.''

"Why don't you just shut up and listen?'' Billings asked. He moved behind the bar, inspected the bottles, opened the refrigerator.

"You're the one needs ears,'' Moria shot. Eddy tensed. Moria rose, moved over to the bar, slammed the door. "I don't want you looking around. Not without a warrant. There's breakable stuff in there. You're too goddamned dumb to know it. Go over there and sit next to your keeper, or show me some paper.''

Billings looked at DaCara, shrugged and stumbled to one of the chairs, sat down heavily, sulked.

"Your name's been coming up a lot lately,'' DaCara said as if nothing had interrupted their conversation.

Moria leaned on the bar. "So?''

"So, I was just about to fax Dallas PD, have them pick you up, ask you to drop in on us down here. Spotting you was just a piece of luck.''

"Pick me up for what? Haven't you guys had enough of that shit? When do you learn?'' Moria shook his head, looked sad.

"Oh, this wasn't an arrest. More like a courtesy call. An invite.''

"Oh yeah?''

"Yeah. You see, I got a morgue full of stiffs down there, and I need you to take a look. See if you know any of them.''

"Me? Why me?''

"Well, some are your 'known associates,' as the rap sheets say. Johnny Ribbon, for one, hooker name of JoEdna—aka Madeline Cohen—couple of citizens who got in the way of some trouble the other night.''

"If you know who they are, why you need me?''

"Well, one of them might be a friend of yours: Bob Cole.''

"Friend, shit," Billings muttered. "They're partners."

Eddy froze. The sweat he felt inside his clothing turned cold.

"Yeah, he's down here. Supposed to be, anyhow: business. We got mutual interests here. Dealerships, that kind of thing."

"Dealerships," Billings muttered. "God."

"Come to think of it, though, I haven't heard from him in a couple days. If you got him, you know him," Moria said. He was relaxed, Eddy thought: casual. "You don't need me to point out Bob Cole."

"Well, it's hard to say. He's in a bad way. No head."

"What're you talking about?"

"No head. Headless fucking horseman." He drew a finger across his throat, pretended to pull up on his own thin hair. "No head."

DaCara's eyes fixed on Moria. He studied him. Moria's mouth dropped open. His head shook as if to clear it, and he almost stumbled as he groped his way back to his chair.

"You're bullshitting me."

"No," DaCara sounded bored. "Straight skinny. No head. Just a body. Torso. Cut off his hands, too: no prints."

"No prints," Moria repeated. His voice was breathless. He took another cigarette from the case. Eddy was amazed at the man's control. His fingers were shaking while he lit it. "So how you know it's Cole?"

DaCara looked wounded. "Mendle, Mendle," he said. "I'm a pro. It's him."

Moria nodded slowly. "You're sure."

"Sure as any flatfoot can be," DaCara said. "But we need a positive. No next of kin. You're his partner. You're the nominee."

Moria smoked, closed his eyes. "He was an old friend. This is a shock. Who would do. . ." He trailed off.

"Thought maybe you could tell me."

"Me?" Moria's eyes widened. "Why me?"

"Cut the shit, Mendle," Billings said. His sulk was over. He took the offensive again. "We know about you. We know what you're into. This soft-soap ain't getting you nowhere."

"You're sure it's Bob. Bob Cole?" Moria ignored the big

cop, concentrated on DaCara. "I mean, he's down here on business. We're supposed to meet him—where was it, Eddy?"

Eddy gave him a blank look, startled.

"That club. What was the name of that club?"

Eddy didn't know Houston. "I'm not sure," was all he could mutter.

"Well, my secretary'll have it. Hey, Kari, uh, Wendi." Mendle called out to the patio. "What's the name of that club?"

"Never mind," DaCara stopped him. "Don't call one of those broads in here. I don't think Teddy's blood pressure can stand it. It don't matter, anyway. You ain't meeting Bob Cole anywhere. He's holding down a slab. He won't be keeping any appointments."

Moria opened his hands: helpless. "You're sure it's Cole. Bob Cole."

"Footprints say so," DaCara said. He also pulled out another smoke, lit it, snapped the lighter closed. "Teddy helped us out there. He was a Green Beret, right? Like you. You *were* a Green Beret, right?" Moria nodded quickly. Eddy saw something cross his eyes. "What the hell happened to you, Mendle?" DaCara's expression changed. "You don't look like A-Team material."

"Looks like dog puke," Billings put in.

"Special talents," Moria muttered, waved his hand, distracted. "I had special talents."

Billings opened his mouth, but DaCara shot him a look. The fat cop reddened again, turned away.

"Bob Cole," Moria looked down at the carpet. "This is a shock. Really."

"No family, you know," DaCara went on. "So we need you to come down. Make the ID. Claim the body, if you want it."

"Of course I want it!" Moria snapped. "If it's Cole, I want it. We go back. Long way. His family's dead. I'll come down. When and where? Tonight?"

DaCara took his time, looked at Moria, glanced at Eddy. "Tomorrow's soon enough. He ain't going nowhere. I'll meet you there. Say, ten."

"Where?" Moria went to the telephone, picked up a pad and pen.

"You know where," DaCara said softly. "You've put enough guys there."

"Broads, too," Billings added.

"Bob Cole," Moria whispered. "Where'd you find him?"

"Buffalo Bayou," DaCara said. "Couple of 'groids fishing down there came up with him, I guess. Was weighted down pretty good. Don't think we were supposed to find him."

"Nobody fishes in Buffalo Bayou," Moria said.

"Niggers do," Billings said. "Niggers don't care what they eat." He glanced out the patio doors. "Some people'll put anything in their mouth."

"Who did it?" Moria asked. "Who you *think* did it?"

DaCara rose. "Goddamn convenient: you showing up. Why'd you say you were in town?"

"Didn't," Moria muttered. He brought a hand up, massaged the bridge of his nose. "Business. Just business."

"Yeah, well let's hope you don't take too long about it," DaCara said. He cupped his hand, tapped ash into it, poured it into the ashtray. "I got enough stiffs to worry about right now. I don't need any more." He started out. "C'mon Teddy. Let's roll."

"I'm looking forward to busting you," Billings said.

"Yeah," Moria said: absent. Lost in thought. "Yeah, it's been a pleasure to meet you too."

"C'mon Marshal Billings," DaCara insisted. "Moving out."

Moria followed them to the door, then he came back. The act dropped. "They move fast. I hoped they wouldn't find me till tomorrow."

He went to the telephone. "Use the other phone. Call down and order those bitches a pizza, tell them to eat it quick then get out of here. We got people to see."

PART TWO

Thursday

8
Al

"What'd'ya mean you got no money?" Red shouted. It was the first time Vicki had heard him sound upset. The sun would rise soon, Tucson was coming up as well. They had been snuffing coke steadily through the early morning. Now, they were out. The aftermath of the drug was having obvious effects on the trio of kidnappers.

Red was the most changed of the three. Ultra-calm up to this point—icy almost—he now squirmed, fidgeted, chewed his cuticles. His voice was louder now, had a frantic, hoarse edge to it. Blackie sulked when he wasn't arguing, wanted to eat. Whatever exhilaration they got from the dope, from destroying the Lincoln, was past. Depression settled into the van like a low pressure system.

"I mean: I got *no* fucking money," Al said. "So there won't be no motel. Sleep in the van. You never sleep in a van before?"

"We got till Friday," Blackie whined. "We got no smokes, no booze, no blow, no food. We don't got shit. We been up two days." He had been begging cigarettes off Al. She finally told him to fuck off.

"Three days," Red corrected.

"Well, too damn bad. I ain't had my beauty rest either."

Vicki thought that it would take more than beauty rest to cure Al's particular case of ugly. She and Red had switched places so he could lie down. He unlocked her cuff from one wrist without her asking. From the swivel seat amidships, she had a good view of the female driver.

Al was fat and manly. She gripped the wheel with pudgy, well-gnawed fingers that spat out of hands large enough to contain all of Vicki's well-manicured digits, even crush them. Her hair was oily, cropped shorter than Red's, and she had a dangling turquoise earring in one ear, a piece of raw granite on a leather string in the other. Ranging up from her grimy lobes, rows of imitation diamond studs raced toward hairy cauliflowered tops. She wore leather pants, creased and cracked, a sleeveless jean jacket with faded biker emblems. If she had a beard, she could be an extra in a caveman movie. Vicki thought: *Neanderthals from Hell,* starring Al, ex-biker, ex-con, addict, bull dyke.

Unlike the other two, Al seemed soothed by the drugs. But she still chain-smoked Marlboros, flicked one butt out the window, lit a new one. The only other sign of tension was the way her tiny, black eyes flicked from the road to the mirror: tight as a new spring inside, but outwardly casual.

And maybe careless, Vicki thought. She could see the speedometer's needle flirting with seventy-five, eighty from time to time. Al had the cruise control on, but when she talked she worked her feet over and kicked up the speed, changed lanes for no apparent reason, never used the turn signal.

"Run it down for me again," Red spoke softly from the rear of the van. "What *exactly* did Cole say?"

"He didn't say shit," Al replied. "Called me Sunday morning to make sure everything was still on line, give me a couple numbers to call him on. Set the money. But he ain't running this show, and you better believe it. Figured that out. Talked to some Gomer when I called in."

"Who?"

"Don't know. But he sounded too stupid to be much. Probably Cole's driver. Anyway, I confirmed the meet, the pickup, the money."

"Sounds weird," Red said.

"It's cool," Al insisted. "Look, I've worked for Cole before. He's straight. This time, he set me up, I set you up. That's the deal."

"Your van?" Blackie asked.

"Right," Al said, ironically. "Cole told me to rent one. You got to have plastic for that. One little detail he didn't think of. All he sent was a plane ticket and five C-notes: that's it."

"That's it, all right," Red said. "Where the hell's the five yards?"

"What you think you been packing your sinuses with? I don't know Phoenix. Took me three hours to score. They don't discount for drifters. And there was the hardware." She reached back, patted the shotgun.

"So, we're broke." Blackie sounded pitiful. "I'm getting ripe. We rode those goddamn bikes all over Hollywood. I need a shower, some sleep, to eat."

"You're the hungriest son of a bitch I've ever seen," Red said. "All you want to do is eat."

"I can't help it if I'm hungry. We ain't had nothing since California, and we're almost to goddamned New Fucking Mexico. I want some breakfast."

"I got a ten-spot left," Al said. "This mother sucks gas. Cole really should have sent me some plastic. You can't run a deal like this on five small bills. Maybe Cole didn't figure on that, but then he's strictly from the Gold Card Club."

"He probably didn't figure you were going to blow the whole wad on nostril powder, either." Red grumbled.

"I didn't hear you bitching about it while ago."

"Well, I'm bitching now," Red said. "We need to get some sleep. We got to watch her." He grabbed the back of Vicki's seat. "We got to be sharp. She ain't just going to sit around and watch us if we pull off and crash. We need some rest. We ain't due till Friday, late. We got time."

"But we ain't got money," Al reminded him. "And I ain't hitting no 7-11 just so you can have a hotdog and a Big Gulp." Red folded his arms, pouted.

The van hummed along I-10, and all three were quiet. With nothing to replace the cocaine rush, fatigue mounted. Al seemed fresher than the two men, but when the argument over money died out, she slumped down in the seat, fingers more casual on the wheel. Vicki knew they'd have to stop soon. Then, maybe, she could get away.

Al switched on the radio, but all she could find was Mexican stations. Polkas and rapid-fire Spanish broke through the speakers' static. Al rolled down the window, let in the crisp early-morning air. It was graying in the east. Vicki could read the billboards.

Red sat up, wiped his eyes. In the cool gray dawn light, Vicki could see they were red, swollen. "Never could sleep in a damn car."

"Me neither," Blackie said. "Especially not when my stomach's growling."

"You guys give me a pain," Al chuckled. "Two days from now, you're going to have more money than you've ever seen in one place at one time, and all you think about is something to eat and a place to lay your pointy little heads. Keep your mind on what's coming."

Vicki also felt tired. Her eyes were heavy, and she imagined splotches, bags already forming under them. Her body was stiff. She stretched her legs out, flexed her toes. Muscles atrophy after twenty-four hours, she reminded herself. Exercise time was seven A.M., every day. She couldn't see any clock in the van, but her arms and legs ached for their workout.

"We have to get some cash," Red concluded. "We could call him."

"No," Al said. "I made the only call we needed to make from Phoenix. Told them the package was on its way. That Disney shit was smart, especially since Cole wasn't there. Never know who's listening on a cell phone." She turned her head, checked Vicki. "We ain't supposed to say shit till we make Texas." Red muttered something, but Al waved her hand. "'Sides, we're out of range for the phone. We won't be able to call nobody till we hit Deming. Military fucks up the airwaves around here, too."

"We'll stop, use a pay phone," Blackie said. "He'll send us some cash."

"Oh yeah." Al's voice dripped satire. "You guys ain't done this kind of work before, I can tell." They said nothing. "Look, there's a plan. People like Cole, they don't like it if things don't go right. We call him, he's likely to tell us to fuck off, leave us hot and holding the prom queen back there.''

"He can't do that,'' Red shouted. "We already got her. It's a done deal. That's why we got to get some rest. We can't let anything happen to her.''

Vicki felt a prickle of pride climb up her back. If she was that important—or if Barbara was—then her position might not be as bad as she thought. She began to put things together: she was worth money to them—alive. They might hurt her, but they wouldn't kill her. That gave her an edge. But she couldn't figure out how to use it. They were screwups, she thought, clowns, flunkies. Somebody else—somebody named Cole—was behind this, and it had to do with Barbara's father— what did she call him? Eddy. They were all just running errands. Even Al, who talked sense, blew their cash on a quick high: kid stuff. It was gone now. So was the money. Things were going bad. Vicki doubted that they would ever reach Texas. When they stopped, she'd make her move. She scolded herself for not running when she had the chance back at the picnic area. This was *not* going to be another Patty Hearst story. She was not going to sit, wait and see what happened.

"We may have her, but till we deliver her, she's just raw goods,'' Al said. "Good-looking goods, but still goods.''

Vicki caught Al's dark eye in the big mirror. She winked, made a puckering sound. Vicki's pride and promise vanished. Fear replaced it.

"So what happens if we call him and he gets pissed and calls it off?'' Red asked. "He needs her, we need him. That simple. There's a pile of money involved here. He won't blow that. It ought to be worth a couple more yards up front.''

"You don't know this guy,'' Al said and shook her head. "If this thing flakes, he could just tell us to stuff it.''

"Stuff it?'' Blackie looked at Al.

"Stuff it. Forget it. Off her and cover our own asses. Guys bigger than him have done it on deals bigger than this. Rather call it off. The deal's not done till delivery's made. If things go sour, I'm not planning to leave any witnesses. How about you?''

Blackie turned his head, stared at Vicki as if seeing her for the first time. She glanced at Red. He also studied her. "I think it'd be a goddamn waste," he said.

"It won't flake," Blackie muttered.

"You better hope it don't," Al laughed. "Otherwise, the only way to get away clean is to leave her dead in a ditch."

"What I am going to worry about is getting food and into a bed," Blackie said. "I'm whacked."

"I'll give you something else to worry about," Al said. "We've picked up a fucking cop."

Everyone started yelling at once. Red jerked Vicki out of her seat, flung her backwards onto the rear cushions, wrenched her arms behind her, cuffed her again, then, before the pain in her shoulders subsided, he rolled her over, pulled out his pistol.

"You can't outrun him in this piece of shit!" he yelled at Al.

"What the hell you want me to do?"

"Pull over," Blackie shouted. "Jesus, it's just a goddamn ticket."

"I got no license, no registration for this heap." Her window was down now, and the desert scenery, lit by the emerging sun, raced past the windows, a yellow blur. Vicki's heart throbbed in her ears. She heard the siren behind them in between its thumps. The van careened, up first on one side then on the other. She spotted a green sign that announced the exit to Rillito was approaching.

"You think I just strolled into a dealership and *bought* this piece of shit?" Al yelled. "It's hotter'n a Arizona prison, so we're stayin' right here." She hit the exit ramp and took the curve. The van tilted.

"She's going to turn us over," Vicki yelled.

Red belted her across the face with his open hand. She barely felt it. The van swerved again, threw both of them off balance. "Shut the fuck *up*!" He screamed at her. He held his left hand high to hit her again. When she cowered, he dropped it. The van fishtailed once more, and he fell to the floor. She flopped over on top of him.

He righted himself, jerked her to a sitting position, jammed the pistol into her mouth, clicked back the hammer. "One word,'' he yelled, ''Just one: your brains are all over the window. Got it?'' She stared at him. ''I said, 'Got it?' Goddamnit! Yes or no?''

She remembered: blinked once.

The van's engine whined. ''Son of a bitch hadn't got no more,'' Al yelled. ''We're going to have to pull over.''

''That's what I been trying to tell you,'' Blackie yelled. Vicki could feel his fear, Red's as well. Any second now she was going to die, she told herself.

''Get me some hardware.''

''No!'' Red said. ''Just take the goddamn ticket. We'll be in New Mexico in two hours.''

''The vehicle is *hot!* If he don't have it on his sheet, he'll have it as soon as he calls it in. We've already run off. I don't know the penalty for GTA in this state. Don't want to find out. We're running, may as well be 'armed and dangerous,' too. Give me a fucking gun!''

Vicki couldn't see behind her, but the siren was close now. Then she felt a surge of power as the van slowed, pulled away once again.

''Get me a gun, goddamnit,'' Al yelled. ''Somebody cover my ass or get me a gun. I ain't taking no chances.''

Blackie scrambled over the console and pulled the shotgun up. He pumped it, checked the load, shoved it down by the driver's seat.

''On your right,'' he said, crawled back into his seat. ''You want to do it, you do it. I ain't shootin' no cop.''

''Big man,'' Al snorted. ''You guys give me a pain.'' She slowed, coasted off the blacktop off into the sand.

''Not too far,'' Red warned. ''We don't want to get stuck.''

''Fuck you,'' Al snorted. She zipped up the window, located the shotgun with her hand.

They sat still. Vicki could see the red reflection of the trooper's flashers shining into the van. Red's face was puffy, blotched. Blackie looked out the window.

''What's he doing?'' Al asked.

''Just sitting there, watching us. He's careful.''

''Smart son of a bitch,'' Al muttered, shoved the shifter high. ''Here he comes. Just be cool. Let me do the talking.''

Vicki slanted her eyes. She could see him clearly. Her side of the van. He got out of his car, squared his headgear, approached the van warily, at a slight angle. Al kept the window up. All the glass in the van was smoke-black. Vicki imagined the new day's sun was blinding in its reflection. He wouldn't be able to see inside.

When he reached the driver's door, Al slid the window down quick, gave him a big smile behind a cigarette floating on her lips. "What's the problem, officer? Wasn't going too fast, was I?" Polite.

His eyes widened a bit, his arm started up, a slight salute, then dropped his arm to his side.

"Could I see your license and registration, please?"

"Hey, I know I was going a little fast, but hey, there's nobody around for miles. Needed to make up some time. No traffic this early. What'd'ya say we just let it go? Huh?"

"License and registration, please."

"C'mon. Gimme me a break. I got a sick woman in here."

The trooper cocked his head. The inside of the van was dark. His flashlight hung on his belt, next to his pistol, handcuffs, other junk. Vicki saw the loop was off the hammer of his gun. He didn't look like a fast-draw artist, she thought. He squinted slightly, peered into Al's window. "Please, ma'am: license and registration. Remove it from your wallet, please."

"Well, hell. Just my luck to draw a prick." Her tone was tired, not angry. "It's in my purse. Just a sec." She turned away, dug around beside her seat, winked at Red when she picked up the shotgun, drew it closer to her. Blackie sat still, stared out the window into the desert.

"Hey, I can't find it," Al said. "How about we just let it go this time. Go get some coffee or something. I'll buy. I date a cop. Really. C'mon. What'd'ya say?"

The trooper took two small steps back. He looked damned good: tough, professional. His name tag said "Martinez." He wore a wedding ring. Charles Bronson in his prime, Vicki thought.

"Step out of the car, please, ma'am."

"Aw . . ."

"Step out of the car, right now." His eyes were fixed on

Al. His right hand now rested on his pistol's butt, casual. He stood at ease: feet apart, chin up, gut in, chest out. The clipboard looked like a baton beneath his arm. "Now, please," he repeated.

"All right," Al said, weary. "If that's the way it's got to go down."

Frustration welled in Vicki's stomach. He wasn't six feet away, just the other side of the opaque glass. His gun was still in his holster, his smile was firm. Red's eyes were on him. Blackie stared out the window. This was exactly what she wanted to happen, she told herself, what she had hoped for: Highway patrol car, flashing lights, rescue, then reporters, TV, Gary, safety. Now that it was happening, she didn't feel the way she thought she would. This wasn't working out at all.

Her whole body was coiled, but there was nothing she could do. The hammer on Red's pistol was still back. The barrel touched her palate. She gagged. Red looked down, distracted, and withdrew the pistol from her mouth. Vicki swallowed.

"I'll be quiet," she said. "Don't put it back in." Her voice was calm, even. Where was her fear?

"Shut up," he said. He held the pistol on her forehead.

The shotgun boomed. Red jumped. Vicki saw the trooper leave his feet, fly backwards. A bright-red stain appeared on his chest, his clean chin flew away from it as if trying to give it more room to grow. He crumpled like a broken doll. *Electra Glide in Blue,* Vicki thought. Only there was no motorcycle. Just one dead cop. Shit.

Her wrists jerked against the manacles, but her voice was gone. She couldn't even scream. She just stared, her stomach churned, ears rang.

In a few seconds, she understood that she had also heard a second, sharper blast near her head. The cocked .22 had discharged into the cushion by her thigh. She wanted to faint, pass out, at least scream. She couldn't. She was numb.

The van bolted out of the sand, left a long strip of rubber behind it as it reached the blacktop.

"Stop! Hold it! Stop, goddamnit!" Red yelled.

He dropped the pistol, moved up behind Al. She braked hard, throwing him forward.

"What the fuck?" Al yelled. "We gotta move! I just killed a cop. A state cop! They *fry* you for that here."

"Back up," Red ordered.

Al hesitated, then shifted to reverse, wandered in a crooked path back toward the cruiser. She stopped when they came even with the trooper's body. Red slid the side door open, leaped out. Blackie opened his door and followed him. Vicki watched them drag the trooper's body over to his car, shut down the flashing lights. They put him down, rifled his pockets, then opened the door and seated him inside behind the wheel. When they returned to the van, Vicki saw that Red's bloody hands held the patrolman's utility belt and accessories: service automatic, cuffs, keys, walkie-talkie, flashlight. And a cracked leather wallet. They piled the equipment in the van's floor, shoved the door closed.

"Twenty-five bucks," he reported after he looked in the wallet.

"Then we eat," Blackie said.

"And sleep," Red said, holding up a VISA card. "Oh shit. Expired."

"Anything else?" Blackie asked.

"Sears card, Monkey Wards."

"Great," Blackie groaned. "We can buy a washer and dryer."

"We better get outta here," Al said. She dropped the shifter down, pulled away at a normal speed.

Vicki turned and peered out the back window. In the early morning sun, the cruiser appeared to be sitting, watching for speeding motorists. The trooper's form was a still silhouette behind the wheel. That far off the interstate, it could be hours before anyone found him. In a few minutes they were back on I-10, rolling east.

"That was something, Al," Red said. "I mean, I never thought you could pull it off."

"She sure blew the shit out of him," Blackie agreed. Al gave a mock bow.

"Always was good with a shotgun," she said. "He was hard to miss. Hate it that he was a cop, though. That goes down hard in this part of the country. Least we still got Prom Queen back there in one piece.''

Red glanced at Vicki. For the first time, she saw him look apologetic.

She dropped her eyes toward the black hole in the cushion, then to the .22 revolver, still and forgotten on the floor. She had just observed a murder. She should be terrified. But she didn't feel anything like fear. The whole thing was too ridiculous to be real. It was like she was watching herself in a movie. She almost expected to hear a director shout, ''Lunch.''

She had nearly been killed, would have been if she hadn't told Red to keep the gun out of her mouth. She had watched two men drag a body over to his car, rob it, then prop it up like a mannequin. She tried, but she could not find any fear inside her, no apprehension. She just felt fed up.

''Uncuff me,'' she said. Red looked up. ''Uncuff me,'' she turned, offered her hands to him.

''Why should I?''

''Because I'm telling you to,'' she said. ''Because if you don't, I'm about to start screaming bloody murder.''

''I don't think that would be too smart.''

''Smart? You're telling me you know from smart? You haven't done a single smart thing since this whole shindig started. Now, you've killed a cop! A *state* trooper! And you're telling *me* what's smart? You people aren't professionals. You haven't the first idea of what you're doing. You're not 'armed and dangerous.' You're just armed and stupid! When they come after you, they're going to bring a fucking army! You can bet they're not going to just walk up and ask you for your gun, either. Not like he did. I don't intend to get shot. Not for you, not for. . .anybody.

''I will *not* be part of your screwups! Not anymore. A person could wind up dead hanging around with fuckups like you. Unlock me. I'm not going anyplace, but with you around, I need to be able to move fast.''

Her eyes fixed on his, then dropped to the cushion. He looked at it, blushed slightly, and then picked up the .22, put it in his belt.

''You can do what you're going to do,'' she said, ''I don't

care. But I'm not going to sit here and let you kill me up by accident. Now, unlock the goddamn handcuffs.'' She turned again. After a moment, she felt the manacles loosen.

"Now, you—'' Red started.

"One more thing,'' she said, massaged her wrists. "You get pissed off at me, you'd better shoot me. You hit me in the face again, I'm going to kick your nuts off. If I can find them.''

Red stared at her. From the front of the van Vicki heard Al chuckle. "Sounds to me,'' she called over her shoulder, "like Prom Queen's got more balls than you do, Red.''

"We'll see,'' he muttered. "We'll see.''

9

Barbara

Homicide Detective Sergeant Louis Sandobal of the Santa Barbara, California Police Department glowered at his stockinged feet propped up on the dashboard of Barbara Lovell's black '67 Mustang convertible. Barbara glanced over at him: unhappy man. He was, however, so damned cute when he sulked, she couldn't resist giving him a big smile. He returned a deep scowl. She laughed.

Right now, she thought, he ought to be on his way to work. He should be worrying about what he was too tired to understand in last night's torts class. He should be thinking that opting for coffee and a doughnut instead of breakfast was bad for him. He should be counting day number fifty-seven since he had smoked a cigarette. He should be thinking what it would be like to be in bed with her instead of hurtling across the predawn Arizona desert at over ninety miles an hour on what he had told her a dozen times since leaving California was a wild goose chase.

"You know," he sighed, "this is just plain dumb."

"There's dumb and there's dumb," Barbara said. She pushed her too-long bangs away from her forehead, glanced in the rearview. Her skin was oily, needed a bath. "You want dumb, try the LAPD. Couldn't care less about anything but their coffee break."

She went over it again, briskly, silently, tried to find something she missed. After standing in the courtyard and watching Vicki drive off with the strange "cousins from Texas," she shrugged, wondered what Vicki was up to now, shouldered her gym bag, climbed the stairs to her apartment. There, what she found angered her. Two bicycles were jammed against the wall. Paint was scratched. Then she saw the telephone, the cut cord, the mess. For a moment she heard her heart in her ears. She raced out, down the stairs. The Lincoln was gone.

She instantly understood: abduction. Panic scaled her spine like an army of ants. She wanted to scream. Then luck smiled on her. She thought. The police cruiser circled the block. She flagged it down, rushed up, and gave the officer behind the wheel what she was certain was a coherent, clear version of what happened. Her professor of criminology would have been proud of her for providing the patrolmen what was, in her view, a complete witness's report of the broad daylight, forced abduction of Vicki Sigel.

The representatives of LA's Finest were unimpressed. "She just went off with them, you say," the younger one asked, stifled a yawn. "I mean, she wasn't resisting or anything?"

"No," Barbara admitted. "She wasn't. But—"

"And you didn't see a gun or anything?"

"No, I—"

"And they're her cousins?" The other, older one pretended to study the notes he took when she finally convinced them to get out of their patrol car, talk to her, come upstairs, see for themselves.

"They're *not* her cousins," Barbara shouted. "I'm sure of that. She wasn't expecting any cousins. I don't think she has any cousins. She had a date tonight. A big date, and—"

"Where did you say she was from?"

"A small town in Texas. . .Something Wells." She searched her memory—blank.

"And where did she say they were from?"

"Texas," Vicki admitted.

The two officers exchanged looks. "Well, I don't think

there's a reason to worry. Maybe they just dropped by, wanted her to show them around. You said they went to SeaWorld?''

''Nobody goes to SeaWorld this time of year!'' Barbara said. They visibly stiffened in response to her tone. ''And what about the bicycles? What about the cut phone cord, the mess they made?''

''You said they were in a hurry?'' the older one asked.

''Yeah, in a big hurry. And one of them had hold of her—''

''Well,'' the younger one tried a soothing voice, ''looks like they were just a little careless.''

''You don't cut a phone cord unless you don't want somebody to plug it back—''

''You know what I think?'' the older one said: a scowl. ''How long you known this Vicki?''

Barbara shook her head. ''A year, I guess. Six, eight months. We're best friends. We work out   ''

''A year, huh? And you say she's from Texas, right?'' Barbara nodded, her brown eyes wide. ''Well, you know there's a lot of nutty people in Texas. Hicks-like, you know, hayseeds. Cowboys, right?''

''What?''

''Well, you know what I mean. Here's these two guys show up on bicycles. Like religious nuts, you know. Mormons. They got Mormons in Texas, don't they?''

''I don't know.'' Barbara was confused.

''Well, I'm sure they do. There was that thing at Waco, right? Branch Davids or something. They're sort of Mormons, I think. You know: one guy, six wives, twenty kids. They send the kids out all over the place. In twos—pairs. Missionary work, you know. People always complaining about them. So, they get tired of selling their Bibles or whatever they're doing, and they just show up here. Unexpected-like. You say she had a big date, and maybe she's embarrassed. She a Mormon?''

''I. . .uh, I don't. . .no,'' Barbara spluttered. She had no idea what religious background Vicki might have. ''I can't say. But what makes you think they were—''

''Well, that's it, then.'' The young one smiled. ''Her country cousins from Texas show up without her expecting them. They turn out to be on some kind of religious mission. She's embarrassed, nervous about it, doesn't want her boyfriend to meet them, so she hustles them off to SeaWorld, gets them out of the picture. She probably was embarrassed that you showed up when you did.''

Barbara didn't reply. She eyed the two cops, concentrated, lowered her voice. ''What about the car, then?''

''What car?''

''The goddamn car! The Lincoln!'' Barbara shouted in their faces, waved her arms. ''They drove off in a Lincoln! Town Car. Brown. Brand-new. If they were on bicycles, where did they get the car?''

''I think Mormons can drive cars,'' the young one said. ''It's the Amish can't drive cars.''

''The Amish aren't from Texas,'' the older one offered. ''They're from Ohio or someplace.''

''That's Mennonites. Mennonites're from Ohio.''

Barbara bit her lip, counted to three. ''The point is that they couldn't have been driving a car.'' She spoke in a controlled voice. ''Not if they were riding bikes. You can't drive a car and ride a bicycle at the same time.''

The officers looked at each other for a moment, sought help. The young one scratched his chin. ''Makes sense,'' he said. ''They can't ride those bikes all the time. That car have a bike rack?''

Barbara had to stop, think. ''I don't think so. It looked brand-new.''

''Well, it might have been in the trunk,'' the young cop said to the old cop, then turned back to Barbara. ''They were out bothering people all afternoon.'' Back to the older cop: ''Must have changed clothes. That's why we didn't spot them. Always wear suits, you know.'' He looked again at Barbara. ''That's what we were looking for. We had a lot of complaints about them. Four, five people called in. Pay no attention to 'No Solicitors' signs, those people. Won't take 'no' for an answer, either. Maybe they knew we were looking for them, just knocked off for the day. Take a break, stash the bikes, head out to SeaWorld, like you said, pick up an old cousin and take off.''

The older cop nodded wisely. ''This, uh. . .Vicki, you said

she's an actress, right?'' Barbara nodded, dumbfounded. ''Good-looking?'' Barbara nodded again. ''Well, that's it, then. Maybe they're 'kissing cousins,' or something.'' He grinned.

''They can marry their cousins,'' the other suggested. He grinned, too.

''I'm telling you she doesn't even live here. She was—''

''No, I don't see much to go on here,'' the older cop nodded, closed his notebook. ''You get a license number on the Lincoln?''

Barbara wrinkled her dark brow in thought, shook her head. ''LC—something. No. It was a California plate, though.''

''California plate?''

''That's right. Can't you two bozos see it?'' Barbara shouted at them. ''Are you complete morons?''

''Look, miss,'' the older one stiffened. ''There's no call—''

''This is crazy!'' she shouted. ''Mormons from Texas driving their bicycles around in a Lincoln with California plates! Are you guys cops or not?''

''Look, miss,'' the young cop offered. ''It's just we don't see any reason to believe—''

''To believe what? That this young woman, this actress, with a shot at meeting a major director at a party, just casually drops everything and jumps into a car with two long-lost Mormon cousins who happen to drop by and find her in an apartment halfway across town from where she lives and they just up and go to SeaWorld?''

''Well, that looks to me like what was going on,'' the older cop said. ''Well, maybe they weren't her cousins. Maybe one of them was her boyfriend.''

''She doesn't have a boyfriend!''

''Who was she going out with on this big date, then?''

''Her agent. Sort of. Look. It doesn't make any sense.''

''We're not paid to make sense out of everything. I just don't see any evidence of—''

''I'd say that all we have is some strange stuff,'' the older cop interrupted. ''People do strange things. This is LA, lady.'' Barbara noted his tone shift, the change from ''miss'' to ''lady.''

''Tell you what: You wait, and if you don't hear from her

in a while—say by tomorrow—you give us a call. We'll come out and see what we see then.''

"Aren't you going to take the bikes?''

"What for?''

"Fingerprints! Evidence! I don't know.''

"I don't know, either, lady. But unless you think the bikes are stolen, we got no reason to take them. They stolen?''

"What? No. I don't know.''

"I don't know, either. Call us if she don't turn up in the morning.''

He turned, left. The younger cop gave her a sympathetic smile, fished a card out of his pocket. "Call us,'' he said. "If you don't hear by tomorrow.''

"Tomorrow, she could be dead,'' Barbara said.

Fifteen minutes later, she was at the pay phone by the corner convenience store, called Sandobal. Like the two cops, he told her he couldn't see what else there was to do but wait. Barbara told him to get his ass ready, that she would pick him up in an hour. She also told him to bring his gun.

"What for?''

"Just bring it, Sandobal,'' she ordered. "I'm taking mine. Oh, yeah. Get a police radio. We may need it.''

Now, in the screaming Mustang, top down, crossing the desert, Barbara at least felt she was doing something. Sandobal pulled a police radio out of a wrecked patrol car. It had no mike, but it would receive. It would have to do, he told her.

He was pissed off. At first, he tried to talk her out of it every mile of the way, hoped she would see reason. The rest of the time, he hid beneath his Mets cap, contemplated his socks. She jollied him, tried to convince him that something awful had happened to Vicki. She needed him, his experience. But she was bored with his attitude.

SeaWorld, Mormon cousins, for Christ's sake. Couldn't anybody but she see how stupid that was?

Tension stretched between them. After another mile marker whizzed by, he sighed, tried again. "What makes you think we'll find them?''

She was glad he broke first, but she answered him with a frown.

"I mean, we're passing a hundred cars a minute—why you don't have fifty tickets by now, I don't know—and you're not even sure where they are, where they're going. Shouldn't you have on a seat belt?"

"I'm sure 'from Texas' was some kind of clue," she repeated for the hundredth time. "I think that was a way of telling me where she thought they were taking her."

"Texas," Sandobal repeated.

"Well, maybe not. But in that direction. And everybody knows that the most direct route to Texas is I-10, so that's the way we're going. Keep your eyes open for a brown Lincoln. They don't have more than a couple hours on us. If it is an abduction, a kidnapping, they won't dare speed."

"Not stopping us," he muttered. He slouched down and looked at his feet again. The radio crackled and spoke. He ignored it. She rubbed her fingertips over the Mustang's wheel. It was a big, sturdy machine, custom-rebuilt, manufactured for handling high speed.

"Texas is a big state," he muttered.

"How would you know? You've never been there. You wouldn't even go through there when we moved out here."

"It wasn't on the way. You said you wanted to go through Colorado. And Texas wasn't on the way."

"I never said any such thing. I just said I wanted to see Pike's Peak. Someday."

"Someday. Well, we saw it, didn't we."

"But we didn't go through Texas." She didn't want to go into that. She had planned to swing through Dallas, see Eddy. But he said no. He was going back to prison, he said. Stay away. It made her mad. She had an idea of trying to find her mother. When they hit Colorado, she gave that up, too: Ellen was only a memory. Eddy had her heart.

"No, we didn't." Sandobal sat up and glared at her. "And I don't think Vicki is going there, either. I think—"

"Look," Barbara sat back, blew out a long breath. "People from Texas don't say 'Texas' when they're talking about someplace specific, especially when they're talking to someone else from Texas."

"What?"

"People from Texas don't say they're 'from Texas.' They don't say—especially to another Texan—'These are my cousins from Texas.' They might say 'Dallas' or 'Houston,' or 'San Antonio,' or goddamn 'Marfa' or 'Oklaunion' or someplace. But they don't say just 'Texas.' Vicki and I are both Texans. See?"

"Okla-what?"

"Oklaunion. It's a town. A ghost town. Sort of."

"I don't get it."

"It's too big. Texas. It would be like saying 'I'm from the USA.' "

Sandobal grinned suddenly. "I tell everyone I'm from New Jersey. So why wouldn't somebody say, 'I'm from Texas.' "

"Sandobal," Barbara gave him a quick, exasperated look, "there are counties in Texas bigger than New Jersey."

He went back into his sulk, put his feet back on the dash, listened to the radio.

Barbara met Sandobal in a coffee shop in Greenwich Village. He was a night student at NYU. She was trying to escape her aunt's clutches, looking for light in the darkness that life in New York had become.

For the first six months, she had gone along with Hillary's program. No choice: she was a kid, her father was a shot-up con, her mother a disappeared junkie. Uncle Quince arrived in his Lexus, hauled her to Houston. She barely had time to throw some clothes into a bag and blow a kiss at Ramona, who stood on the porch and cried the whole time.

She spent no time in Houston. Uncle Quince told her it would be "easier for everyone" if Hillary was appointed legal guardian. Eddy agreed, Quince said. He drove her to Hobby, gave her a quick good-bye peck on the cheek. Aunt Hillary took it from there. Forty-eight hours after leaving Fort Worth, she was in New York.

At first, there were a lot of tears. She loved Eddy, idealized him: center of her life. The sudden separation from him, from friends and familiar surroundings in Fort Worth, was hard. Tears soon gave way to despair. Barbara moped around her room, refused to go out. Called Quince every night, begged to come home. He told her New York was home.

One of the hotels Hillary owned was in midtown. They lived in the penthouse, forty-four floors up. Good view of the river, better of the park, private pool, private tennis court, gourmet kitchen. Every need provided.

Hillary enrolled her in an exclusive private school. She was surrounded by daughters of diplomats and politicians, tycoons and international drug dealers. Two or three of the fathers were screwing Hillary in the afternoons. No one seemed to mind. It was all so civilized. She was, at first, shocked, then overwhelmed, then entranced. She adapted. Hillary made it easy.

Life was idyllic: opera, theatre, dance, symphony, museums. A limo instead of a school bus, private tutors for French and music, a personal dance coach. For her sixteenth birthday, they took a shopping trip to Paris on the Concorde. Hillary was rich. New York was richer. But she still missed Eddy.

She wanted him to love her again. She wrote long letters to him, didn't brag. She just wanted him to know she was okay, but that she missed him. She gave the letters to Goldie, Hillary's maid, to mail. She never had a reply.

Barbara also thought about her mother, but she only had a name and a state: Ellen, Colorado. It was hopeless. On a whim, she called her grandfather in Windthorst, told him she was his granddaughter.

He said, ''There's been enough whores in my life. I don't need to hear from another one.''

Barbara made excellent grades in school. She was bright. She didn't like most of her classmates, hated her aunt's friends' kids. A steady parade of preppy boys was invited for lunch, dinner, tennis, and sailing excursions. Each was thrust upon her, each presented to her as one might present a prize puppy to a prospective buyer. Hillary recited a boy's pedigree, his accomplishments, his physical attributes right in front of him. Most of them just stood there grinning, fingering hundred-dollar ties and shuffling Italian loafers around. About all Hillary omitted was their breeding potential.

But that wasn't entirely ignored.

More than once Barbara came out of her room to find some

freshly shaven young man perched on the Chinese silk sofa in the living room, a bottle of wine open in front of him, the house empty, soft music on the stereo. She made polite conversation, sipped the wine, then ushered them out. She wasn't stupid. She knew what she was expected to do. It made her sick.

One afternoon, a surprise visitor refused to leave. His name was Jim, he said, son of an ambassador, friend of her aunt's. He was blond, handsome, well built, rich, obnoxious as hell. She had a glass of the wine he brought, hinted, once, twice, then blatantly asked him to go. He sat on the sofa, grinned at her.

"Your aunt said you'd play hard to get."

She stormed out of the room, went to the bathroom. When she returned, he was still there. On the sofa, naked, his erection pointing at her like an accusing finger.

"C'mon," he said, patting the sofa beside him. "Take it in your mouth. It won't bite."

She picked up a magazine and swatted at him, at it. Clipped it just enough to sting. While he rolled away from her, she grabed a poker from the fireplace and attacked him, threatened to kill him. She meant it. He grabbed his pants and scrambled out the door.

She confronted her aunt, who denied everything, pleaded ignorance, blamed the whole thing on Barbara's natural allure, dismissed the whole thing as something she needed to get used to. "You're going to marry money. I can feel it," she told her.

One or two nights a week, when Hillary passed out, Barbara slipped away, took a train to the Village, prowled the bistros and coffee shops, occasionally sat in corner bars and taverns and sipped a beer and talked to anyone who would listen. She always was home by ten. It was all the freedom she could manage.

She was careful. She never drank too much, always made sure to be polite, chatty with Hillary. Mostly, she missed Eddy.

It was then Barbara met Sandobal. A thick wet snow, the last of the season, was falling. She came into a crowded, smoky coffeehouse two blocks from NYU, discovered that the only vacant seat was at his table. He was reading through a shock of long, dark hair by the dim, red light of a decorative candle.

He wore a cheap overcoat, Mets sweatshirt, faded jeans. A filterless cigarette dangled from his lips. She thought: Eddy.

"Mind if I sit down?" she asked.

"Whatever you like. Free country," he muttered. He had a thick accent: Jersey. "But I'm not buying. I'm tapped out." He still hadn't looked up at her.

"I'll buy," she said. "What are you having?"

Then he looked at her, crushed out his smoke. His dark eyes ran from her suede beret over brunette hair down her expensive leather coat to her designer boots. "Coffee," he said. "Black."

She could tell he fell in love with her at that moment. She was barely eighteen.

He was a cop, which amused her, and he was completely different from any boy she had ever met. Small, wiry, but strong, somehow deeply confident. His swarthy complexion, perpetual five o'clock shadow, brooding eyes appealed to her. She couldn't hide her opulence from him—her clothes, her jewelry screamed money—at first, he was standoffish, reluctant to talk to her. But that didn't last long. They met a half-dozen times at the same coffee shop, same table, drank black coffee until he finally asked her out, took her to a movie, bought her dinner, took her to bed.

The sex was good, but they found something more important than romance: friendship. Her aunt's private dick found them.

Auntie Bitchie threw a "screaming fit"—so Barbara described it to Sandobal. She threatened to call his commander, have his badge, get him arrested for corrupting a minor. Barbara pointed out that she wasn't a minor any longer. Hillary didn't care, forbade her to go anywhere alone. Barbara said she'd go where she pleased: standoff.

She never told him about Eddy.

Hillary made plans for them to go for two weeks in the Bahamas after graduation. Half the graduating classes from a half-dozen prep schools were to be there. Hillary planned for Barbara to make a selection for the upcoming collegiate year. Or for life. Hillary went down early, left Barbara a ticket and money for a beauty treatment, a summer wardrobe.

In the meantime, Sandobal made detective, and better, was offered a job with the Santa Barbara PD. It was part of a program set up with a law school out there. He would study nights, work days. Same routine, but this time in California.

"I'm going to learn to surf," he said, grinning through the perpetual cigarette.

The news upset her. She wasn't in love with him, but he was her only friend, her rock. He was in love with her, and that made things awkward. But he was sweet. They slept together, but it wasn't expected. He never demanded anything except a smoking section in a restaurant. He never took her for granted, never treated her like something delicate. To him, she was as tough as he was. He was honest with her. But she wasn't honest with him, and she hated that. She didn't want to lose him, didn't know how to keep him, didn't know if she truly wanted him. Not forever, but for a while, and he was leaving. California was a different country, and she didn't want to go.

When she conjured Sandobal's face, she understood that what attracted her to him wasn't love, not even infatuation. What attracted her to him was the fact that he was not rich, not like any of her aunt's friends. It was what she saw the first time they met, what looked up at her from through the gray smoke with eyes that cut through bullshit, got to the truth. He saw her for what she was, what she came from, and he loved her for it. He was her friend. Then Barbara heard from Eddy.

She saw the letter from Fort Worth on the hallway table where the new maid left it with the other mail to be forwarded to Hillary. The return address was only a box number, but scrawled in pencil across the top of the left-hand corner was a single word that caught her eye: "Lovell." It was addressed to Hillary, but she didn't hesitate before ripping it open. The message inside was clear.

Hillary, you bitch,
Tell me where she is or, so help me God, I'm coming to get her. I'll find you. I know how. Even Quince admits I still got rights. You call him. You've got a week, or I'm coming up there to get her. You don't want me in New York.
Eddy

Light burst in front of her eyes. The room spun, reeled, then settled back into place. Eddy still cared about her, still loved her, wanted her.

She picked up the telephone, called the prison. They wouldn't give her any information. She called directory assistance in Fort Worth, then Dallas, but there was no Eddy Lovell listed. Then she called Quince.

"Where is he?"

"Barbara? This is—"

"Where the is he, Uncle Quince? Tell me how to reach him."

His breath filled the line with noise. "I don't know."

"I want to talk to him."

"Barbara." Resignation was in his voice. "I really don't know. He calls me. I don't know where he is. Fort Worth, maybe. Dallas, I guess. Living with some prostitute. All I have is a box number."

She looked across the room into a gold-framed Louis XIV mirror, saw a stunning, graceful girl standing by a five-thousand-dollar antique *escritoire,* dressed in a thousand dollars worth of high-fashion casual wear, her hair carefully clipped and combed by a two-hundred-dollar-an-hour hairdresser, her nails filed and polished by a fifty-dollar-an-hour manicurist. She wondered who that girl was. What happened to Barbara Lovell?

Quince was still talking. She wasn't listening.

"You tell him to call me," she said. "Or you get his number, and I'll call him."

"I want to speak to Hillary."

"She's on vacation," Barbara said. "I'm going to sit right here and wait for Daddy to call. He gave Hillary a week. I'm giving you a night."

Quince didn't reply.

"I don't think you really want him paying you a visit. Do you, Uncle Quince?"

"Barbara, listen—"

"I've got his box number. I can write to him. But I want you to have him call me. See that he calls," she said. "By tomorrow."

The truth was she didn't want to write to him. She didn't know what she would say.

She telephoned Sandobal, shocked him by asking him to come over. When he arrived, he found her dressed in nothing but a stained Dallas Cowboys sweatshirt she found among her oldest clothes. He was overwhelmed by the penthouse, but she barely gave him time to look around before she pulled him into the bedroom. She had never wanted him more.

"I'll find him," she told Sandobal later. They sat naked on the bed, ate delivered Chinese with four-hundred-dollar-a-bottle champagne she found. "And I'll tell him what they did, what they said."

"Not a good idea." He held up his hand.

"Why not?"

"Look: he's been in the joint. He's on parole, probably broke, looking for work, and—I hope—trying to stay straight. He doesn't need you to worry about. He sure as hell doesn't need you showing up, dumping a load of shit on him about Hillary and your uncle. He might do something stupid."

Eddy called the next day. At first awkward, almost cold, it turned into a warm reunion. She teased him about being a gangster, a con. She wanted him to know she wasn't ashamed of him, that she was proud to be his daughter. He teased her about becoming a rich society girl. They finally relaxed, talked for two hours. She tried to sound happy, normal, confident. By the end of the talk, it was like they had been apart for weeks, not years. She cried, but she didn't let him know. She got a number for him, gave him Sandobal's address in Brooklyn, told him to write her there, call her there. He didn't ask why. When it was over, she cried some more.

She made up her mind right then to tell Hillary off.

The next morning, she called Sandobal, told him she was going with him to California, but that she wanted to have her own place when they got there. He was hurt by that, but she jollied him out of it.

She had money for the trip to join Hillary, but she added to it, drew out all the cash she could, then bought a blank, framed canvas from an art shop. She drew an enormous hand with the middle finger extended, left it hanging over the sofa. Beneath it she wrote in a flowery hand: "Love, Barb."

They heard about the exploding car on the radio. The report was vague, guarded, and they had to stop and buy a road map to find the approximate location. They located a State Police office in Wintersburg, parked, went inside. AHP Sergeant Barry Newland wouldn't give them much.

"You're way out of your jurisdiction," he told Sandobal when he flashed his badge, said they were looking for a missing person. Newland was six-four, two-thirty, granite and hard-cooked sand. He looked at the young Santa Barbara detective: shapeless corduroy coat, Angels tee-shirt, Mets cap, stained khakis, worn-out sneakers. " 'Less you give me cause, I see no reason why I should tell you anything. You authorized to bring a police radio into Arizona? You need clearance for that, I think." He looked at Barbara: crimson wind-suit, nice cross-trainers, great eyes, great figure. "She with the department, too?"

Sandobal hesitated. "We have reason to believe that a woman, a friend of hers, was abducted."

Newland allowed an eyebrow to rise. "You mean kidnapped? That's federal. Now you telling me you're FBI?"

"It's just suspicion." Sandobal's voice was not strong. Barbara nudged him over.

"Look, a friend of mine was taken from my apartment."

"In Santa Barbara?"

"In LA."

"But he's—"

"A friend. Right now, there's no police report. But we have reason to think she was taken by force. Against her will. We're just trying to trace this car. This Lincoln. All we want to know is if the car that blew up is the same car. The report we heard on the radio said it looked like it was a Lincoln Town Car."

Newland studied her. "I can't tell you anything," he said. "Not without authorization from the commander."

"Where's he?"

"At the site."

"Where's the site?"

"You got a radio. You find it." He turned and walked back to his desk. Sat down. "I'm not telling you anything till I hear from the lieutenant." Barbara's mouth opened, but his hand went up. "That's the menu, folks. You can sit and wait, or you can go back to LA. You say your name was Sandobal?" He made a note. They left.

"It's hopeless," Sandobal said.

Barbara set her mouth, steered the Mustang back out onto I-10, headed it east.

"We don't even know where it happened."

"It happened on the interstate," Barbara pushed the car smoothly through the gears. "That only runs two ways. We've seen what's behind us. Let's see what's ahead."

It didn't take them long. Police cars, ambulances, firetrucks were jammed along the highway next to a picnic area: lights flashed, cops and firemen milled around. Acrid smoke hung in the morning atmosphere. The blackened ribs of two semitrailers smoldered in the parking area. Nothing else was visible. Traffic was routed across the bumpy, sandy median, where a series of bright-yellow cones split the lanes. Cars were backed up on both sides for miles.

Barbara steered off to one side, let traffic pass, got out. They couldn't see much but the maze of emergency vehicles across the way. An angry trooper spotted them, waved at them to move on. Barbara ignored him, stared at the scene. He stalked across to them.

"You got to move," he yelled over the noise of cars honking, drivers' yells. Hands on his hips, mirror shades. "You're blocking traffic."

Sandobal flashed his badge, too quick for the young trooper to read it. "You need any help? I'm a cop."

"All we need is for you to move on."

"What kind of car was it?" Barbara asked.

"What?" The trooper's eyes narrowed. "What's that? Who wants to know?"

At that moment, a sheriff's cruiser bumped around the outer perimeter of the picnic area, the vehicles surrounding it. He headed east, down the closed-off interstate. No big hurry.

"C'mon," Barbara shouted. She leaped behind the wheel, peeled out almost before Sandobal could get inside, shut his door. She pushed her way along the shoulder by the slow-moving rubberneckers, honked and raced the Mustang's finely tuned engine until they were free.

"You want to tell me what the hell you're doing?" Sandobal asked her.

She pointed to the sheriff's car, said nothing else. After a while, it pulled into a Terry's Tourist Trap restaurant. "That guy will tell us what we want to know. Small-town sheriffs love to talk."

She was right.

"We got no ID on the car," Deputy Sheriff Enrique Cortes admitted over coffee Sandobal bought him. Barbara gave him a smile, looked at his face: craggy, pock-marked, deep-set, kind eyes under bushy gray brows: somebody's grandfather "No plates," he added, sipped the coffee. "Motor numbers blown up. All the plastic parts burned. Except for the doors. Blew all the doors clean off. One went nearly a hundred yards. I got a daughter living in LA," he said, suddenly sad. "Ain't seen her in two years."

"I know how you feel," Barbara said.

"Families just ain't what they used to be. Thought Reagan was going to fix that. He didn't. Bush didn't do no better. I swear, it's enough to turn me into a Democrat in spite of that cracker from Arkansas." He forked a piece of apple pie into his mouth. "World ain't what it was," he said around his chewing. "This used to be a good job."

"Was it a brown Lincoln?" Sandobal asked. He was tired, Barbara saw. Losing patience.

"Yeah, that's right. Brown Town Car, they figure. New. Blew the doors off, like I said. Nothing much left of the chassis, frame, or wheels. Just a black spot. Twisted metal."

"Anybody inside?" Barbara asked, afraid to breathe.

"Don't know yet. I doubt it, though. I mean, it went sky-high. Saw the fireball twenty miles away, they say. That's why I'm here. Happened about two-thirty, quarter of three. Got a call from a rancher, friend of mine. Lives over that way. Thought it was a meteor. Two trucks went up with it. Semis. One carrying flammables. Two drivers dead. One hell of a mess. Can't tell why it happened. Gas tank, I guess. Glad the state boys are handling it. Won't need me 'less somebody has to get out in the desert. Get their boots dirty.''

Barbara sighed, sipped her own coffee. "Do they know anything?"

He reached into his shirt pocket, pulled out a greasy notebook. "There was some other trucks parked there. The two that blew up, couple of others. One driver they talked to said he saw a van—Ford or Chevy, maybe a Dodge—he ain't sure, but full-sized, custom job—pull in, bunch of people hanging around the car. Then they took off in a hurry and stopped a ways off. Then the car went up. Then one of the trucks. This guy's windows busted out, and he was knocked cold. Lucky to be alive, you ask me. He was carrying cattle. Half was killed by the concussion.''

"He got no other description? Of the van? Just a big van? License number?''

"Nope. No way to tell if it was involved or not. Excuse me." He pulled out of the booth and made his way to the restrooms. "I got to call in. Radio in the car's busted.''

"Barbara," Sandobal said, his eyes suddenly especially sad. "Give it up." He reached over and took her hand.

"Give up?''

"You—we got nothing. Nothing. Not one thing. A car blew up. They *think* it's a Lincoln. You *think* Vicki drove off in a Lincoln. You *think* it was a new one, you *think* it was brown.''

"I'm sure of all that.''

"They're not. They're not even sure what happened here. Some kind of accident. Look: you're tired. So am I. Let's just find a motel, get some sleep. Or whatever." He grinned. She grimaced. "Later on, we'll go back, call LAPD if Vicki's still missing." Her eyes sharpened. "Okay," he said. "We'll call the FBI. Hell, I'll call them personally. From the office. Make it official as hell. But let them handle it. This is way out of line. You know it as well as I do.''

"But if that was the same car. If she was kidnapped, and if—''

"Okay, okay." He put the palm of his hand out, stopping

traffic. "Let's say you're right. She was kidnapped—abducted—they're heading east, just like you say. They're going to Texas. They were driving a brown Lincoln. Now, the Lincoln—if it's the same Lincoln—is in about fifty million pieces, and now we're chasing either a Ford or a Chevy or a Dodge van that may or may not have had anything to do with it." He paused, lit a cigarette he squirreled from the sheriff's open pack. "Can't you see how crazy this is?" He wiped his mouth quickly. "It's insane, girl."

She looked out onto the parking lot. Desert heat rose in waves over the interstate. Cars and trucks whisked by.

"You've got no evidence she was kidnapped," he said. Again the hand, stopping her. "Think about it. What do you have? A messed-up apartment? Couple of bicycles. Couple of boys. A crazy story about SeaWorld. You know, Vicki's not the most stable of people."

"Sandobal!"

"She's not. She alley-cats around all the time. She's not a bad person. But she's—"

"Flighty," Barbara offered.

"Yeah, that's good. I might have said 'flaky,' but 'flighty's' good. The point is that even if she did go off in the Lincoln—even if it was *that* Lincoln—you got no reason to think they made her go against her will. They're probably holed up someplace, and she's banging both of them."

She ignored that. "Then you admit that it could be that same car that blew up."

He pulled his hat off, wiped his hand through his dark hair, sighed. "Yeah, yeah! For Chrissake, I admit it. But you got to come up with something to make me think that there's more to this than a joy ride with some cousins back to Texas."

Barbara scowled down into her cold coffee. Sheriff Cortes returned and picked up his hat, his cigarettes.

"It's been nice to meet you folks, and I'm obliged for the coffee. I just called in, and they want me back down there."

"Why?" Barbara asked. She ignored the frown of disapproval from Sandobal. "They didn't find. . .they didn't find any bodies, did they?"

"No. They're pretty sure it was empty. The truck was blown

sky-high, but there wasn't nobody in the car. That's why, now, they're thinking maybe there's more to this than they thought before. It wasn't no accident.''

"Why?" Now Sandobal was interested.

"Well, for one thing, them doors I told you was blown off the car. Well, they didn't have no door handles. Somebody took them off. Neat, on purpose."

"So?" Sandobal offered, watching Barbara's eyes staring at him: triumph.

"Well, they don't know what to make of that. But they also think some kind of high explosives was used on that car. They found a timer. Or part of one. Guess somebody blew that car up on purpose."

"Yeah," Barbara leaned forward. "Anything else?"

Cortes looked around, then leaned down and almost whispered. "Well, this ain't for public consumption, but since you're a police officer, I guess I can tell you. A van, just like the one they think was here last night—a Dodge, they say—is now involved in the murder of a state trooper over near Tucson."

10

Houston International

Earline Gilroy's favorite movie of all time was *The Fugitive*. She saw it twelve times. She admired the way Harrison Ford used every trick of the trade to elude the cops until he was in the clear. Now, she was discovering that being a fugitive wasn't all it was cracked up to be: Earline was scared.

Standing in front of a ticket counter in Houston International, nearly ten thousand crisp one-dollar bills packed tightly into the heavy pink Samsonite pullman she received for high school graduation, a passport and a ticket for Paris in her purse, she should have been relaxed. She wasn't. She wanted to throw up.

Earline, aka Heather Lockhart, had never been on an airplane before. She had never been in an airport before. Reared a country girl, she spent most of her life in Houston trying to figure out where the next month's rent was coming from. The only asset she had was mile-long legs, naturally curly shoulder-length dirty-blonde hair, a fuck-me smile, and large, firm tits. Such assets converted her from Earline from Elgin to Heather from Houston, a girl with a willing nature and a reasonable rate.

The lines at the counter moved but didn't shorten. Earline

was bewildered, kept looking around, waited for someone to grab her, haul her off. She had dyed her blonde rinse to a cheap dull red, wore heavily tinted shades, donned a frumpy floor-length overcoat to cover her athletic legs, oversized breasts. The disguise made her feel conspicuous, too much like Heather trying to look like Earline.

She stared at the airline schedule, tried to make sense out of the lists of numbers and times: confusion. She had no idea how to find her plane, what to do with her bag. Except for a couple of quick trips up the interstate to Dallas and one wild weekend on South Padre with some free-spending New Yorkers, she had never been anywhere in her life but Elgin and Houston. Earline only knew one way to travel: cable TV.

The passport, ticket, and cash were all part of the deal. They would get her out: out of town, out of the business, out of Heather, out for good. She'd figure out the rest later on. Right now, the priority was to stay alive.

She lugged the heavy suitcase down the long ticket counter, tried to decide which line to stand in, wondered if she should show her credentials to anyone, wondered how in God's name she got on top of such a low-riding wave.

She couldn't wait to see Paris. One of her old high-school chums went there, fell in love with it, moved there. Earline hadn't kept in touch with her. But she was sure she could find her. She wondered if she could learn French.

Her tickets were for the 8:20 flight. Now, it was after eight. She tottered under the weight of the bag until she reached the security check-in down a long concourse. She had no idea if this was where she needed to be, what she needed to do. One place looked just like another. TV monitors and announcements for boarding calls, arrivals and departures gave her a bewildering list of information that made little sense. Everyone was in a hurry, no one paid her any attention.

The suitcase was crammed full: too heavy. Surely they didn't expect her to drag this bag on board an airplane. Surely someone would come forward to help her. She had seen movies about flying. There were supposed to be people around to help travelers. She looked around expectantly: no one.

The line at the metal detectors was long, and the morning

crowds were irritable. Her heavy coat made her sticky, steamy. Her flight would leave without her. Panic welled.

She spotted a man—a skinny cowboy—walking toward her. Too fast, too deliberate. He looked right at her beneath a dark hat brim. Raw fear took root in her gut. She felt a tightening around her neck. She grabbed her bag, shouldered her purse, moved away: wrong direction. Another man—another cowboy—moved toward her from there. She spun around. There was the line, a bar—closed—an open air gift shop: no escape. She hefted the bag, dropped it. Reached into her purse for her blade.

A large black man in a black uniform came forward from nowhere: photo ID and a smile. He was tall, had a thick neck, close-shaved head. Muscles strained his white shirt beneath the uniform coat. His broad face warmed her: liquid eyes. She glanced at the cowboys. Two stood nearby, pretended interest in the TV monitors. She gave the uniformed man a helpless grin.

"Can I assist you, miss?" he asked, reached for the Samsonite pullman.

She hesitated briefly, thought of the money inside, then relaxed. His hands were large, firm-looking. He looked professional, trustworthy. The two cowboys waited, watched her from the corners of their eyes.

"Miss?" the black man said.

She looked at him. He smiled again—handsome. She felt a little sorry for him for some reason. "I'm a little confused," she said. She extracted her ticket, thrust it out toward him. "I'm supposed to be going to Paris."

"This is the wrong gate," he said. "Wrong concourse." He took her bag, her ticket, turned. "You want the international gate." She followed. He walked quickly, she had trouble keeping up in her high heels. The cowboys followed.

"Best hurry," he said over his shoulder. "They've already boarded."

They turned down another concourse, then he made an abrupt left toward an unmarked door. "Customs is this way," he said. "Passport check." She nodded, glanced over her shoulder: nervous—no cowboys.

He opened the door, held it wide for her to follow, let it hit her in the butt when she came through. She paced behind him. It was dark, like a closet. Curious, she thought.

The plain metal door opened into a long, narrow, empty hallway, closed automatically behind them. She was confused again. He turned, gave her another broad smile, set down the suitcase, then came around hard and slapped her, broke her nose.

Her head bounced off the wall hard. Bright lights filled her eyes, she tasted blood in her mouth. "Oh, shit," she said.

He slapped her again, harder this time. A bell rang in her ears, more lights flashed. Pain webbed from the bridge of her crushed nose. She felt herself blacking out. Everything was fuzzy.

He grabbed her arm, shoved her down on the floor. She scraped her elbow, felt skin peel away. She looked into his hand. A long, sharp knife pointed down. "Told them you were more trouble than you was worth," he said. "Should've done you when we did the other bitch."

Something caught his attention. He made a choking sound, stumbled backwards, a shocked look on his face. Blood gushed out of his mouth, his liquid eyes rolled back, then dropped forward, fixed but unfocused. A dark stain covered his white shirt behind the photo ID.

Heather-Earline, half-blind with pain, looked up into the shadowed face of the lanky cowboy. He needed a shave, he was ugly, but to Earline he was gorgeous. In his hand was a large black pistol. Blue-gray smoke trailed up from the silencer on the end of the barrel.

"Earline," the cowboy said, lightly moving a finger up to touch the brim of his hat. "There's some gentlemen'd like to have a word or two with you. Now, let's don't have no trouble."

Detective Sergeant Gregory Abraham DaCara sat with his shoes propped up on a two-inch stack of paperwork covering his battered desk. An unlit cigarette dangled from his lips, formed in their perpetually sad smile. His eyes were half closed. The crooked smile was partly natural, partly affected, the result of years of giving bad news to good people. His eyes were tired.

DaCara's telephone was buried somewhere beneath the official rubble beneath his shoe soles. He was unconcerned about having to find it. If it rang, it would probably be for Billings. Billings had been getting calls all day. DaCara tried not to care. He failed.

Like most detectives in the squad room of Houston PD, DaCara had no private office, only an overladen desk in a large, impersonal room filled with overladen desks. Also under the clutter was a photo of his ex-wife, his seventeen-year-old daughter, a baseball signed by Joe DiMaggio, and a huge red crawfish, a symbol of his famous gastronomic capacity. He held the department record for consuming the tiny crustaceans at the annual crawfish boil. He should. He was the genuine article: bona fide coon-ass. Cut his teeth on crawfish, boudain, étouffée, seafood gumbo.

Around the squad room, the buzzing of electronic communication devices vied with the rattle-tap of old IBM Selectric typewriters, the light clack of computer keys. An indignant perp's angry voice sometimes disturbed the well-scrubbed atmosphere beneath the fluorescent lights of the room. Telephones buzzed, beepers beeped. Once in a while, someone laughed. Mostly, there was a steady hum.

DaCara was a career cop. Never wanted to be anything else, except rich. He'd shot four men in the line, killed two of them, never hesitated or felt a regret. Police work was war. He wasn't a good guy, didn't see himself that way. He just happened to be on one side, perps were on the other. He was a soldier, perps were the enemy. The enemy's motive was money. Always. Where there was money, there was crime.

DaCara was smart. A smart cop stayed alive, especially in a cesspool like Houston. DaCara had been alive in Houston for twenty years, had four commendations, five citations for bravery, held the departmental record for homicide collars and convictions. "Without conviction," DaCara liked to say, "a collar don't mean shit. And," he would add with a sad smile and a new cigarette, "I got conviction."

What he didn't have was money. DaCara liked to gamble.

He lit his smoke, drew in a lungful: a calculated and deliberate violation. HPD was a smoke-free environment. He deliberately tapped the ash from the lighted coal over the opening in a Pepsi can, put the cigarette back onto his lips.

Across the squad room, several heads snapped up when tobacco odor drifted toward them, brought scowls. He smiled back, drew in again, and entertained them with a series of smoke rings. There was no gold higher than sergeant on the floor, and he was a sergeant. No one could make him put it out. Sooner or later, the lieutenant'd hit him with a fine. He didn't care. He had no intention of paying it. The prospect of him sitting in a cell, busted for smoking, was too ridiculous to contemplate. Right now, he had a problem, needed to think, and without a smoke, that was impossible.

The problem sat at his smaller desk in front of a computer terminal: United States Marshal Theodore Billings. The fat federal cop tapped keys, swore low, studied the screen. He had a AAA map unfolded on his desk, covered with scraps of paper on which he'd scrawled notes. DaCara smoked, studied Billings's back. Yes, he thought, Billings was a major problem.

He was also, in DaCara's opinion, a major joke. But DaCara wasn't laughing. Billings wasn't that kind of joke.

He studied the thick federal officer, contemplated the sweat rings beneath Billings's arms, the regulation haircut. He studied the straining suspenders holding Billings's trousers up, noted the belt, observed the roll of fat pushing out of Billings's collar, weighed the Glock 9-mm automatic in the shoulder holster, the extra clips strung along the strap. He wondered what Billings was doing there. It stumped him.

DaCara wasn't a man who collected aphorisms, but he believed in one: "Parallel lines never meet; look for the perpendicular."

Houston was the "Unofficial Murder Capital of the Western Hemisphere." Bullshit, DaCara thought: TV tabloid trailer stuff. There were more killings every hour in Mexico City or São Paulo or any of a half dozen other American cities than took place in Houston in a bad week. New York and Miami— to say nothing of LA and Chicago—were close rivals. Oklahoma City outran Houston two weeks out of three. But somehow, a killing in Houston especially a bunch of killings—elevated the city to the news quicker than anywhere else. That meant bad PR. The lieutenant hated bad PR.

But lately, even DaCara had to admit that Houston was exceeding its overgrown reputation as a fertile homicidal garden. The shootings at Red's Steakhouse the other night prefaced a wave of mysterious killings that should be connected, but somehow weren't. He enumerated the dead, sought a perpendicular line: Bob Cole, a major player, dirty as a pair of old socks, but no arrests, no convictions. Johnny Ribbon, pimp, street scum, but connected. His number came up. Headline for a day, page three by the weekend, out of the paper entirely a week later.

Aside from Cole, Johnny's only significant "known associate" was one of the biggest bosses in Houston: Boot Town. Managed his stable for him. Boot Town might have a reason to take out an uppity Negroid—DaCara never used any other word for African Americans—who maintained connections with New York, LA. Even with Cole.

As for JoEdna—the hooker—she was Cheez Whiz. Titty dancer-prostitutes were common as mosquitos in Houston. She had more busts than a balloon factory. She'd have gone down sooner or later, anyway, probably head first in some motel's toilet. Or she'd just get into the tub, open a vein, take the long vacation: Happens every day, DaCara thought.

Pimps and hookers didn't last long, and when they bought it, even when they bought it big and loud, it wasn't worth getting heated up over. Just clean up the mess, round up a couple of suspects, question them, listen to their lies, check their alibis, then kick them all loose, let them kill each other, bust the one left standing when the smoke cleared. Saved paperwork. Nobody was going to attend any funerals.

But Bob Cole was different. And his connection was Moria Mendle. Parallel lines. Then there was this Lovell character. Was he the perpendicular? Billings thought so. But why? DaCara couldn't figure *that* out, either. Where was the money? DaCara chain lit another cigarette, crushed the other out on the side of the trash can, risking fire.

"Hey, DaCara," another detective yelled across the room. "You going to cut that out, or what? You know the ordinance."

"Fuck you," DaCara yelled. "I'm thinking here."

"Can't be," the other cop shot back. "I can see both your hands." Laughter. Two female detectives looked away, tried not to be embarrassed. DaCara had balled both, but not at the same time. Both were pretty, both were good, until they decided that an affair with a mere sergeant might retard their careers. Women cops, DaCara thought: basic waste of good pussy.

Billings—whom DaCara called Teddy, because it annoyed him—hunched his shoulders, didn't laugh, said nothing. He was a smoker, too. But he was also a fed. Feds didn't laugh. They obeyed the rules. Usually.

That's what worried DaCara most about Billings. He only obeyed some rules, the ones that didn't matter. The ones he broke, he broke on purpose. Billings was different from any fed DaCara had ever known.

Billings was foisted on DaCara by the lieutenant, who didn't give the detective any choice in the matter.

"I work alone," DaCara protested. "I don't like partners."

"You and he are married," the lieutenant said. "Till he gets tired or you get retired. You don't like it, take some personal days."

That, DaCara knew, would please the lieutenant, a smarmy little penis of a kid who hadn't spent more than two years on patrol before being bumped up to detective, who went gold shield before his suits went out of style. Never hurts to be the son of a councilman, DaCara thought. His own father had been a shrimper. The lieutenant also lobbied for the No Smoking ordinance in the building. DaCara took that personally.

The rationale for federal interest was the automatic weapons used in the steakhouse hit. That should have called in AT&F. Instead, a fat click with ears and a marshal's shield shows up. Another parallel line?

DaCara didn't believe for one minute that Billings cared about automatic weapons. His interest was elsewhere. But where?

DaCara got up to pour himself a cup of coffee. It was thick, black, bitter and decaf, made that morning while most of the detectives in the squad room sat around, diddled their yogurt cups, ate croissants.

DaCara always went down to Rudy's and picked up a double fried-egg sandwich, hash browns, a chocolate shake. The onions gave him heartburn, but he loved them. He also loved to watch the grimaces while he wiped grease from his chin, doused the potatoes with ketchup. Hell, he thought, years ago breakfast break meant talking baseball, football, anyfuckingkindof ball. A *good* break meant talking horses, maybe making a little side bet on the daily double. The only ball these buttheads talked was golf. That was no game for a cop, no game for a man. Women played golf.

If they knew he played the ponies as much as he did, they'd have his shield. It cost him his wife, his daughter, his home, already. If he didn't hit this weekend, it could cost him more than that. DaCara lit another cigarette.

He went back to his desk and fingered over a file. It was the preliminary report on the newest homicide: Will Dudly. DaCara was an Oilers fan, when they were winning. Which wasn't often. He remembered Dudly from the days when he was good for two touchdowns against any team in the league. It hadn't lasted long. DaCara also remembered the six arrests and four convictions Dudly took for drug possession. But that was later.

A security guard at Houston International found Dudly's body a half hour ago. The Harris County Sheriff's office handled it. Dudly was found in a security hallway swimming in most of his bodily fluid. He was dressed as a skycap, 9-mm hole right through his phony picture ID. Nobody saw or heard shit. That meant a silencer, a pro hit.

He remembered that Mendle was scheduled to show up. He looked at the clock: 9:55. If he came, that meant something. If he didn't, that meant something else. DaCara wasn't sure what meant what.

There were dried blood stains on Dudly's pants. They were doing the autopsy now. DaCara told them to rush it. Dudly became another parallel line.

DaCara leaned forward, picked up another piece of paper, the autopsy on Bob Cole. Cole's head and hands had been burned off. Not cut off, not sliced away, and not ripped off:

burned off. His genitals were also seared, as if electrodes had been attached to his cock and balls, to the tender areas under his arms, around his rectum. Painful fucking way to die, DaCara thought. Just right for Bob Cole.

The restaurant shooting was a distraction. Throw around some bullets, leave some bodies, keep the cops guessing. But that scenario didn't sell, at least not for the most likely suspect: Mendle. Wasn't his style. Besides, Mendle didn't have motive. There was no money. No money, no motive.

Then Billings showed up, as if he was hovering over the city and dropped down out of nowhere. DaCara originally figured him for a hotdog, willing to build a frame out of something federal-heavy to pin on Mendle. DaCara didn't care. He wouldn't mind seeing Mendle go down on a bum rap, even if it helped out a federal cop. And he would have figured Billings was the type to set up a solid frame. But it was a stretch, a perpendicular line, maybe. But it was dotted.

He looked up again at the clock. Would Mendle show? He'd wanted to put a tail on him, but the lieutenant wouldn't authorize the overtime.

The phone rang. Billings covered the mouthpiece with his hand, swiveled away from DaCara. Who was this guy? He was acting less like a cop every minute. DaCara dropped the second cigarette butt into the remnants of the coffee, looked at Billings. What kind of cop spends a whole afternoon staring at a computer?

"You mind telling me, Teddy, what the fuck you find so interesting?"

Billings didn't turn around. "I'm looking at a lot of different shit."

DaCara pretended to look over Billings's shoulder. He had no faith in computers. You want answers, you go out, get them. It wasn't easy, but then, police work never was. That's why it was called "work."

Billings's hands played across the keyboard. His fingers were blunt, square on the ends. He wore a small gold ring in the shape of a marshal's badge on his wedding ring finger, and had a plain, steel-cased watch on his wrist. A deep scar ran across the back of his left hand, like a tattoo had once been there.

Billings looked every inch the rube. Every fed DaCara had ever dealt with had been slick. They dressed well, were strong, handsome, confident and efficient: professional pricks. Billings was a prick of a different stripe: rogue bull. But the fancy pistol, the way he maneuvered the program on the screen, told DaCara there was more between Billings's cauliflowered ears than beer gas, more to his background than handling warrants and escort duty. Billings played the part of the hick lawman, the beast, the slob too well. Overacting, DaCara thought.

The phone rang again. Billings snapped it up before DaCara could move. Might as well go for real coffee, he thought.

Billings took some notes, tapped some keys, then swiveled around. "Got the prelim-ME report on Dudly," he said.

DaCara's eyebrows moved, but just slightly. "And?"

"Nice little tidbit." Billings moved the mouse, a new screen popped up. He sat back, smiled.

"You waiting for a drumroll?"

"The blood on his pants is O-negative."

"And?"

"He was A-positive."

"Okay."

"Well," Billings smiled. Small white teeth framed under narrow, porcine lips. "Guess who has O-negative?"

DaCara glanced at the pile of papers under his feet. "Bob Cole?"

"Bingo."

DaCara pinched the bridge of his nose. "Maybe. But not perpendicular."

"What?"

"Circumstantial as shit."

Billings looked hurt. Then the phone rang again. Billings snapped it up.

DaCara glanced up at the clock: 10:05. Billings put down the phone, leaned back, smiled. "You can relax. That was the tail on Mendle."

"We don't have a tail. Not authorized."

Billings's eyes flickered, but he shook his head. "They've

gone to a place called Pap's Cafe. Owned by some guy named Boot Town.''

DaCara watched the perpendicular line ease into place. He relaxed. ''Now we got Bingo.''

11
Boot Town

Eddy Lovell sat in a worn booth with cracked vinyl upholstery, rubbed his eyes. They stung from cigarette smoke, no sleep. He'd been sucking 7-11 coffee from Styrofoam mugs for the past eleven hours. The fresh portion of inky liquid in the cracked mug in front of him did little to calm his acidic stomach. Neither did the eggs-over, limp bacon, greasy home-fries, margarine-slathered toast next to the coffee.

He stared at protoplasmic yolks in front of him, fought back a gagging sensation. It had been a long night. It was shaping up to be a long day.

The restaurant was Pap's Cafe, once the pride of Telephone Road. Splendid in its late forties modernity, it used to boast the most complete menu anywhere on the south side, was a regular stop for Houstonians on their way to or from work downtown: hot coffee, creamy shakes, generous hamburgers, quality steaks, seafood, wholesome breakfasts served twenty-four hours a day, beer and wine available after five. Pap's Cafe was the place for anyone more interested in eating than in being seen eating. It wasn't fancy, it wasn't expensive, it wasn't fashionable: it was good.

Now, the menu was reduced to one laminated eight-by-ten

card offering sparse choices for the day's three squares. Everything came with fries. It all tasted the same, half-frozen and undercooked: grease on ice.

Eddy looked out through the dust-streaked windows. The streetside parking lot, once capacious, inviting, surrounded by palms, magnolias, oleander was now landscaped with yellowed Johnson grass, a variety of stumpy trees that somehow took root and forced their way up through the rotten blacktop, cracked cement. The back lot was now occupied by an unmatched add-on building with high, narrow windows, unpainted sides. Everyone parked in front, in between chughole puddles big enough to swallow a Honda.

There were no Hondas in the parking lot. The vehicles of choice were modified bobtails or six-bys, usually fitted to carry bottles, cans, glass, or assorted construction equipment, tools, supplies. Some never carried anything other than debris. Sometimes they carried wetbacks, sometimes corpses. There were a handful of pickups, one or two doolies with stock trailers, lowboys attached, a Peterbilt tractor rig with a rusted fender. There was only one import, a Datsun pickup belonging to an auto parts store. An old Harley leaned against a bent handrail.

Off in the corner, near the Telephone Road entrance, with Hedge's shadowed form barely visible in the back seat, squatted Moria's battered Buick. It was parked nose out to the street: Fast getaway, Eddy thought.

Pap's Cafe's clientele reflected the variety of their vehicles. Gimme caps, greasy cowboy hats, hardhats, faded pipefitter's headgear were the most prominent: jeans and workboots crowd. There were some ponytails, some earrings, more uniforms: Coca Cola, Budweiser, Texaco, Napa. Men laughed, talked, bickered about last night's ball game, swilled coffee, packed cholesterol in with the caffeine and calories, tobacco and toot. All hiding from their jobs, their wives, all getting an early start on waiting out quitting time, so they could go somewhere else, get loaded, get laid, talk about what a bitch life was.

All of them waiting to see if there was anything they could do for a little spare change, anything they could do for Boot Town. Working-class America: always willing to lend a hand. Like a rock.

All night, Eddy had not stopped thinking about the nearness of Hobby airport, about the need to get away. There hadn't been much else to do but think about that all night. There hadn't been much chance to split, either. He wasn't sure he could, or even that he wanted to.

The visit from the cops left him feeling naked, scared. Billings was a jerk, but DaCara knew his stuff. His focus was on Moria. But Eddy was nervous. Right now, Moria was all he had, his only wall against. . .against what? He didn't know, couldn't decide. He had become one of Moria's people, part of his organization. Part of murder.

That it happened shouldn't have surprised him, but it did. He'd known for years that when you get involved with the wrong people, you can't avoid them later. The feeling was uncomfortable, now that he recognized it. Every time he tied up with somebody, every time he got in bed with somebody else—Ellen, Raul, Dodd and Henderson, Tommy Bodine—he got burned.

He wondered how long it would take this time, how long before he made his mistake. Then he wondered if the mistake hadn't already been made. He might have made it when he followed Moria into Pap's Cafe to meet Boot Town.

Boot Town himself sat in a corner booth behind the one Eddy occupied alone. The large table was designed to seat six people. With Boot Town present, though, more than three others would have had to squeeze to fit. Other than Moria, though, the only people nearer than Eddy were Boot Town's two bodyguards, cowboys. They hovered over him like hawks, ready to pounce on the big man's every need.

If Boot Town weighed three hundred pounds, it was because he'd been on a month's diet, Eddy thought. It was common knowledge that he lived in the apartment built onto the backside of Pap's. Never left it. All he ate was food cooked in Pap's kitchen. Years of greasy calories had taken their toll. Boot Town looked like an ad for American sloth.

Though he always wore heavy shades and an oversized cowboy hat, the Boss of the South Side's skin had seen no light that wasn't artificially generated in years. It was pale, pasty. Even his huge lips were nearly white. In addition to the hat and its Diamondback band, he wore a lime-green, western-cut leisure suit, a pair of custom-made, bright-yellow lizard skin boots: size fourteen. A ponytail trailed down his back. But it wasn't for style. He just hadn't had his hair cut in years. He might look like an overdressed, oversized hick—a fat joke— but Eddy and everybody else knew what Boot Town was. Nobody fucked with Boot Town.

"Spics and spades," Boot Town said sadly into his coffee cup. It was a tiny cup, a demitasse, actually. His hammy fingers could have crushed it without effort. It contained Boot Town's favorite drink, espresso. He was the only one in Pap's who ever drank espresso, ever ordered it. "That's the whole god-damn trouble with this town, ol' hoss. Always was. Too god-damn many spies and spades."

Moria sat across the table from the big man. He had on a sports coat, cotton trousers, all white. He nodded, said nothing, stared into a cup of cold coffee. He was tired, Eddy saw, impatient. But he sat quiet. No one talked until Boot Town was finished.

"Time was," Boot Town said, sipped his beverage, "when a white man could run a decent little operation. Make an honest bill or two. Maybe run a few hookers up on Montrose, get a little table action going over on the west side or out in Pasadena, maybe do a little booze here and there. Then everything god-damn changed. Affirmative fucking Action."

"Yeah," Moria muttered. Boot Town continued to rave.

Eddy knew about Boot Town from guys in the joint. He was The Man in Houston, the Boss, the operator. Once tall, handsome, he had been a bull rider on the rodeo circuit. He made a pile, then retired, went into a different kind of livestock trade: whores. Ran hookers all over town. Back in the old days before Houston went wide-open, he ran a quality bootlegging operation. He'd been busted fifty times, never convicted. Claimed he had the best lawyers in Texas. Claimed nobody dared mess with him, not even the feds. Claimed he'd put more men face down in Buffalo Bayou than "Sam Goddamn Houston ever did."

The word was he was connected to bigger boys, men who ran Houston from glass-and-steel office buildings. Boot Town had power because he knew who they were, how to talk to them. He did for them, they did for him. His claim to power was influence, and his claim to control was money, and, he often said, always with a fat wink, his claim to money was pussy.

It was his favorite topic. He warmed to it.

"Ain't a swinging dick anywhere don't want to get his wick wet with some high-quality strange now and then. Hell, I supply bankers and politicians, judges and district attorneys, preachers and prophets, oilmen and cattlemen, visiting diplomats, movie stars, and ball players. Pillars of the community, one and all. If they can get it up, I can find them a place to put it."

Moria nodded. He'd heard all this before. Eddy marveled at his boss's patience. Moria was not a tolerant man. He had a low threshold for bullshit. But he had to back off where Boot Town was concerned, that is, if he wanted Boot Town's help. And he did.

Reclusive as he was, nothing went down in Houston Boot Town didn't know about. If you wanted somebody found, Boot Town would find them: for a price.

At the same time, Eddy wondered if maybe Boot Town might not be losing it. Pap's Cafe was shabby, even compared to Bishop's, and while he was still a major player, the man was grotesque. It was only a matter of time before one of the big cowboys guarding him decided it was time for Boot Town to retire. Eddy thought: empty saddles.

He wondered if Boot Town had decided it was time for Cole to retire. Maybe Cole and Moria both. Maybe that's what this was all about. It wouldn't be hard, get them to the back room, have one of those cowboys put them away while the fat man laughed, slurped more coffee, told more stories.

He looked the two cowboys over. The one called Bodie laughed at Boot Town's every joke. He wore a nicely tailored jacket, though it was warm in the cafe. When he leaned over to pour more espresso into Boot Town's cup, Eddy noticed the heavy revolver beneath his arm. Bodie saw Eddy notice, smiled.

Eddy pretended to scratch his back, checked his piece. He was glad he had one of his own, glad it was loaded, ready. Above the bar was the customary sign warning patrons that carrying firearms where alcohol was sold was a felony. Half the people in the place were heavy. Eddy smiled back, sipped his coffee, lit another Camel, waited.

Boot Town and Pap's was the last stop on a long list. Too goddamn long, Eddy thought. They had talked to everyone Moria could run down. Gang leaders black and brown, shylocks, gamblers, small-timers, high rollers. Eddy's butt ached from sitting around, waiting until Moria got around to business. His mind ached from anxiety. Nobody knew a goddamn thing. Boot Town was a last resort. As usual with most last resorts, it was about to pay off.

Moria made the call around midnight. When he hung up, he shook his head. "I hate to call that fat fuck," he said. "Hate to give him the satisfaction." They were coming back from Pasadena where Eddy had stood in a wet alley, watched Moria go through the motions with a white supremacy gang leader. He didn't know a thing, didn't know who Moria was, told him to take his "white nigger," meaning Eddy, and his "personal nigger," meaning Hedge, get the hell out of town.

"Dumber than shit," Moria reported when they took their time driving away. Then he called Boot Town. Boot Town promised that Moria's problems would be solved.

"So, back to the hotel?" Eddy wanted to get someplace he could think.

But Moria Mendle took no man—not even one like Boot Town—at his word. "Hell no," he said and barked an address on the north side. "Not if I can figure this out first, get to that bitch before he does." He sighed. "Don't trust the fat prick." Moria shook his head. "But he's got the network. He can find her if anybody can. I hate asking him to do it. He won't forget it. It's going to cost me in the long run."

The night wore into morning, they got nowhere. The only thing Eddy learned was that nobody liked Moria. The only thing Moria learned was that nobody knew what happened to Bob Cole. Nobody knew where he might find Heather. Even fewer gave a damn.

Moria had his own theory of root problems. "Houston's

changed," he said. "Time was when this was a good little town for business. Now, it's overrun with losers, street punks and Yankee Yuppies looking for a hook. Every one of them's got a hard-on and no place to put it but up my ass."

All night they drove. They met people in bars, clubs, back alleys, warehouses, hotels and after-hours joints. Nobody knew shit. Or nobody was talking. Eddy mainlined coffee, Moria stayed on the phone, Hedge squatted in the back seat, a loaded shotgun across his knees: careful.

The sun came up. Moria told Eddy to swing by the hotel where they grabbed showers, changed clothes. Moria found two of the girls still there, asleep in the living room, warm, naked, seductive when they stirred, hanging all over them.

Eddy shrugged his off, took a shower while she went back to sleep on the bed. When he came out, Moria was just finishing with the other one. Gave them a C note apiece, threw them out. "Whores," he said. "I'm sick of hanging around with whores. The only whore I'm interested in is the one I can't find."

Then the call came from Boot Town while Moria was bathing. Eddy took the call, then reported: "He's got her."

Moria came out toweling off his thinning hair. "Goddamnit," was all he said. He was ready in five minutes. Eddy was seated, waiting.

Hedge came out of his bedroom, unbathed, unchanged. He went automatically to the door. "Boot Town?" he asked.

"Yeah," Moria nodded. "Fat son of a bitch. Might have known.

Now, they'd been there nearly an hour. To talk to Boot Town, you had to eat his food, listen to his bullshit. It was a toss-up which would make you sick first.

"What happened to Bob was a goddamn pity." Boot Town found the subject at last. He sipped more coffee, frowned bitterly. "I always liked ol' Bob. Weird as shit, Yankee as they come, but stand-up guy. Sometimes he got in my face a little. But that was all right. He'd stand up."

Moria had said almost nothing, let Boot Town run down.

He told Eddy as they drove down Main and onto Telephone Road, he dreaded the meet as much as anything. ''Fat son of a bitch has to talk for an hour before he gets down to business,'' Moria said. ''Wants you to hear his whole political philosophy, wants you to agree with him.'' He stared out the window at business owners rolling back heavy bars, disarming alarm systems. ''Wonder what this is going to cost me?''

Eddy only grunted in reply. They picked up a tail leaving the hotel—a van—he was sure, but he hadn't spotted it until they were nearly there. Could have been behind them all night. He started to drive on, make a pass, try to shake him, suggested it to Moria. Moria looked back. Blue Chevy van. Old model, nondescript. Cell phone antenna off the rear window.

''It's probably DaCara's boys,'' he said. ''We're just going to eat breakfast. Maybe he's hungry, too.''

The tail made a pass when they pulled in, then came back, parked across the street in a convenience store lot. Eddy watched it. The windows stayed up. Nobody got out.

From time to time, people came in, sat down, ordered, ate, left. Eddy watched them all. No one seemed out of place, but given the variety of tired, overweight, hopeless faces he found when he scanned the room, it wouldn't be hard to blend in. A dark man—maybe an Arab, Eddy thought—got out of the van, walked across the street to the parking lot. He never glanced at the Buick. He came in, sat in a distant booth near the kitchen, ordered coffee.

''Would you look at that?'' Boot Town demanded. ''Hell of a note. Man can't even conduct a little business without that kind of shit going on.''

The waiter took his time. Everyone stared at the man. He was small, had neat, wiry hair cut close, a full handlebar mustache. He rose, went to a pay telephone in the corner, made a call. The room fell silent, but he spoke only a few words, then returned to the booth, sat down, drank his coffee. The only noise came from the kitchen: clanking, sizzling. Then he rose, left a bill on the table, left. He returned to the van, got in. It didn't move. Conversation resumed in that end of the cafe.

''I'm here to see Heather,'' Moria said, when Boot Town's

attention returned to his own coffee. "Already killed a whole damn day on that."

The huge face looked up, blew his cheeks full, a gesture of helpless sympathy. "Yeah, I know," he said, disappointed. "Should've called me soon's you hit town, ol' hoss."

"I need to talk to her," Moria said softly.

"Yeah, I know," Boot Town repeated, now extracting a thin brown cigarette and balancing it on his fat lower lip. "I got a good man working on her right now."

Moria's eyebrows shot up, then lowered. "I don't want a 'good man working on her,' " he said: even. "I want to work on her myself."

Behind the dark shades, Boot Town's eyes drifted toward Eddy. He sighed, lit his smoke, sat back. A lungful clouded up toward the grease-stained ceiling. "All in good time, ol' hoss. We know our business."

"You said you had her. So if you've got her, I want to talk to her. That's all you need to know," Moria said.

"Wrong!" Boot Town's hand slapped the table, made the coffee cups jump. "I need to know plenty more than that." Then his smile widened again. Eddy thought of a picture of "Mr. Sun" Barbara always kept on the wall of her room. It always struck Eddy as more frightening than fun, but Barbara loved it. Boot Town was loving this.

"I just need to talk to her," Moria said. "She's my property."

"Was." Boot Town blew smoke out, covering Moria. He turned to the lanky cowboy with the espresso pot. "She's mine, now."

Moria started to say something else, but Boot Town held up a fat paw to stop him. "Hold your water." He consulted a pocket watch. "Ought to be about done." He looked up at Bodie. The cowboy nodded.

"Phone," the big man said. Bodie produced a cellular unit. Boot Town flicked it open, punched in seven digits. Eddy was surprised the man's fingers could work the tiny buttons. He spoke softly into the handset.

He looked at Moria, winked, spoke clearly. "I want her awake." His voice dropped once more to a low whisper. He snapped the phone shut, beamed another Mr. Sun smile at Moria.

"I got a stake in all this. Losing Johnny is tough," he said. "And it's personal. About the best spade I ever had. Knew how to handle that pussy. Kept himself clean, kept them happy. Hell, if he'd been white, I'd've adopted him. He was just plain good."

"He was a saint among men," Moria said with no trace of irony.

Boot Town nodded sadly. "Just so you know who's running this show." Moria nodded once, sharp. Boot Town crushed out his smoke. "Let's go."

They rose, moved aside. Boot Town struggled to extricate himself from the booth. Moria waited, his expression blank while the large man stepped off toward the kitchen, flanked by two cowboys. Moria fell in behind. Eddy waited until his boss gave him a nod, then he rose, checked the van. Still parked across the street. A black Chevy Caprice, brand-new, pulled in, opposite end of the lot. No one got out.

"You coming or what?" Moria yelled at him. Eddy joined in the small procession. No one in the cafe looked up.

Boot Town marched through the smoky kitchen to a small door, waited until one of his men opened it. Then he stepped through, disappeared. Eddy couldn't believe a man with that much bulk could move so fast. Bodie, one hand inside his coat, stood to one side, held it open for Moria and Eddy.

The room behind Pap's kitchen was a dim, broad rectangular hallway that led to other, brighter rooms twenty yards beyond. The walls were covered with a heavy, spongy material: sound-proofing, Eddy thought.

What next caught Eddy's attention and held it was in the center of the hallway. There, beneath a bright spot light, squatting on a rusty, old-fashioned kitchen step stool, naked, her arms tied behind her, her legs strapped down, gagged, wide-eyed with fright, was the girl who held Cole in front of the steakhouse. She looked better on the tape, Eddy thought.

"Moria Mendle," Boot Town said amiably, ambled to the

center of the room, blowing smoke from his cigar all the way. "I think you know Earline. Or should I call you Heather?"

Moria stepped forward, took one look into her face, spat into it. She flinched as if scalded.

"She's done told us all she knows," a tall thin man with no front teeth stepped forward. He had a small instrument in his hand. Eddy recognized it, a hotshot. "And that ain't much," he went on. Earline's legs, stomach, and sides of her hips were crisscrossed with deep red marks, web-shaped burns. Only her breasts were unblemished. They were large and firm, with soft pale nipples. Centerfold material, Eddy thought.

"Oh yeah," the man added, glanced at Moria, "had to kill us a nigger out to the airport. He was after her, too. Busted her nose."

Boot Town's bushy eyebrows shot up. "No shit? Goddamn, Earline, you *are* in demand! Makes me wish I'd had you over a time or two, myself." He turned, waved his fat hand. "Uh, Moria, this is Crackers. Call him that 'cause he's crazy. But he usually gets what we're after. Crackers, this ol' hoss here's Moria Mendle. Mr. Mendle to you. Don't know the muscle."

"Eddy," Moria said, nodding toward Crackers. "Eddy Lovell."

Crackers nodded, lifted a single finger to touch the spot where the brim of a hat would have been had he worn one. Creases in his well-oiled hair suggested he did most of the time. "'Lo. Sorry for your loss." He meant Cole, Eddy decided.

"You kin to Quincy Lovell?" Boot Town asked.

Eddy shook his head. "Not anymore."

"Don't blame you. Prissy son of a bitch, ain't he?" Eddy nodded.

Moria studied Earline. "I wanted to talk to her myself," he said, flat.

"Tough," Boot Town said. "Was my spade got greased. This is my town. I kill my own snakes."

"And you charge for it," Moria answered.

"Business. Don't you forget it."

Moria moved forward. He was so short, he could almost look Earline in the eye. Eddy could see veins in his neck pulsing. "Heather," Moria said. She raised her eyes to him. They were dull with pain. "Why'd you set up Bob Cole?"

She stared at him, her eyes, red-rimmed, pled for mercy.

Moria reached out, slapped her hard. Her head snapped to the right. He slapped her again, left. Eddy stepped forward, then caught himself, turned away. Not now, he told himself.

"Seems she was working for these galoots from out of town," Crackers said. "Put her on the spot. Told her they were going to put the big hurt on Cole. That was it, but she ain't too clear on details. Wasn't nobody supposed to get killed. She was very clear on that."

"Galoots?" Moria asked, distracted. "Who?"

She shook her head. Didn't know. Tears flowed down her cheeks, made new trails in the salty tracks of the old ones. The edge of her mouth bled.

Eddy looked at her again. He saw Monica, saw Princess, saw Barbara. He even saw Ellen. Every woman he knew was reflected in Earline's eyes. His stomach hollowed. She was dead, he thought. He was looking at a dead girl. Unless he did something to stop it. He glanced at Crackers, at Bodie and the other cowboy who had taken positions down the hall, toward the light. Breath was hard to find in the narrow room.

"She had this on her," Crackers said. He handed over the airline ticket, the passport to Boot Town. "And this." He kicked the pink Samsonite. It fell open. Bundles of cash mixed with new clothes—still tagged—flowed onto the floor. "There's near ten grand there," Crackers said.

Moria looked at the money, then up at her again: disgust. Eddy saw him reach into his pocket. He stepped forward, couldn't stand it. He put his big hand out on his boss's shoulder. Moria flinched as if burned.

"She's just a kid, Moria," Eddy whispered. Moria held his hand steady for a moment. Then relaxed. Sighed. "She's not who you're after," Eddy added.

"So who *am* I after?" Moria asked her. She shook her head. "She has no idea who they are?" Moria looked at Crackers.

"Said one was a nigger. Another was some kind of A-rab. Nigger may be queer, way he talked."

"Goddamn! I knew it," Boot Town hooted.

"Give her the money, the ticket and passport," Crackers read from a small spiral notebook he found in his shirt pocket. "Had her thinking she was supposed to get out of town. Then, they turned the tables on her. She don't know why." He looked up. "Or so she says."

"You believe her?" Boot Town asked.

"Looks like they planned to kill her, if that's what you're asking. Keep her quiet, is my guess. The money was bait."

More tears. She nodded vigorously.

"Ungag her," Moria said. Crackers looked at Boot Town.

"Too risky," the fat man said. "There's folks out there," he tilted his big hat toward the door.

"Ungag her, Bernie," he said. Boot Town's head snapped around, his fat face showed rage. Nobody ever called him Bernard, Bernie, or anything but Boot Town. He had killed men for calling him anything else.

"You're pushing me, ol' hoss," he said in a low voice. Then he shrugged. "I can see you're upset, so I'm going to cut you some slack. But don't push me." To Crackers: "Go on. Do as he says."

The gag was a handball, stuffed in her mouth, covered with a towel, bound with a shock cord. Crackers removed it, handled the saliva and blood-stained ball with his fingertips. "Spits a lot." He wiped it on his jeans. She immediately gasped, gagged, gasped again. Worked her jaws. Then began sobbing more. Blood ran from her nose.

"I'm sorry," she choked out. "I swear I am! Nobody was supposed to get hurt. I didn't have any choice. They—"

"Shut up," Moria said. He waited. "Shut up," he repeated softer. "Tell me about them."

"Who?" she looked up at him. Crackers snapped the hotshot. The spark was purple in the subdued light of the hallway. She flinched, struggled against her bonds.

Bodie, standing behind her, put a hand on her shoulder, slid it down to heft her left breast. "Best you answer the man," he said. "Them's real nice titties. I'd hate to see 'em all scratched up."

She swallowed, looked at Moria. "Who?" she demanded, confused. "Bob? Oh, it was—I saw him! They had this wire or something around his neck. They wanted him to tell them something. They burned him. Set him on fire! They cut off—''

''Tell me about the men,'' Moria said. ''I don't want to hear about Bob.''

She stopped, heaved slightly, breathed deep, held it, let it out slowly. ''There were two of them, at first. Two men. One was black. One an Arab of some kind. Then there was this white guy. But he wasn't there long. I'd never seen them before. They called Johnny. Asked for me special. I thought it was a double, maybe a triple, you know?''

Moria nodded. ''Go on.''

Eddy leaned forward. Moria might have been her father, getting the story of a wild night out from his wayward and repentant daughter, not grilling a naked, tortured whore.

''They offered me money. A lot of money.'' Her eyes slanted down toward the bundles on the floor. ''Told me they would send me to France. To Paris. I always wanted to go there. They knew that. Knew everything—'' She bit her lip. Her teeth went all the way through. Blood flowed down her chin. ''Oh God! I never wanted this to happen! It was supposed to be a kind of joke.''

''Nobody's laughing,'' Boot Town said.

''Tell me about them,'' Moria said sternly.

She shook her head. Her newly colored red hair, matted as it was, swayed across her face, left damp tendrils over her eyes, stain where sweat and tears had taken the dye. Her nose was twisted out of shape. ''They were just men. Good clothes. Lots of money. Took me to their hotel.''

''Where?''

''Hilton? I guess. I don't remember.''

''Crackers,'' Boot Town said. The man stepped forward. The hotshot sparked.

''I *don't remember!* Please!''

Moria stepped forward, backhanded her again, hard across the mouth. Two drops of blood hit Crackers's face. He flinched. Moria made a fist.

Something went off inside Eddy's head. He stepped forward slightly, rose to the balls of his feet. He didn't care what she had done, why she had done it. He would not let Moria hit her again, wouldn't let Crackers sting her again with the electronic zapper. He wouldn't. His fists doubled. Before he could move, he saw Crackers step back. Her eyes had rolled up, her head lolled. She was out.

Eddy realized he was holding his breath. He wanted to be sick.

A large pitcher of water sat on a table near the door. Crackers picked it up, splashed her full in the face with it, ice and all. She shook her head, blew blood out of her nose, her mouth.

"Answer quietly, or I'll have him gag you again," Moria said. Her dress was on the floor. He picked it up, wiped her face with it. Pushed the hair out of her eyes, strangely gentle. A caress. "Which hotel?"

"The Hilton. Maybe the Marriott. It was a busy week."

Moria nodded, satisfied. "Go on."

"They just gave me the money. The other stuff. Told me what to do. Said they'd send me to Paris. Johnny was in on it."

Silence greeted this.

Boot Town lit another smoke. "I don't believe that."

"Well he *was*. That's what they said! They said he *had* to be in on it, so they could talk to Bob." Her voice was rising again. She caught it. Dropped to a whisper. "They gave me the gun. It wasn't even loaded. They said for me to hold Bob still while they pretended to scare Johnny off. All I had to do was keep Bob quiet. They'd scare Johnny and JoEdna off. Make it look like a robbery or something. They'd put us in the car. Talk to him. Take me home, then to. . .to the airport. That's what they said. That's all I know." She looked from face to face. "Johnny *had* to be in on it."

Boot Town looked at Moria. Shook his head. "Hate to say it, but it makes sense, ol' hoss. You're going to have to take my word that I didn't know nothing about this. But it might be true. Can't trust a spade. Not when there's money involved."

Moria gave him a narrow look, turned back to Earline. "Who were they?"

"I don't know their names," she said. "They were just men. One was black, one was white. The black guy was tall and had kind of gray hair. Wore glasses."

"What kind?"

"Those—metal kind. You know. Rims like shiny metal. Steel."

Moria nodded. "Anything else?"

"He had taste. Good suit. The other guy—the white guy. He was kind of tacky."

"How?"

"Just tacky. All rumply. Slouchy." She shook her head. Sweat and tears still mixed. She took a breath, went on: "The white guy was short, fat, kind of bald. He had a scar."

"Where?" Moria asked.

"On his cheek."

"What about the Arab?"

"Just an Arab," she said. "I can't tell much about him. Mustache. Short, I guess." Her eyes widened. "And there was another guy. But I couldn't see him real good. He stayed in the other room. Didn't come out but for a minute. They were all weird. They talked funny," she repeated. "Except the white guy."

"Funny how?" Moria asked.

"I don't know. Like foreigners. Not like a Mexican. I draw a lot of Mexicans for some reason. I know how they talk." She licked the wounds on her lips. "He talked. . .just funny. I don't know."

"Could have been anybody," Boot Town said.

"I only saw them that once. They didn't want me to do anything. They just wanted to make a deal. I thought it would be okay. It was a joke. They sent the money to me in a package. The ticket. The passport. They came by mail." She looked down. "I don't even know where they got my picture."

"No names." Moria wiped his mouth. "Tall black guy, short white guy. Could be anybody." His eyes flicked to Boot Town, to Eddy, back to Earline.

"That's all I know." She sobbed again. Tears started again. "That and that they killed Johnny and JoEdna. They tried to kill me. But I got away."

"And ol' Bob. Killed the shit out of him, too," Boot Town put in.

"And you have no idea why?" Moria asked.

She shook her head, gulped air. Shock and panic were taking over.

"Think!" Moria yelled. Eddy was shocked by his voice. Unlike his usual tenor pitch, this was deep, commanding. "You said they wanted to know something. What?"

"They wanted to know . . ." she trailed off, started crying again. Her eyes were wild, rolling around the room, going from face to face. "Oh, God!"

"Wanted to know what?"

"They wanted him to tell them something."

"What?"

"They just kept hurting him. . . ." Again she collapsed. Fear boiled up inside her, bubbled over, became tears. Blood still ran from her broken nose.

Moria went over to her once more, slapped her again. Eddy made no move to stop him. Stupid little bitch, he thought. Got in over her head. Couple of strangers flash a little money, she sold out everybody she knew. The videotape rolled through his mind. She was lucky she wasn't just gunned down right then. He wondered why she wasn't.

She gasped from the blow, but in a moment, she sobered. She was spent. "All he said," she wheezed, "was a word. I don't even know what it means. But he said it. Then, they killed him. They. . .oh God!" She sobbed, choked. "They cut off his head! I saw it! They cut *off his head!*"

"What was the word?"

"I ran away. I just busted out of there and ran."

"What was the word?"

She cried. Fresh blood ran from her nostrils. Moria raised his hand to slap her again, but Eddy caught it. "Let me," he said.

He went over to her, put a large finger beneath her chin and lifted her face to him. Her face was streaked with blood, mascara, red dye, tear tracks. Her lips were chewed raw. Her eyes red-rimmed and swollen. "Don't let them hurt me?" she whimpered. "I can't stand it anymore." Her eyes closed, opened, focused. "I'm so scared," she whispered.

"What was the word?" Eddy asked. "Tell them, they'll let you go."

She swallowed, nodded, swallowed again. "I don't know what it means."

"Tell them," Eddy said in a soft but firm voice. "Tell me."

"Balmorhea."

"We run the nigger," Crackers said. Earline was now still, silent, in shock. Her eyes stared at the knot of men who stood around her, oblivious to her pain, to her nakedness, to the terror that now kept her silent. She no longer sobbed. Quiet tears ran down her cheeks, mixed with blood from her lacerated lips, crushed nose, traced across purpling bruises, dripped from her breasts to her thighs, then to the floor.

Eddy couldn't stand to look at her any longer. He moved into a corner near the door. His stomach roared. He didn't know what would happen next, but he would not let them hurt her anymore. He had promised her they would let her go. He intended to keep that promise. At the same time, he was desperate to leave the smoky hallway, to be outside.

"What nigger?" Boot Town asked, dragging Eddy's thoughts back into the room.

"One we greased at the airport. Nobody from Galveston. Used to work the docks. Hell, used to play for the Oilers. Name of Will Dudly." Something went off in Eddy's mind, something dim and distant. He knew Will Dudly. "Pretty good tight end in his day," Crackers went on. "Come out of Nederland over yonder." Crackers put a finger beside his nose. "Had a habit, done time. Rape, I think. Dope maybe. Been an odd-jobber lately. Anything for a buck."

A scene rose up in Eddy's memory. His tryout with the Oilers, years ago. The guy in the locker next to him at the camp: number fourteen draft pick out of Nederland, Will Dudly. But there was something else, too, something he was almost sure of.

"And he was after her?"

"Had her. Said she was there when Cole bought it. Someplace over to Pasadena. Says she seen it. Didn't see much else. She had a blade." He went over to her purse, brought back a slender knife, no handle, lightweight.

"Here," Crackers said. "Careful, it's sharp as midnight. She didn't have it out, though. If Bodie and me hadn't showed up when we did, he'd have cut her. With this." He held up a stiletto, equally sharp, bone handle.

Moria took Earline's blade. Ran it across his arm, shaved away hair. "So that's it?"

"I don't think we know any more than we ever knew," Boot Town said. He nodded toward Earline. "Nothing left to do but clean up the mess." He glanced at Moria, then down at the girl. "We'll make it quick."

She made no noise, bit her lip again, drew fresh blood.

Eddy had had enough. "Let her go," he said.

Moria stared at him.

Boot Town's mouth opened, and his cigar almost fell out. "I don't think I heard that, ol' hoss." His voice was hard. "And I don't take orders from muscle. Anybody's muscle."

Eddy looked at Moria. "I told her we'd let her go if she told you what you wanted. She did. Let her go." He mentally checked the pistol. His heart raced. Every eye in the room was on him.

"You think that's smart?" Moria asked him softly.

"I think it's right." He looked at her, met her eyes. "She didn't kill Cole. Didn't even set him up. She's as much a mark as he was. She just got lucky." He looked at the knife Moria still held in his hand. "She's not a player." He stepped between her and Boot Town, looked at Moria. "Let her go."

Moria gave him a long study. Then he pushed past Crackers, past Boot Town, went behind the stool, cut her wrists free. Her arms dangled. Her fingers were bone-white, dead.

"Get her into some clothes. Let her clean up," Moria said. "Get her something for these burns. Doctor her lip. Tape her nose up. Give her back her fucking money. Drive her to the airport and buy her another ticket. Stay with her until she gets on the goddamn plane."

"Hoss, I don't care what this side of beef says. She set up your best friend. That there's blood money."

"That's right," Moria said. "Cole was *my* best friend. All you lost was a worthless pimp. A pimp who set up my friend and got what was coming to him. This," he looked down at

Earline, "this girl's a patsy. She doesn't know shit. I don't know if you're in on this deal or not. I'm taking your word that you're not. For now. So keep on my good side. Let her go." He looked up at the huge man in front of him, softened his tone. "Call it a favor. Send me your bill for the rest."

Boot Town hesitated, glanced at Eddy. "You're going soft." Moria refused to look at him. To Crackers: "You heard the man. Let her go."

Crackers stepped over, took Earline's blade from Moria, cut the bonds holding her feet. She stayed very still, made no attempt to cover herself. Her arms dangling, feet now akimbo.

"Listen, Moria. I liked ol' Bob. I didn't have no reason to put him down. But even if I did, I wouldn't have done it that away. You've known me too long to think I would." Boot Town sounded hurt, sincere.

Moria nodded. "Let's go," he said to Eddy. He opened the door and passed back into the hubbub of Pap's dining room.

When they got to the car, Eddy fired it up and turned the a/c on high. It wasn't yet noon, but the temperature was already pushing the mercury up. He couldn't imagine how Hedge stood it, sitting out there, windows up except for a crack to blow smoke through. The big man's skin was slick with sweat. The shotgun still rested on his lap.

Eddy noticed that the blue van was gone. But the black Caprice was still there. Men inside.

Moria pulled out his handkerchief, wiped his face, sighed. "Don't ever put me on the spot like that again," he said.

Eddy didn't hesitate. "I wasn't going to let them kill her."

"Or me?" Moria's eyes turned up, locked with Eddy's.

"Or you."

Moria sighed, broke contact. "I hate this kind of shit. And I'm shot."

Eddy nodded. He felt grit behind his eyelids, but he was wired with coffee and adrenaline. His mind wasn't on sleep. It was on a ghost from his past: Will Dudly.

He remembered reading about the big tight end, remembered reading about his troubles with girls, money, drugs and hot cars. He also remembered who had represented him, who had managed his contracts, then kept him from doing long, hard time when he blew it: Quince.

Now, there was a connection, which in a roundabout way made the connection Eddy, and that was no connection at all.

"Feel like a little road trip?" Moria asked. He pulled the map from the glove box, unfolded it, peered down at it.

"Where to?"

"Here," Moria's chubby finger fell on a spot in the middle of nowhere. "I got a feeling that whatever answers there are, we're going to find right here."

Eddy leaned over, looked where Moria's manicure pressed down: Balmorhea. He shrugged, settled, his mind working when he pulled out of the parking lot, onto Telephone Road. They were two miles away when Pap's Cafe exploded in a thunderous fireball that broke every window on the block.

12
Quince

"I can't understand for the life of me why anyone in his right mind would want to live in this damned town."

John Quincy Adams Lovell—Quince to anyone who wanted to think they were friends—stood in his office, his hands locked behind him. He stared out over the hazy, smog-laden midday skyline of Houston. A good view from twenty stories up. Beneath him coiled the congested confluence of expressways of the nation's largest southern metropolis.

To his right, visible through the huge plate glass wall of the office, the towers of the medical center thrust through hazy smog. Behind him, through another glass wall, the spires of Westheimer and the Galleria shimmered in dirty sunlight. Quince's office occupied the corner of the building. He sometimes called it the "apotheosis" of his career, sitting on top of a pile of recycled steel and glass looking out over a sprawl of steaming urban shit: Houston.

"It's your town," Hillary offered. She was comfortable on a leather sofa, her third bloody maria in one hand, an unlit pink cigarette in the other. Her ice-blue minidress showed off long legs, matched the frames of her sunglasses. Her hair: perfectly blonde. Her lips: perfectly red. "You chose it."

Quince, like Eddy, was a large man: bullet-headed, six-two, body of a linebacker. Quince never played ball. Quince never played anything. His hair, curly, full, prematurely gray at the temples, set off a broad, handsome, clean-shaven, baby-soft face. Suit: Italian. Tie: Japanese silk. Shoes: English leather, handmade. His nails manicured. Cuff links matching emeralds, shirt custom-tailored, combed cotton. Everything about him said money.

That was his ticket for most all his life, that and the degree from Harvard Law on the wall. Money and the right degree. Together, they got him where he was, made him what he was: image.

But the image of money was not the same as money. The image of strength was not quite the same thing as being strong: lessons Quince never quite learned.

"I didn't choose anything," he said, picked up a small porcelain cup, sipped from it. The coffee was bitter. He liked it that way, reminded him of his life.

"There was always a choice," Hillary sniped. "I made my choices. I was very well connected."

Quince focused again on the traffic chaos below. A headache crept around his temples, threatened to squat. "Still are. Most of the time, from what I hear. Takes a water hose to get you loose most of the time."

Hillary turned her head away. Crudity was his only weapon against her.

Mitchell Jensen, a well-dressed black man in his forties sat at a small glass desk off to one side, his back to the room. His attention was focused on a computer monitor, but he chuckled. Hillary shot him a mean look.

Quince asked Jensen, "Any word?"

"No. I'm making sure everything is in place for the exchange."

"I thought that was Cole's department," Quince said.

"It is," Jensen replied. "Or was. It's ours—mine, now."

"Nice," Quince muttered to himself. "I wonder what else can go wrong."

"Almost anything," Jensen said. "They're not professionals." It amazed Quince that he could hear so well. Almost everything about Jensen amazed Quince. "They're Cole's people. He said he only worked with the best, but I can assure you, they are *not* professionals."

"That's comforting," Quince said.

"Allowing Mr. Cole to handle this was a mistake from the beginning."

Quince nodded. "I know."

Jensen turned around. "People like him. They have no subtlety. They aren't careful."

"And you are?" Jensen only returned the look. "Oh, sorry," Quince continued. "I forgot. You *are* careful."

"I know my business."

"Do they know? These people? About Cole?" Quince asked.

"No," Jensen said. "Nothing has been released to the press. Even if it had, it's a local matter. Not exactly a headline for CNN."

"But you are going to tell them."

"Of course. It will be obvious when Mr. Cole fails to appear."

"How will they take it?"

"They shouldn't care," Jensen said. "That much money has a way of smoothing out such matters." He took a beat. "They can like it, or not. Or," he paused, shrugged, "they're expendable. You know my position on that."

"Honor among thieves," Hillary said.

Jensen sighed, sat back, ran a hand through his graying hair. "Right now, our only concern is to find out precisely what they're expecting to happen. We have the name of the place, but we don't know the arrangements."

"I thought it was a straight trade. Money for Barbara. Simple."

Jensen offered a plastic smile. "It's been my experience, Mr. Lovell, that nothing is simple. Not in my business. This is far from simple."

Quince felt a numbness creep over him. He needed to speak, to instruct. He had lost control, knew it. He wondered what ever made him think he ever had it. Jensen was running things. Jensen scared the hell out of him.

"We should have handled it my way," Jensen said.

"The way you handled Raul Castillo?" Quince asked. The numbness grew, became general.

Jensen looked away. "I remind you that the delay in that matter was entirely your doing. In the end, Mr. Castillo proved most uncooperative. He panicked, and what happened to him was an accident. Overzealousness, actually. I reacted to that. It won't happen again. We can only hope that your brother will prove to be more cooperative. With your niece as a bargaining chip, I expect he will."

Hillary looked up. "Quince?"

He put up a hand to stay her question.

"And Moria Mendle?"

"He's done his work, however unwittingly. He's brought your brother here, which is convenient. I'm not interested in him, except insofar as your brother is concerned. Our information is that he can control him."

"Information you got from Cole."

"Cole assured us that Mr. Mendle could handle your brother."

"You're going to kill him, too, aren't you?" Hillary put in. "Not that I care. Who is he, anyway?"

Jensen gave her a distasteful look. "No. Not unless it proves necessary. I imagine we can persuade Mr. Mendle to be cooperative. Where Mr. Cole and Mr. Mendle differ is that Mr. Mendle understands business."

"But Cole was his friend," Quince said. "What if Moria put things on a personal level?"

"He won't. He's in the dark. He's spent most of the morning looking for the prostitute."

"I thought you paid her off, sent her out of the country."

Jensen's mouth made a thin line. "We did. She proved. . ."

"Uncooperative?" Hillary offered.

"The important thing is that the operation is still proceeding according to plan. Mr. Cole's absence is only a minor problem."

"House of cards," Quince said wearily. "A goddamned house of cards. Nobody knows what anybody's doing. Nobody can trust anybody. How in the hell did I ever. . ." He shook his head, rubbed his eyes, looked at Hillary, who returned an ironic smile. Definitely a headache day. He hadn't slept in two days, not since Cole's murder. Hillary's early-morning arrival didn't help. He wanted to lie down, to rest.

"When the time comes," Jensen went on, "we make the exchange, your niece will be safe. Your brother will see reason. Mr. Cole's people become rich. Mr. Mendle becomes richer. You become the richest of all. Everyone is happy." He took a breath. "Relax." He looked briefly at Quince. "This is not the way I like to do things," he said. "But this is the way you set it up."

"You go at Eddy the way you went at Raul, you'll kill him, or he'll kill you, and nobody will have anything," Quince said.

"I doubt your brother is as formidable as all that."

"You don't know him," Hillary put in. "He's a brute."

"Brutes can be handled," Jensen said.

"Brutes can cut your balls off and shove them down your throat," Quince said. "You don't get a stranglehold on him, he will. He's capable."

Jensen smiled again. "Well, we have that stranglehold now. And she's on her way. Just as Mr. Cole arranged it. So, relax. Things are moving. All we need is to make contact with your brother, explain the situation, then make the exchange."

"Works for me," Hillary put in.

"Shut up, Hillary," Quince said.

"Don't tell me to shut up, big brother," Hillary said. "*Mister* Jensen and I put this deal together in the first place. It was you who blew it. You and your so-called contacts. Where did you find those two clowns, anyway? What were their names? Dot and Mendleshon?"

"Dodd and Henderson."

"God. Sounds like a CPA firm. Trust a lawyer to come up with that. If you had gotten someone who knew what he was doing, Eddy would be dead, Barbara would be well-matched, and I would be sunning myself on an island someplace, looking at all the pretty boys. But now, you're blowing it again. I'm just along for the ride. I need a drink," she added with a sigh. "I hope Barbara comes out in one piece."

"You mean comes out *as* a piece," Quince corrected. "A piece you can barter on the sex exchange. Why don't you admit it, Hill. She's just bait."

"Don't be vulgar. My God, you're worse than Eddy." Hillary returned to the sofa, sat, recrossed her legs. She tapped her cocktail glass with a long nail. "Make me a drink. That's all I want."

"And the money," Quince added. Hillary looked away. "You don't give a damn about anything but the money. Why won't you admit it? We're all in it for the money," he said. He rose, went to the bar, mixed her fourth bloody maria of the morning. It astonished him how she could drink so much, remain so lucid.

Jensen spoke again: "By Monday, all of this will be a memory."

"A bad memory," Hillary said, accepting her drink. "But these people who have Barbara: How do you know when they don't see Cole they won't run away."

"They'll merely think Mr. Cole worked for us."

"I thought so, too," Quince muttered. He felt the headache more now, setting up camp.

"That problem is over. Mr. Cole is dead."

"Noticed that," Quince said.

"He consistently refused to provide details of the exchange so we could cover for him, protect him—protect your niece, not incidentally. We had to know where the exchange point would be." He shrugged. "Mr. Cole became a problem, and the problem had to be solved."

"I don't see why you had to kill a half-dozen people in the process," Quince said.

"That has nothing to do with you. Mr. Cole was a well-known police character."

"Never convicted."

"Never charged," Jensen said. "But they know him, know about many of his activities with Mr. Mendle. By arranging things the way we did, we threw suspicion far away from us. I think things came out very well for a change."

"Matter of opinion," Quince muttered, sipped his coffee. It was cold. He scowled. His head began to throb.

"It was only a small inconvenience," Jensen added. "A slight miscalculation." Then he smiled again. "It probably would have happened, anyway. In an operation such as this, there can't be any loose ends dangling." Quince suddenly wondered if he was a loose end, as well.

Jensen continued, "At this point, it doesn't matter. We're still on schedule. My associates are keeping an eye on Mr. Mendle, Mr. Lovell. I am monitoring Miss Lovell's progress. By Saturday, we'll have her under our care. We'll have made the deal with Mr. Lovell. I'll be gone from your lives, and everything will be back to normal. To coin a phrase, 'everything will be cool.' "

"Right," Hillary said with irony. "You guys are the 'cool brothers.' For all we know, they could be dead somewhere in the middle of the desert."

Jensen looked at her evenly. "Ms. Lovell, please understand. The profile is right, and I'm following their every move." He swung around to the monitor, clicked the mouse. "At the moment, they should be approaching New Mexico."

"How do you know?" Hillary asked.

Jensen tapped the monitor. "I can intercept military satellites on this," he said. "I have access to all communications from the various law enforcement agencies. I know they blew up the car they stole in Los Angeles—right on time, according to Mr. Cole's original plan—and I am plotting their course based on a formula of speed and distance, compensating for rest stops. I also know that they have a blue-on-gray Dodge van, which one of their party stole from an airport parking lot in Phoenix."

"Slick," Hillary said, bored.

"I also can monitor any calls they make from their cellular telephone. Any of three different telephones, actually. Cole's, and the two they have."

"You can tap them?"

"No. But I know when they call and what numbers. Last night, they placed a call to Mr. Cole's car telephone. My guess is that they confirmed the exchange, probably the payoff amount as well with Mr. Mendle."

"You guess?" Hillary asked.

"I cannot account for their every move, hear every word. Even the best technology has limitations," Jensen said.

Quince said nothing. Cole insisted on handling the kidnapping himself, used his own people. He never trusted Jensen. With good reason, Quince thought.

"I'll hand it to Mr. Cole," Jensen admitted. "It was a smart place to arrange the exchange. Remote, quiet. After they've arrived, we'll meet them."

"Not in person!" Quince said: alarm.

"Yes, in person," Jensen said.

"That was not the plan!" Quince said. "You were supposed to bring her here, to us. Barbara wasn't supposed to know we're involved."

Jensen looked at him evenly. "But you *are* involved. With Mr. Cole absent, things have changed. You can wait in the car, if you wish. No need for you to be exposed to these people. I and my associate will be there. But your niece will have to know you are involved. She must be persuaded to cooperate."

"She'll be kicking and screaming," Hillary said.

"That is precisely why the two of you must be there. To convince her of her best options. Keep her calm. We make this very simple. After the exchange is made with your brother, Miss Lovell goes with"—he glanced at Hillary—"with whomever she wishes. You'll be paid. Everybody's happy."

"And Eddy?" Hillary asked.

Jensen's mouth tightened. "He'll be compensated, if he wishes. But, I somehow doubt Mr. Lovell is going to survive this transaction. As you say, your brother is highly excitable."

"He'll tell you to shove it," Quince said, "if he knows we're involved."

"Mr. Lovell has no choice in the matter. If he wants to see his daughter again. And he will, I assure you. I have his profile." He tapped the monitor again. "He'll accept the chance to save her. Do you think he's going to risk her safety for something he doesn't even know he has?" Jensen smiled again. "There's nothing to worry about."

"Who's watching Eddy now?" Quince asked.

"Two of my associates," Jensen glanced at his watch, "reported a while ago that they're stopped. Having breakfast. One of my people will call for me shortly when he arrives downstairs."

"I don't want Christy taking that call," Quince said, nodding toward his door and secretary beyond.

Jensen's eyes widened. "I thought you said she could be trusted."

"I said she could be trusted to keep her mouth shut. But the way things are going. . .I don't. . .." he trailed off. "She's been asking a lot of questions lately."

"I'd like to ask a few questions, if you don't mind," Hillary said.

Quince ignored her again. "House of cards," he repeated. "One misstep, and the whole thing blows up. I *don't* want Christy picking up the phone and taking any suspicious messages. I don't want her to become. . .."

"Expendable?" Hillary smirked.

Jensen shrugged. "Very well," he said, rose. A handsome man, he wore an expensive version of the corporate power suit: silk shirt, paisley braces, French cuffs, light-colored loafers, argyle socks. He was fresh-faced, handsome beneath steel-rimmed glasses, well built beneath his shirt. But there was hardness behind his eyes. Something there suggested there was only one role he should play in a lawyer's office: client.

"You do that," Hillary said softly. "Bring me a bagel or a danish or something, will you? I haven't eaten today."

"Not watching our figure, are we?" Jensen asked.

"Not watching yours," Hillary shot. "Just bring me a bagel." Jensen left the room. "God, Quince," she said when the door shut. "How can we trust that person?"

"I thought trusting him was your idea," he said. "You found him, sent him to me. Or did he find you?"

"Oh, yes. This is all my fault," Hillary said with mock surprise. "I keep forgetting. You weren't at all involved."

Quince studied her. When had she become so completely intolerable? "You met in the Bahamas. He approached you. So you said. You sent him to me. That's what you said. You do need to keep your story straight, Hillary."

"It's straight," she said. "You were desperate. I just gave you an opportunity. Put you in with the right people. You set up the first deal."

"That deal went sour," Quince said.

"Thanks to you and the Frick-and-Frack twins."

"It wasn't their fault. Raul Castillo blew that."

"And Eddy went to prison."

"And you got Barbara." He looked at her evenly. "You blew that."

She looked out the window. "Jensen came to me," she said. "He knew everything. I thought it would be easy. I wasn't supposed to be involved."

"Who does he work for?" Quince asked. "He scares the shit out of me."

"What makes you think he works for anybody?"

"Everybody works for somebody."

"Who do you work for?"

He sat down at the desk, sat down heavily. His headache followed him like an invisible mob. She lit a cigarette. "This building is smoke-free," he said.

"Too bad." Hillary filled her lungs, snapped her gold lighter shut. Twin blue-gray jets sprayed from her nostrils. "I do *not* want to be there when they make the—what's the phrase?— the exchange?"

"He doesn't seem to be giving us a choice. That wasn't an invitation."

"So I noticed. All this was supposed to be easy. Fly in— fly out. Get Barbara. Collect the money. Kill Eddy. Easy."

"God, you're cold-blooded."

"I can give you a list of names who would testify otherwise."

"Is he one of them?" Quince nodded toward the door.

Hillary sniffed in more smoke. "I'm a warm and caring human being. I dote on my niece, and I want her back in my care."

"You want her back in your control."

"Don't split hairs."

"You forgot the part where you get paid off," Quince said.

She waved her fingers in the air, dismissed the remark. "So I get here and find that she's being brought bound and gagged—"

"Nobody's bound and gagged her. If everything goes right, she never will be. Nobody will."

" 'If everything goes right.' Quince, my dear brother, when

in your entire life did *anything* go right?'' She stood, paced, glanced around the office. ''No wonder you owe money to everyone you meet. Do you do any work here? Shouldn't there be some papers or books or something? I've never been in such a sterile office in my life. There's not even a magazine.''

''They're all online,'' Quince said, gestured toward the computer monitor on his glass-topped desk. Four other monitors were stationed around the room. ''I can call up anything I need, any magazine, even law books.''

''Why would you need those?'' Hillary's eyebrows raised above her glasses' rims. ''Were you thinking of starting a practice or something? What a novel idea! Your creditors will be thrilled.''

''You know, Barbara was right. You have become a bitch.''

''I did not *become* anything,'' she said. ''I've always been a bitch.'' She ran her hands over the front of her skirt, smoothed wrinkles that weren't there. ''So what's the latest problem?''

''It's complicated.''

''I've an aptitude for complication. Besides, nothing about this has gone right. Not from the beginning.''

''Cole was double-crossing us. Or he was going to.''

''You're surprised? God, Quince, you're so naive.''

''Cole was apparently dealing. His leverage was that he was the only one who knew where the exchange for Barbara would be made. He wanted more money. A lot more money.''

''How much?''

''Five hundred million.''

Hillary stared at him. ''How much?''

''You heard me.''

''So?''

''So, Jensen grabbed Cole. Dealt him out. Tried to make him talk.''

''And?''

''And he talked. At least, he told them where.''

''So, where?''

''Place called Balmorhea. An old resort. Out in West Texas.''

''Does our little brother know anything about this, about Barbara?''

''No.'' Quince rubbed his head. The numbness was totally

gone. Pounding pain in his temples an unwelcome replacement. "I don't know. He has no reason to. He doesn't contact me anymore."

"That's not surprising. You've spent most of what you laughingly call a career setting little Eddy up one way or another." She took a beat. "Just how sure are we that Cole didn't tell Eddy about the whole thing? Maybe he already knows about Barbara. . ."

"Cole was out of the picture before Barbara was. . .uh, handled."

"Kidnapped," Hillary said evenly. "The word you're looking for is 'kidnapped.' Not 'handled.' Why don't you just say it? That's what it's been from the beginning: a kidnapping. And this Cole person is not 'out of the picture.' He's dead. Murdered. You always were squeamish." She examined her fingernails. "And imprecise. But I'm still worried. You know how I love Barbara. Couldn't stand anything to happen to the little bitch. Kidnapping is somehow inadequate justice for what she did to me."

"What she did to you?"

"She was ungrateful," she said. "But it's what she can do *for* me that matters now."

"Christ. Haven't you given up on that? She's a full grown woman, for Christ's sake."

"I'm sure I have no idea what you're talking about." She waited, finally asked, "What's our cut?"

"Cut?"

"Right. Are you hard of hearing? What's our cut? How much?"

Quince sighed. "Jensen says fifty million."

"Each?"

"Half and half."

Hillary sighed. "Wouldn't it be nice to think so." She stiffened, changed tacks: "But you're sure he's dead?"

"Who?"

"This Cole. This gangster, this hood, this double-crosser. He's dead?"

"Oh, he's dead." Quince shook his head, closed his eyes. "Like a herring, as the saying goes."

"Mackerel," she said.

"What?"

"Mackerel. The expression is 'dead as a mackerel.' God, Quince, you can't even get a cliche right."

Quince rubbed his temples. The headache was now fully resident, a beaut.

Hillary rose, went over to the window to see what, if anything, had captured her brother's attention. Oversized panes were dirty, stained with soot, smog. Architects hadn't figured that cleaning them would be a life-threatening chore, too rich for the owners' insurance company. The windows stayed filthy.

"Who is this Maria person?"

"Moria. Moria Mendle. Cole's partner. Eddy's boss. Eddy drives for him."

"How do you know he won't figure out everything, try to make his own deal?"

"He doesn't know enough. He sure as hell doesn't know who killed Cole. If we're lucky, he won't find out. Once Eddy knows we have Barbara—"

"*They* have Barbara."

"Once Eddy knows he has to deal to save Barbara, Moria'll go along. Or he can be bought off, like Jensen said."

She snapped her long fingers. "Or he can be killed, too! Brilliant!" She scowled. "God."

Quince rubbed his chin, felt bristle. He had failed to shave that morning.

Hillary paced up and down in front of the window. In heels, she was remarkably tall. She stopped, cocked a hip, spoke to the filth-streaked glass in front of her. "Barbara's all right, isn't she." It was a statement, almost a threat.

"She's fine. And what do you care?"

"I care," Hillary said. "How do you know she's fine? Have you talked to her? This hare-brained scheme. . ." she trailed off. "What's stopping them from merely killing her, dumping the body? Just claiming they have her? I don't know why I let myself be a part of this."

"You know why as well as I do," Quince said. "You need money. As much as I do," he added. Hillary didn't move. Accepted the blow. Quince continued, "If you hadn't fucked things up so badly in New York, none of this would have happened. We never would have started this. We could have handled this ourselves, another way, dealt with Eddy ourselves without involving anybody.''

"It shouldn't have to be handled. It should have been done right in the first place. Those two idiots you hired. . ."

"I didn't hire them. They came to me. All I did was give them Raul. Raul gave them Eddy."

"And that was a surprise to you?"

"That was—never mind."

"And where are they now?"

Quince shrugged. "Out of the country, if they're smart. If they show up, we'll take care of them."

" 'Take care of them'?" She laughed: dry, hollow. "It's ludicrous. Like a cheap gangster movie. I expect to see Jimmy Cagney at any moment."

"You're getting old," Quince said. She spun on him, but he stared her down. "Barbara was the best bait you had. Get her to sleep with some society kid, maybe get knocked up, maybe marry him. Either way you hook into the family fortune, cash in on the family trust. In the meantime, you'll screw the father, older brother, or maybe just a friend in the bargain. The rich don't like scandal. They pay well to keep it quiet."

"What are you suggesting?"

"Don't you think I know how you operate? How you started operating as soon as you got her there? Jesus. There's not a pimp anywhere couldn't take lessons from you."

"That's not fair," Hillary said. "She's. . .she's my niece."

"She's one good-looking piece of ass," Quince said bitterly. The headache was now full-flower, spread across his forehead like a blossom. "She was your ticket to middle-aged comfort, respectability. She's all that stood between your image as doting aunt and reputation as round-heeled whore."

"You should know about image," she spat back at him. "You've made it your life's work."

"And you blew it," Quince went on. "You ran through the sheik's money like it was an hors d'oeuvre, but you forgot to check on the main course. I told you to settle for cash, but you had to have property, hotels, casinos. They cost money to run, money to keep, money to sell. So now you're broke, old, and in trouble. Mostly broke.''

"You're broke, too. You think I don't know how much you owe?''

"Owing is one thing. You can owe forever. But you haven't got forever. Your tits droop and your ass sags. You've got so much plastic in you if you stood near a fire, you'd melt.''

"God, you're vile.''

"Our one chance was to keep her in reach, where we could use her to deal with Eddy, and you blew that. Now we have to do it another way.''

"Your way?''

"*Another* way. Maybe when this is over, you can make your peace with her, bring her back to Manhattan. With her in tow and the money you'll make on this deal, you can hang on to some of your assets, maybe get a little more cosmetic work, then you can still draw a fly or two to your honey pot before it shrivels up for good.''

"You're *unbelievably* vile,'' Hillary said: a critique, not a denial.

"Without her and what she might pull in for you—direct or indirect—you're headed for a packing case under a freeway.'' He massaged the bridge of his nose. "So are we all.''

"I want to talk to her. To Barbara. When this is over, I want to talk to her. Make it up to her. I can do her a lot of good.'' There was a sadness in her voice. Quince nodded, his smile thin, savage. "Well?'' she demanded. "What's wrong with that?''

"Why don't you let her go, Hillary?'' Quince asked. "Jesus, this isn't that hard to handle. In two days, you'll be back in New York, or Paris, or wherever the hell you want to go—with more money than you've ever had in your life, even when you were married to Mr. Middle Eastern Oil. What the fuck do you care what happens to Barbara?''

"The money's not important. Barbara's all that matters to me.''

"Jesus Christ,'' he swore. "You're sicker than I am.'' He rose, poured himself more coffee from an insulated carafe on the edge of his desk. From a small box on the credenza, he removed two small white pills, popped them into his mouth. He didn't know what they were, only that they worked. Jensen kept him supplied. Only took them when he had to. His eyes wanted to pop out. "You just screwed everything up, Hillary."

"Fuck you, Quince," she said, dropped her cigarette butt into her drink glass.

Jensen came back into the room, noiseless. Hillary visibly straightened herself. Quince held his head. Jensen carried two pastries, placed them on Quince's desk. Hillary glanced at them, looked away, disgusted.

"When my associate arrives, he'll call on your private number. I gave Christy the day off. Told her you and I were going to a resort." He winked.

Quince shook his head. He no longer had control of his own secretary.

Jensen sat down at the computer, clicked, moused, then sat up, erect. "I don't like this." He punched more keys, sat back, read the monitor.

"Something's wrong," Hillary said. "Something's definitely wrong. I can see it. What is it? Is it Barbara?" Quince didn't move. Jensen read, clicked. "You want to tell me what's going on, Mitch? Or are we supposed to guess?"

"Mitch?" Quince thought. When did it become "Mitch?"

"They're in trouble," Jensen said.

"How?"

"Don't know for sure yet. I'm monitoring traffic for Arizona Highway Patrol. They seem to be in trouble. State trooper has been killed."

"Christ!" Quince shouted. His head wanted to explode. He moved behind Jensen. "What happened?"

"It's sketchy yet," Jensen said, clicking keys. "They apparently just found him. It might not be our people, but the coincidence is too likely to ignore. A Dodge van is involved."

"Where are they?"

"A moment, please." He read the screen, clicked, read some more. "This was west of Tucson. They *should* be halfway across New Mexico by now," Jensen said. "But I don't know."

His screen filled with a map of the Southwestern United States, then zeroed in on Arizona.

"No calls? To Cole or anybody?"

"None this morning." He touched the mouse, clicked: New Mexico jumped to the screen. "Not unless they used a public phone. But they were instructed not to do that. If they stay on the move, they won't have cellular service until they hit Deming or Las Cruces, maybe not until El Paso. Of course, they could stop anywhere."

His speech was so precise Quince wondered if he mentally rehearsed his lines before he spoke. His contractions seemed strained. There was no trace of an accent, no particular inflection. He even pronounced "Las Cruces" and "El Paso" in correct Iberian Spanish. His constant suspicions about Jensen gathered, swirled suddenly, like a tornado. This man was no mere player.

"If anything happens . . ." Quince ran his hands through his hair, then composed himself, spoke solidly. "You make sure nothing happens. Understand?"

Hillary stood very still. Her mouth open, her eyes moving from Quince to Jensen, back again. "Exactly how much control do you have over this situation?"

"Sit down and be quiet. Please." Jensen glanced at her, nodded, then returned his attention to the monitor.

"This is out of hand," Hillary insisted. Her voice raised.

"Shut up!" Jensen ordered. "I am trying to think." Her head raised, her back arched as if he had slapped her. For a moment, the only movement in the room was his hand adjusting the mouse. "It is them. No question. For some reason they've killed a state trooper near Tucson."

"They've caught them?" Quince asked.

"Not yet."

"Are they chasing them?"

"Not yet," he said, leaned back, read the screen. Quince and Hillary glared at Jensen's back. "They have no idea who they are. No witnesses, apparently. Everything is confused. Most of the authorities are still tied up with the exploded car. Some civilians were killed there."

"Civilians?" Quince thought aloud. "What do you mean—"

"Very sloppy business," Jensen cut him off, then chuckled. "The whole state's in a panic. Half the police in the Southwest are on alert."

"That's great," Quince grumbled, sat back. "That's just great."

"Well, actually, it is. They're looking for one thing, not another. Classic misdirection. It will be all right if they have enough sense to change vehicles."

"They didn't have sense enough not to kill a policeman," Hillary said. Her voice was softer now.

"For the last time: Shut up, Hillary." Quince cut her off gently.

"Oh," Jensen spoke. "What is this?"

"What now?" Quince wasn't sure he could take another upset.

"Some detective made a missing person inquiry near where they blew up the car. Arizona State Troopers have filed a query on him."

"That must be a coincidence." Quince tried to sound hopeful.

"Could be, but that's close. Let's see. Name: Sandobal." He clicked keys. "Detective out of Santa Barbara?"

"Sandobal?" Hillary asked.

Jensen swung his chair around, surprised. "You know him?"

"That's the name of the cop Barbara ran off with. That's her boyfriend. He was a policeman in New York. Had a job out there. That's why—"

"I see," Jensen said, turned again, clicked keys. The screen went blank. He picked up the telephone, punched buttons. "I'm sending one of my associates out to monitor this in person. I should have done that already."

Hillary rose. "I'm going home, boys. Back to the city. I can't handle this." She seemed numb, confused. "Send me a check."

Jensen spoke to someone on the phone, his tone flat, even.

Hillary walked unevenly over to his desk. "Did you hear me, Quince?"

"Make another drink, Hillary," Quince said. "You're in too

deep to quit.'' He forced himself to rise, go to the bar. ''So am I,'' he added.

She dumbly eased herself back onto the sofa, dazed. ''I can't for the life of me figure out how I let myself get into this.''

Quince said nothing, mixed her another bloody maria. As an afterthought, he poured it out, turned over a tumbler, filled it with straight vodka, took it to her.

Quince's private line buzzed. He picked it up, listened, nodded. ''Very well,'' he said, replaced the instrument, stared at Jensen. ''Your *associate is* downstairs. Name he gave was Robin.''

Jensen stood. ''I will be back in a few hours. You might try to calm down.'' He looked at Hillary. ''Calm her down.''

''Where are you going?''

''To arrange a meeting,'' he said. ''Oh, and by the way. When I return, I'll need a writ.''

''What?''

''A writ. *Habeas corpus,* I believe.''

''Why?''

''Well, they don't know it yet, but your brother and his employer are about to be arrested.''

13
Vicki's Angels

Vicki Sigel had never felt more soiled. Not even when she was a kid working on her aunt's farm killing chickens, cleaning out the hog pen, worming cattle. Sticky grit ground between her toes, a sour film coated her teeth, dark lines appeared under her fingernails. She didn't want to contemplate the state of her hair, her complexion.

Crammed as she was against the doorjamb of a battered '75 Volvo station wagon, she was miserable and uncomfortable. The car had no air conditioning. Al refused to allow anyone to put down any windows in the back. The farther they went into the Southwestern desert, the hotter it was. Vicki's underarms were wet, her crotch sweaty, slimy moisture collected behind her bent knees, on the insides of her elbows. She believed she might stink, which upset her more than the visible signs of grime.

And her stomach ached. If it was hunger, if it was fear, if it was anger, she didn't know. She wasn't conscious of any of those. She didn't know what she felt anymore. Disappointment, maybe. Everything had a surreal, dreamlike quality, more like a movie with every passing mile. She wanted it to end, one way or another.

No one said a thing, though. Not Al, not Blackie, not Red. The Volvo bumped on, taking each uneven section of the interstate with a rough bounce. The suspension was shot, Vicki analyzed. Too many years rocking around the desert and driven by a complete idiot: Professor Jeffrey Kingston, Ph.D.

Al slouched behind the wheel of the wagon. The big woman's hands played across the steering wheel casually, but Vicki could see from the side that her eyelids drooped. She allowed the Volvo to drift from one lane to the other, did nothing to avoid a chughole or road hazard. A cigarette dangled from the big woman's ugly mouth. Ashes covered the front of her biker outfit.

Red sat opposite Vicki in the back, Blackie was in the front passenger seat, the top of his head visible over the rest. He emitted a gurgling snore: fitful.

Between Vicki and Red, riding the hump, Professor Kingston—recently the handsome director of a University of Arizona field trip—sat bolt upright, hands folded neatly on the wiry hair of his bare legs. Sweat ran rivers down his stubbled cheeks, lips fixed in a grim, thin line, eyes focused on absolutely nothing at all.

Vicki realized with a sudden measure of relief that it was not she but he who was the source of the sour body odor she smelled. But it wasn't mere perspiration. It was something that came from deeper within: terror.

Dressed in desert khaki shorts, thick wool socks, sturdy hiking boots, twill shirt, and a floppy, battered fedora, he reminded Vicki of a cross between Indiana Jones and Forrest Gump.

"We got to hole up someplace," Al broke the silence. "El Paso, maybe."

"Can't," Red muttered. "Got to stay on schedule." He was only half-awake. The dead highway patrolman's service automatic, a 9-mm SIG Sauer, rested on his lap. Vicki caught Professor Kingston eyeing it from time to time. There was no danger he would make a move. He was too certain that he was about to die. He probably had no idea how to use the big pistol anyway. Vicki sure as hell didn't.

"Well, we ain't going to make it," Al said. "I thought we

could, but we can't. We got too much baggage, now, and we got to stay sharp. Can't do that without some Z's. Not without another car. Every cop from Denver to Dallas has this one on the hot sheet by now. It's still six, seven hours on the road, and I'm whacked.''

''It's farther than that,'' Red said. ''Hell, it's two hundred past El Paso, at least.''

''And I'm starving,'' Blackie said, suddenly rousing himself.

Al snarled, ''Why don't you shut the fuck up?'' Next to Vicki, Professor Kingston tensed. Vicki was surprised. He was already wound tight. But he turned another revolution every time one of them shouted.

''Why don't you go fuck yourself?'' Blackie replied.

Al grumbled, ''All you want to do is eat.''

''And all you want to do is sleep,'' Blackie said.

''And all both of you want to do is argue,'' Red put in. ''I can drive us in.'' He tried to straighten up in the backseat. ''I can drive. Get me some coffee, I can make it.'' He glanced at the professor. ''But we need new wheels.''

''I don't know why we don't get on a side road,'' Blackie whined. ''Might be someplace safe to stop and eat on a side road.''

''There ain't no side roads in the fucking desert,'' Al said. ''Maybe you ain't noticed, but this ain't the LA suburbs.''

Red continued: ''The only thing I don't know is what we're going to do with Teach, here.''

Blackie sat up, turned around in the seat. The line of his left jaw was dark red. His open mouth revealed a ragged gap where a tooth had recently been. Purple bruises circled both eyes, his nose was smashed. His shirt was stained with blood. His knife came up in his hand. ''I got an idea or two.''

''Just put me out,'' Kingston said hopefully. He had said it before. Each time with the same intonation. Vicki had invented a nickname for him: Rerun.

''I won't say anything,'' he whined. ''Not till you're gone. I give you my full assurance of that. Really.'' His voice broke. It gave Vicki a headache.

''You're a piece of work, Teach,'' Al said. ''You know that?'' She made a kissing noise with her mouth. ''I'm getting to like you. I think we'll keep you around. I never did no P, H, and D before.''

"Look," he said, pleading, "I've got a wife, kids.''

"I got a hernia," Blackie growled. "So what?''

"Your mind wasn't on no domestic pussy this morning.'' Al laughed. "You and Suzie Supertits back there wasn't exactly mapping out strategies for some goddamn Little League game.'' Kingston's jaw set. "Just how long you been banging that little twat?" Al asked. "Bet she was *all* U.S.D.A. sweet meat. That about right?'' Kingston said nothing, stared at Blackie, who grinned, exposed his dental gap.

"She ain't so tough no more, though, is she, Teach?''

"Just put me out," Kingston repeated, teeth grinding.

Blackie laughed, faced front abruptly. Slouched down again.

Al glanced at him, smiled. "Wish we had her instead of him. He's not worth a shit. Might have got some mileage out of her. Sometimes, I don't think you got a brain.''

"Lighten up," Red said wearily.

Al scooted around, settled her rump in the Volvo's seat. They hit a bump or hole in the blacktop. The car skidded to one side until she wrenched it back under control. Kingston lost balance and leaned against her. Her nostrils filled with his odor. She gagged.

"Goddamn car rides like a log wagon," Al complained.

Vicki squirmed away from Kingston, shoved him over, rough. "Get the hell off me," she barked. He turned another revolution, she sensed.

"You've got my car," Kingston said. "I don't have anything else. Why *not* just put me out someplace?''

"If you'd had some fucking money, you'd already be out. One way or another," Red said, squirmed next to him, tried to move away. "This is the most hard-luck outfit I've ever seen. Can't do anything right. I thought all you college teachers was rich. Where's your money, anyway?''

Kingston licked his lips. They were already cracked and chapped, but his constant attempts to wet them with a dry tongue over the past several hours brought a fine webbing of blood. "You don't carry money on a dig," he said. "You don't need any.''

"So how were you going to pay for the gas and shit back there?"

"The university—the school—we have an account. I don't—you just don't carry money on a dig."

" 'You don't carry money on a dig,' " Al mimicked Kingston's whine. "Teach, I've changed my mind about you. You're giving me a pain in the ass."

"I've already got a pain in the ass," Red said. "And it's crowded back here. Why *don't* we dump him and go on?"

Al looked in her rearview mirror, swerving dangerously out of her lane. A passing semi blew its horn. "Fuck you!" Al yelled back.

"Be careful, goddamnit," Blackie yelled, reaching for the wheel. Al slapped his hand.

"I told you," she said, "there might be some use for him later. Things could go sour fast."

"Thought you said—"

"I know what I said. I'm just saying I've been thinking about it. Guy who answered the phone last night when I called didn't sound that sharp. Cole only hires sharp people."

From what she could see, Vicki doubted that.

Al lit another cigarette, crushed the empty pack and dropped it on the floor. "I also been wondering where the fuck he was. I mean, this is too big a deal to leave the details to some redneck flunkie. He should have been there to take that call himself."

"You think somebody might've whacked him?" Red asked.

"I think things could get weird. That's all I'm saying. I think we might need a little insurance."

"We got her," Red argued, jerked a thumb at Vicki.

"Yeah, but for how long?" Al said. "We're supposed to turn her over, then get the payoff. That's her gig. What happens then? Where's the next move? How do we know we don't go driving off right into a SWAT team? Cole's double-crossed better fuckoffs than you guys."

"What about you? He ever double-cross you?"

"He knows better," Al said. Then she sighed, nodded toward Kingston. "But there's always a first time." She winked into the rearview. "Right, Teach?" To Red: "He might come in handy." She ran her hands over the wheel. "Already has, in a way. Least the fucker had smokes."

They came upon Professor Kingston by accident. After putting nearly a hundred miles between themselves and the dead highway cop, they approached the New Mexico state line. It took a long while to come down off the adrenaline rush from shooting the trooper, but they finally leveled enough to pull into a roadside cafe to spend the dead cop's cash on gas, food. Red worried about the van being recognized, but Al claimed that roadblocks would be up soon, that the Dodge was too big, too obvious, and too hot to keep.

Blackie bitched about wanting food, though. Vicki needed to pee. Red also wanted to stop. And they needed fuel.

The cafe was a hold-on place: Mom and Pop's. A gas-station-grocery that had sprung up when the interstate was first built. It hung around when the chains popped up with modern dining rooms, truck washes, expensive curio shops, adult video and massage parlors. It had one advantage, it was the only stop in forty miles either way. And they fixed flats. Big sign said so.

Dusty, sandy parking lot, potted miniature sequoia cacti, tumbleweeds, "Biggest Shakes in the Desert," ice, snacks, hamburgers, hotdogs, cherry cider, and "Clean Restrooms." Gas was two bucks a gallon—"Cash Price"—pump it yourself, wipe your own windshield, check your own oil. Actually: fix your own flats.

Mom and Pop—if that's who they were—stayed inside under the clanking swamp coolers and cooked, rang the register, laughed at the tourist suckers, planned to retire in Florida.

Al stopped on the frontage road, checked it out. "We got enough cash for a tank of gas. That'll take us all the way," she said.

"And won't feed us," Blackie complained.

"Why not just use your big gun?" Vicki asked. She still felt feisty, assertive: then.

"Shut up," Al said. "We'll park, order some food, then fill 'er up and drive away."

"That'll throw off suspicion," Vicki said sweetly.

Al ignored her. "They might call the local cop, but I doubt it. If we handle it right, they won't know we're gone till we're across the state line." She looked at Red, who was strangely quiet. "I hate doing half-assed shit like this," she said.

"Just do it," Red muttered. "I need to stop."

Al guided the van up beside the gas pumps next to a beat-up '75 Volvo wagon with an open hatchback. On the passenger side were the rest rooms and a row of refrigerated ice boxes. She and Blackie got out, went in to order some food. "Watch her," Al ordered Red.

"I need to go," Vicki said. Red nodded, opened the door for her, took her to pee.

"Don't get any ideas," he said, fell in behind her.

Since killing the cop, Red had changed, become quiet, more serious. He barely looked at her, only gestured with the cop's ugly automatic. He moved like he was sleepwalking, idling, not revving as he had been. That put Al in charge. That worried Vicki.

Red knocked on the door marked "Women," listened for a second, pushed the door open, looked quickly inside, stepped back. "Hurry up."

She entered the restroom alone. Red remained outside, pistol in his hand, down by his side, hidden by his leg. She started to say something—"Don't you want to watch, too?"—but his half-closed eyelids, listless manner warned her not to push it. She pulled the door to, thumbed the door lock.

The "Clean Restroom" was a typical, old-fashioned roadside toilet. Five-by-five, dirty sink, filthy commode, coin-operated Kotex machine on the wall, pull-out tissues to cover the seat—empty—no toilet paper. No window. The floor was slippery from something wet leeching up through the gray concrete then running into a drain in the concave center. Light came from a single bulb overhead, protected by a metal cage. Reeked like an outhouse.

She rolled down her blue sweatpants, sat, briefly wondered if the flimsy door was strong enough to prevent their breaking in, taking her if she refused to come out. It wasn't. A crack ran from top to bottom, let in a quarter inch shaft of light.

She read the graffiti that covered the walls, the sink. She

was surprised. Women didn't usually write graffiti in restrooms. Most of it was collegiate: Greek letters, school names, phone numbers complete with area codes, offers for blow jobs, anal intercourse: nothing interesting.

For a moment, sitting there, alone at last, listening to the urine run out of her, she wanted to cry. What strength she had flowed away with the body fluid. She was too tired, too hungry, too frustrated to go on. But she had no choice. If she refused, they'd just drag her, hit her again, mess her up worse. She felt sick to her stomach. She wiped with some coarse paper towels provided on the sink, repaired her clothing, stood and looked at herself in the cracked, fly-specked mirror.

If Gary saw her now, he'd write her off, never tell anyone he had known her. God knows he wouldn't want to sleep with her. She wondered if any man ever would again. Fatigue rings framed her eyes, her hair strung down in a greasy mess, her lip split, a red mark sang from her cheek. She tongued a tooth she suspected was cracked, but it felt okay. Tears welled in her eyes, even so. She bent down to turn on the tap, thought to bathe her face, wash her hands: no water.

That almost did it. The room seemed to close in on her, squeeze her to death. She almost screamed. She would have, she would have, except she suddenly noticed a small, gold, plastic tube resting atop the dark streaks of grime that covered the sink: lipstick.

Her heart pounded. Breathing stopped. The tiny room spun. She looked behind her to see if Red had somehow sneaked in, was watching, laughing at the sudden rush of false hope. She gasped in jerks of air. The tube seemed to glow, struck by a light from the crack in the door.

She picked it up, pulled the cap, twisted the base. It was nearly gone, only the smallest amount remained on the pointed tip: burnt orange. What kind of tramp wears orange lipstick? Vicki was repulsed. She put aside the thought, bit down on her sore lip to punish it. "Angels," she whispered. "Angels wear orange lipstick."

She knew what to do, had seen it in too many movies not to know. She reached over the sink to write on the mirror. Her hand stopped before the orange stain touched the first dark fly speck. She turned and studied the door. If Red opened it to look in after she left, checked, he'd see the mirror first thing. She thought about knocking out the bulb, but it was a foot above her reach, protected by the wire cage. The walls were too dirty, too covered with graffiti, stains, cracks to find a spot. She stood, panic swelled. There wasn't much time. Decide: act.

She twisted around, searched the tiny room for a space where she could write something that only a person using the toilet could read. The only clear area was over the commode's tank. Women wouldn't see that, not casually.

She turned again, slowly this time, studied the entire space. Then she saw it: the door. The stuff scrawled and drawn on the door was mostly at eye level or above. There was a blank space about halfway up, directly in the sight line of anyone sitting on the commode, bisected by the shaft of light.

She knelt down, felt moisture seep through the knees of her sweats, didn't care. She took thought, remembered, then wrote in large letters, careful to conserve what remained of the lipstick, not to smudge it too much:

Help! Vicki Sigel! K-napped! 2 men, 1 woman. Armed! Danger! Call Police! Blue Van! Heading for TX—Bal-More-Λ?? Tcx——

The door banged under the lipstick's fading point, bounced inward. Vicki jumped back, fell next to the commode. Her throat closed. Sweat sprang on her forehead. A bright-orange streak ran from the X to the edge of the partition.

"What the fuck's taking so long?" Red demanded. "Why's this locked?"

Vicki swallowed, breathed deep. Her abdomen pumped on its own. She placed her hand on it, forced it to still. Swallowed again. "Just a goddamn minute!" she croaked out. She was surprised to hear her own voice sound so convincing, so ill. "Sick. Don't feel good."

"Open the fucking door! Get your ass out here, now! I'm coming in!"

"Just a minute!" she barked back at him. She wanted the same tone she had used with him before. "Let me get my pants on."

She stood, dropped the lipstick case into the toilet, pushed down the handle. For a moment, she didn't think it would flush, then water gurgled weakly from the tank, swirled around the plastic gold in the center of the bowl. It disappeared. She turned, opened the door.

Red's hand jerked her outside. She felt his fingers bite down into her flesh. Bruises on bruises.

"What the fuck were you doing in there?"

"Throwing up." He pushed her toward the van. "There's no running water," she tried to explain. "I got some on me, tried to clean up."

"You blow beets more than anybody I ever seen," Red grumbled. He glanced at the dark stains on her knees, even inspected her wet bottom. Nodded. "You're losing it, sweet-meat," he said. They reached the van, he slid open the door, pushed her into the midships seat, grabbed the handcuffs, looked at her a second, hesitated. She decided not to resist, stuck out her hands. He brushed them aside, then clamped one bracelet around her ankle. The other end he fastened to the metal seat bracket.

He looked around the parking lot. Except for the open Volvo, it was empty. Traffic up on the interstate hummed past, shimmered in the desert heat.

"I'm thirsty," she said. "My mouth—"

"Shut up," he ordered, winced. He was in pain: a cramp. "I got to take a dump. Now. You sit quiet. You say anything to anybody, you're going to get hurt, and they're going to die. Bet on it."

He walked deliberately to the women's restroom. Vicki felt panic once more swell in her chest. Why would he go in the women's? This wasn't right. The men's room was right there. Right there!

Her orange angel spoke, though, gave her a thought. She leaned forward, stuck her head as close to the open passenger's window as she could, manacled as she was.

"Hey! There's no paper in there."

Red stopped, his hand on the women's restroom doorknob. He turned, frowned at her, opened the door anyway. Vicki saw her orange angel flying away into the blue sky. Her hopes trailed behind.

Red opened the door all the way, stuck his head inside, then one foot. The automatic was up, ready. He peered into the gloomy interior quickly, then nodded, backed out, shut the door, gave her one more glance. With one hand already unbuckling his belt, stepped through the next door marked "Men."

Vicki breathed. She sat back, sleeved sweat from her face, scratched beneath the metal anklet, sighed. Maybe, she let herself think, maybe at last this nightmare will be over. Someone will see what she wrote. Someone will call the police. Someone will come for me. For the first time, she relaxed, let herself drift in the dry heat of the desert. She wished she knew where in Texas Bal-More-A was. She'd never heard of it. But the cops would know.

Her eyes closed. She thought: Sleep. As soon as they ate, got on the road, she would sleep. She listened to the buzz of insects.

She didn't see Kingston and his companion come out of the store. They moved behind the van. Then they came back around to the ice boxes on the other side, next to the women's room. Vicki heard them then, came fully alert.

"Have you ever seen such a gross woman?" a laughing female voice asked.

"Nosy, too," a man agreed. "Bet she's gay. She sure looked you over."

Vicki sat up, peered out through the van's side window. They moved together, deposited some sacks filled with various supplies on the ground.

The girl was a blonde bubble. She walked close to the man, too close: clear skin, blue eyes. Vicki could read them. In love. Or in lust. They wore the costumes of modern desert scientists. She thought: Explorers.

He was tall, slightly stoop-shouldered, but well built, maybe forty. His arms were muscled, tanned. His hands hard, his eyes hidden behind Ray-Ban aviator sunglasses. Her Oakleys were pushed up on top of her head.

At first, Vicki thought they were going to the restrooms. She almost panicked. If the girl went in, saw the message, came out screaming about kidnappings and vans, it was useless. They would all be killed. Again, her orange angel seemed to fly.

She strained to lean over to speak to them. They weren't ten yards from the van. Shouldn't be hard. Red's warning echoed in her mind—"they'll die," he said—but she shied from it. People have already died. Fuck him. But what to say? Her orange angel was mute.

The couple opened the ice boxes, looked inside. Vicki relaxed. They were after ice. With any luck at all, they had already been to the restroom, if they had to go. It was going to be okay.

"Maybe not," Vicki thought she heard the voice of her angel again, angry now. She snapped her head around. Through the back window of the van she spotted Al, Blackie coming out of the small office-cafe-grocery. Their arms filled with bags: burgers, shakes, fries. Grease already soaked through the white paper. They were arguing. No angel. The voice she heard was Al's.

"Hey." Al stopped dead, stared at the pair next to the ice machine. Delight spread across her face. "You guys need a hand?" Kingston, his Indiana Jones hat askew, his arms full of freezing bags of ice, hesitated, nodded. Al dropped her food on a rickety picnic table propped against the side of the building, rolled up to them. Blackie stood stupidly behind her for a second.

"C'mon," Al commanded. "Put that shit down. Give us *a hand.*" She made a gun of her finger and fist, pulled the trigger in Kingston's direction. "Hurry up!" Blackie paused, dropped his food next to hers, scooted to the van.

He opened the passenger door, looked in. "Where's Red?" Vicki shrugged. "Shit," he said. He glanced at Al, who gathered ice into her big arms. Blackie leaned across the seat, popped the top up on the console, removed the .22 pistol. It had been there all along. Vicki was pissed at herself for not having thought about that. Blackie used the door for cover, shoved it into the back of his trousers, pulled his shirt down to hide it. "Be quiet," he hissed. "Or somebody's going to die."

"What are you going to do?" she demanded—distraction. "I'm hungry."

"Shut up. We don't need any more trouble." He turned on the key to the van, slid the windows up, glanced at Vicki, then shut the door and strolled over toward the trio, who ferried the ice toward plastic coolers in the hatch of the Volvo. Vicki moved from her seat, looked out the side window. The cuff held her ankle, pinched the flesh. Red marks already were visible. They weren't five yards from her. Could she get their attention? What should she do if she did? Her pulse pounded again. She felt freedom, rescue, sensed it. How to grab it? How to make this work? She strained to hear her angel.

She glared through the window, silently commanded them to look at her. A faint hope of catching the khaki-clad professor's eye fluttered. Maybe she could signal him somehow. She wished she had kept the lipstick. She could scrawl "HELP" backwards on the window. Maybe he would see it, run inside, call the cops. The image of him rescuing her made him appear different to Vicki. He looked strong, decisive, she thought. She could see the co-ed's eyes. They never left him. Vicki sneered silently: True love.

He kept his back to Vicki.

Al smashed bags of ice on the sandy ground, helped fill the coolers with bottled water. The man shuffled around next to her. Al was doing everything for him. He removed his sunglasses, twirled them on one finger, let her work, watched her hammy hands. He was trying not to stare at her, at her outfit, her tattoos, her greasy, razored hair, grotesque earrings.

Vicki could hear their conversation. It was stifling in the van with the windows rolled up. A wet sheen covered her, felt sticky beneath her clothing.

"No shit," Al responded. She smashed down another bag of ice, tore it open, dumped it in. "What're you digging?"

"Hopi ruins," the man said. "We may have discovered one of the earliest Hopi villages in this part of the state. We think it was a stopover for traders heading north."

"We've been at it nearly a week," the girl put in: chirped, Vicki thought. "We've found some awesome pots." Vicki eyed her critically. She was cheerleader-pretty, perky as a chipmunk.

Perfect complexion, perfect eyes, perfect tits: braless, bold. Vicki hated her. Her legs were deeply tanned, firmly muscled with well-shaped knees. They dropped straight from tight little hips beneath short, short khaki pants to ankle-high army green socks worn under heavy hiking boots. It took great calves not to look dumpy in such an outfit. Vicki's envy inched up a knot. Her attention wandered. She could pull it off, she thought. But she would wear sandals. Hiking sandals. Show off her feet. Besides, heavy boots like that could cause blisters, bunions, corns, God only knew what else.

"Gee," Al said. Blackie moved around the front of the van, stood watching the man spread ice around in the cooler. Vicki saw the pistol bulge. "I've never seen such a thing. Mind if we tag along, take a look?"

The professor stood up, banged his head on the hatch lid. The girl moved to touch him in sympathy, but he stepped away, looked directly at Al. "Well, actually, this is a college class. A field trip. We're part of—

"I'm sure you won't mind a few extra students," Al said—cheerful. "I'm a fast learner. How about you?" In a swift maneuver, she pushed Blackie forward, extracted the pistol from beneath his shirt, jammed it into Kingston's side. "This is our tuition. Tell you what, I'll ride with you, and you can teach me stuff as we go. Suzie here can ride in the van. Blackie?" Blackie seemed confused. Didn't move. Kingston also stood where he was, frozen. His dark eyes were wide, sunglasses dangled from his fingers.

"My name's not Suzie." The girl, standing slightly off to one side, still hadn't seen the gun, was annoyed. "It's—"

"Shut up, Darla," Kingston said in a high, whining voice. To Al: "Don't do this." He gulped a breath. "I beg you." Al grinned in reply. His voice rose a notch in tone. "Do we have to do this?"

"You bet, schmugums," Al said. She puckered her lips, made a kissing noise. "Get in the fucking car, Teach."

"Jeffrey?" Darla asked. She still stared at him, puzzled. Then, at last, she came awake. Her blue eyes found the gun, took it all in, her brow furrowed, she yelled, bellowed. Al stepped back.

Darla took a short hop, spun on one foot, came around in a full circle. The heel of her left hiking boot neatly clipped Blackie in the side of his jaw. Vicki heard the smack, saw Blackie reel backwards, crumble.

"Hey!" Al yelled. Blackie was down, spitting blood. Al was off balance, retreating.

Vicki leaped forward. She strained to reach the horn. Before she could touch it, a cold, round object inserted itself beneath the sweatshirt's hem, pressed against her flesh. She turned her head, saw Red's ugly smiling face. He had eased the door open and leaned over the passenger seat. The ugly automatic pistol poked her side, pushed its way against her lower ribcage. "Be cool," he said. "Don't say a fucking word."

She wilted, then drew a breath. "Get that away from me. Remember what happened last time."

"Hey!" Al yelled again. Vicki snapped her head around. The girl fell into a crouch, both hands formed into blades, oscillated in front of her narrow blue eyes, freckled nose, her perfect knees pumped slightly to keep her weaving, moving, off target. Her mouth was a thin line of concentration: absurd, but dangerous. Al held the pistol on the professor, then on her. They were too far apart for her to cover both of them at once, the man too close to risk taking her eyes off of him for an instant.

"Let him go," Darla said in a loud, even voice. "Let him go, now!"

"Darla," the professor quaked. He was still rooted where he had been, but he summoned reason. "She's got a damned gun."

"Let him go!" Darla repeated. She began to move, one foot stepped deliberately over another, maneuvered her between Al and the van's driver's side window, widened the gap between her and the professor. Red shoved Vicki back with one hand, stepped into the van. He spread himself across the passenger's seat, leaned over, turned the key, ran the window down, then rested the barrel of the pistol on the driver's door's opening.

"I warn you," Darla growled, "you harm him, and I'll drive my fingers through your throat before you can shoot again. I'm trained!"

Vicki sat back, strained against the shackle on her ankle, watched through the rear window. Red glanced at her. He put a finger to his lips. She was stupefied. Her mind raced. She saw the cop, the state trooper in her mind. Her stomach turned over. She couldn't accept it. The van's window glass muted everything, insulated her, like a TV screen. She felt detached but at the same time involved.

Al looked nervous. Darla confident. Vicki sensed an uncanny calm descending on her. This might turn out all right, after all, she thought. The idea swam over her as the scene in front of her eyes took on another meaning. She thought: *Co-Ed Rangers.* Gary would fucking love it! She could play it! She'd have to change her exercise program, work on the legs differently, build up some muscle, get a tan, maybe a dye job—hell, it was time. She couldn't name five women in Hollywood who could remember their original hair color. Maybe Chuck Norris would like it. He needed a sidekick, somebody who had sex appeal *and* talent. Vicki wondered how much karate lessons cost.

Red sighed, shifted his weight. Al formed a nasty grin: a dare. Reality snapped back. Vicki flexed her legs. She might be able to do something to help the girl. Red was prone, stretched out, leaning over the console, holding the SIG on Darla. It was only a few feet or so to the back of the girl's head. He couldn't miss. Unless something spoiled his aim.

Vicki thought she might be able to kick his arm, maybe knock the gun out of his hand, force the barrel up, away. Then Darla could take out Al, then Vicki could deal with Red. She thought she could. Her hands were free. She could kick him silly, scratch him, gouge his eyes. Get the key, get the gun.

The image of herself holding Red hostage at the point of the ugly automatic appealed. "Just blink, don't talk," she heard herself say.

She stared out the window, glanced at Red, calculated the trajectory necessary to kick him just right: just behind the elbow. Her heart beat a tempo in her ears. She could do it. She *would* do it. She glanced again at Darla. The girl had an orange bandanna tied around her long blonde hair. Orange, Vicki thought: the color of angels. She's my angel!

Another thought hit her: It was over. Her spirit soared. Darla saved her! They worked together. Cops would come. Then the press! She'd have the pitch ready for Gary before the weekend. What an angle! She'd play the heroine who saved herself from the Armed and Insane Kidnappers. Darla could play her: the Victim. Shit, she could team up with Darla. Maybe they could get a third partner. Fuck Chuck. Maybe Farrah Fawcett might come on as the matron, the trainer, the boss lady who ran the show—Bingo! A series. Fuck film. You're in, you're out. TV is steady work. Sexy costumes—lots of leg, and *no* nude scenes. She'd worry about the cleavage later. She wasn't above a little plastic in that area, if that's what it took. The idea took physical shape in Vicki's mind. They might get more than a series out of it: tee-shirts, toys, Saturday morning cartoon, the whole enchilada: *Vicki's Angels,* she thought. No, *Power Co-Eds,* or *Student Desert Rangers* — something: not original, but surefire. They'd take it to Fox.

Darla had circled as far as she could. She was about to make her move. Al looked nervous, trapped between Vicki's Co-Ed Angel and the Volvo. She started to move the .22 one way, then the professor would shift his weight, so she moved it back.

"Hey," Al said, still grinning her challenge. "Nobody needs to get hurt. You've put on a nice show. Now, just be a good little twat, and we'll all be on our way. If you're nice, I'll let you take me around the world later on."

Vicki tensed, ready to kick the pistol out of Red's hand at exactly the right moment: Cue Vicki, action! she thought.

"Put the gun down," Darla ordered. "Put it down and back away. Now!" Behind her, on the ground, Blackie rolled over. His chin was bright red, his mouth bloody. He spat out a tooth. His eyes were glazed. He looked up and stared at Red, then at Vicki.

Al saw him, visibly relaxed. "That just ain't going to happen, girlie."

Blackie sat up, gathered his legs beneath him.

No, Vicki thought. This is *not* in the script. To this point, Vicki had believed that Blackie was all bluff. He always played with his big knife, showed it to her, bragged about it. Red had said he liked to cut people. She remembered what Blackie said about it at the rest stop in the desert. She thought he was just trying to scare her. Impress her. Maybe he was. She had read somewhere that men who carried big knives had a problem with their masculinity. Blackie was ripe for that kind of problem. He wasn't the brightest member of this gang of idiots, anyway.

But he wasn't bluffing. That wasn't in the script, either.

He found balance, came up smoothly: Snake, Vicki thought. Darla had forgotten about him, counted him out. Vicki saw the flash in the desert sun. She opened her mouth to warn her co-ed savior, her partner, her angel. Her leg tensed for the kick. Her hands became claws. But there was no cue, no action, no time. Blackie slid the slick blade into the girl's side beneath her rotating arm. He ripped in quick, then up, then out. Blood jetted behind the point, dark as motor oil, pooled red on the yellow sand.

"Shit," Vicki said.

Red chuckled. "He does like that blade."

If Darla felt the blow, she ignored it. She spun on her toes, her left knee cocking, and she kicked Blackie in the groin. He grunted when the air rushed out of him, rose up, his face forward. The knife fell into the blood. Her left hand formed a half fist, smashed into his nose. Her right followed, then her left again. His head snapped back and forth, he dropped backwards, spewed blood. Red brought the pistol up, aired back the hammer. Darla didn't see it.

Vicki sensed another hope. It was impossible, but Darla was still on her feet, still going, still bleeding. She readied again, poised her foot to kick, flexed, recovered, started to turn on Al, but before she could make the rotation, strength left her. She looked around. For one quick moment, her blue eyes locked with Vicki's, focused a question, then dropped to her ripped side, saw the blood, rolled backwards.

Her pretty mouth formed a silent *O*. She slid down smoothly into the scarlet puddle beneath her.

Red relaxed, thumbed down the hammer, withdrew the pistol, sat back. "Good girl," he said.

"Fuck you," Vicki sighed. "Just fuck you."

Al was already moving. She shoved Kingston into the driver's seat of the Volvo, jumped in the back. His hat fell off. Vicki strained to lean across the van, ripped her ankle pulling against the handcuff, pushed her face against the glass. The girl lay with one beautiful leg twisted beneath her, her perfect breasts heaving with every laborious breath, her orange bandanna and blonde ponytail soaking up the muddy blood. Her blue eyes closed.

Al jammed the pistol into the back of Kingston's skull hard enough to bash his forehead into the steering wheel. She leaned her head out the door. Blackie was still down on his knees, his hands pressed into his groin.

"Get the fuck up and follow us," she said. She slammed the door, and the Volvo peeled out, spraying sand and gravel onto Darla's bloody form. And onto Blackie. He struggled to his feet, limped into the van.

"Where the fuck were *you?*" he gasped out at Red. His face was pale, smeared with blood. He hunched forward. More blood ran from his mouth. He fired up the van. "I got a fucking hernia. You know that?"

"Had to see a man about a dog," Red said casually. Blackie grunted, drove the van forward out onto the highway, followed the Volvo up onto the interstate. "Don't worry," Red added. "I had you covered."

"Yeah? Well, why'd you let her kick me?"

"Didn't seem like she was big enough to hurt you."

Blackie said nothing, rubbed his jaw, spat out the window. "Broke out a whole fucking tooth," he said. "Just broke it out." He held his nose. "Busted my nose, too. Jesus! I think I'm ruptured."

"Serves you right," Red said. "You guys ought to have your own show."

Vicki let the remark pass. Then she bent over and vomited. "There she goes again," Red said in disgust.

They left the interstate and made the vehicle exchange at Cotton City, New Mexico, way to the south. The van was running on fumes, they drove off the road and dumped into a dry wash just out of sight of what passed for a highway. They transferred the weapons, the light totes to the Volvo, tossed out two of the three coolers. There were drinks, some snacks: beef jerky, chips, other junk. The main item of value, though, was a carton of cigarettes.

Vicki accepted one, smoked it, felt better than she expected to. She refused the junk food, though. Took some orange juice, gnawed on a piece of jerky, smoked some more. It was turning into a long day.

Now she sat miserably next to the professor and stared at Deming, New Mexico rolling past. It was a pretty town, striking green in the middle of the big, yellow desert. For the past half hour, no one had said a thing. Kingston still, sat ramrod straight, his eyes glared. She noticed that his sunglasses were neatly folded in the V of his shirt. She reached over, plucked them away. He didn't move. Didn't look at her. He didn't have a clue that she was as much a captive as he was. She put the glasses on. The world darkened.

"Hollywood," Red said: chuckled. "You look like a movie star."

"Bet your sweet ass," Vicki said.

Kingston scooted closer to her.

"For the last time, fuckhead, move over," Vicki ordered. "It's crowded enough back here." He flinched away.

She rested against the window, searched the rolling desert. A huge billboard appeared. It advertised the blandishments of Mexico, enticed visitors with a dark señorita dressed in a bright-orange peasant's blouse. She reminded Vicki of Carman Miranda. She held an equally bright orange drink in her hand. The sunset on the ocean in the background was also tinged with orange shades.

Orange, Vicki thought: Orange Angels. The señorita was orange, but there were no more angels in sight.

14
Special Crimes

Barbara and Sandobal had steered the Mustang into Mom and Pop's while Darla McKnight was still lying, dying in a muddy pool of her own blood on the sandy driveway beside the ice boxes. It was an accidental stop. Sandobal refused to go another mile. He needed to piss.

"Just go," Barbara told him. "I don't want to stop till we need gas. Go ahead. It'll cool you off."

"I'll drive at breakneck speed halfway across the wasteland with you," he replied, "but I'm damned if I'll do it soused in my own personal waste."

"Breakneck speed" hardly described Barbara's driving. Except for a gas stop, she kept the souped-up Mustang pegged at ninety most of the way. Aunt Hillary told her she could have any car she wanted for high school graduation. Sandobal knew about the Mustang. It had been ordered by Daryl Strawberry just before his last New York drug bust: Shelby engine, bored out, 380 cubic inches, 300 horses, ready to run, would turn the quarter in 5.5 on wet pavement. Speed was not a problem.

Their only extended break had been at the site of the state trooper's murder. From the radio, they learned that the suspect vehicle was a blue-on-gray late model Dodge van. On the hot sheet, stolen from the Phoenix airport. They didn't learn much else. Barbara knew Vicki was in that van.

Sandobal also knew things: His California badge wasn't going to carry him very far in Arizona. His casual attire and scruffy physical appearance didn't lend a lot of weight to his claim to be a lawman of any sort, not with superstrake state cops. His strong eastern accent—wasn't going to cut much water with these guys, either. He had explained all this to Barbara five or six times. She knew it by heart.

They pulled up to the site where the patrolman was shot, tried to talk to the trooper assigned to keep people away. He wouldn't give them shit. He also wouldn't listen to any story about possible kidnappers who might have blown up a Lincoln, who might be in a van, who might be heading through on their way to Texas, who might have been the same perps who whacked the rookie patrol cop.

"You got any idea how many vehicles—vans and otherwise—are heading to Texas?" the trooper demanded. He pointed to the interstate. "You're going east, where the hell else *would* you be heading? You can't miss Texas. Now, move along. We got zero tolerance on rubbernecking when a cop's been killed."

But they had the radio. Rather than hang around, try to learn any more from the dozens of cops and reporters milling around the dead trooper's cruiser, Barbara pushed the Mustang hard. The machine responded: eager. Sandobal squirmed. They zipped past trucks and cars, Barbara kept the needle posted at ninety on the rare curves that appeared on the gray highway. The broken white line turned into a rope rushing beneath the black car's wheels.

But Sandobal's bladder was hurting. And, Barbara admitted, she was thirsty. When they spotted Mom and Pop's, she decided: Pit stop. But as they pulled off the highway, onto the frontage road to find the driveway, they found a problem.

Fisher Gropnek, known to all who knew him as Pop, knelt over the body of a young girl who was trying her best to bleed to death beneath the shade of a huge umbrella that Mom—Gladys—held over them. Pop used what he remembered from his training as a Navy medic in World War II to staunch her bleeding with towels. He doused the open wound with baking soda, fed Darla single-serving plastic bottles of orange and tomato juice.

"I called the damn cops," he shouted as soon as the convertible ground to a skidding halt next to them. "That was near an hour ago."

"Forty minutes," Mom corrected, checked her wristwatch.

Sandobal jumped out while the car still rolled. He started toward them, stopped. "You check her out," he yelled to Barbara. "I got to go!" He ran to the men's room.

Barbara, already out, moved to the girl. She was conscious, her face pale, lips blue: shock. But her pupils weren't dilated, she breathed. And bled. "What happened?"

"Damn me if I know," Pop answered. He offered Darla more juice. Most of it spilled out of her mouth, ran into her sand-and-blood-matted hair. "Come out to see if some yahoos who was here was gone, if they'd stole anything, and I found her just laying here in the dirt. Somebody stuck a knife in her, you ask me. I seen this kind of thing before. I was in the Navy."

Barbara examined the wound: deep, ragged. "She's hurt bad."

"I can see that. I'm Navy-trained."

Sandobal came out of the men's room: fly still open. He rolled the girl over, pulled away the blood-soaked towels. "Get some ice."

Barbara went to the ice boxes, pulled out two bags, brought them over. Sandobal smashed them on the ground, ripped them open, pulled a clean towel off the bundle in Pop's hand, wrapped fistfuls of ice inside them. He pressed the pack into the wound. Blood flowed through his fingers, but he pushed the ice in deeper.

"I called that damn 9-1-1, and they wouldn't answer," Pop complained. "No sir. Nobody answered it at all. Had to call on the long distance."

"They ain't come, anyhow. This child is hurt bad!" Mom put in.

"You don't have 9-1-1 service out here," Sandobal explained. "You have to live near a city to have that."

''They have it on the TV! I seen it on the damn TV show. They say, if you have a situation like this one here, just pick up the phone and call 9-1-1. They come running.''

''You have to have the service.''

''I have the TV. That ought to be enough.''

''Why didn't you move her inside?''

''You don't move somebody hurt like that,'' Pop answered. ''Could be cut up inside. Could kill her. Don't want no lawsuit.''

''But you called an ambulance?''

''Told you I called! Near an hour ago. Called the damn 9-1-1. Nobody answered there. Then I called the cops on the long distance. Near an hour!''

''Forty-two minutes,'' Mom corrected. She hadn't moved, kept the shade over Darla's body. ''Poor little thing,'' Mom added. Darla's eyes wanted to roll back. ''Just a child.''

Sandobal pinched Darla's cheeks, slapped her face lightly, put ice on her lips. ''Call again,'' he ordered. ''Keep calling. Tell them it's an emergency.''

''What do you think I told them, you damn fool! That long distance costs money! This wasn't none of our doing.''

Sandobal looked up at him: angry. He held Darla's head in one hand, but with the other, he pulled his badge out, flashed it in Pop's eyes. ''I'm a police officer,'' he said. ''Go call the fucking highway patrol. Call them now!''

''There's no cause for foul language,'' Mom cautioned. ''I let Pop swear a little, but there's no—''

''I'll call them,'' Barbara leaped up, raced toward two pay telephones mounted near the driveway's entrance.

''Them don't work,'' Mom called.

''Damned yahoos keep them tore up,'' Pop added. ''You'll have to use the phone in the store. Don't stay on long. The long distance costs money!''

Barbara turned and ran toward the store. ''I think the bleeding's stopped,'' Sandobal said. Pop only nodded.

A full ten minutes later, the ambulance, followed by an Arizona Highway Patrol cruiser, pulled in. EMTs leaped out, took over. Barbara and Sandobal stood back. The trooper stood around a moment, looked for someone to arrest. Darla was out. The cop helped the EMTs put her on a gurney, shoved her toward the ambulance.

"You may have saved her life," the trooper told Sandobal when he came back. "But it's touch and go. They got her on life support." He wore a name tag identifying him as Gomez. Mirror-lensed Ray-Ban aviators hid his eyes. "The ice. May have done the trick. That and the juice. Quick thinking."

"I give her the damn juice," Pop put in. "Learned that in the Navy."

"She's not out of the woods yet," Sandobal said, wiped his bloody hands off on his Angels tee-shirt.

"No," Gomez admitted. "They're scared to move her, to drive her, even. They've called for Life Flight. Now, what the hell happened here?"

It took a while to piece it together. Pop explained that two people, a man and a woman, came into the store just after the girl—Darla—left.

"Nice girl. Good-looking little thing. Little flighty, I think—" Pop started to go on about Darla, but Gomez turned the discussion to the subject that more interested him: "The yahoos."

"Why attack her?" he asked. Pop shrugged. "What did they look like?"

"One was a man: short, dark, nervous type. Kind of chunky."

"Sounds like the one named Blackie," Barbara whispered to Sandobal. Pop went on about the other one.

"Was a woman," Pop said. "Didn't think so at first: ugliest thing I ever seen: big, fat, ugly, damn near bald-headed. Looks like one of them damn Hell's Angels we get through here time to time, though I never heard no motorcycle. Thought it was a man at first, leather britches, tattoos and all, even with the earrings. But then I seen her ta-tas."

"Ta-tas?" Gomez stopped writing, pen poised in midair.

"Ta-tas," Pop said, held his hands in front of his chest, palms inward. "Out to here."

"Breasts," Gomez clarified, glanced at Barbara, suppressed a smile, finished his note.

Pop nodded. "Ta-tas. Titties. Out to here. Big old floppy

things. But ugly. Damn ugliest ta-tas I've ever seen.'' Mom blushed, moved off a pace or two. Pop didn't notice. "One went left, the other went right. No damn brassiere, don't you know? Course, Little Bit over yonder never wore one, neither. But she was nice to look at.''

"Pop!" Mom said.

"Hate to see the other one naked," he went on. "Might've been one of them damned hermaphrodites. I seen one of them in Hong Kong once. Had a pecker and ta-tas all at the same time.''

"Pop!" Mom repeated.

"I was in the Navy," he added.

Sandobal took Barbara's arm, pulled her away. "Was there a woman with them? In LA, another woman?''

"No," Barbara said. "Unless she was already in the car." She was weary of explaining to Sandobal what she had seen, that she hadn't dreamed it up. He had already insisted—twice— that she call LA, try to reach Vicki. She did. No answer. No answer at Gary's, either. No sign of her at the spa, or at the temp pool where Vicki still worked from time to time. She left messages that she would call back, to leave a message on Sandobal's machine if anyone heard from Vicki. Thus far, no word.

"Could the other guy, the redhead, could he have been this woman?" Sandobal pressed. "Disguised?''

"He didn't weigh more than one-sixty," she said. "No tattoos, and no 'ta-tas.' " She now smiled. Sandobal joined her at last. But Barbara didn't enjoy it. She shook her head, flipped her hair. "He was male. I don't know where the woman came from.''

"Same place the van did, possibly," Sandobal said. For a moment Barbara let herself hope that Sandobal finally believed her. But then, he turned and frowned into the sun. "If it's the same van. If it's the same people. If any of this means anything. It all could be coincidence.''

Anger rose. *"If,* my ass," she said. "What do you think this is? A tourist attraction? See Arizona: blown-up cars, dead cops, stabbed girls? You stuck your *hand* inside her, for Chrissake! What does it take to convince you?''

Her voice attracted Gomez's attention. He left Pop, strolled over to them.

"He says you're a cop. Can I see your shield?"

Sandobal visibly shrank, but pulled out his badge and ID, handed it over. Gomez studied it through his shades.

"Long way from home, Detective."

"Sergeant."

"Sergeant. Still a long way."

"Sort of a vacation."

The trooper looked at Barbara, at the Mustang. "There's an officer the other side of Tucson still looking for that Ford. He said you flew past him like your ass was on fire. Clocked you at ninety, and if he hadn't had to go two miles for a crossover, he'd have your butt in jail."

"I doubt it," Barbara said.

Gomez was unimpressed. "No way for a cop to be driving, I don't care where he's from."

Barbara smiled. "I was driving," she said. "Sergeant Sandobal here was asleep. I get a little crazy sometimes."

Sandobal shot her a look. Gomez caught it. "You on a case, Sergeant?" Sandobal shook his head. Barbara looked away. "It wouldn't have been you who was flashing his badge over in Wintersburg earlier this morning, would it?" Again, Sandobal shook his head. Gomez turned his golden lenses on Sandobal, sighed. "More than one Santa Barbara cop running around Arizona today, think?"

"I'm sure I don't know," Sandobal said. "We just came in here to get something to drink. Use the toilet. Stumbled into this mess. I couldn't get the old man to do anything by yelling at him, so I showed him my badge to get him moving. That's it."

"We need to be going," Barbara said.

"What's your hurry?" Gomez asked.

The sound of an approaching car caught their attention. A light brown Ford Taurus sedan with a mounted antenna crunched into the driveway.

"Wait here," Gomez said. He started away, Sandobal's shield and ID still in his hand. "Your fly's unzipped," he said over his shoulder.

"Detective," Sandobal said quietly, nodding toward the car, repairing his pants. "Figured one to show up."

The driver, a balding burly man with an ugly scar on his face, a rumpled brown suit on his body, got out, spoke to Gomez. He entered the ambulance, pulled the door to behind him. In a moment, he emerged, spoke briefly with Gomez, moved over to them.

"You Sandobal?" he asked. Sandobal nodded.

"You got any connection to what happened here?"

Sandobal opened his mouth to respond. Then stopped. "Who the hell are you?" he asked. The man showed a wallet with a badge. "Curtis Fletcher. Inspector: Special Crimes."

"Special Crimes?"

"That's right. State Police."

"So?"

"So, I'm now in charge of this investigation. You want to tell me what you're doing here?" He shifted his weight. "Oh yeah: we know you've been running around all over the state asking a lot of questions, so you can stow the bullshit." He nodded at the ambulance. "You aren't going to tell me this is your missing person?"

"No," Sandobal said. "We just ran into this."

"Ran? From where to where? What're you doing here?"

Barbara was tired of being ignored. She took a breath, stepped in. "He's with me," she said, drew Fletcher's attention. "He's helping me. I'm looking for a friend of mine. We—" She looked at Sandobal, who hung his head in embarrassment. *"I* have reason to believe she was abducted. Kidnapped."

"Kidnapped?" The man squinted in the bright light, glanced over his shoulder at Gomez.

"We—that is *I*—think that the people who hurt that girl may be the same people?"

"Why?"

Barbara swallowed. Her throat was parched, scratched. At last, she thought, someone is going to listen. "Get me something to drink," she ordered Sandobal. "A Coke." He hesitated, Fletcher nodded, and he went to the grocery.

Mom and Pop remained where they were, watched and glared

at Sandobal. ''Twelve-ouncers is eighty-nine cents, plus tax,''
Pop yelled. ''Leave some money by the damn register.''

Barbara took a breath, patiently went through it. Fletcher
eyed her closely. She saw he didn't believe her.

''Sigel? If her name is Sigel, then who are you?'' he asked
when she finished.

''My name is Barbara Lovell.''

Fletcher stiffened: slapped. ''What?''

''Barbara Lovell. L o-v-e—''

He swallowed hard, stared at her. ''You got ID?''

Barbara went to the car for her gym bag, pocketbook. Sandobal came up with two Cokes, a pair of cheap sunglasses.

When she handed him her California driver's license,
Fletcher examined it closely, then stood back and looked at
her, expression serious. He said something softly under his
breath, then turned and looked up at the sky, as if searching
for something. Then he took a breath, glanced at Sandobal.
''And you're in on this?'' he asked.

Sandobal shrugged. Barbara made a noise with her throat.

''I'm asking some questions,'' he admitted.

''Is there a report? Do you have a warrant? Anything?''

Sandobal shook his head. ''This isn't official.''

''Well, I don't know how they do things in California,''
Fletcher said, ''but in Arizona, we tend to frown on people
running solo investigations, official or otherwise.'' He looked
hard at Sandobal, then at Barbara. ''Even if they are cops.
Maybe you should call the LAPD. Let them—''

''I did call them. Or I talked to them,'' Barbara said. ''They
didn't believe me.''

''But you expect me to,'' he smiled, but there was no humor
in it. He glanced at Mom and Pop, who waited patiently under
Mom's umbrella for the business to conclude. Mom mopped
her forehead with a handkerchief. Pop glared at Sandobal: the
Cokes, the sunglasses.

''Them things cost money,'' he muttered irritably.

''I suggest you just go on home,'' Fletcher said, handed her
license back to her. ''We've got things here under control.''

''I can see that,'' Barbara said, with sarcasm. ''Hell, you've
been here five whole minutes, and you've already got the sus-

pects in custody. Problem is that it's the wrong suspects.'' The weariness that had been flocking overhead lit on her shoulders, pushed her down. ''Christ,'' she sighed. ''You bureaucratic types give me a pain.''

Fletcher studied her, a small, sad smile on his face. ''I'm just a cog in the wheel. Wait here,'' he said. He went back to his car, picked up a telephone from the seat. He punched buttons, frowned at the telephone, tried again.

''Too far out for cell,'' Sandobal surmised. ''Why not use the radio?''

Fletcher went over and spoke to Gomez. The trooper shrugged, came over, handed Sandobal back his credentials.

''Are you carrying a weapon?''

Sandobal shook his head.

''It's illegal to do so,'' he said. ''Even if you have a shield.'' ''My gun's in the trunk.''

Gomez nodded. ''Listen. I'm going to cut you a break because of what you did for the victim—the girl.''

''A break?'' Sandobal was puzzled.

''On the speeding. On impersonating a police officer.''

''Imperson—'' Sandobal spluttered.

''Operating out of your jurisdiction and using invalid credentials constitutes impersonation of a police officer,'' Gomez explained. ''Unless you're in hot pursuit,'' he added. ''Look, we're having one hell of a day. We got cars blowing up in picnic areas and somebody's declared open season on state troopers. One of ours was killed today.''

''Yeah, we know,'' Barbara said.

Gomez gave her a serious look. ''We got reason to believe the same people who did this may have been the ones involved in that shooting.''

''That's what I've been trying to tell you!'' Barbara shouted.

He gave her a different look: patient. ''There's a major manhunt going on, and we're too shorthanded to worry about you running around, getting in trouble. Soon as Inspector Fletcher lets you go—*if* he lets you go—I suggest you head back to California.''

'' 'Inspector Fletcher'? He's giving you orders?''

''Right.'' He spun on his boot heel, went to his cruiser.

Fletcher was again trying his telephone. He shook it hard, then tossed it into his car: disgust. He stalked over to the twin pay telephones on the corner of the driveway.

"He's got a radio," Sandobal said, his brow wrinkling. "Why the phone?"

They watched Fletcher pound on the switchhook of the near telephone.

"Damn yahoos keep them busted up," Pop observed. "Some people'd do anything for a quarter."

"You reckon we could go back inside now?" Mom called across to Sandobal.

"Beats me, lady," Sandobal said. Then, he softened. To Pop: "I put a twenty by the register."

"You got change coming," Pop insisted.

Sandobal tapped the sunglasses, whispered to Barbara, "Not much."

Barbara opened her Coke and went back to the convertible, got in, glowered at the windshield. Sandobal went with her, leaned against her door. Neither spoke: frustration.

Fletcher gave up on the phones, then came over to them, breathing hard. He glanced at Barbara, at Sandobal. "You wait here," he said. To Pop: "Do you have a telephone inside?"

"Course, I do," Pop responded.

"I need to use it. Those don't work."

"Could have told you that," Pop noted.

"What's wrong with your radio?" Sandobal asked.

Fletcher ignored him, followed Pop inside. In a few minutes, he was back, Pop right behind him. He approached Sandobal. "You need to call in. Talk to your watch commander. Now."

"What?" Sandobal asked. "Why?"

"Because I said to. They're looking for you all over. Talk to your watch commander. Call in, now. Do it."

"Who'd you call?"

"He called your boss," Pop said, outraged. "Ratted you out. Said you was 'causing a disturbance.' Didn't say diddly about you saving that girl's life. Ought to give you a medal. Sounded to me like he was trying to get you busted down. I want four dollars for the call. Four more for the other one you made."

Fletcher idly pulled a handful of bills out of his pocket, dropped them on the ground behind him. Kept his eyes on Barbara. Pop's mouth dropped open, but he scooped up the bills. "You're big for your britches, ain't you?"

"Who did you talk to? What did you tell them?" Sandobal demanded.

"I did my duty." Fletcher turned to Barbara. "Now, you—"

Sandobal stepped between them. "What department did you say you were with?"

Fletcher wheeled on him, furious. "I said, 'Call in.' Do it now. You're in a world of shit, Sandobal. Take my word for it. I'm doing you a favor. You picked the wrong state to play cowboy in. Call in, get the fuck out of here."

He stalked over to Gomez's cruiser, stopped, conferred with him. Gomez gave Sandobal a long look through his shades, nodded, then Fletcher returned to his car and drove off, hit the frontage road, disappeared around a curve into the desert heat toward New Mexico.

Sandobal looked at Barbara. She could read him. "Don't do it," she said. "Just ignore him."

"Wish I had a fucking cigarette," he said. He went inside to call in, Pop right behind him, warning him of the cost of the call.

"They want me to come back. Now." Sandobal's Mets cap was tilted back over his sweaty hair. He still wore his rumpled coat. The desert temperature was over 110°. The Angels tee-shirt beneath was stained with dried blood. He peered at Barbara over the top of the sunglasses, awaited comment.

Barbara did not respond. She sat, one knee cocked beneath the Mustang's steering wheel, the other straight out. Her face was fixed, brown eyes straight ahead, studying the interstate across the frontage road.

"That's what they said."

Barbara shrugged, took a sip of her tepid Coke. She frowned. "If the Life Flight ever gets here . . ." She trailed off, uncertain how to finish the sentence. She wanted to go on, felt Vicki moving away.

She looked past Sandobal off into the desert, wondered how much she really needed him: not much, she thought. Heat waves shimmered above the giant sequoia cactus, yellow sand. Two large birds flew great circles in the distance, rode the thermals, patiently waited.

Sandobal coughed, impatient. She stretched her arms over her head. Sleepiness swarmed around her, wanted to light. She wanted to let it, close her eyes. Instead, she yawned, pulled the bottle of Coke up from between her legs, sipped again, frowned again, brushed her bangs away from her forehead again. They left a wet trail.

"So?" Sandobal asked, his eyebrows rose, pushed his cap higher on his forehead. "You going to take me to the airport, or what? They expect me to be on duty in five hours. I can catch a flight from Tucson, just have time to shower and shave. I—"

"Fuck them," Barbara said.

Sandobal's eyes widened. "Beg pardon?"

"You can't go back. You can't just give up on this."

Sandobal sighed, turned, leaned against the car. "Yeah, what the hell. It's only a job. A career. What the hell."

"They're going to fire you if you don't come back? That's ridiculous."

He didn't say anything.

"They said that? That they would fire you?"

"That was the gist of it. They said if I didn't have my butt back in the Santa Barbara station by six o'clock tonight—their time—my ass was grass." He hunched his shoulders slightly. "Oh, yeah. I'm on report for taking the radio. That's department property."

"Why?"

"Why what?"

"Why would they give a damn?"

"About the radio?"

"No, about you." She sat up, stared through the bug bodies dotting the windshield. "I don't mean 'about you.' I mean why would they demand that you come back?"

"All I know is that I need to get my butt back to Santa Barbara by six o'clock tonight, or—"

"Your 'ass is grass.' "

"Right."

"And you believe that?"

Her eyes remained focused on the windshield. She couldn't look at him.

"Hell, yes, I believe it. What the hell else am I supposed to do? I'm too short-time not to go for it." He sighed again, pushed the glasses all the way up on his long, bent nose. "To tell you the truth, it pisses them off what I'm doing. I'm out here, all by myself—"

"I'm here."

"All by myself," he repeated: a point. "With no right to be here. I'm just a citizen in this state—in any state, in any city outside Santa Barbara."

"Okay, okay," Barbara said, resigned. "I get the point."

"No, you don't," he said.

She tossed her head again. He wasn't so cute anymore.

"Well, are you going to take me to Tucson, or not?"

She fixed her stare once more on the buggy windshield. "I'm thinking about it."

Pop came crunching up toward them, seething. Mom was right behind him. "That girl may be dying in there! Ain't nobody going to do nothing but stand around here and jerk off?" he demanded.

"Pop!" Mom admonished.

"Well, hell's bells," Pop raised his fists and shook them at the sky. "Girl laying in there bleeding to death. No damn 9-1-1. Said they called for a damn helicopter, but do you see one? I don't! Cops calling all over the damn country. This is one crazy business, you ask me. Something's screwy."

"Is that what you're going to do?" Barbara asked Sandobal.

"Go back? What else? There's a flight in two hours. They're taking care of the reservation. All I have to do is be on it."

"Tucson's in the wrong direction," Barbara said.

Sandobal took off his glasses, cap. He rubbed his face, smeared grit across it. "I give up," he said. "Just get me to the goddamn airport. Any airport. We'll figure out the rest later."

Barbara looked at him, nodded: too tired, too pissed off to

argue. She wanted to lie down, sleep. But she decided that she didn't want to sleep with him again. She wanted him out of her sight. "Okay," she said.

The ambulance door opened, and an EMT came out, stared at the sky. His hands were stained red, as was the front of his uniform. He lit a cigarette. Mom and Pop drifted toward him, so did Gomez. Sandobal hesitated, joined them. Barbara waited, then got out and walked over as well.

"Life flight's coming from Deming," the technician said. "Tucson's chopper is grounded. Big storm coming. Wind. Rain, likely."

"How is she?" Pop asked. "She going to make it?"

"She's holding on. Might make it. I don't want to drive her if we can help it. Holler at me when that chopper shows up." He crushed out his cigarette, went back inside.

"Let me ask you something," Gomez said to Sandobal, walked beside him and Barbara back toward the Mustang, "Cop to cop." He looked at Mom and Pop, who were peering at the sky. "What did you do to piss that guy off?"

Sandobal looked at the interstate. "Who? Oh, Fletcher?" He looked at Barbara. "Don't know."

"Who is he, anyway?"

"You don't know?" Barbara asked.

"I don't know shit," Gomez said. "He's an inspector. Outranks me. Gave me orders to do whatever he said. And he had plenty to say, especially where you were concerned. He wants your ass back in California, pronto."

"Yeah," Sandobal said. "He was pretty clear on that point." A thought struck him. "He said he was with Special Crimes. Does—"

"Are you goldbricks just going to stand around here and admire the heat all day, or are you going to do something?" Pop came up.

"Well, Mr. . . . uh, Grupnek," Gomez consulted his notes quickly. "I think we've done about all we can—"

"What about them yahoos cut that girl?"

"We've got an APB out on the van. In fact, it's already wanted. We should pick it up any time now. New Mexico Highway Patrol has—"

"What about the professor?"

"Who?" Gomez looked at Sandobal, confused.

"The professor. Kingston. Guy she was with," Pop clarified. "You ask me, there was more than teaching going on there." He glanced over his shoulder, checked Mom. "I can't believe he just stood there and watched them cut that girl up."

"What guy?" Somehow, amidst all the talk of ta-tas, the trooper had missed the fact that Darla was with someone.

"She was with this guy: Kingston. Professor of some kind. Least that's what everybody called him. Everybody but her, that is. Ain't that right, Mom?" Mom nodded. Pop continued: "That's right. They come for ice and drinks and stuff all the time. Got gas. Got an account. Probably got them a motel room over in New Mexico, 'less I miss my guess."

Mom's mouth dropped open. "Pop!"

"Don't tell me. I was in the Navy. Anyhow, they left together. Come out to get ice. Then them yahoos come in. Then they left. Then we find the girl. Don't know what happened to the professor. Reckon they got him is my guess."

"What?" the trooper yelled. "*What* was his name? Did they have a car? Jesus! Why didn't you tell me? I thought she lived here."

"Nope. She just comes here with the professor. Every couple of months, like I said. They're working over to Flat Mesa. That away." He pointed vaguely toward the desert. "Have one of the European cars."

"Volvo," Mom offered.

"A Volvo or something," Pop confirmed. "They come in and gassed her up this morning. Got some drinks and snacks." He paused. "Box of rubbers—sorry, Mom: This is official. Went for ice. Last time I seen them till—"

"Goddamn!" Gomez yelled. He pulled out his notebook, started scribbling. Sweat coursed down from his hat. He threw off his Ray-Bans. Barbara was surprised: blue eyes. "Why didn't you mention this before? Half the goddamn cops in the country're looking for a van? What color is the goddamn Volvo? You got a license number?"

"There is no cause for foul language—" Mom started.

Sandobal stood off to one side, listening. Barbara took mental

notes as well: brown Volvo, older model, Arizona plates but
no license number. Professor's name was "Kingston" or
"something like that," Pop said. He hadn't been seen since he
left the grocery-office with the girl—"and the rubbers." Gomez
rushed over to his cruiser, put it on the radio. Barbara and
Sandobal followed, left Pop and Mom arguing over details of
description.

"Well," Sandobal said, as soon as Gomez returned. "Seems
we do have a missing person after all."

Gomez whirled on Sandobal, pushed him back. "Look," he
said. "I don't know who you are or what you're doing here,
but I've got orders, and I'm telling you to get the hell out of
here: now."

Sandobal's temper flared. He jumped back into Gomez's
face. "What the—"

"You're out of line, Sergeant." Gomez said. "And you're
out of your depth. I don't know who the fuck that guy is, that
inspector, but he wants your ass back in California, pronto."
He pointed toward the interstate. "I have to go. There's a
chance they doubled back to Tucson, and I'm the only one out
here. Everybody else is looking for a goddamned van."

"We've got a kidnapping," Barbara said. "We have a perfect
right— "

"My problem starts and ends right here!" Gomez yelled. "I
need forensics out here. We've got tire tracks here! Fingerprints,
footprints." To himself: "Jesus. Soon as that chopper gets here,
this place is going to be a mess. And there's a storm coming.
I'll have to go for a tarp—" He turned, stared at Sandobal,
spoke quietly. "One cop to another, get out of here. I don't
have time for your bullshit."

"Okay, okay," Sandobal, still angry, put up his hands. "I'm
on a flight to LA in two hours. No problem."

Gomez went over, grabbed Pop, escorted him off to one
side. Mom followed with her giant umbrella. Sandobal rubbed
his chin, thought.

"Well?" Barbara asked.

"I need to make another call," he said.

"You're still going back?"

He sighed, looked around: desert and the buzzing of passing

vehicles up on the interstate. "I need to make another call."
He started toward the store.

She slumped, drained off the Coke. It sat on her stomach
like acid.

Gomez left Pop, entered his cruiser, peeled out of the driveway. He crossed the frontage road, bumped across the median,
shot over the eastbound lane. When he hit the westbound, he
was picking up speed, lights flashing.

No sign yet of Sandobal. "Well, I guess I'll just go pee,"
she said to him, although he was gone. "Then, I'll drive you
to Tucson. Damnit."

She got out, walked to the women's room, opened the door.
Foul, sour odor hit her nostrils. The toilet had overflowed:
disgust. She thought she would wait. How far back was Tucson?
Could she hold it? She decided not. She took a deep breath,
held it, went inside, closed the door.

She was out in less than a minute, still pulling up the running
suit, tripping, almost falling down as she raced for the car.
Sandobal was already there, in the driver's seat, breathing hard,
sweating. The engine was running.

"C'mon," he said. "Let's go, now!"

"I know where they are! I know where they're going. There's
a—"

"C'mon," he said. "Let's go. Now!"

"But I need to tell—"

"Now!" he said. "Get in, now!"

She jumped in. He fired the engine, slammed the Mustang
into gear. She saw the butt of his service revolver sticking out
of his waistband.

"What the hell is going on? I thought you were going back."

He shook his head. "Hold on!"

He swung the big car onto the frontage road, pushed it
through the gears, catching rubber in the first three. Speed
climbed, they rounded the curve. In the distance ahead of them,
just before the entrance ramp, Fletcher and his car blocked the
single-lane blacktop. He picked his spot well. On either side a
deep ditch descended into a culvert: no turnoff, no way around.

The balding scarfaced figure was confident, leaned casually

on the car, one foot crossed in front of the other. Brown man on a brown car, smiling. His scar glowed red in the heat.

"Hold on tight," Sandobal yelled through gritted teeth. There was enough room behind the Taurus for them to pass. Just enough if they were perfect. Fletcher reached inside his jacket. The distance between the racing nose of the big Ford and the tail of the brown Taurus closed. Barbara had the sensation of leaping off a high dive, seeing the water rush up toward her face. She was thrilled: terrified.

"Sandobal!" she screamed.

Fletcher produced a large silver automatic. Barbara could see the silencer. He fired twice, the bullets ricocheted off the windshield's slanted glass, leaving crazy star patterns in front of Sandobal's face. Fletcher saw they were going to try to shoot the gap. He stepped to his right, toward the rear of the Taurus, took aim once more.

Sandobal jerked the wheel to the left, hard, then to the right, then left again: miscalculated. They wouldn't make it, not clean. The Mustang rose on two wheels as they reached the Taurus's rear end, struck it hard, knocked it out of the way: glass and steel, squealing tires, shattered plastic.

Fletcher's body thudded against the car. He dropped his pistol, leaped, landed on the hood, grabbed a windshield wiper in one hand, hung on. He was pressed against the windshield, the ragged end of his collarbone, stark, white, sharp, jerked out of his shirt, stabbed his neck. Sandobal pushed the big Ford on past the wreck, hit the entrance ramp with a bump. Fletcher's head bounced hard on the windshield, and blood spilled out his mouth and nose. The splintered bone stabbed him over and over again in the neck and throat. His left hand fastened desperately to the top of the windshield while the Mustang careened, swerved.

"Get him off! Get him off!" Barbara screamed, but she couldn't hear herself over the Mustang's engine, wind tears. Fletcher's blood-filled mouth opened in a scream of his own. Below the knee, his right pants leg was an empty, ragged, bloody tear. Blood splattered over the top of the windshield, dotted Barbara's face and hands. His breath against the red-streaked glass made a crimson fog.

Now Sandobal yelled, penetrated her horror. "Get him off, for Christ's sake." Barbara gave him a wide-eyed stare: How? The collision with the Taurus snapped something in the Mustang's suspension. Sandobal gripped the steering wheel with both hands, fought for control. The wheel wobbled. "Get him off! I can't see!"

Barbara hoisted herself, held onto the windshield, pounded Fletcher's fingers, had no idea what she was doing, what they were doing, why. Fletcher clung to the top of the windshield, a death grip. His nails were white, bloody teeth clenched. He released the wiper arm, tried to get both hands up, pull himself over on top of her.

"Get him off!" Sandobal screamed. "Get him off, now!"

She looked for something—anything that would work: a knife, a tool, anything. An empty cassette tape case was in the floorboard, cracked. She grabbed it, smashed it hard against the dash: splinters. With one more horrifying look into Fletcher's tormented face, she jammed the jagged plastic into his fingers. Blood spurted out of the wound, filled her eyes, she jabbed him again, and again. He let go.

He rolled off the right fender into the slipstream down the passenger side, hit the pavement. Barbara turned, saw him bounce twice, then spin over and over in a grotesque somersault onto the sandy shoulder of the highway into the cactus and yellow dust, out of sight.

Sandobal let up on the gas, slowed to eighty, then seventy. Control returned, though the wheel vibrated dangerously. He sat back, sweat poured from beneath his cap. Dots of Fletcher's blood covered his face like freckles. Her hands were covered as well: warm, sticky, red.

She lowered her head into her hands, breathed deeply for a moment, then looked at Sandobal, who kept his eyes in front of him, fixed on the highway.

"He was a cop."

"That was no cop."

"Who was he, then?"

"Don't know." He eased their speed up to a point where the vibration became violent, came down again. "Think we broke something."

"No shit? Jesus, Sandobal!" She looked back: nothing. "What the hell's going on?"

"We're looking for a brown Volvo," he said. "Two men, anyway, maybe three. And one woman who looks like a man. Remember the ta-tas." Quick grin, then a frown. "And Vicki," he added.

"I know where they're going," she said. He looked at her, surprise on his face, belief. She was relieved. She told him what was scrawled in burnt orange lipstick on Mom and Pop's restroom door.

He nodded. "Never heard of it, but hell, that doesn't mean a thing. I never heard of Arizona either, and look at me. I'm the Lone Fucking Ranger."

"You're not so alone," she shot.

"Right, Tonto," he said, smiled. "Tonto looked better," he added.

She found a towel in her workout bag, began wiping blood off her face. She then wiped his face, forearms while he drove.

Overhead the Life Flight from Deming passed them, then started its descent. Barbara looked at Sandobal, noted the firmness in his hands on the wheel, dark determination in his eyes. She decided that maybe she was wrong. She might want to sleep with him again after all.

"I don't understand," she said. Then she narrowed her eyes. "What happened? How did you know? Who did you call?"

"He wouldn't use the radio. Wanted a regular phone. Why? I called Arizona State Police. They never heard of a cop named Fletcher, and there's no such department as Special Crimes."

15

Habeas Corpus

The walls of the Interrogation Room 2-A of HPD were typical
of other interrogation rooms Eddy Lovell had been in: modern
acoustical tile on the ceiling and three walls, fake mirror—
one-way glass—on the fourth. A cheap, brown Formica-topped
metal table was dead center, one stiff, short, uncomfortable
steel chair pulled up: Eddy's seat.

Opposite him were two other chairs, same color as Eddy's.
Same design but thickly padded, easier on the ass. They were
taller by two inches. HPD paid a professional consultant-
criminologist two hundred grand to figure out if a suspect was
two inches lower than his interrogator and seated on a chair
that bit his butt, he would be more apt to cooperate.

Eddy could have told them that in two minutes. All he would
have charged was a pack of smokes. He'd confess to killing
Jimmy Hoffa if they'd give him a single cigarette. But the only
appliance in the room was a portable tape recorder on the table.
In Dallas, Eddy remembered, there was also an ashtray. World
going to hell, people blowing up people with firebombs, scyth-
ing them down in front of public restaurants, cutting off their
heads, and all the suits downtown could think of to do was ban

smoking. Made Eddy want a cigarette. It was the only thing he and DaCara would have agreed on.

Across the table from Eddy in the more comfortable chairs were Detective Sergeant Greg DaCara and United States Marshall Theodore Billings. DaCara chain-smoked, flicked his ashes into a Diet Coke can on the floor. Billings leaned forward, round elbows rested on the table. His thick fingers played with Eddy's file.

"Why don't you make it easy on everybody, Lovell," Billings said: fourth time. Eddy was bored. "We know you're not smart enough to pull this off. You got no motive, anyhow. Mendle don't pay you enough for this kind of action. Hell, he don't have enough. Tell us what went down. Mendle's going away, so's his muscle—what's his name?" He glanced at DaCara, who returned a sad smile.

"Nguen Long." DaCara pronounced it "New-jew-inn." Looked confused. "What the fuck kind of name's that, anyway? Vietnamese?"

"Montagnard," Billings corrected. "File says he's like a mountain tribesman of some kind. Refugee. Somebody brought him back from 'Nam."

"Brought him back?" DaCara asked. Billings nodded. DaCara shook his head. "Most guys just came back with the clap." He turned to Eddy. "You two suck buddies or something?"

Eddy shook his head. "I thought his name was Hedge."

"Yeah, well, what the fuck," Billings said. "These days, you ain't cool 'less you got four or five AKAs." He pointed a finger in Eddy's face." You don't got none, asshole, and you ain't cool." He offered a fat grin. "Look, Lovell, I checked: You're damn near clean. You just drive for that short little fuck. In exchange, he gives you a nice little salary and a shack job with a twenty-buck-an-hour hooker. Dyed redhead named Queenie."

"Princess," DaCara corrected.

"It's a lousy deal," Billings went on, "even for a dumb-as-shit low-ball loser like you. You don't owe Mendle a fucking thing. It's all falling apart, now. Firebombing's a federal rap. You tell us what you know, maybe you can walk on this. Hell, you can be back in Dallas by Sunday, banging that hooker, watching the Cowboys. You don't even have to testify." Billings leaned back, laced his fingers over his fat stomach. "Nobody's going to believe you, anyway. Nobody believes a con."

"So why're you asking me?" Eddy asked. He reached in his pocket for a smoke: empty. Took everything away when he was brought in. All he had in his pockets was lint.

"You can save us some time," DaCara spoke up softly through blue-gray breath. His sad smile inched up a bit. "Look, I don't know if you had anything to do with that grease ghetto going up or not. I really don't give a shit. It's a damned loud way to kill roaches and rats, but it's effective as hell. Saved us a lot of trouble down the road. High-speed urban renewal. But what I want to know is what the fuck's going down? Why's my city all of a sudden filling up with stiffs? Why are they all tied in some way to Moria Mendle?"

"Why don't you ask him?"

"Mendle's a sawed-off little scumbag with a big mouth," Billings put in. "He's nut-deep in shit. We could nail him anytime, but he was too small-time to worry about. Till today. Why'd you guys whack Bob Cole?"

Eddy almost smiled at Billing's interrogation technique: regular prime-time TV. He shook his head. "Got me," he said. "I was in Dallas at the time. You can check with my girlfriend."

"Why'd you torch Pap's Cafe?"

"We didn't."

"Who did?"

"Beats me."

"Let's take it from the top," DaCara sighed, reached for Eddy's folder, pulled a Bic pen from his pocket. "What the hell were you doing in Pap's Cafe when you were supposed to be at the morgue putting the ID on Cole?"

Eddy went through it again. In a way, it was easy: he didn't know shit. But at the same time it was tough: they were looking for somebody to squash: Eddy was ripe. Billings played with the tape recorder, turned it around and around. It wasn't running—not yet.

Eddy had no idea what Moria told them, didn't know how

much they knew about where they were last night. When in doubt, tell the truth, was always Bodine's advice. The problem: Eddy didn't know the truth. But neither did the cops. They knew he was there, probably guessed that Moria had business with Boot Town. That was it. If they knew or cared about Earline, they didn't say so. Eddy thought about Will Dudly. How did he connect to all this?

Hell, Eddy thought, he had more questions than the cops. He wasn't any closer to the answers than they were, either.

One thing was certain: they'd been watching Moria, not Boot Town. He had to be careful about what he said, to let Moria do the talking, just answer their questions, stay with the truth, at least with the facts as he knew them. He wouldn't mention Boot Town.

When they brought him from Holding to Interrogation, he had been in custody six hours. He was hungry, tired, sleepy. He guessed they had Moria on the grill for a couple of hours, anyway. If he'd given anything up, Eddy'd be booked and basted by now. Wouldn't need him. If it was Moria they were after. He wondered where Hedge was, if he was alive.

He continued the story. The black Caprice picked them up within minutes of the explosion at Pap's Cafe. They heard the boom—hell, everybody in south Harris County heard the boom—but they knew nothing about it. They'd just turned off Telephone Road onto Main Street. Moria was studying the road map, Hedge was smoking. The Chevy came up beside them, forced them into the curb. Moria was yelling, cursing, looking for his piece. Hedge was out the door in a flash, shotgun up. The windows on Eddy's side of the car exploded. Hedge went down, the shotgun went off. He disappeared. The Buick took a half-dozen hits. Nobody else was hurt.

Eddy lay down across the seat, pulled his automatic, then heard the cop's voice on the PA for them to put their hands up, throw out their weapons. Eddy pulled out his shirttail, wiped his prints off the pistol's grip, buried it under the seat, shoved his hands up, rolled out onto the ground: routine.

Moria still had his piece in his hand when they got to him. He waited until they came for him, jerked him out, threw him over the hood of the Buick, cuffed him, Mirandized him. He was yelling for Hedge the whole time. But Hedge was gone.

Eddy hadn't done anything. He was just the driver. Even if they tied the Beretta to him, he had a permit for it. He just didn't want a cop to have a reason to shoot him. Billings looked like just the cop to do that, too. It was no surprise to Eddy that Billings was the one who cuffed him. But they didn't book him, weren't that sure. He clung to that point. He wondered if they booked Moria.

"So you were on your *way* to the morgue when we picked you up," DaCara repeated wearily. Eddy nodded. "Just *happened* to stop in the greasiest ptomaine tavern in Houston to have some ham and eggs, just *happened* to leave the place five minutes before it went into orbit, just *happened* to be heading downtown when we pulled you over. That it?"

"Well, we left out resisting arrest, consorting with known felons, possession of a concealed weapon," Billings added. "Shit, Eddy. When they get through with you, you're going to be too old to get it up."

Eddy sighed. "There was no felon in the car." Billings snorted. "At least, none I know about," Eddy added. Moria had a full pardon, expunged record. So he said, anyway.

"That's it?" DaCara repeated. "All that just fucking *happened?*"

"That's it," Eddy said. The two cops looked at him: liar. Pissed him off. "Look," he said. "I'm just Mendle's driver."

"You carry a gun."

"I got a permit."

"Cons can't get permits," Billings grumbled.

"I got one, anyway. It's in my wallet. Or it was." DaCara frowned at that. Eddy continued: "We stopped, had breakfast. Moria talked to some people."

"Who?" DaCara brightened.

"Don't know. We didn't sit together."

"Bullshit," Billings growled. "You're a piece of work. You know that?"

"So we leave after we eat. Then we get pulled over by you assholes. We didn't know you were cops. Black Chevy. Came out of nowhere, ran us off the road. Could have been anybody.

This isn't the safest town in the world. You guys do a shitty job of keeping the streets safe.''

DaCara reddened. Billings smiled.

"When you ID'd, I rolled out, turned over, didn't say shit. You got nothing to hold me for," Eddy went on. "Either charge me or cut me loose.''

"Or what? You'll get a fucking lawyer?" DaCara yelled. "You can get a shit-load of lawyers. But they won't help you. How come your gook boyfriend's riding around with a loaded shotgun in his lap?''

"Ask him.''

"We will. He took a load of double-ought: dead-on. What's he made of? Iron? You don't know when there's a guy behind you with a loaded 12-gauge?''

"I just make sure his seat belt's fastened," Eddy said. "I'm a driver.''

"Yeah, and I'm—" DaCara trailed off.

"A prick," Eddy muttered.

DaCara's eyes narrowed. "I'm going to nail you, Eddy boy.''

They were quiet again. "Maybe your buddy Long will talk," DaCara said. "Maybe he might have something to tell us when he crawls in and asks for an aspirin. Maybe he won't like being charged with accessory to murder.''

"He might be facing deportation, too," Billings muttered. "Got to check on that.''

Murder: The word floated in front of Eddy's mind. He fought to keep control of himself. What did they have? "So, who was I accessoring?" he asked.

"Maybe yourself," Billings shot. "Maybe your boss. Maybe you're some kind of sicko. Hell, Eddy, maybe you're the torch.''

It had been a good job. A guy they picked up, put in holding next to Eddy, told him it was all over the news: radio, TV. Pap's Cafe went up like a firecracker stand in high wind. There were eight dead, sixteen seriously injured, five more critical: burned. At first, they blamed a gas leak—that was the obvious—DaCara and Billings thought different. They were sure

HFD investigators would find evidence of a bomb, would link Moria to the blast.

Eddy had no idea who was hurt, who was dead. His first thought was of Earline. Poor stupid little cunt. Wrong place, wrong time: classic.

"What makes you think there was a torch?" Eddy asked. It was hot in the room—another of the consulting criminologist's ideas: keep the temperature high, uncomfortable. But Eddy wasn't sweating as much as Billings. The man looked close to having a stroke.

The two cops glanced at each other. DaCara now seemed calm, recollected. He ground his cigarette out beneath the table, let sparks fall on the floor, dropped the butt into the Coke can, leaned forward.

"Let's face it, Eddy," he said. "You're on a short string. It's only a matter of time before Mendle gives you up to save his fat ass. He's already given up Long, claims he didn't know the big gook had the shotgun, either. Claims he didn't know it was cops pulled you over. That's bullshit, too. Hell, we don't exactly qualify for any award for disguise around here. You guys think we got a quota for bullshit, though."

He leaned back, pulled another smoke out of his pocket. "In a while, Moria'll claim you blew the place. Save his own ass. Probably finger you for Cole, too." He held up a hand. "We know you're alibied out on that. Don't mean you didn't set it up. You already have a couple of hookers in your personal stable, and Cole ran with hookers. We already know the hooker you guys been all over town looking for was there this morning. It's all one piece. Looks like gumbo, now. Time we finish, it's blood sausage. We'll put it together."

Eddy blinked. He didn't want to, but he did. He forced himself to remain steady. He now knew the tail had been with them all night. How had he missed it? He'd been careful. But they knew about Earline. That brought the blink.

"What does the broad have to do with Cole?" DaCara asked rapid-fire. "We know they were together the night Cole got whacked. Was she in on it? Were you? What does Boot Town have to do with Cole? What does Moria have to do with Boot Town? What does Boot Town have to do with the broad? What do you have to do with any of this? Answer me, you son of a bitch.''

Eddy stared at him, confused. He wished he knew the answers to half these questions.

Billings continued the quiz: ''You know a guy named Will Dudly? What does he have to do with the broad? How come Dudly's holding down a slab at the morgue right next to the broad? How come she's in the next pew?''

''She's dead?''

Billings smiled. DaCara nodded, said, ''Her name was Earline Gilroy, by the way. Aka Heather Lockhart. Doesn't matter. She's a crispy critter, now,'' DaCara said, shook his head. ''So's most of the muscle Boot Town kept around. So's most of Pap's customers.''

''And Boot Town's going to be on a liquid diet himself for a while,'' Billings put in. ''If he makes it at all.''

''He'll make it,'' DaCara said. ''Too fucking fat to die. And when he makes it, he'll talk. Bet on it. Going to be so pissed off, he'd give up his own mother. So, there's no reason for you to keep quiet, Eddy. Why not let us in, now? Let's clear this shit up. We can both take the weekend off.''

Eddy kept still. His mind was working. If Boot Town was alive, he'd spill his fat guts. Convinced Moria did it. It was as good a guess as any.

''Otherwise,'' DaCara went on, ''I'm going to charge you with accessory to arson and murder. I'm not shitting you. I got enough on you for that.''

''You don't—''

''We got plenty,'' Billings said. ''Even if you beat one, we'll get you on the other. You're going back to the joint, fuckhead. At the very least. Firebombing's federal, like I say. You'll be lucky to draw El Reno for life. Better grease your ass, bend over, and get ready for it. They got a whole new crop of bull queers since you was away.''

Eddy shook his head slowly. He hadn't done a thing. Neither had Moria. He didn't think. Couldn't be sure. He remembered Ralph the Mouth. ''Business,'' Moria had said. Was this just business, too?

He went over it again. He remembered the guy in the blue

van who came in, looked out of place: Arab. Earline talked about an Arab. Same guy? Houston was lousy with them. Every convenience store had a full staff of ragheads punching buttons, pretending to speak English. Had that guy known she was there? Brought in a bomb? Could be. Everybody else looked regular. That guy stuck out.

Damn, Eddy swore. This isn't the way to go. He was angry and afraid at the same time. Loyalty has its limits, and he hadn't ever really felt any loyalty to Moria. What did the guy do? Give him a job? Was that enough to go down for murder? Not that kind of murder. El Reno: shit. He'd get the needle and the eighteen-minute good-bye for this kind of murder, even if the dead were all scum-buckets and cokeheads. He wouldn't take the fall for that.

He then thought about Cole. Maybe the bomb—if that's what it was—wasn't meant for Boot Town at all. Maybe it was meant for Moria. Maybe Cole's hit was a warm-up bout. Main event still to come. The game was heating up: too many bodies, not enough suspects. Too many players, all after the same thing. And nobody knew what that was.

It was time for the sidelines. Even the best sometimes has to leave the game, save his ass. Bodine's advice loomed large in his mind. "Everybody gets burned," he remembered the carrot-topped coon-ass saying, "it's just a matter of when." He made up his mind. He was not going to be burned again. But the big problem remained: he didn't know anything. He was trapped. Now, he wanted a lawyer, said so.

"What for?" Billings responded to Eddy's request. "You ain't been charged. Right now, you're a material witness to a possible arson. That's it."

DaCara leaned back. "You know something, you'd better tell us. I give you my word you're okay." His sad smile turned down, serious. "Eddy, I don't know you. Don't like you. You're a con with a long sheet. You hang with scum. That makes you scum. But I'll shoot straight: I got nothing on you, nothing to hold you for, nothing to drop on you. But I'll tie you up for a month if I have to, put you on the extended tour. You'll be drinking cold soup and fighting junkies for toilet paper the whole time.

''You tell me what you know, what Moria knows, I'll kick you loose: no charges, no bail. I know where to find you. Teddy here's got jurisdiction just about everywhere, and I'll sic him on you if you rabbit. He'd just as soon kill you as piss on you anyway, so you're better off cooperating with me.

''You don't need a lawyer. You need me. Help me out, I'll see you walk. Maybe you can get another job. Maybe you can't. But you can stay out of the joint. That's the deal.'' DaCara's dark eyes peered into him.

''C'mon, Eddy, try us,'' Billings said: Mr. Warmth.

''Here,'' DaCara pulled his smokes out, offered one to Eddy with a grin. Billings scooted the tape recorder over to him. Eddy leaned over and accepted a light from DaCara. Billings punched a button on the recorder.

Eddy pulled smoke into his lungs. He still had no idea what he was going to say.

The door to the room opened, and both cops spun around, angry at the interruption: uniform. ''His lawyer is here. With paper. Got to cut him loose.''

Eddy was led down the hall and through a door ahead of DaCara and Billings. Billings cursed loudly every step of the way. DaCara just shuffled along, shook his head.

Moria was already out. He stood by a counter, filled his pockets with personal items. The bag with Eddy's goods was next to it. Eddy stopped one step into the room. Next to his boss stood a well-dressed black man: intensely familiar, but Eddy couldn't place him. One of Moria's lawyers, Eddy thought. He was well dressed—cream-colored suit, cranberry shirt, silk tie, fancy braces, tasseled loafers—flashy—short graying afro, steel-rimmed glasses.

The guy beamed. ''Sorry I took so long, Mr. Lovell,'' he said. ''Traffic.'' Eddy nodded, stepped up to the counter, accepted the plastic inventory bag, put things away.

Moria took a breath, turned to the clerk behind the counter. ''What about his gun?''

The clerk looked at him, blank. ''Pardon?''

''His gun. Beretta. 7.65 millimeter. He's got a permit to

carry." He turned to DaCara. "I know you won't give me mine, you fuck. But he didn't even have his on him. I want him armed. He's my bodyguard."

"Why you need a bodyguard?" Billings asked. "You planning to blow up another building today?"

"Give him the piece," DaCara said to the clerk. He nodded toward the lawyer. "This isn't over. With any luck, they'll shoot each other, soon as they decide which one whacked Cole."

Moria spun around, moved quickly for a man so short, pudgy, stepped around Eddy to face the detective. His glare was filled with hate. "Did it ever occur to you that maybe I was the mark today? Maybe whoever took Cole down might have me next on his dance card? I mean, we *were* partners, you know. It's not impossible. Or maybe you'd just like to see me dead." DaCara didn't react.

Moria's eyes suddenly softened. "Let me tell you something, DaCara," Moria said. "You're a good cop. First-rate flatfoot. Do your job, collect your paycheck, go home and bang the cunt *du jour* senseless. Drop a bundle on the ponies. Come back to work. You don't take any shit, and you leave people alone."

"Mostly," DaCara said: a smile.

"And I got to tell you—off the record—sometimes you're closer to right than you ought to be. Sometimes, you fucking scare me, you're so close." DaCara nodded. Moria moved closer to him, leaned close. "But this time, you're wrong. You can believe that or not. You were wrong about me before, and you're wrong about me this time. You write that down. You fucking memorize it."

"I'm watching you," DaCara said.

"Watch close," Mendle said. "You might learn something." To the clerk: "Give him his fucking gun."

DaCara shrugged, nodded to the clerk, who also shrugged. "Didn't find no gun."

"Bullshit!" Moria said.

"We didn't," the clerk replied, held up a clipboard. "Didn't look for it, didn't find it. You ain't been charged, so your car ain't been impounded."

DaCara grinned. "It ain't been waxed, either."

"It's out back," the clerk said, confused. "It's shot to shit, though. They towed it, left it. Two flats."

"Let's go," Moria said, stalked out the door.

"Eddy boy," Billings said. "Keep one thing in mind: While DaCara's watching him," he thumbed toward Moria, "I'm going to be watching you. You get a hard-on, I'll be the one who cums."

They left HPD by the front door. The bright damp heat of Houston twilight smothered Eddy when he followed Moria and the lawyer outside. He stopped, lit a smoke, watched the black man follow Moria down toward a black Mercedes sedan.

"This your car?" Moria asked. "We need it. We have a lawsuit here, right?"

The man stopped, looked back at Eddy, then down at Moria. "No."

"Why the fuck not?" Moria demanded. He looked at Eddy. "Where'd you find this guy? He the one got you that great plea bargain?" He looked again at the man. "They pull us over for no reason. Shoot my bodyguard, shoot my car. Shoot at me. No 'Stop, Police.' No nothing. Haul me in, hold me five, six hours. No food, no phone call. That's got to be actionable."

"I think we need to have a talk," the man said.

"Fuck that. *My* lawyers'll know how to handle this kind of shit. But we got no time now. We've got someplace to go. Should already be there."

"I don't think you'll be going anywhere."

"Yeah, well. We're leaving." Moria dismissed him with a wave of his hand, stepped around to the passenger side, opened the door. "Send me a bill. Add a couple days' lease on the wheels."

"Mr. Lovell?" the man turned to Eddy, crossed toward the car. Moria eased into the passenger side. "Mr. Lovell?" the man repeated. "I'm sorry. We really haven't been introduced. My name is Jensen, Mitchell Jensen." He stuck out his hand.

Eddy stepped back slightly. "I think we met before." Jensen smiled.

Moria stepped out of the car. "What the fuck? Isn't he your *lawyer*?"

Eddy shook his head, looked at Jensen's plastic smile. "I don't think he's anybody's lawyer."

"*You* didn't call him?" Moria demanded.

Eddy continued to ignore the offered palm. It dropped. "I hope this doesn't indicate a racial prejudice, Mr. Lovell."

"I'm just careful who I get close to," Eddy said. Moria stared at him. Eddy's eyes swept the parking lot, the street. Jensen maintained his smile.

"Mr. Lovell, I think it's time we had a talk."

"I got nothing to say to you," Eddy growled. Moria was gape-mouthed. Jensen stood still, neat and cool in the steaming atmosphere. But there was an odor about him: danger. Eddy tensed. "Who the fuck are you?" he whispered. "What do you want?"

"Mr. Lovell, Mr. Mendle, please." Jensen stepped closer and turned slightly so Moria could see when he opened his coat. The butt of a Desert Eagle .357 rode easy in an underarm holster. Eddy was shocked. He had worn the pistol through the whole procedure inside. That was more than risky: stupid. How the hell did he get it through the metal detectors? "I assure you, I mean you no harm." Eddy doubted that.

Moria also saw the pistol, slapped his hand on the Mercedes's roof. "Jesus Christ! We're right in front of the fucking police station! Call a cop!"

"Mr. Mendle," Jensen said, his face, eyes now formed into a mask: deadly. "Please keep your voice down. At this moment a high-powered rifle is aimed directly at your head. One more loud word, and your skull and its contents will simply vanish. No one will hear a thing."

Moria turned, scanned the buildings behind him, the parking lots, the shrubs and trees: nothing. "You're bluffing." But he lowered his voice.

"I assure you, I am not. My associate has you in the crosshairs at this moment. You might be interested to know it's an experimental rifle. Israeli design: antiterrorist. Only four kilos fully loaded with a nine-round magazine, twelve millimeter, built in miniscope, infrared, laser-guided, and absolutely silent without the benefit of some cumbersome noise-suppression device. Accurate to within six millimeters at five hundred meters.''

He held up his hand, flat to the buildings opposite. Eddy saw a pencil point of scarlet light on the exact middle of his palm, tracing his lifeline.

''Amazing, really,'' Jensen continued. The point of light disappeared. ''Oh, and the ammunition is also experimental. At present, it's loaded with a special antipersonnel cartridge. The actual projectile contains highly compressed amounts of an exceedingly volatile explosive. Also amazing. If the rifleman is good, he can completely destroy—'vaporize' is the correct word, but I hate to be dramatic—a human body with carefully spaced hits.''

Jensen's eyes slanted to HPD Headquarters. ''It also works wonders on gasoline tanks, hot water heaters, other explosive appliances as one might find in a commercial restaurant. Wouldn't you say?'' Another smile. ''So please disregard any plans you have to overpower me or escape.''

He stepped back, buttoned his coat. ''My personal sidearm is also available to me. It's very light-weight in spite of its size. A special synthetic alloy, undetectable by conventional devices. Also experimental. And while it's neither so powerful or so accurate as the long arm, it's equally deadly. I qualify as Expert with it. So I suggest you join me. We shall take a little ride, have a little talk. Mr. Mendle, if you please.''

''Shit,'' Moria said.

''If you please, Mr. Mendle.'' Jensen's smile turned down: serious.

''Aw, fuck,'' Moria said. His face fixed with anger, he scooted into the front seat.

16
Blackie

The battered Volvo station wagon groaned through a heavy dust storm into the parking lot of Sarge's Liquor, Beer, Wine— Checks Cashed! on the western outskirts of El Paso, Texas. Dark blue exhaust trailed from the tailpipe, evaporated into the wind that raced across Interstate 10.

Most of the way since Las Cruces, the boxy vehicle was blown along more by high winds than engine speed. A biting norther pushed the gale, gusted past sixty, carried cutting sand, dust, and bits of desert flora on its chilly blast. It howled, obscured sound outside the car.

Vicki slumped against the back seat passenger door, groggy with fatigue. Her anxieties took on the smooth texture of worn cloth. Only half aware the car had stopped, she didn't care what happened next. She only had one thought: a bath. It was a growing fantasy. Bigger than rescue. Rescue had deteriorated in her imagination to only a vague hope.

Rescue was a scene she saw in a movie once. A bath she could visualize.

"Wha'd'you think?" Al's voice half-whispered. There was an edge to the atmosphere: cold and wet, incongruous with the desert landscape. In the distance, the Franklin Mountains loomed over the city. Mexico was in sight across the river beneath an airborne layer of yellow dirt.

"I think this weather sucks," Blackie said. "This whole thing sucks."

"You suck," Al said. "I wasn't talking to you. Red?"

"It's your show," Red replied. He sagged low in the seat. "We need new wheels. Need to move." He shrugged. "You're driving. I'm back here with the baggage."

Vicki automatically resented being called "baggage." She started to say something, decided she didn't care, closed her eyes.

Al wiped her mouth with her stubby, tobacco-stained fingers. "Yeah." Parked nose-in on the side of the white stucco building was a burgundy minivan. "I'd say that Ford's the best ticket."

Blackie raised up, looked over the Volvo's dash. "A minivan?"

"You see anything else?"

A Toyota pickup and Nissan Maxima shared the other end of the parking lot. Neither would hold the entire group. Blackie sighed, shook his head.

"What's the deal?" Red asked.

Silence. The Volvo idled raggedly. The tech's needle kept swinging up and down. To the east of Las Cruces, a banging erupted from the engine, then the whole car stopped. It took an hour to start it again. Blue smoke belched out of it every time Al shifted.

"I have a thought," Professor Kingston piped up.

Vicki turned her face toward him. He hadn't said a word in miles, hours. He had just sat, sweated, stared straight ahead. He also stank. Before it had just been a wisp of body odor emanating from his salt-caked shirt. Now, it reeked, filled the car, more since the wind closed them in, made the interior closer, dank.

What had Darla seen in him anyway? she wondered. The image of the girl fallen, bleeding into the sandy mud filled her mind momentarily, then blew away with the dusty wind. Another scene from another movie. She shrugged.

No one responded to Kingston's offer: tacit approval. He ran his tongue over his chapped, scabbed lips, continued. "I would be more than happy to volunteer to go inside, find out who is driving the van, then tell them that they have no choice but to let you have it."

"What?" Al snickered.

"I'm sure I could do it," Kingston said. His voice was level, confident. "You have guns, knives. I've seen what you can do. Whoever owns that van would see reason. I know it. They wouldn't want to get hurt or—" He broke off.

"Or what?" Al laughed.

"Or—" Kingston's eyes raced around the Volvo, sought help.

"Or killed," Vicki said. Her voice was choked, throat dry. She swallowed dust, went on. "He knows what a bunch of lunatics you are, so he could warn them that you're going to kill them."

"Shut up, Barbara," Red said quietly.

"Give me a cigarette," Vicki responded. Red hesitated, then reached for a pack in his pocket. He shook one out and leaned across Kingston to light it for her. She felt lower than ever before: ready to die. Taking up an old habit seemed the exact thing to do. She drew in the smoke, cracked the window, noting Red's eye on her, making sure that was all she was doing. She blew the smoke out the opening.

"Well, we just going to sit here all day or what?" Blackie snarled. "I think we just need to go. Take the fucking Ford. Boost it, if that's what you want. I'd hold out for a better set of wheels, though."

As if responding to his wishes, a new midnight-blue Suburban turned in, pulled past them, made a wide swing, parked next to the minivan. They all gaped at it. "Man, he's got TV in that fucker," Blackie said. He sat up, put one hand on the door, drew out the SIG.

"Cool it," Al said. "Let them get inside. I can wire that turkey in a heartbeat."

A man—late fifties, small goatee, jeans and boots, no hat over his silver hair—got out, fought the wind toward the door of the liquor store. There, he stopped, took thought, glanced at the Volvo, then pointed his key ring at the Chevy. Headlights flashed, the alarm was armed.

" 'I can wire that turkey in a heartbeat,' " Blackie mimicked, slumped back. "Shit."

"I could still take him," Al suggested.

"Not out here," Red said. He glanced at the access road behind them. Rush-hour traffic was building. The man opened the door of the liquor store wide, allowed another man to come out, sack in hand. He got into the Ford, started up, pushed out against the wind.

"That cuts it down," Al said. "I say we go for the Suburban."

"Wait till he comes out? Grab him?"

"Shit, no," Al barked. "We got enough fucking hostages. I'm bored with Teach, though."

"And he stinks," Red said.

Vicki looked up, startled. She thought she was the only one who noticed. Incredibly, Kingston started sweating anew. A brine delta marked the side of his face. She started to agree with Red, then stopped herself. Why should she care? Whose side was she on, anyway?

"Mine," a voice inside her answered. She had better be on her own side.

Al eased the Volvo into a slot just off the storefront window: right angle to the Suburban, killed the engine. It coughed, dieseled, gave it up.

"We'll go inside, grab the keys, be out in a flash," she said. "What're you drinking?" Red shrugged, looked out the window. "Okay, me and Blackie. Hold the fort. This time, try to keep an eye on things. Anybody pulls up looks like we can't handle, honk or something."

Red nodded. "Try not to fuck it up."

"Fat chance," Vicki said.

Al hesitated, took a breath. "This ain't in the plan. But we got no fucking money, this car's for shit. I'm crashing, and you boys've looked better. We're okay for time—got till tomorrow—but we need to get off the road, and we need wheels to get back on. This place's good as any."

"So?" Red said, impatient. "Take the keys, grab some cash, let's split."

Al didn't move. She sighed. "It ain't *your* ass. Is it? Sometimes, these joints got hotshots running them, sometimes hot-shots got guns.''

"We got guns.''

"Right,'' Al said. She sat still, her hands gripping the Volvo's wheel.

Vicki studied her, stunned. Al was afraid.

"Anything goes bad, you whack Teach here. Get Prom Queen, haul ass. We'll catch up. Make sure she stays healthy.''

"Gotcha,'' Red said, bored.

"Let's do it.''

She picked up the shotgun from the front floorboard, looked at Blackie, who was now holding the dead trooper's shotgun, had the cop's SIG Sauer in his belt. She nodded, pulled the handle on her door, when Kingston spoke up again.

"I don't think you've thought this through.''

His voice was still strong, but panic trembled beneath the words.

"What is it, Teach?'' The old Al, but relieved, glad for the delay.

"You'll have to pardon me for saying it this way,'' Kingston started.

"What the fuck's he talking about?'' Blackie demanded. Red and Vicki looked at him. "That guy's going to be back out here in a sec.''

"Listen,'' he said. "Please don't take offense, but you two go in there, looking like that, and the owner—the 'hotshot,' as you call him. He'll hit an alarm button—if he has one—as soon as he sees you.''

"Looking like what?'' Blackie demanded. But Al turned around and looked at Kingston. The fear was gone, but Vicki saw something else behind her small, mean eyes: understanding. And growing anger.

"Well,'' Kingston licked his lips, now bloody from chap and a raw, dry tongue. "Look at you. I mean you, uh. . . sir,'' he lifted his hand in Blackie's direction. "You've been bleeding.''

"Yeah, well, your little Kung Fu pussy had something to do with that.'' Blackie touched his broken nose, battered jaw.

"Nevertheless, the first thing anyone's going to do is notice you. Then, they'll see your. . . uh, weapons. Then. . .'' he trailed off, his hands open in helplessness.

Blackie snorted, didn't disagree.

"And you," Kingston took a breath, relieved: still talking. He looked at Al. "Forgive me, really. But you don't look exactly like the average weeknight customer. You're dressed—"

"What the hell?" Al scowled at him, glanced down at her biker clothes. "These are my fucking *colors,* man! Nobody fucks with my fucking colors—" She reached across and grabbed Kingston's shirt, bunched its sweat-dampened fabric in a fist and pulling him forward. "I've hurt people *bad* for saying something about my fucking colors!"

Kingston's face blanched. His eyes went wide, white behind his glasses. His mouth opened, moved, but he didn't say anything.

Al wrenched Kingston forward, smashed his face on the car's bench seat. Blood ran from his nose. "Now *you're* fucking bleeding, man," she said. "Now *you're* the one who's had a fucking accident." Fresh odor permeated the car's interior, urine: hot. Vicki gagged, choked.

Al shoved him backwards. "Watch him," she said. To Blackie: "Let's go."

"He's right, you know," Vicki said. She clenched her fists, swallowed her nausea.

"What?" Al spun around in the seat, knuckles ready.

Vicki swallowed again, slipped her cigarette butt out the window: casual, unconcerned. Inside: boiling. She forced a shrug. "I don't care what color you think you are. You go in there carrying guns, and anybody seeing you is going to start screaming bloody murder soon as you're inside the door."

"Well, fuck me!" Al laughed. "Now, Prom Queen's going to give me advice. Tell me, Queenie, just how do you hold up a liquor store?"

Vicki sorted quickly through what she felt. Just a numbness, a quiet numbness. "I personally don't give a shit what you do. Nothing would please me more than for you to bring every cop in Texas right here, right now. But him—" She looked at Kingston, wrinkled her nose. "He stinks. He's peed all over himself. I will not go another mile sitting next to a walking toilet.''

Al, Red, and Blackie all looked at Kingston's soaked crotch. "I'll be damned," Al said.

"I can't stand it anymore."

"Tough shit," Blackie said.

"Take him with you," Vicki said: an order. "I'm telling you. I'm *not* sitting next to him." She glanced at Kingston, who stared straight ahead: deer in the headlights. Blood leaked out of both nostrils, streamed over his lips. He shook all over. "Take him, leave him. I want him out of here. Now."

"You're nuts. C'mon."

"Wait," Red spoke up. "She's right."

"You, too?"

"Yeah," he said. "Me fucking too. She's right. He stinks like a goddamn bus station, and he's scared shitless or we'd be up to our necks in that, too. I'd just as soon nobody else gets killed on this shift. But if somebody has to fall, may as well be him. You and Butthead go in there like goddamn Bonnie and Clyde, the hotshot's going to start blasting. This asshole'll make a good target." Red nodded at Kingston. "You said he was our insurance, a hostage. Take him, use him. Get us some decent wheels and leave the son of a bitch inside. I don't want to look at him anymore."

"Do I geb a vote ib dis?" Kingston asked, blood bubbling fresh out of his nostrils.

"Shut up," Al ordered. She looked at Red for a long moment. "All right," she said. "C'mon. But you give me one ounce of trouble, Teach, you're dead. That's Lesson One."

Every Thursday afternoon for more than six years, Lieutenant Colonel Beryl T. Raymond, USA (Ret), drove in from his ranch on the Texas-New Mexico border some thirty miles north of the El Paso city limits to chew the fat with Sergeant Major Raymond O'Leary, also USA (Ret), owner-proprietor of Sarge's Liquor, Beer, Wine—Checks Cashed!—Sarge's for short. They had much besides the military in common: both loved the desert, both were widowed, both were making prosperous post-career careers doing precisely what they wanted to do. Colonel Raymond raised goats for fun and profit. Sergeant O'Leary ran his own business. Life after sixty was very good.

At the same hour every Thursday, Colonel Raymond entered Sarge's, went to the cooler, pulled out a can of Foster's Ale, opened it, sat at a card table next to the counter in perfect violation of Texas State liquor laws, drank it while he shot the shit with Sarge. If no other customers were present, Sarge picked out a cold one for himself, joined in an illegal brewsky with the only brass hat he ever liked.

That afternoon, their usual confab was delayed by a middle-aged Hispanic woman, shopping for a cash-bar reception. She was in the back, collecting mixers to add to a collection of bottles of whiskey, gin, and vodka she had toted to the counter in front of Sarge. She had no idea what she was doing.

"What kind of mixers do you carry?" she called from the back.

"Tonic, maybe some sweet soda. 7-Up.," Sarge replied with a wink at the Colonel. "Some people use fruit."

"Fruit?"

"Lime and lemon."

"Do you sell those?"

"You'll have to get those at the supermarket."

The door blew open. Al, Blackie, and Professor Kingston came in on a gust of moist dirty air. Sarge only glanced at them, scowled at their scruffy appearance, at Kingston's bloody face. The Colonel immediately spotted the long weapons dangling in their hands.

"Stickup," he announced: matter-of-fact. Sarge's head swiveled toward the door.

The Colonel jumped to his feet, turned the card table over, spilled the remains of his Foster's, ducked for cover. Al blasted the table. The Colonel caught a load of double-ought in his shoulder and arm, rolled to his right. The woman emerged from an aisle with several large bottles of tonic and Sprite, which she dropped, broke, allowed to spew. She looked at the guns, the blood spurting from the Colonel, screamed.

"Shut the fuck up!" Al yelled at her. She pushed Kingston forward in front of her, kept him between her and Sarge, who remained behind the counter, at-ease, calculator in hand. Kingston bumped into a cardboard cutout of Troy Aikman in his best quarterback form, arm cocked for a long pass. Blackie raced over and covered the Colonel. He scrunched beside a stack of beer cases, clutching his shredded arm to his body, his face clouded.

The woman's screams continued: no breath. Al walked over, slapped her with the barrel of the shotgun. She dropped to the floor.

"This is a robbery," Blackie said, panted, glared at Sarge. Kingston stood as still as Aikman's likeness. "We don't want to hurt nobody."

"No shit?" Sarge growled.

"Shut up," Al ordered, went to the counter, looked down at the woman's chosen goods, swept them off onto the floor. "You got an alarm?"

"Goddamn right I have an alarm," Sarge said. "What you think? I'm stupid? This is El Paso! That's Mexico across the river." He met Al's gaze evenly. "You a man or a woman?"

Al stopped. "What the fuck's that supposed to mean?"

"I just want to know for the description I'm going to give the cops. Don't want them shooting some other butt-ugly shit-for-brains thinking he's you."

Al grinned. "Whoo! This one's got a mouth and a half. I like that, sugar plum. What you say you and me get down. I like it doggie-style. How 'bout you?"

Sarge held his at-ease posture, "I wouldn't fuck you with a rusty pipe," he said.

Al lifted the shotgun, pulled the trigger. The blast threw Sarge backwards into the shelf of half-pints, a scarlet tear opened across his white shirt. Light left his eyes before his body slid to the floor.

"Shit," Blackie said through the gray-blue smoke that filled the room. "Why'd you do that?" Al was silent, her face closed, dark.

The Colonel moaned. "Son of a bitch," he said. Blood squirted from his lacerated arm. "You didn't have to kill anybody."

"We want the keys to your car. The Suburban," Blackie said.

"Fuck you," the Colonel said through clenched teeth.

Blackie poked the wounded arm with the barrel of the shotgun. The older man cried out. "Look, old man," he said. "You can see we ain't fucking around. We want the keys to the Suburban. Now."

"Kiss my ass," the Colonel groaned.

He tried to pull his feet under him, but Blackie knocked him backwards. "Stay down, old man. Give me the keys."

"Up yours," the Colonel replied.

"Here," Al said impatiently. She came over, clipped the Colonel on the jaw with the butt of her shotgun. He went prone, she rolled him over, fished around in his pockets. "Man, he's got a whang on him," she said, digging deep into the Colonel's khaki trousers. "Too bad we ain't got time to play."

Blackie moved away, eyed Kingston: hadn't moved. The professor's eyes were wide, blank. "Go back there and get the fucking money out of the register." Kingston stood still, didn't look at him. "I said *move,* motherfucker!" Blackie yelled in the professor's ear. Kingston's feet began to shuffle as he slid slowly around the counter. "Open the goddamn register and get the fucking money. Put it in a sack or something."

Kingston stood behind the counter. Blackie went to a display of potato chips, beef jerky, other snacks, grabbed a handful. "While you're back there, get me a sack, too. We've got to eat, or I'm fucked." He dumped several packages of food onto the counter. Kingston was now standing, still as before, right behind the register, his feet in between Sarge's splayed legs. Blackie raised his shotgun with one hand, fired just to the right of Kingston's head.

Bottles smashed, splashing Kingston with broken glass, liquor. Kingston didn't move. His eyes only blinked with the noise. Otherwise, no movement.

"Get a fucking sack," Blackie said slowly, as if Kingston were a child. "Open the fucking register, and bag up the money. Then get another sack, and fill it with the fucking food. You got that, fuckhead?"

Al stood in triumph, dangling a set of keys with a car alarm remote on it. "Got 'em." She looked at Kingston. "I thought he told you to move!"

Dumbly, Kingston opened the register, took a brown paper bag, began shoving in wads of bills and coins.

Al picked out three large bottles of premium bourbon. "Put those in, too." To Blackie: "Want some beer?"

Blackie didn't respond. He had found a long cooler containing packaged meats and cheeses. He lay his long weapon down, carried armloads up to the counter. "We're going to get something to eat out of this deal. Swear to God!"

"You're a pain in the ass," Al said.

"Fuck you." He went back for a second load. "I been hungry since we started this. I want to eat. You may go on cigarettes and spit, but I need to fucking eat!"

Al went for another bottle. The woman, forgotten on the floor, came to, rose to her feet. She staggered a bit, dazed, looked around, opened her mouth, tore out a louder scream than before. Al's head snapped around. "Jesus Fucking Christ!" Her arms were laden with a case of beer, shotgun held tight under her arm. "Shut that down!"

Blackie stopped rummaging in the cooler, looked up. "Goddamnit," he swore. "I hate this shit." He looked at his own weapon two feet away, shrugged, pulled the black automatic from his belt. He stuck out his tongue slightly, took aim at the screaming woman. "I hate to do this, lady."

A small red hole appeared just over his left eyebrow. The back of his head opened, most of his brain flew out. His knees buckled, folded, he slumped to the floor.

Al gaped at him, then she identified the noise that reached her over the woman's shrill screams: sliced through her ear like an icepick. She spun around, still held the beer, spotted Kingston, a .44 Magnum revolver in his hand: three-point stance. A perfect blue circle of smoke formed over the pistol. His thumb went up, aired back the hammer as he made a slow rotating turn toward Al. She dropped the beer. Kingston fired. She dropped to the floor. Kingston's bullet tore into the open mouth of the woman, ricocheted off a solid gold tooth, then sliced down, into her throat and out between her shoulder blades, sprayed Sarge's display of fine aperitifs with blood.

"Thanks, Teach," Al huffed. "Bitch was driving me crazy."
Kingston fired again.

Al stayed down, slipped in the mixture of gore, spewed soda
and booze covering the space in front of the counter. The
Colonel reached out, kicked the shotgun. It skittered away.
Kingston continued to rotate a few degrees, fired in single,
measured shots, each one tearing through glass and alcohol.

"Goddamn, Teach!" she yelled, scrambling out of his sight
line, enduring the shower of sticky liquor he brought down on
her. "That's some shooting! Regular Dirty Fucking Harry!"
She slowly counted, moving her lips: three, four, five, six. She
heard the empty click of the hammer on an empty casing.

Kingston also heard it. His eyes blinked, came to. He dropped
behind the counter, shoved Sarge's body off to one side, scrambled away. Al pulled herself erect, brushed wet, broken glass
from her clothing. She went over, looked down at Blackie's
body. The back of his head was ripped as if a bomb had gone
off inside. Jagged pieces of skull and hair smashed open on
the floor beneath sharp edges of bone.

"Shit," Al sighed. "Red's gonna be pissed off about this."
She turned, found the shotgun, checked the load. "Hey, Teach?
Where are you? We got a final exam to take." She started for
the counter.

She stopped, tilted her head when a new sound came to her
ears: sirens. They were distant, growing closer. "Just like the
old fart to hit a silent alarm," she muttered. "Can't trust nobody
these days."

She went to the glass door, looked out. Traffic snarled on
the access road. "Didn't count on rush hour," she said. Large
raindrops spattered against the building, wind raked the parking
lot with muddy grit. "Or a storm."

She wandered back to the counter, grabbed a bottle of bourbon, opened it. She tilted it, drank, let the whiskey run down
her fat chins and onto the front of her shirt.

"Let me have a shot of that?" the Colonel asked. He had
found a sitting position, leaned against a stack of beer cases.
Blood spilled out of his shoulder. Only gore-greasy threads of
skin and muscle remained of his arm.

Al stepped over to him, careful of the slick floor. "I swear," she said, "you two guys got more balls than any bull biker I ever met."

"Yeah, well." The Colonel accepted the bottle from her in blood-stained fingers, tilted it up. He swallowed twice, then again. "Jesus," he gasped. "This is sorry whiskey." He took another swig anyway, handed it back.

"Keep it," she said, grinning. "You're dead, anyway."

"Don't count on it," he growled. "Hell, I've hiked forty miles of hills hurt worse than this: full pack." He drank again. "Wish you hadn't killed that son of a bitch," he said. "Best goddamn noncom I ever met." His eyes glazed, rolled. He fought for consciousness. "Used to—" He stopped, stared, died.

"Hey, Teach," Al yelled, "you coming?" She waited a beat, listened again, grabbed the automatic from Blackie's dead hand, stuffed it into her belt. She picked up the sack on the counter, grabbed a bottle of tequila, went for the door into the howling wind and mounting thunderstorm.

Vicki saw Al, and held her breath. Red sat behind the wheel of the Volvo, and she once again wore the handcuffs: right ankle to left wrist. The motor was running. It took almost the whole time for Red to start it. From where they parked, no part of the inside of the store was visible. She heard the muted thunder of gunfire over the wind. First the thumps of the shotguns, then the sharper, higher pitched cracks of a pistol: hope.

She waited, chewed her raw lip. Fatigue forgotten, she now wanted cops, sirens, flashing lights. Her fingernails cut into the palms of her hands. She wanted someone—anyone—to come rushing out, save her. *Bonnie and Clyde,* she thought. No. She didn't want that kind of final scene. Too dangerous. *The Getaway?* No. They got away. *Chinatown.* Yeah. That'd do. One shot and Faye Dunaway was dead. Risky, but one well-placed shot. It worked.

She looked around. Reality: they could shoot the tires off the Volvo, she imagined. They could come and wrench her door open, pull her out, kill Red. She wanted Red to die. The thought shocked her.

She looked at her captor. His chewed fingers pressed white on the wheel, his teeth clenched behind a grim expression, muscles of his jaw flexed. "C'mon, c'mon," he breathed. Then, from far off, she heard the siren. At last, she thought.

Al burst out into the storm, pointed toward the Suburban, yelled something that tore away in the wet wind. She raced past the front of the station wagon, waved her shotgun for them to follow. She keyed the alarm and ran around to the driver's side.

"Let's go." Red killed the Volvo. Vicki didn't move. He unlocked the cuffs, opened his door, looked at her, sighed. "I said, move." She stayed still. He pulled the .22 up from his lap. "Don't make me hit you again," he said. "Don't make me hurt you."

"Why?" Vicki asked. "You falling in love with me?"

Red's eyes were bloodshot. Orange stubble creased his chin. No angel here, she thought. She could smell his breath: tobacco and fatigue, rot. "Just move," he said. "Move, goddamnit. I'm out of threats."

She studied him, decided, opened her door, stepped out. The wind tore her, filled her eyes with dust. Cold rain matted her hair to her forehead. He came up right behind her, pushed her forward.

They piled into the Suburban. Red took the middle seat, Vicki the back. She looked at the twin rear doors, but before she could think about possibilities, Al fired the engine. Red's door wasn't quite closed when she peeled out backwards, shifted down, headed for the access road.

"Where is he?" Red asked. Al ignored him. "Where is he?"

Red looked back, Vicki joined him. Traffic was heavy. They had to wait. Seconds ticked. Vicki planned to see red police lights at any second. An odor struck her senses. It was sweet, cloying, vaguely fruity. But there was another odor, stronger. Vicki recognized it. She had tasted it enough lately: blood.

"Where the fuck is he?" Red asked again.

Al said nothing, just patted the steering wheel with her fat fingers.

"Where is he?" he demanded again. "Ain't he coming?"

She looked intently at the slow-moving cars. "Didn't make it."

"Didn't make it? What the fuck's that supposed to mean?"

She peeled into traffic, narrowly missed a concrete truck, then fishtailed, straightened out, floored it around cursing commuters.

"Teach took him out," Al said, sighed. "Twinky little son of a bitch had more balls than we thought."

"Shit!" Red swore. "Shit, shit! I knew that was fucked."

"Better shot, too," Al concluded, chuckled.

Just before they pulled around a curve in the road, Vicki spotted Kingston standing in the parking lot, pistol in hand: helpless. Al found the entrance ramp, pushed them into the fast lane, weaved through traffic. When it was clear ahead, she sat back, eased back under the limit. Her face was grim in the rearview, creased. Vicki shuddered. She felt sad, couldn't say why. Should be triumphant. Blackie was dead.

Then she knew: Kingston. He was free. She was still a prisoner, a prisoner of killer-assholes.

Red slumped down, rubbed the bridge of his nose. "Knew this was fucked," he said. "Knew it. Knew it!"

As they sped down the interstate, Vicki finally saw her flashing lights. They penetrated the fading sunset's filtered rays as they sliced through the blowing, blinding dust like sharp points, almost lasers, red and blue and white.

They were on an ambulance, not a police car. They screamed past her, beyond the median barrier, flickered through the chain link, passed rapidly through the heavy five o'clock traffic moving city workers out to suburban homes, far from the dirt, grime, crime of the inner city. She watched them until they completely faded away into the dusty, rain-splattered, wind-blown southwestern desert, and night closed around them.

17
Jensen

It was full dark when Eddy pulled Jensen's black Mercedes into the parking lot of the Medical Arms Pavilion. He got out, preceded Moria and the black man into the lobby, onto the elevator. Jensen dictated their destination. All the way from HPD they were tailed by the familiar blue Chevy van. It pulled in behind them. A small, wiry man emerged from behind the wheel. From the rear came the same Arabic-looking guy Eddy saw in Pap's that morning. No surprise there, Eddy thought. The duo fell in behind them, they passed through the lobby. But they took a separate elevator, already knew the floor.

They passed the same security guard from the night before. He gave Moria a smart salute, waited for another tip: nothing. Eddy gave a long look to the old geezer's rusty .38. He saw the Arab, saw his companion see the look. He moved ahead, quiet.

When they reached the room, it smelled of cold pizza, cheap perfume, stale sex. Moria and Eddy were instructed to sit. Jensen's companions positioned themselves with care. The thin one removed a Desert Eagle of his own from his coat, smiled. The Arab, casual, played with a knife. Jensen went to the bar and made himself a drink: sparkling water and ice.

"I'll have a beer," Moria said, jovially. "Seems like the thing to do." It was his first utterance since leaving HPD.

Jensen nodded, obliged. He brought the Löwenbräu over to the short man, almost in the manner of a butler. "Oh, I'm being rude," he said. "Anything for you, Mr. Lovell?" Eddy shook his head. Moria's eyes never left Jensen.

"Let me introduce my associates. This," Jensen indicated the Arab, "is Mr. Fizer. And he," indicating the smaller man, "you may call Robin."

"Does that make you Batman?" Eddy asked.

Jensen smiled. "In a manner of speaking, you might say so." He extracted a long cigar, unwrapped it slow. "I tend to show up at the first sign of trouble."

"You hang by your heels and shit on the floor?" Moria asked.

"Let's just say I never fly blind," Jensen came back.

Jensen returned to his drink, took it to a chair, sipped and watched them with amusement. He extracted his pistol from his coat, a silencer from his pocket, began screwing it onto the barrel. Execution, Eddy thought. "So," he said, "at last we meet."

"I don't know whether to thank you or fuck you up," Moria said.

Jensen glanced at Robin. "Under the circumstances, I think a thank you would be in order. You could be eating prison dinner at the moment."

"Who are you?" Eddy asked.

"I'm a lot of things," Jensen said. "In a way, I can be whoever I choose to be." He smiled. "I can be your friend as well. If you cooperate."

"I choose my own friends," Eddy said.

"Your associate, then."

"Fuck you," Moria said, sipped his beer. "Why don't you just lay it out? Speak your piece, get out of here."

"Mr. Mendle," Jensen said, weary. "You are no longer important to me. Your principal value was to deliver what is important to me: Mr. Lovell."

Moria looked at Eddy. "There he is. Have fun. Can I watch?"

Jensen smiled again, turned his body to completely face

Eddy, studied him, lit the cigar. "Mr. Lovell's whereabouts are of supreme interest to me."

Moria's eyes sparked. "What kind of interest?"

"Monetary," Jensen said. "That's the only kind that has ever appealed to you, isn't that correct?"

Moria looked at Eddy. "He doesn't have a pot to piss in."

"No," Jensen nodded. "But he has something I want. He will give it to me, and he will profit, and so shall you, for your service. If he refuses, he will suffer, and so shall you, for his lack of cooperation."

"What do I have?" Eddy asked.

Jensen cleared his throat. "Recently, you met with an old partner of yours, Raul Castillo. Correct?"

Eddy now knew where he had seen Jensen before: Dallas. The cigar, the nice suit. He was the guy in the VW Golf, the guy who had pulled in when he was talking to Raul, the same guy who sat outside the hotel and waited all night after Raul left. Something ugly and dark crawled up Eddy's back.

"You can deny it if you wish," Jensen went on. "But I was there. I saw you talking, and I believe there was an exchange of some sort."

Eddy conjured Raul's frightened face before him. "You want to call it that. I gave him a couple bucks."

"I *do* want to call it that. At the time, I couldn't imagine him parting with the only thing that was keeping him alive. But he did. Apparently." Eddy shrugged. "Exactly what did Mr. Castillo give you?"

"A hard time," Eddy said. His mind shot to Dallas, ricocheted off the fourth floor of the Sheraton, then beelined to California: Barbara. He glanced at Moria, who seemed bored. Careful, Eddy thought. "I gave him a couple of yards," he admitted.

"Come, come, Mr. Lovell," Jensen said. "Mr. Castillo passed to you a briefcase. Correct again?" Eddy said nothing. "A briefcase you had been an accomplice in stealing." He rolled the cigar in his mouth. "Inside that briefcase were some compact discs. Two, to be precise. So, what I want is really very simple. I want that briefcase. Actually, I want those CDs."

"Nothing on them," Eddy said. Should he admit he no

longer had them? Or was the prospect of having them all that kept him alive?

Jensen's eyebrows shot up. "Oh, that's where you're wrong, Mr. Lovell. There was a great deal on them."

"What?" Moria put in. "The Supremes' greatest hits?"

Jensen's eyes stayed on Eddy. "Hardly."

"What the fuck's going on?" Moria now was angry in a different way, different direction: Eddy. "You working some deal on the side? You know I—"

"Nothing of the kind," Jensen interrupted. "This is old business." He sipped his water, sat back. "A few years ago, Mr. Lovell here was involved in an armed robbery, supposedly of a Purolator van."

"Yeah, so what? I know that."

"The briefcase was the item taken from the van, for which Mr. Lovell here received not only a bullet through a kidney, but also a prison sentence—lucky you weren't charged with second-degree murder, Mr. Lovell. That was the plan, after all: to leave you with the entire blame. Mr. Castillo set you up, you know. He, in turn, was set up by your brother."

Eddy winced. "My brother? What does—"

Jensen waved the cigar, dismissing. "It's not important. What's important is that Mr. Castillo gave you the same brief-case, those same CDs. Correct?" Eddy stared at him: poker face. Jensen smiled, continued: "Things went awry. Mr. Castillo wound up in possession of this singular item and its contents."

"You mean all they got was some music?" Moria laughed.

"No, not music," Jensen said. "Hardly that. What they 'got' was information." He sighed: patronizing. "A computer program, to be exact. A golden version of a highly sophisticated program. Very sensitive, very secret." He smoked, examined the cigar's tip.

"A computer game? Big fucking deal."

"Hardly a game, Mr. Mendle. This was a program, an application. It took a team of top experts nearly a decade to develop it."

"Bigger fucking deal."

Jensen frowned. "Their records and processes are on one of

the discs. The program itself is on the other. Both are necessary in order to access the information they can provide.''

Moria no longer laughed. ''What kind of information? What are you, some kind of spy?''

''That's not your concern. But it is mine. As I said, Alpha and Beta versions of the program had been transported for months along that route. Taken for testing, then returned. No problem. No reason to suspect that this time would be different.''

''But it was,'' Eddy said. Jensen nodded. ''Dodd and Henderson,'' Eddy said. Jensen nodded. ''Double-cross,'' Eddy said.

Jensen nodded once more. ''And not the last, I'm afraid. All they were required to do was to acquire the briefcase, pass it to me, accept payment, and all would be well.''

''But they blew it?'' Moria asked.

Jensen nodded. ''They were a poor choice for this operation. A poor choice, indeed. I fear your brother had a hand in that, as well.''

''Quince?'' Eddy smiled. ''Quince couldn't steal a quarter from a telephone.''

''I have to agree with you. He's fundamentally inept. But what he could do was to put me in touch with those who could do the required work.''

Eddy shook his head. ''Bullshit. Quince's a big-time lawyer. He doesn't know that kind of people.''

''Your brother, alas, does know that kind of people.''

''Shylocks?''

''Precisely.'' He drew on the cigar. ''Some years ago, your brother came into a little money. Your parents were killed quite unexpectedly, I recall.''

''Not much money,'' Eddy said. ''The cut was small. Our old man was broke.''

''Not so broke,'' Jensen smiled. ''The estate came down to just short of three million dollars to be divided equally among you.''

''Bullshit,'' Eddy started. Then stopped. ''Take the money and run,'' Quince told him when he cut Eddy a small check, handed him the keys to the old Caddy. It was possible. Quince had screwed him before. So had Hillary. It was more than possible, Eddy concluded.

"Your brother has expensive tastes. Political ambitions. You recall he ran for state office. He spent—well, he threw away almost all of it."

"So?"

"So, he grew used to the lifestyle. Cars, multiple residences, fine clothing, lavish vacations, expensive gifts for his . . . lovers. He also grew used to blackmail."

"Shakedown?"

"Yes."

"So he blew it all."

"Every penny. And he borrowed. Heavily. At first from small-time moneylenders, then he moved out of town, sought new sources when the old ones became too burdensome—or too acrimonious—to manage. He went next to Dallas, found new sources to finance his secret life as well as his public image."

"Dodd and Henderson?" Eddy asked.

"Precisely. And one of their associates, a gentleman who provided some association for them: Robert Cole."

Moria sat up. "Cole? What's Cole to do with a couple of small-timers?"

"More than you might think, Mr. Mendle," Jensen smiled. "But that is all old business, as well. Messrs. Dodd and Henderson were inept at usury, as you learned all too well, Mr. Lovell. They were less well prepared for armed robbery. When they needed help, they turned to your brother, who sold them you to acquit his debts to them—and to Mr. Cole.

"That would have been the end of it, but Mr. Castillo unfortunately foiled their plans. He absconded with the briefcase and left them, as you know, holding the bag. Or, more precisely, holding no bag at all."

"So why didn't you handle it yourself, handle Raul, if you're so slick?" Eddy asked. "He wasn't hard to scare." That, Eddy thought, was the only fact he was sure of at the moment.

Jensen shrugged. "I couldn't. Not at that time. I was far too close to the matter to do more than suggest. And your brother insisted on a degree of discretion, relied completely on Mr.

Cole to handle Mr. Castillo until it became clear he could neither locate him nor deal with him. But again, we are mired in old business.

"The point is that the briefcase and its contents belong to us."

"And who is 'us'?" Moria asked. "Who the fuck are you? You haven't answered that question, yet."

"Suffice to say, Mr. Mendle, that that is none of your concern, either."

"All this for a computer program?" Eddy asked. He knew nothing about computers. To him, they mostly caused trouble.

Jensen smiled. "It's an action-data program. Interactive search and coordination. Something like scientists use to isolate specific DNA molecules, atomic clusters, things of that sort."

Eddy looked blank.

"This was the golden, the final version. The omega, if you will,"

Jensen said. "That program, in the right hands, could give an organization—or individual—almost godlike powers."

"Right. Like Space Invaders," Moria drank deeply from his beer. "Some fucking Nintendo game. Jesus. We can just pick up another one at WalMart."

"Hardly," Jensen said. "This program can give anyone the—well, the wherewithal to know everything there is to know. About everyone."

"Meaning what?"

"It means that with this program and a name, just a name, I can find out everything about anyone."

"Bullshit."

Jensen nodded. "Yes. That's appropriate, for that is all that's worth knowing about most people. But we are not interested in most people. We are interested in very special people."

"Such as?"

"International terrorists," Jensen said. "Organized crime bosses, headmen of drug cartels, or, perhaps, leaders of hostile states. For that matter, heads of our own state: governors, senators, congressmen, presidents. To say nothing of corporation heads, CEOs, union leaders. The world runs on information, Mr. Mendle. Knowledge is power. Power is, well, money."

Moria was listening now. "This program operates at such a high speed that within a matter of hours, for example, we can find out anything, no matter how confidential."

Moria chuckled, but less comfortably. "Like what?"

"Like PIN numbers, for example."

"So? What're you going to do, run up my long distance bill?"

"If used properly, this program can produce the account and PIN numbers of any individual. It will also deduce passwords."

Moria looked at Eddy, who shook his head. He had no idea what Jensen was talking about. "That, I know, is bullshit," Moria snorted.

"No," Jensen said. "Everything we do, not only in the way of business, but pleasure as well, becomes part of a numerical profile. We are born—birth date, size, weight, even hospital identification code. We grow up—social security number, credit card numbers, addresses, telephone numbers, insurance policy numbers, etcetera. All of this is really public information, unprotected, open to view. Businesses don't even protect it. Too many people need access to it. Credit card numbers are protected, of course, but anyone can break those down. Again, too many people need access to those data.

"That's why there are PIN numbers, passwords. For individual protection. If you have them, you feel safe. You made them up. Only you know them. But if we have some information, we can obtain more. The result is a complete profile of any individual: hobbies, proclivities, pastimes. With those data— and this program—we can deduce your most privately conceived secrets."

"So?"

"So, what if you have bank accounts in Switzerland or the Grand Caymans or anywhere? What if you have millions of dollars put away you would prefer no one else to know about? Particularly the IRS or your family? Well, in that case, all that's needed to break in is—"

"A PIN number," Moria said. "Like you said. Big deal. Nobody's going to put that kind of information on some fucking computer."

"Of course they do. Banks have records of all PIN num-

bers—they have to. How else would they know when to allow
anyone to have access? And they're on computers, and there's
access to them, but the security is too tight to break. That's
not the way to go. Bank records are accessed by computers,
and they, in turn, are protected by passwords of their own.
These are generated by other computers, and they change them
all the time.''

"I'm listening, Jensen."

"People—individuals—don't change passwords. Not routinely. They don't even write them down, particularly people
with something to hide. You, Mr. Mendle, are a prime example.
Most of your assets are hidden. Correct? Protected by PIN
numbers.''

"People don't put those things into computers, either.''

"They don't have to. If you have enough personal information, you can find a PIN number or a password.''

"You couldn't find mine. I don't care what kind of snooping
you're doing.''

"Oh?'' He reached into his coat pocket, produced a small
notebook, opened it. "You have—or had—an account at the
Mexican Federal Bank in Mexico *Banco Federale*, correct?''
Mendle stared at him. "At the time we ran your profile, you
had close to a half-million dollars on deposit there. That would
have been nearly three years ago. Your password to access that
account was ARAS213—the name of your late daughter spelled
backwards, if I'm not mistaken, along with the date of her
birth—March twelve—also backwards.''

"How?'' Mendle asked.

"Oh, that was easy. It was a demonstration to convince Mr.
Cole that our enterprise was worth his interest. Based on nothing
more than information he supplied us—none of it having to
do with your finances, I might note—we had your personal
password in fifteen minutes. It wasn't even a challenge.''

"I don't get it,'' Eddy said. "I don't see how some computer
can . . .''

"The program works like a huge mathematical vacuum.
It absorbs then reads a personal profile, digests everything,
matching telephone records, travel itineraries and the like,
where you most probably deposit your assets, then converts

the data to a series of numbers. It then tries them in various sequences until it finds the one that works.

"If you hadn't been so obvious as to use your daughter's name, it might have taken longer. You wouldn't be careless with that much money. But you don't want to forget your password. So you picked something you would never forget. Most everyone does. Dates, names, significant numbers such as golf handicaps or even shoe sizes."

Moria's face darkened. "So, Cole wanted my money. Wasn't satis—"

"Ah, no," Jensen interrupted. "Mr. Cole had no interest in your money. Nor, for that matter, do I. It's a paltry amount compared to what's at stake here, I assure you. We are talking about hundreds of millions of dollars, perhaps billions."

"Okay, you got lucky with me," Moria said. "But it could take forever to figure out somebody else's, somebody with that kind of cash."

"No. The program is trained to discard the obvious first. It works at a high rate of speed. It can dial a telephone number so rapidly that all you hear is a click." He snapped his fingers. "Shorter than that. A single click for an eleven-digit number. It can process over a hundred billion bytes of information in less than two hours. In a day or so at the most, it can come up with the proper codes and passwords to invade anyone's most private sanctuary."

"So you can find out my password. So you draw out a couple of thousand from somebody's ATM card?"

"It's bigger than that, Mr. Mendle," Jensen grinned. "Much bigger. Let's say we run a profile of a drug dealer who has millions stashed away in a bank in Rio. Let's say we come up with a PIN number and password for that account. We access his account by computer, arrange a wire transfer to our bank in, say, Tokyo. We handle the whole thing at midnight, Japanese time, so there won't even be a check or notification until the next morning, but then it's too late. We'll have moved the money again. It's gone. There's no paper trail."

Eddy began to see.

"It was developed, of course, for law enforcement. Originally,

Jensen said. "International law enforcement. The political possibilities, once they were obvious, moved it to top secret status and out of private hands. The Purolator truck was a ruse, a front. The men shot during the robbery were not, as you doubtlessly deduced, Mr. Lovell, actual guards."

"CIA?" Moria ventured.

Jensen shrugged, smiled. "If you like. Again, suffice it to say that there are many uses of such a program. The right people would be willing to do almost anything to obtain it. It really is a marvelous device."

"Slick," Moria said. He sipped his beer. Frowned, set it aside. "And you think Eddy has it?"

"I'm certain of it. Mr. Castillo did not have it when we . . interviewed him. The only other logical place is in Mr. Lovell's possession."

Eddy felt sweat building beneath his shirt. He again retrieved the mental picture of him packing a sock-wrapped pistol between the CDs into the battered briefcase, using it as a mailer, shipping it to California.

Barbara. Her face swam up in front of him. He'd put her in the middle of this.

"So you're not some kind of cop?" Eddy asked. His heart was thudding now.

Jensen laughed. The other two men in the room also laughed.

Eddy stopped listening. All he could think of was Barbara. Did she still have the case? Didn't matter. He wasn't telling this bozo squat. He figured he knew just how they had "interviewed" Raul. Thus far, Jensen had been cordial, almost friendly. But now, he turned his eyes on Eddy once more.

"There's a great deal at stake, here," Jensen said. "We have gone to a great deal of trouble to find out where those CDs are. After the robbery, Mr. Castillo disappeared utterly. We tried to reach him through his sister. No luck there."

"What did you do to her?" Eddy half rose in anger.

Jensen put up a hand. "Nothing to upset you. She had lost touch with her brother. We allowed her a small vacation to her homeland."

"Chicago?"

"Well, no," Jensen said. "A touch farther south than that. But she's not important."

"Not to you," Eddy growled.

"No one harmed her," Jensen said. "We merely talked with her, then moved her out of the way. She's in Mexico, I believe. Or possibly South America. I really do not recall. She is alive and living well."

Eddy wanted to believe that. "And Raul? He alive and well, too?"

"He proved more difficult. He was very good at hiding. We tried to reach him through every associate he ever had. No luck there, either. Then, he turned up on his own, trying to gather money together. Ironically, he planned to go to Mexico, as well. We knew it was only a matter of time before Mr. Castillo came to you, Mr. Lovell. And so he did. Indeed, you were the last person to see him before. . .before he met with an unfortunate accident of his own."

"Accident?" Eddy snapped. "You people are full of fucking accidents."

Robin, still in the corner, laughed softly.

"He could have saved himself a good deal of anxiety," Jensen said, "merely by turning them over to us. He knew we were looking for him. He knew how to contact us."

"Through Cole?"

"Through Mr. Lovell. The other Mr. Lovell. Your brother." Jensen smoked, thought. "But he ran. He was stupid."

"He wasn't stupid," Eddy said. *Yes, he was,* he thought.

"The only remaining question is, are you stupid? Where is the briefcase, Mr. Lovell? Where are the CDs?"

"Who iced Bob Cole?" Eddy asked, using the word deliberately. He saw Moria sit up straight.

"Ah," Jensen smiled, distracted. "Yes. Mr. Cole. I fear Mr. Cole was also part of a little plan of his own devising. He was a chronic underestimater, and he, too, was stupid."

"And you also arranged his 'accident'?"

"Yes," Jensen said. He pulled on the cigar once more, sighed out the smoke. "Mr. Cole became greedy. Attempted to deal on his own."

"Cole would have told me," Moria said. "He didn't work on his own."

Jensen looked at Moria as if he were an idiot. "When you went to prison, Mr. Mendle, who was it suggested you locate Mr. Lovell, seek his protection?" Moria stared. "Mr. Cole, wasn't it? And who suggested you hire Mr. Lovell when he was released? Why, do you think? You already had protection, and a driver. Hedge, you call him. He, also, was Mr. Cole's acquisition, I believe." Moria nodded, numb. "Mr. Cole, you see, was the liaison, the connection. A connection that ran from Eddy Lovell to Quincy Lovell, thence to Messrs. Dodd and Henderson, to Mr. Castillo, to Cole, and now, it seems, to you."

"So you killed Cole."

"To be blunt, I did. I apologize for the theatrical mailing. The idea was to bring you here without undue delay. It worked, as you can see."

Silence descended on the room. Jensen's cigar smoke wafted in the lamplight, like a blue cloud. Eddy's mind sorted through things, Moria was in a funk. "I want the briefcase, the discs, Mr. Lovell," Jensen said.

"People in hell want ice water," Eddy said. He half believed the bullshit about computers, pin numbers, banks. If he could hand over the damned discs, walk away from all this, he thought, he would do so in two seconds. But Barbara had the case, had the CDs, or at least she had them for a while. He couldn't give Jensen either without giving him Barbara. That, he would never do.

The telephone rang. Jensen jumped slightly, looked annoyed. Robin, who was seated closest, picked it up.

"It's for him," he indicated Moria.

"Careful what you say," Jensen warned. Moria rose, went to the telephone, like he expected the call. Robin put his pistol to Moria's head. Fizer kept an eye on Eddy.

"Hell, no!" he spoke after listening. "Tell them no. Well, hell! All right. No, it's all right." He hung up. Jensen looked a question at him. "Security guard. Downstairs. The old fart." Moria returned to his chair, shook his head. "Said some women are coming up here."

"Women?"

"Couple hookers. Were here last night, this morning. One of them lost a set of keys. Thinks they're here." He looked at Eddy, who nodded back.

"Tell them to come back later," Jensen said, agitated.

Moria shook his head. "Can't. Already on the elevator. They slipped the doorman a twenty to let them in while that old geezer wasn't looking. They know I'm up here. Afraid I wouldn't let them come up if they called first."

"Don't answer the door," Robin suggested, sat.

"Won't work. They'd just go down, get that old cop to come up and check. The doorman and guard saw us—"

Jensen lost patience. "We'll send them away when they arrive. You answer the door," he barked at Robin. "Give them some money. Two hundred. Apiece. That will suffice. It will have to. Now, where were we?" He put the cigar down in an ashtray. "Ah, yes. Mr. Lovell was about to tell us where the CDs are." He resumed his smile: plastic.

"Fuck you," Eddy said. "I'm not telling you shit."

Jensen sighed again, smiled sadly, now. "Your brother said that would be your response. Your sister confirmed that."

"Hillary?" Eddy felt bile rising. *"She's* in on this, too?"

"Some family you got," Moria put in.

Jensen smiled. "She said you saw yourself as a man of honor. Is that right?" Eddy clenched his fists, said nothing. "Well, actually, she said you were a pig-headed rogue bull. She is fond of mixed metaphors."

"She's fond of mixed drinks," Eddy said, shook his head. She never quit.

"She said that the only way to get to you was through something—actually through some*one* you hold dear."

The pricking fear Eddy felt before began anew, laced up his back.

"You might take some comfort, in light of recent events, that it was all arranged by Mr. Cole."

"Cole? He arranged what?" Moria demanded.

Jensen ignored him. "You deliver to me the CDs, intact and properly preserved, Mr. Lovell, and you will see your daughter, Barbara, again. Alive."

Eddy came out of the chair, his hands set for Jensen's throat.
Robin was ready, moved quick. His pistol rose and came down
on the back of Eddy's head like a club as Eddy reached Jensen's
knees. He fell, stunned. Robin produced a sap from a pocket,
raised it.

"No," Jensen said. His voice was level, but his hands were
shaking. "I need him lucid. We don't want another 'accident.' "
He glanced at Moria, who sat still, watched. Robin turned Eddy
over, pushed a foot down on his throat, held his automatic's
barrel on his forehead.

"So, you and Cole cooked up a little kidnapping, a little
extortion," Moria said. "Now, *that's* like Bob. Fits him."
Moria reached for the cigarette box, extracted one, lit it. Eddy
lay still under Robin's foot. "Now, where *was* Eddy's daughter?
LA? That explains Johnny Ribbon. He's connected there. Or
he was. Took care of that, too, didn't you?"

Jensen was composed. "Mr. Cole decided that there was
more at stake here than what he was offered. He felt that his
part was worth considerably more than we were willing to pay.
In short, his avarice led him to try to deal on his own." He
looked at Moria. "I am sorry," he said. "I know you were close.
It wasn't personal. He overreached. He became expendable."

Eddy's eyes were open, fixed on the ceiling. His mouth was
forced shut by the pressure of Robin's shoe on his throat. "If
you hurt her," he said through clenched teeth, "I will rip you
apart, you fucking nigger—"

"Please, Mr. Lovell," Jensen cautioned. "No prejudicial
remarks. I'm sensitive about that."

"Where is she?"

"That," Jensen said, "presented a different problem. We
didn't know. Mr. Cole arranged things on the West Coast. He
insisted. He was not forthcoming with the precise location of
the exchange. At least, not without persuasion."

"And Heather?"

"An unfortunate pawn. As were Mr. Boot Town and his
loyal patrons." He touched Eddy's shoulder with his foot. "But
we're getting nowhere. What I need is the briefcase and its
contents. What you need is your daughter. What Mr. Mendle

needs is a price for his cooperative silence. Can we make an arrangement on that basis?''

The doorbell rang.

''That's the hookers,'' Moria said, rose. ''I'll get rid of them.''

Jensen laughed. ''I think not.'' He pulled up his Desert Eagle, trained it on Moria, nodded. Fizer rose, went to the door. Robin watched him, kept his weapon handy, covered Moria. Moria eased back into his chair.

''How you doing, Eddy?'' Moria asked. ''Get you anything? Like up?''

Eddy started, choked. ''Son of a—''

Fizer reached the door, stuck his pistol in his pocket, opened up all at the same time. There was a muffled explosion. Fizer left his feet and came leaping backwards into the room over the tiled entryway, propelled, flying. The front of his shirt was black with powder burns. The entire back of his coat was blown out, ragged, red.

Robin and Jensen looked up. Moria sprang from his chair, flung his body against Robin. They rolled onto the sofa, upturned it.

Eddy was off the floor. His left hand circled Jensen's throat. His right forced the pistol up, away from him. Four shots spat through the silencer before Eddy heard the satisfying crack of Jensen's wrist. The handsome black face twisted in agony, mouth opened to scream. Eddy's left hand closed on Jensen's throat, stifled him. The pistol fell, Jensen's wrist cracked again.

Moria and Robin tumbled on the floor, rolled over and over in the sopping remnants of Fizer's insides. A blur raced across Eddy's line of vision: Hedge.

Eddy pulled himself to his feet, Jensen's throat firm in his left hand, his right arm dangling, shattered. His face was a mask of agony, his mouth open, tongue thrust out. His left hand tore at Eddy's fingers.

Moria continued to tumble with Robin. The thin man was quick, kept eluding Moria's grasp, but couldn't bring his pistol to bear before Moria would knock it away.

Eddy shook Jensen. ''Where is she?'' He smashed Jensen's

injured wrist onto the bar. Jensen struggled against the pain, went limp.

Hedge stumbled down into the sunken living room. He lifted the shotgun, smashed the butt down twice on the back of Robin's head. Moria rolled over, covered with sweat and blood, panting. Robin lay still, bleeding, dead.

Jensen collapsed, eyes rolled back. Eddy relaxed his grip, grabbed his cream-colored lapels, held him off the ground, shook him. "Where is she, you son of a bitch?" he yelled into Jensen's face. "Talk to me!" Jensen's head lolled on his shoulders. Eddy dropped him, stood back—a mistake. As soon as his feet touched the carpeting, Jensen jumped slightly, spun around and caught Eddy squarely on the jaw with the heel of his shoe. Eddy reeled, stunned, stumbled into Hedge, who, in turn, collapsed onto Moria. Eddy scrambled to his feet, turned to attack, but Jensen was out the open door: gone.

Eddy raced after him into the hallway. The elevator doors closed. He bolted for the stairs around a corner at the opposite end of the hall, reached the fire door, burst through, leaped five steps at a time down, raced the elevator to the lobby: too late. He rushed past the astonished guard, then the doorman, arrived outside in time to see the blue van peeling away, joining the traffic on Main Street. Eddy loped after the taillights, then stopped, helpless. He spun around, looked for a vehicle. The parking lot was quiet, empty. He saw Jensen's Mercedes, ran to it, jerked on the door. It was locked. Eddy kept the keys, he remembered. He searched his pockets: nothing. Then he remembered his windbreaker upstairs.

He pounded the top of the car in frustration. He didn't even wince when he heard more than felt his little finger break. Tears of frustration filled his eyes. "Goddamn son of a bitch," he said.

The doorman and security guard, his ancient pistol drawn, approached him. "You got some kind of trouble?" the guard asked.

Eddy opened his mouth to answer, remembered the mess upstairs.

"No," he said. "Just a . . . a joke."

The guard smiled, reholstered his piece. Eddy trudged past

him to the elevator. His clothes were drenched in sweat, but his pounding chest, burning eyes were not caused by the fight, the chase, or even the frustration of losing Jensen. There was no sensation at all from his broken finger. The pain he felt when he looked into the mirrored walls of the elevator was deeper. The only face he could see looking back at him was that of his daughter.

It was all falling together: Quince, Hillary, Cole, Barbara, even Raul. It all now was in place. And there was only one place that could be: Balmorhea.

Four hours later, across town in a crumbling duplex on West Main street, a telephone rang. Houston Police Detective Sergeant Greg DaCara grunted, swung his muscular legs over the side of his bed, turned on a lamp, lit a cigarette, coughed, pushed aside a stack of racing forms, picked up the cheap, no-name brand phone next to his bed. "Yeah?"

A crisp, wide-awake uniform informed him of a multiple homicide, discovered in the Medical Arms Pavilion Hotel, near the medical center.

DaCara was fuzzy, tongue thick, eyes stuck together. He sucked in the smoke, coughed again, listened to the report, let his right hand stray behind him, rubbed the plentiful rump of the brunette hooker next to him. He hated this. She was the first half-decent piece of ass he had had in months. He hired her to help him get over the three grand he lost that afternoon. It was money he didn't have, couldn't get, money that was going to shitcan his career for good. He hired her for the night, planned to have her twice more: shit.

"Pretty messy," the watch commander said, concluding the report.

"Anybody we know?"

"Nope. All out-of-towners, from their IDs. Which are bull-shit."

The detective's brain shifted, stalled, then smoothed into overdrive, made a perpendicular turn. "Medical Arms?" he repeated. "What apartment?"

"No apartment. They were in a dumpster, alley. Junkie found them. Security guard called it in."

"I'm coming over," DaCara said. "Take a look."

"No need."

"I'm coming over," he repeated. "Moria Mendle at home? He's a resident there."

"Mendle?" A pause. "No Mendle on the witness list. They finished the door-to-door about a half hour ago. No Mendle."

"I'm coming over," a beat. "Call Billings."

"Who?"

"Never mind, I'll do it."

He hung up. Crushed out his butt, wiped his face with his hands, checked the clock.

"Come on back, sugarloaf," the whore said, half turning toward the light, eyes shut. "I'll charge you up for another round."

He looked at her. He wanted to. He stood, went to the bathroom, pissed, came back in, and opened his wallet, found the number to the cheap motel where Billings chose to stay. Another oddity. Normally visiting feds stayed first class: Hilton, Wyndham, someplace with room service, saunas, and waitresses in short skirts, black mesh stockings. He dialed, asked for 122, Billings's room: no answer.

"Fuck it," he said. It was on Main, almost on the way. He'd have to pick the fat prick up anyway.

"That's my idea, sugarloaf," the whore said, sleepy. "Come on and come. I need some sleep."

He pulled a fifty from his wallet. Half what she expected, but he wouldn't be back, dropped it on the table. "Don't steal nothing," he said. "I'm still a cop."

He dressed, went out, and got into his car, '85 Olds Cutlass. The weather felt still, heavy, humid. Storm coming, he sensed. He steered up West Main toward downtown. Used to be a good neighborhood, he thought. Now, it's gone to shit. Like everything else in this town.

He wheeled into the Warbonnet Motel, a holdover from the sixties when the Astrodome brought in the chains, buried the independents. The room was on the end of a wing. He parked, pounded on the door. No answer. Again: nothing.

He went to the office. A pimply kid in an Oilers jersey held down the night clerk's job.

"Billings," DaCara said. "Room 122. Where the hell is he?" He flashed his badge. The kid looked confused, checked the computer, then the file.

"We got no Billings."

DaCara felt like pulling the little punk over the desk. "Yeah, you got a Billings," he said instead. "Big guy. Doofus. Federal marshal. Probably gets a discount. Room 122. I dropped him off here last night."

The kid checked again. "Nope, no Billings." He checked the computer. "That room—122. Been vacant all week."

DaCara was about to explode. He glanced out the window, made sure he had the right motel. "Look, kid. I'm on a homicide investigation. You're obstructing me. You want to see what the inside of a drunk tank looks like at two in the goddamn morning, that's your business. But it'd be one hell of a lot easier if you'd just come across. Now, I want a guy named Theodore Billings. Federal Marshal."

The kid gaped at him.

"Big guy," DaCara went on. "Ugly. Stupid-looking."

Light, a smile. "Oh, I know the guy. He came in here when I went on duty. You're the guy. DaCara, right? Knew it was Italian. Couldn't remember."

"It's not Italian," DaCara said. "It's Cajun. And—"

The kid turned around, reached under the key cabinet. "Just a sec."

"And?" DaCara repeated, "Where the fuck is he?"

"I dunno," the kid said. "Gave me this to give to a cop named DaCara. But you didn't have on a uniform or anything . . ." He shrugged, he handed over a small package, neat, tied with string, DACARA printed in block letters on the top.

DaCara turned it around, ripped it open. Inside was a small cardboard box wrapped with a pair of suspenders, a belt. DaCara sat on a chair, put the box on his lap, studied it. The kid studied him.

"You got nothing else to do?" he asked. The kid shrugged, moved back.

DaCara unstrung the suspenders, the belt from the box,

opened it. Inside, precisely arranged, all facing up, bound with a bank wrapper, were two six-inch stacks of one-thousand-dollar bills.

And a note: "Thanks for the use of the hall," it said. "Teddy."

DaCara sat and looked at the money for a beat, then closed the box, rewrapped it, went to his car, got behind the wheel, then reopened it, looked again. He wondered if the whore was still back at his apartment. "Fuck me to tears," he said.

PART THREE

Friday

18

El Paso

"I'm telling you, quit blaming yourself." Sandobal stood dripping in the middle of the dingy motel room, sparse towel around his waist. Wiry, curly hair covered his chest. A three-day beard beneath his dark eyes gave him an appealing rough look. At the same time, there was something fragile about him. Turned Barbara off. She used to see strength in him. Now, all she saw was Sandobal.

He should never have left New York, she thought. Maybe she shouldn't have, either.

"You just pushed yourself too hard. Pushed that car too hard." He went back into the bathroom.

Barbara sat on the bed, open telephone book in front of her. She leaned back, looked out the window. The parking lot was a sea of orange light washed by sheets of rain: eerie. Rain in the desert, she thought.

Earlier, it rained mud. They barely got the top up on the wobbling Mustang in time. Huge drops passed through the dust-laden wind. Mud pelted the vehicle, blocked her windshield, made the remaining wiper useless. Sandobal panicked, jerked the car beneath an overpass. He'd never heard of such a thing: Yankee, Barbara thought. She refused to wait out the storm, replaced him in the driver's seat, pulled out into the bizarre storm, pushed ahead, fast. He warned her to slow down, especially in the rain. She should have listened.

Before, the Mustang was only damaged. Now, it was wrecked. Towed into Hernando's Body Shop in Ysleta, outside El Paso, a mile from the Borderland Motel. Barbara put it there. In the wind, rain that swept in from the northwest, she lost sight of the white lines. Something snapped underneath the vehicle. She veered off a curve, ran up onto a guardrail, nearly rolled.

They were all right: bumps and scrapes. The Mustang wasn't—broken axle, busted ball joint, for openers. Two tires ruined, a wheel bent. None of that included the damage done to the right side of the car from the collision with Fletcher's Taurus.

The tow-truck driver dropped them at the first motel they came to, told them it would be the next morning before anybody could look at the car. "Get a storm like this," he told them, "makes for overtime. We don't see much rain out here. Get some snow in the winter." Snow in the desert, Barbara thought. That would be something for Sandobal to see.

Now, they were without wheels. Barbara wanted to rent something right away, keep moving. Sandobal nixed the idea. "Soon as they find Fletcher, the first thing they'll do is put out an APB," he said. "That state trooper, Gomez, thought he was a cop. They might not double-check, may not care. Hell, for all I know, neither of them may have been cops." Barbara wiped her eyes confused. "It doesn't make any difference. If we use a credit card, get our names onto a computer, we're caught."

"But they don't know *my* name," Barbara argued. "The trooper never asked for it, never checked my ID. The only one who did was Fletcher. He's not likely to tell anyone, not if—" She bit off the thought.

"No," Sandobal said, softly. "He's not likely to say anything to anybody."

His statement hung ominously between them. Sandobal had never killed anyone, not in the line, not otherwise. Neither had she, but he took pride in the fact. She had never considered it. Didn't want to confront it. Now, though, it confronted her.

She shuddered. "He tried to kill us. If he wasn't a cop—"

"I don't know who he was," Sandobal almost yelled at her, caught himself, calmed. "But he had a shield. Gomez didn't question it. I'm not sure why I did. I don't know who he was." He looked into the mirror. "I don't know who anyone is. Not anymore."

"Cops don't use silencers," Barbara added quietly.

Sandobal nodded. "He was no cop. He was a player."

"A what?"

Sandobal rubbed his chin, needed a shave. "Maybe—" He broke off then, stripped off his wet, muddy clothes, went in to shower.

Barbara pushed the problem to one side. She refused to let it intrude on her purpose—their purpose, now. But it did anyway. She knew he was right—*they* were right—but she couldn't reconcile her actions with anything that made sense. Did Fletcher have anything to do with Vicki? That question, too, refused to reconcile. And it, too, would have to wait.

When the storm hit, the Mustang unevenly galloped through the miles, put Arizona, most of New Mexico behind them, Sandobal said nothing, kept his hands firmly on the wheel, kept his eyes on the road ahead. Then, all at once, he started talking, wouldn't shut up, kept going over it, outlined his suspicions about Fletcher, tried to convince Barbara, himself that they were completely justified. She thought he was rehearsing a speech: a defense.

As they approached the Texas border, Sandobal made Barbara recite the message on the restroom wall a dozen times. He pulled over, bought a map, tried to find a place called "Bal-More-A." It took a while. Barbara had never heard of it, had no idea how to spell it. She scanned all the place names in the map's index, finally figured out the transliteration—Balmorhea. A small, black dot just five miles off I-10. The places around it had strange, alien names: Brogado, Toyahvale, Sargosa, Verhalen. There was a lake and a state park: that meant rangers, cops. It was on the way to Fort Davis, on the way to Alpine, on the way to Mexico. On the way to everywhere. But it wasn't anywhere. Not anywhere special. Like everything, it made no sense.

But the restroom door message was from Vicki: no question. Balmorhea was the place. No question there, either.

She looked for a rental. She avoided national agencies, sought a local. There were six, only one open twenty-four hours. The woman who answered said they had nothing available until the next morning. Then, a Ford F-150 Supercab was due for return. She reserved it, thankful that the woman on the phone hadn't asked her for a credit card number to hold it. "It's brand-new," the woman said with a thick accent. "You got to have insurance."

"I do," Barbara said, hung up, leaned forward, put her head in her hands.

Sandobal came out of the bathroom again, started to speak. She cut him off. "I just wish—never mind." She explained the rental arrangement.

"That's probably okay," Sandobal replied. "We need something to eat, some sleep." He glanced out the window. "Storm's slowing everything down. And it's dark out there. We don't have a shot at seeing them if we run right up on top of them. How far, anyway?"

"About two hundred," Barbara said. "More." She glanced down at the soggy road map. "That's three, maybe four hours."

"Two, the way you drive."

She scowled at him, but he didn't see. He returned to the bathroom. She stood, stretched. He was right. She felt dirty, soiled. Her muscles ached, head throbbed. She struck it on something during the crackup. Sandobal had a bruise on his leg, his right arm was badly scraped. Lucky, she thought again. Could have died. Twice in one day. Must be some kind of record.

She stripped out of her wind-suit, leotard, then looked at herself in the mirror. No bruises, no lacerations, no wounds of any kind. Streaks of Fletcher's blood, rain-splattered mud still marked her face, but everything worked okay. Just the headache: lucky.

Sandobal came out again, hair combed back, naked. He stopped, looked at her looking at herself. She blushed, didn't cover up. "First thing in the morning, you go pick up the rental," he said. "The manager said he'd give us a ride some-place if we needed it. Best if we're not seen together." His eyes ran up and down her body. There was a catch in his voice. "What we need is something to eat."

Barbara ignored his leer, attitude, obvious wants. She padded over and flipped on the TV: news.

"You call for pizza?" Sandobal asked.

"It's after midnight. No one delivers after midnight."

"There's a place just up the road," Sandobal argued. "I saw their sign. Said 'All Nite Delivery.' "

"Don't tell me. Tell them." She nodded toward the phone. "I called four places. Same story: no delivery after midnight. That was," she consulted her watch, "two hours ago." She looked out the window again. "I don't blame them."

"But they're open?"

"One place is. Taco Pizza Express. It's on the highway. By the place you called the tow."

He nodded, went to the window, looked out. "Maybe the manager's still up. I'll try to borrow his car."

She gave him a look.

"I've still got a badge. Maybe it's good for something."

"Aren't you afraid to show it? What about your famous APB?" Mean, she thought.

He shrugged. "I should be back by the time you're out of the shower. It's only a couple miles." She nodded. "You want me to pick up some clothes? Fresh clothes?" He plucked his stained, filthy tee-shirt off the floor, smelled it.

"At this hour?" she asked. He shrugged. "I doubt you could anyway," she said. "Unless you have cash. I've barely got enough on my credit card to cover the rental."

"That's probably more than I've got on mine." He pulled on his jeans. "How come you have more money than I do?"

Barbara nodded. "You forget, I'm the poor little rich girl."

He smiled. "That's why I love you."

She didn't return the smile. "Don't get used to it. There's nothing to spoil a nestegg like financing a wild goose chase across the country at eighteen percent."

He sat down beside her. "Now *you* think it's a wild goose chase?"

Barbara shook her head. Her hair was too dirty, oily, too pasted by muddy rain to her forehead to move. "I don't know, Sandobal," she said. "I'm just scared."

"That's why you need some sleep. Food. I got maybe thirty, thirty-five bucks. That's enough." Sandobal picked up his jeans, shook them out, put a leg into them, frowned. "This shirt smells like I died in it."

"I'll wash it out."

He ignored socks, worked bare feet into muddy sneakers. "Take a shower, get some rest. I'll be back." He started to the door, stopped. "I swear, Barbara, we'll find her, find out what's going on. The way I see it, we have no choice." He checked the rain-swept parking lot. "Don't take any calls or open the door."

She looked at him. "Seriously?"

"Seriously." He was out, gone. She stood still for a moment, shivered in spite of herself, went to the door and latched the chain.

The shower was hot. She let the water course down her olive skin, sluice between her breasts, her legs, wash away fatigue. She tried to piece together everything into a solid whole, couldn't. It was all a jumble, a crisscross pattern of blown-up cars, frightened looks, bloody girls, fake cops who died horrible deaths right in front of her, because of her. Or because of Vicki.

Tears started. She had held them back all afternoon. Now they came. She sobbed into the near-scalding water, dipped her crown beneath it, boiled away the doubt. Her mind raced from image to image, searched for sense. She shuddered with frustration. Everything everyone—stood in the shadows, just out of the light.

She raised her face to the hot spray, breathed deeply.

Why was she doing this? For Vicki. Who was Vicki, anyway? A flighty girl with no common sense: Actress-Model-Whatever. Wanted to be a star, but probably would never make it. Too many AMWs wanted that. They were friends, sure, but that was because they were both out of place, out of order, both seeking something they wouldn't recognize when they found it.

But she was a good person, a good friend, a sister, in a way. She was honest, loyal. But would she do something like this for Barbara? For anyone. She was basically self-centered, spent all her time at the movies or chasing people who were in the movies. Would she drop everything, race around all over the country, kill people if Barbara was in trouble? The question washed away in the shower. The obvious answer was no.

Dump or not, the motel had pretensions, the water stayed hot. She poured from the complimentary shampoo bottle, scrubbed her hair, her face, soaped her body, then let the water flood it all away. Maybe the best thing would be to go back. Hitch to the airport, use what was left on her VISA. Get home, call the cops again, the FBI. Let them handle it.

Then she imagined Vicki writing the note on the restroom door, holding her breath, fearful. It was smart to put it there. But how could she know anyone would see it in time to do any good? Criss-cross, she thought.

Later, Sandobal lay next to her, asleep. The clock on the TV said it was after four. He had returned with pizza, found her toweling off from the shower. She made him strip again, then used the remainder of the complimentary shampoo and bar soap to wash their clothes in the tub. His shirt was permanently stained, so was his jacket. Socks were a total loss. She hung the wet clothes in the bathroom under the full blast of the overhead heater. Her wind-suit was nylon, leotard was thin enough to dry quickly. His clothes would still be damp, but he could wear them.

They sat cross-legged on the bed, naked, ate the pizza. He complained about the quality with every bite until it became funny, then absurd. They laughed, silly, then she looked down and saw that he was no longer hungry—for pizza. She pushed the carton off the bed, and they fell back together into a tangle of giggles and long kisses that soon gave way to moans of pleasure. She wanted to let go, to forget everything, break the tension. For a few minutes, anyway, she forgot about everything but Sandobal. He might not be what she wanted, not forever, but he could fuck like a rabbit.

Now, hours later, sated, relaxed, she lay awake, stared at old water stains on the motel's ceiling. She got up, walked to the window, looked out. The rental would be ready by nine, nine-thirty: gassed and ready to roll.

Outside, the front had passed, the thunderstorm was over. Now, only a light, chilly north wind blew out of a star-dotted sky. They didn't twinkle, just sat there, waited, patient: tiny points of distant light as complex in their arrangement as anything she could think of. Yet, somehow, they made sense. Nothing else did.

She lay down again, glanced at Sandobal. He had maybe twenty bucks left on him. She had her VISA, couple gas cards, maybe ten, twelve bucks in ones. That would carry them to Balmorhea, but what then? And what the fuck *was* Balmorhea? A place on the map. What would they find when they got there?

Once more, she eased out of the bed and reached for the light, picked up the TV's remote. She turned it on, muted it. Blue light illuminated the room. She glanced at the screen. Four-thirty in the morning, they were showing the news: sports, even. As if anybody up at that hour would care.

She noticed Sandobal had picked up a pack of Pall Malls, his old brand. He had smoked three, four of them. She knocked one out, snapped a match to fire, and breathed in the smoke. It felt good. "Fire and water," she whispered when she exhaled. "Purging."

She went to the chair where they had dumped everything they retrieved from the battered Mustang: her purse, a light jacket, her gym bag, a battered metal briefcase containing her pistol. There were deep scratches on the latches, the sides were dented. She spun the combination, opened it, checked to make sure the S&W .38 Eddy sent her was still there. She held it up in the gray light of the TV. The blueing was perfect.

She remembered the day she received it. At first, she couldn't get the case open, couldn't figure out the combination. Then she remembered the odd phone message. She played it back, tried the number: 3006. It snapped open, revealed the CDs and the pistol. The disks were blank. She tried them on her player, got nothing but hiss and pop, so she put them back inside. A gag gift, she thought.

There was nothing funny about the pistol. She was thrilled with it, but it scared the hell out of Vicki. Poor Vicki, she thought, never imagined that Barbara might be chasing her halfway across the country, gunning for bad guys with the same weapon.

She aimed it at a print of a bullfighter on the wall, sight right on his heart, eased back the hammer: snap. Again. snap. And again. Three through the chest. She wondered if she could actually use it against a man. It wasn't the first time she had asked herself that question. The answer had always been yes. The way she felt now, she wasn't so sure.

She picked up the box of cartridges, opened the pistol, loaded it. She knew that she should keep the hammer down on an empty chamber for safety. She didn't care. Six chances were better than five. But she knew also the problem wasn't the ammunition. It was guts. She snapped the gun closed, rested it on her naked thighs. Sandobal's weapon, a Colt Python .357, nickel-plated, was next to the box. She picked it up, checked its load also. Five chambers, one empty.

She looked at him and felt sorry for him all at once. He was angry, scared. Not of the bad guys—whoever they were—but of other things. His career was in the toilet now. By refusing the order to return, he had screwed himself. Unless. . .her thought trailed off. Unless, what? Unless they caught the bad guys. Somebody big was pulling strings, moving things behind the scenes. But Sandobal didn't believe in big. He only believed in Sandobal. She admired that in him.

But now that Sandobal was committed, Barbara moved to new questions. Who were these bad guys, these "cousins"? Who would kidnap Vicki? Why? Vicki didn't know people like that. Barbara hadn't questioned motive before, only that Vicki was in trouble. If it was an abduction, a rape, why go all the way to Texas? If it was for money—well, that was stupid. Vicki had no money.

Tomorrow, she thought. She replaced the pistol in the brief-case and walked to the bathroom. It was already tomorrow. It would be light in two, three hours. She checked their clothes. Hers, all but dry. His still wet. He'd bitch about that. She didn't care.

She returned to the room, sat on the edge of the bed. Sandobal rolled over, groaned a little. His arm looped over, reached for her, missed, settled for her pillow, curled it toward him. Why wasn't she sleepy? Why didn't she crave sleep? Why didn't she crave Sandobal? Vicki once told her that the best part about making love was cuddling afterwards. Barbara had never found that to be so. She'd never been a cuddler. She wished he wasn't there. She would feel less dependent, more confident. He was in the way. She would be better off alone. Not just now, but permanently. She decided that when they got back, she would see less of him. She was fond of him, always had been. The sex was good: no question. But there had to be more than fond, more than sex.

She looked at the muted TV screen, watched the flickering images of cops in yellow slickers at a crime scene in heavy rain. Bright lights from the strobes gave everything the eerie spectacle of disaster: bodies covered with blood-soaked blankets, shots of the interior of a liquor store, broken glass, ruined shelves. A young reporter with an umbrella spoke earnestly into the camera. This was made earlier. Rain sheeted the background. Barbara shrugged: other people's problems.

She remembered something one of the guys at the gym had said about El Paso: "East LA East. Crime, drugs, Mexicans, whores, and everybody trying to fuck everybody else at once."

Barbara decided to turn it off. Suddenly, the screen was filled with a mug shot of a dark-haired man with a sloped nose, large brown eyes. Barbara sat up straight: Blackie. She groped for the remote, turned on the sound.

". . . Michael LeRoy Stone," the announcer's voice continued, "was found dead at the scene, apparently shot fatally in the altercation by Professor Jeffrey Kingston, a professor from the University of Arizona, who was originally thought to be a suspect—"

The screen flickered. A man was being led away to a police car. He wore desert khakis, hiking boots, handcuffs.

"Sandobal!" Barbara yelled. "Look at this!"

Sandobal rolled over, groaned, came alert. An interview with Kingston was taking place behind the pretty announcer's voice-over. "I'll be damned." He rubbed his face.

Images on the TV screen flashed back and forth between the liquor store, Kingston, a variety of police officers. Then another mug shot of a lighter featured man, Rusty Malory, the reporter identified the suspect.

"That's them," Barbara said. "One is the guy called 'Blackie.' The other is 'Red.' " The reporter gave descriptions of the men, their prison records and history of violent crime. The camera panned across Sarge's Liquor.

"God, we drove right past that place," Sandobal said, "just on the outskirts, right on the interstate. Ambulances and radio cars everywhere." Vicki shushed him, thumbed up the sound.

"—according to Kingston. One of the female suspects is a woman in her forties, dressed as a Hell's Angel,"

Barbara held her breath.

"—the other woman, who went by the name of 'Barbara,' was, according to Kingston, a female in her late thirties wearing blue sweatshirt and -pants—"

"Vicki!" Barbara said. "She's calling herself 'Barbara.' Why?"

"He said they were all part of the gang," Sandobal said.

"She'll love that part about 'late thirties.' "

"—whose idea it was for the gang to use Kingston as a human shield. Police believe that the suspects could have made their getaway in a 1994 Chevrolet Suburban belonging to Beryl T. Raymond, another victim of the shooting, found dead at the scene."

"I'm confused," Barbara said.

"I'm not." Sandobal pulled his legs over the side of the bed. The reporter was going over the facts again. At last, the scene shifted to twin anchors in the studio, who broke for a commercial.

"So? Why is she calling herself me? Is Vicki somehow mixed up in—"

"They think they have you," Sandobal said.

"What?"

"They think Vicki's you. She's going along with it. Look:

342   *Clay Reynolds*

it makes sense. They came to your apartment, grabbed a girl who apparently lived there. They think she's you.''

"That *doesn't* make any sense. She doesn't even *look* like me. Besides, there's no more reason to kidnap me than to kidnap her.''

"I thought you were rich.''

She let the remark pass. "There's no reason in the world to kidnap either one of us.''

"Well, all I can see is that they think she's you, and she's going along with it. At least, they're calling her 'Barbara.' I don't think they're rapists. Hell, they're pros, ex-cons.'' He rubbed his eyes hard. "This looks like a straight kidnapping for ransom.''

Barbara shook her head. Sandobal shrugged, grabbed a fistful of sheet, pulled it over himself, lit a cigarette, started channel-surfing.

Barbara walked into the bathroom, pulled on her leotard. Her head spun. She stared into the mirror, looked into her own eyes for an answer. It made no sense. Vicki was—nobody. But she was nobody, too: almost.

In the mirror, her reflection showed family characteristics: high cheekbones, straight, even teeth, full lips bracketed by slight dimples. She saw a resemblance that once had flattered her, then made her resentful enough to deliberately ignore it: Hillary. Their coloring was different, but there she was in a darker, younger version: Auntie Bitchie. She didn't know why. But now she knew who.

The room reeled, settled. She stumbled back into the bedroom, started to speak. He held up a hand for silence. "They're putting together a composite sketch of you—of Vicki. This Kingston guy's totally zoned—but they're going to make him a hero. He apparently shot Stone—the one you call 'Blackie.' He says the other woman, named Al, is some kind of transvestite or transsexual, remember the 'ta-tas'? They're moving east. No surprise there. He didn't know where they were going, but we do.''

"Balmorhea.'' Barbara's voice shook. She sat down on the bed.

"We ought to call the state cops,'' he said. She started

shaking her head, but he was ahead of her. "We need to let them know she's not part of the gang. I don't know how he could think—"

"You'd have to know Vicki," Barbara said. "It's something—I don't know." She shook her head again. "Role of a lifetime," she thought aloud. "She's trying to protect me."

"Protect you from who?"

She picked up the phone.

"Who're you calling?"

"My Aunt. Hillary. She's behind all of this."

Sandobal launched himself across the bed, slammed his hand down on the switchhook. Barbara glared at him. But there was concern in his eyes. He took the receiver from her hand, replaced it. "Why?"

She reminded him of her aunt's fury when she found out she was seeing Sandobal. "She's crazy. And I'm going to call her and tell her that the joke's on her. That I'm sitting in a motel room in Texas with the very man she—"

"Don't," he commanded. Barbara looked at him: perplexed. "If you're right. If your aunt's crazy enough to actually hire criminals to grab you and haul you back, then what is she—or they—going to do when they realize they grabbed the wrong girl?"

"She'd just tell them it's a mistake."

"And they'd just turn around, drive Miss Vicki back to LA, maybe give her a pat on the bottom and say, 'Whoops! We're sorry'?" Barbara began to see. "And there's Fletcher. What about him?"

"I don't know."

"I don't either. But he could be some kind of PI. With the kind of bucks your aunt's got, she could afford somebody who could get dummy credentials as good as he had, could convince a state trooper that he was a state cop." He stopped, stared. "He seemed more intent on killing you than kidnapping you."

"Maybe it was you he was trying to kill."

"It doesn't matter at this point. They've killed a half-dozen people. They're out of control."

"But Vicki —"

"You make that call, Vicki's dead. Right now, they think

she's you, so she's worth something.'' He paced, still naked, unaware how silly he looked. She smiled. ''No, we know where they're going, and we've got to get there before the payoff, if that's what's going down. We've got to move.''

She looked at him. Now, she knew why she wanted him with her, why she couldn't leave him. His strength was in action. She picked up the phone, punched numbers.

''Who are you calling now?''

''Eddy.''

19
Interstate 10

At dawn, Eddy Lovell stood beside Mitch Jensen's black Mercedes, a pumpjack in his hand. He filled the tank, watched the traffic on westbound I-10 whiz by on wet pavement. An imaginary swarm of angry gnats buzzed around his head: fatigue. He ignored it. His hand was bandaged, two fingers taped tight together to form a makeshift splint. The car had a deep dent just above the driver's seat. Reminded, he pulled a small bottle out of his pocket, popped two Advil into his mouth, chewed. The hand only hurt when he moved it. Another pain was constant.

The north wind had a bite to it, but the rain had stopped. Eddy tugged his windbreaker around him. It was cold, but his anger kept him warm. He felt the tug of Jensen's heavy automatic in his waistband.

Inside the Mercedes, Moria slumped against the front door, asleep. In the back, Hedge lay across the seat. Three hours on the road. Three days with no sleep. Only Eddy was wide awake, running on hate, fear, worry. He had a single thought: Barbara.

He had called Barbara's apartment three times. The phone just rang. He thought of calling her boyfriend, Sandobal. But he had no first name, no address. Anxiety boiled in his gut.

The gas pumped slow. He felt like a whore: paid for, used. For more than a year now, he had been ready when Moria called: quiet, steady, docile. It started in the prison yard, continued when he got out. Too easy. Eddy was tired of it. He had to admit the short fat prick was sticking by him, standing behind him. Of course, Moria had a stake in all this. Bob Cole. But that wasn't enough, Eddy thought. Moria smelled money.

"We're going to get those fucks," he said, kept saying it almost every five miles since they left Houston. Eddy had no doubt about that. His only question was how.

When he stumbled back into the room after losing Jensen, Eddy's first thought was to get the Mercedes's keys, go for Quince, Hillary. He knew where Quince lived. He planned to rip out his faggot heart, make Hillary eat it while he watched.

But when he came into the apartment, he stopped, took stock of the carnage, chaos. Fizer's body, cut almost in two, sprawled in the middle of the floor, a stunned expression on his swarthy features. Robin's corpse, facedown, lay next to his partner in a lake of brains and blood. Behind them, on the sofa, lay Hedge. He, too, was bleeding, running a river into his lap. Beneath his ripped tanktop was an ugly, seeping hole. Moria leaned over him, applied towels, ice. Hedge reclined, his green eyes in their perpetual half-shut pose, the 12-gauge still in his hand, still on the job. "Get him?" Moria asked, didn't look up.

Eddy shook his head. His hand was throbbing, head also. He found the windbreaker, hefted it: keys. Moria fussed over Hedge. "Get some sheets from one of the beds. Got to wrap him up before he bleeds to death."

"We're across the street from sixteen different emergency rooms," Eddy said. "Call a fucking ambulance. I got business." They were going to pay, he promised. They'd hate the day they ever even heard of Barbara.

A sharp pain erupted across the back of his head, dropped him to one knee. "What the fuck?" His vision blurred: Jensen he thought. He shook his head, rose, spun around, fists clenched Moria. The short, pudgy man had a sneer on his face. His eyes were focused, intent clear. He held Robin's Desert Eagle silencer off. Eddy opened his mouth. Moria came up quick, snapped the barrel of the gun across Eddy's jaw, knocked him down again. Eddy tasted blood.

"Get the fuck up," Moria ordered. "C'mon. Get up. Been wanting to hurt somebody all day. May as well be you."

Eddy's head raged. He gathered his feet beneath him, charged Moria, head down, shoulders square—never touched him. Moria took one neat step to the side, brought the pistol butt down hard on the back of Eddy's lowered skull, sent him headlong across Robin's corpse. He lurched to his feet. Moria stepped forward, held the pistol on him. "Get a grip. Don't want to kill you."

Eddy stood still, panting, hurting. "I can't—"

"You're still on my goddamn payroll." He stepped forward, wheeled the big pistol around, leveled the barrel between Eddy's eyes. "I want it clear that we work together on this thing, or we don't work at all."

Eddy glared at him, rubbed his head. "This is personal."

"Fuck that."

"Jensen said my brother, my sister—my daughter. They got my girl!"

"Heard him. I was here," Moria said. "Think. He's been gone—what?—ten, fifteen minutes. How long to make a call? Dickhead like that probably got a phone in every pocket. Wherever they were, they're gone now. Running scared, is my guess. I'm the only one knows what a pure pussy you are. They'll hold up. Wait on pretty boy to join them. Then they're on their way."

"Where?"

"To that place—that Balmorhea. Where else? It's the only thing that makes any sense. We need wheels."

"We got Jensen's Mercedes," Eddy said.

"Good." Moria nodded. "Never liked that Buick anyway. Reminds me of Cole. That son of a bitch." He thumbed down the hammer, looked at Eddy.

Eddy thought. "My sister has her own plane," he said. "If they fly—"

"Fuck that, too," Moria said. "They can fly if they want. The deal goes down tomorrow afternoon. Late, you said. That's what you said, right?'' Eddy nodded. ''That's when we'll be there. We'll have a little meeting. On my terms this time. Let 'Batman' hang by his fucking heels.'' He paused. ''Look: You're not the only one's been jerked off here. Cole was playing his own game. The prick. Now it's my game. Our game. Personal is shit. Personal is charging in there, making a fool of yourself. Get everybody killed, your girl, too.'' Eddy looked at him. ''I hate to agree with that son of a bitch, but he's right. This is *not* personal. It's business. Straight business. This is money.''

Eddy swallowed hard. Bodine's face flickered in his mind. ''Okay.''

''Okay,'' Moria said. ''We've got work to do. This place is a mess.''

It took nearly two hours to put things in order, haul the bodies down the stairs, dump them in the alley dumpster. Hedge stayed on the sofa, quiet, breathed in a low gurgle: punctured lung, Eddy thought. He never explained how he eluded the cops, made his way there, called upstairs, tipped Moria off that the cavalry was on the way. He said nothing. No wonder Moria was so cool while Jensen carried on.

Eddy taped his broken finger, poured antiseptic on Hedge's wound. It seeped but no longer bled freely. How he was alive, Eddy didn't know. They both popped pain killers. Eddy took four Advil, Hedge eight. His hand still throbbed, but his headache went away.

He found Jensen's Desert Eagle under a chair. Robin's automatic rode in Moria's waistband. Hedge, Eddy thought, wouldn't have the strength to lift his shotgun, but the big man surprised him. When they were ready, he rose on his own and walked unsteadily down the back stairs. Eddy brought Jensen's Mercedes around. Hedge collapsed into the back seat: blood on leather.

''All right,'' Moria said as Eddy eased the black car off of the loop and onto I-10. ''Looks like you're the man with the answers. Like the cops say: 'Take it from the top.' ''

* * *

Eddy finished filling the tank, glanced quickly at the shards of light from the rising sun, then entered the office, flipped two twenties down in front of the clerk, a sleepy young pregnant girl.

"Getting chilly out there?" she asked. He nodded, went for coffee, picked up two packs of Camels from a counter display. "Folks say it'll be wintertime 'fore we know it, but I lived here all my life." She looked to be about seventeen, reminded him of Barbara. "I'm telling you we still got a lot of heat coming."

"Heard that," he said.

She pushed his change over to him, gave him a smile. He hurried back to the car. Moria and Hedge slept on.

When they left Houston, Eddy started telling Moria the story. He detailed his association with Dodd and Henderson, told about the busted robbery, getting shot, copping the plea. He told him about Quince, about Hillary, how they took Barbara from him. Moria listened without comment. Eddy got to the part where he and Moria met, then he trailed off. "You know the rest."

"What about the CDs Jensen's so hot to have?" Moria asked. "Did this guy, this Castillo—he pass them to you?"

Eddy hesitated. "Yeah. I didn't know what they were. He didn't either."

"He tell you they were hot?"

"No. Only that they weren't worth anything. Figured whoever was after him would think he blew the money or whatever was supposed to be in the briefcase. They'd just kill him when they caught up, found nothing but a couple of blanks."

Moria took this in. "But they're not blank?"

"Guess not."

"So, where are they now?"

Eddy lit a smoke.

"You're going to have to trust somebody."

A mile passed. Eddy said nothing. The discs were his only ace. And Barbara had them. Moria smelled money. Big money. Eddy wasn't crazy. He'd go through him and Barbara to get them. "They're safe," Eddy said.

"Have it your way," Moria said. "But you got to tell somebody sometime."

Eddy stared straight ahead.

"Ah, fuck you," Moria snorted. "Fuck you."

It was good to be moving again. Cold wind buffeted the car,
but the tires hissed smoothly along the damp pavement. The
last Mercedes Eddy drove was the bobtail truck: piece of crap.
This car handled easily, slid along the early morning interstate,
skimmed the tops of small rises, pulled smooth toward the
rapidly clearing western horizon. Eddy cracked the window,
felt the cool freshness of a rain-washed morning. He kept the
needle just over eighty, lit a Camel, slid it over to his left hand.
Behind them, the sun rose on a damp, cool landscape, its rays
tinted everything orange under an azure sky filled with the
bright points of fading stars.

Moria was awake, quiet. They hit early rush in San Antonio,
were delayed by jammed traffic in the interchanges downtown.
Then they were out of the city, moving against traffic, heading
west: four, four and a half hours to Balmorhea. Moria was
asleep again. Eddy was hungry, didn't want to stop. He hadn't
eaten since the breakfast he mostly ignored the day before. His
stomach hurt. The cigarettes, coffee weren't helping. Then, he
had another thought: Eddy wanted out. Not just out of this.
Out for good.

Soon as he saw Cole's head, he should have walked. But
they had Barbara by then. They had her now.

In his mind, she was still a kid, a jerky, gangly teenager in
braces. He thought of her voice on the phone, smart-ass but
still a kid. She was going through hell for something she could
have turned over easy: his fault. Most of what happened in his
life was his fault. Wrong people, places, wrong everything. He
needed to fix this. For her.

Ahead, he spotted a green sign announcing the distance to
Fort Stockton: impossible. His stomach growled, another urge
hit him. He also thought he ought to call Monica. He remembered what Raul said. "Hurt my chick, man," he said. Killed

her, Eddy recalled. Eddy needed to know that Monica was all right. He didn't worry about Princess.

He steered onto an access road, into the parking lot in front of a log building: Hill Country Tavern. A large sign announced twenty-four-hour breakfast. Just like Pap's Cafe, Eddy thought, maybe worse. Moria stirred awake, looked around. "Got to eat," Eddy said. "Take a leak."

Moria rubbed his face. He looked back at Hedge, nearly out, breathing heavy. Blood soaked through the makeshift bandages, dried, caked. "Leave him sleep," Moria said. Eddy locked the car.

The parking lot was still wet from the passing storm. Inside, morning travelers jammed the booths. Babies cried, but most people spoke in hushed tones. Aromas filled the bright atmosphere, coffee, fresh bread, bacon. The restaurant was warm, homey. It reminded Eddy of the way things were a long time ago. He could barely remember a normal life far away from guns, gangsters, pimps, prostitutes. He and Moria took a booth, sat silently, sipping coffee from the self-serve bar, watched the parking lot through the window.

Eddy made a decision. The second he had Barbara, he was leaving. Fuck them all. Get Barbara, go. No revenge. Bodine was right. Moria was right. This wasn't personal. It was business, and now business was over.

He doubted Moria would like that. Moria had a long arm, might find him anywhere, might send somebody after him. Eddy knew too much. Guys who knew that much didn't just walk away. Eddy thought of the bag of money at the locker in Dallas. Get there, grab the money, maybe take a cab out to DFW, then—what? He had no idea.

Costa Rica, he thought. He'd never been there, wasn't sure exactly where it was. But it sounded like a place where a man with cash could hide for a while. He liked the image: beaches, beer, blondes. Barbara. She could even bring her cop, if she wanted. If he wanted. Eddy didn't care. He was committed. A vision of sun-swept sand filled his mind. He looked around for a waitress, was ready to order, eat, go.

"You think there'll be cops?" he asked.

"Doubt it," Moria said. He had the map in his pocket, looked at it. "Place is so far out in the tulies, probably the last action they saw was when Jesse James held up a stage coach."

The waitress, frizzy and bright-eyed, buck-toothed, big-titted, broad-hipped, grinned at them when she took their order.

"You're a big'un," she said to Eddy. "Bet you want the Bull Rider's Breakfast."

Eddy ordered a cheese omelette. She was disappointed.

20

Flight Plan

Hillary Lovell's Lear Jet raced down the westernmost runway of Hobby International Airport, spun off the hissing wet tarmac, tucked its wheels, shot up through the sticky gray rainclouds, rose steadily away from the sudden golden light of the sun.

The pilot, Terry Hildebrandt, knew how to please his mistress. He'd worked for Hillary for three years, knew she liked to have her desires anticipated. They caught the gap in thunderstorms just right, gained altitude. The wet, windy cold front passed behind them.

The interior of the plane, designed for the comfort of Hillary's ex-husband, was set up like a comfortable den: a place where important people could have important discussions while traveling to important places. Six plush captain's chairs faced each other amidships, each with a separate table, reading lamp, footrest, telephone. A well-stocked wetbar was fixed against the forward bulkhead, astern there was a fold-down queen-sized bed, silk sheets: Hillary's addition, Quince decided.

"Just how bad is it?" she asked. She sat back in one of the portside chairs, crossed her forest-green leather jumpsuit-covered legs, sipped a vodka martini from a frosted glass.

"It's bad enough," Jensen said. His right forearm, wrist,

hand were thick, wrapped in bandages. His shirt and tie were askew, stained with sweat. His suit lacked crispness. The steel-rimmed glasses were gone: he squinted, needed a shave. His eyes were heavy, dark. For once, he looked less than perfect. For once, Quince thought, he looked human. "But our losses are acceptable, so far," he finished. An unlit cigar rolled in his fingers.

"Acceptable," Hillary repeated, lit a pink cigarette. "Yes. That's a nice word. A professional word. You're *such* a professional."

Quince laughed: dry. He sat across from her, next to Jensen. He slouched. He felt old, older than Hillary. She looked thirty. The cup in his hand held coffee, straight and black. He ignored it, let it slosh on his trouser's leg.

"I've got a headache," he said. Hillary ignored him. "I do," he insisted. The pain in his temples was now fully resident: lease signed.

"I don't know how you could approach him that way," Hillary said. "He's too unpredictable. Could have killed you."

"He didn't," Jensen responded.

Behind her, porthole-sized windows revealed morning light. Quince looked up, put his fingers over his brow, shielded his eyes. She donned a pair of sunglasses. Light seemed brighter at twenty-five thousand feet, he thought.

Hillary sipped her drink, smiled. "Balmorhea?" she repeated. "Sounds like the title of a Pinter play. Once more: Just where is this exotically named place?"

"About two hundred miles from El Paso, give or take," Jensen replied.

"Charming."

Balanced on Jensen's knees was a powerbook computer hooked to a telephone cord. He clicked the mouse occasionally with his left hand, read the screen, frowned.

"Something wrong?" Hillary asked.

"Haven't heard anything for a long time," he said. "There's trouble up and down the interstate. All the way from LA. An abduction. A murder. Armed robbery."

"Our people?"

Jensen shook his head. "I doubt it. I don't have any names,

anyway. Not on Mr. Cole's people.'' He shrugged. ''Probably not connected.''

''What about that cop: Sandobal?'' Hillary asked. ''Barbara's friend?''

Jensen shrugged. ''No word on that, either. That was supposed to be handled. My associate is out there. He left a voice mail. It was garbled. Something about things being wrong, that he would fix it. I don't know. No word since, and he doesn't answer his phone.'' He ran a hand across his eyes. ''He's a good man.''

''As good as the two you ran out on?'' Quince muttered.

Jensen shot a look at the lawyer. ''I did *not* run out on them.'' He dropped his eyes to the computer again. ''Besides, they failed to do their job properly. They were trained.''

''Good help's so hard to find, these days,'' Hillary noted.

Jensen said, ''My associate, Mr. Fletcher, is not just 'help.' When he learns something, I'll hear from him. There were no further calls at the office after I left?''

Quince shook his head. ''We were out of there by three. What about your cell phone?''

''Batteries are dead.''

Quince and Hillary observed him coldly. He was a different man from the day before, from any time before, less confident, less sure of success. Made sense: he had met Eddy.

Quince could barely suppress an ironic smile. Jensen would learn. You don't just knock Eddy down, count him out. He'd tried that for years, but Eddy kept coming back. He repeated like a bad meal. The only relief he felt was that they were out of Houston, out of Eddy's reach. For now.

After Jensen returned for the dummy writ, then left again without much explanation, Quince decided to leave the office. Hillary was drunk. He suggested they eat an early dinner. It didn't help. She drank more at the restaurant, refused to talk to him, just looked around the dining room at the sparse late afternoon crowd, scouted for anything that looked wealthy: Horny, Quince thought. He hustled her out, took her to his condo. They retired before the evening news came on. They were already asleep when Jensen called from a convenience store on South Main.

"Eddy's on the loose," he yelled. "And he's crazy." His voice was high, frightened. It was the first time Quince had heard him refer to Eddy as Eddy. Like everyone else, it was always "Mister" this, "Mister" that. Jensen was nothing if not formal. Now, though, he sounded scared. "He knows you're in on the deal, and he'll come for you."

"He knows?" Quince yelled into the receiver. "How in God's name—"

"He'll be coming for you," Jensen said. "Get out of there." He gave them an address, a time to meet. An hour later they were at a motel near Hobby. Jensen came in with weapons and the portable computer.

"I don't want to carry a gun," Quince said when Jensen offered him a pistol. Jensen turned to Hillary.

"Don't be ridiculous," she said, accepted the small, black automatic for herself. "It's cute."

He gave them details. Eddy went mad, he said. Moria was no help at all. Two men were dead, and he was hurt. After he called them, he had his wrist set at Ben Taub, but refused a plaster cast: no time. He left the van, took a cab to the motel. Then Hillary called her pilot. "Can't leave," she said.

"We have to," Jensen said. "There's not an option."

"What there is, is a cold front," Hillary explained. "Terry says nothing smaller than a jumbo jet's going west out of here for a couple of hours." He was right. But the front passed, the rain let up, and as soon as he could, Jensen convinced the pilot that their business was urgent enough to merit a chance. They went to the airport, took off illegally.

"So we're flying into El Paso?" Hillary speculated.

"Alpine," Jensen said. "It's the closest we can get, actually. Well, Fort Stockton's closer. But too small. We'd attract attention."

"And we won't in, uh, Alpine?"

"The last thing to attract attention in Alpine was an earthquake. I doubt everyone noticed that. Alpine was the plan from the beginning."

"Awfully damned sure of yourself, weren't you?" she asked. Jensen squinted at her. "How so?"

"My plane. That I would use it, not fly commercial."

"I could have gotten another plane," Jensen said, gingerly lifted his bandaged arm, winced. "You surely know by now that I leave very little to chance."

"All I can see is a broken arm and one scared little black rabbit," Hillary said. "You refused our advice and left Eddy to chance, and he broke your arm. You're lucky he didn't break your neck." Jensen said nothing. She glanced out at the early morning sky.

Quince shifted his weight. "I don't understand why you tried to rush things? What purpose—"

"I had an idea," Jensen interrupted. "If we could make the transaction there, in Houston, everything would have come off quietly. We would have circumvented Mr. Cole's people's further involvement."

"Left them hanging, you mean," Hillary corrected.

"Left Barbara hanging," Quince added.

"We could still have handled that," Jensen said. "Mr. Fletcher—"

"That was not the plan," Quince argued.

"No, but neither was their finding the prostitute who set up Mr. Cole," Jensen said. "One of my people, Robin—"

"The *late* Robin," Hillary added.

"Yes. Robin saw them taking her into the back of that place. His partner, Mr. Fizer, followed Mr. Mendle and Mr. Lovell there as well. It was a foregone conclusion that they talked to her. I don't know how much she knew, what she might have told them."

"You made damned sure no one else knows that, either," Quince shot back, sitting up slightly. "I cannot believe you blew up an entire building. A place of business. Killed innocent—"

"Distraction," Jensen said. "And it was necessary to eliminate the prostitute. I needed to talk to your brother and his employer, to find out what they told the police. That was their second interview, you know."

"I'm sure they said nothing," Hillary offered. "Eddy has never been too popular with the police. Isn't that right, Quince?"

"A firebomb," Quince said, "Christ! Impersonating an attorney with a fake writ. My God, Jensen. You're supposed to be better than that.''

"It almost worked," Jensen said, shrugged. "Unforeseen development."

"It almost got you killed," Quince said. "It *did* kill two of your men."

Jensen's face lowered, expression darkened. "They were expendable."

"Expendable," Hillary said as if she had never heard the word before.

"I miscalculated," Jensen said. "That's all. Who could have expected Mr. Mendle's bodyguard to show up? He was wounded, badly. I saw it. Shot point-blank. He should have died on the spot."

"You're panicking."

"I'm not panicking," Jensen said. "I'm exercising damage control. We will meet Mr. Fletcher in Alpine, I'm certain. He'll drive us to Balmorhea. We'll trade for the girl, then we'll reenter negotiations with Mr. Lovell. Nothing's changed."

"Two men dead, and nothing's changed," Quince moaned. "Jesus God."

"Two?" Hillary asked. "There's a whole cafe full of dead people."

"And," Quince added, gaining strength, "we mustn't forget Cole and his friends. People died in that little escapade, too. I don't know how much of this 'nothing's changed' the world can take. Al Capone didn't kill this many people. You're the Pro from Dover, aren't you, *Mister* Jensen? Do professionals always leave so many corpses in their wake?"

Jensen gave Quince a long look. "Nothing's changed. The only significant new element is that Mr. Lovell is aware that we have his daughter."

"And of our involvement," Hillary put in.

"He doesn't know where she is," Jensen continued, "doesn't know where we are. He has no idea when or where the exchange will take place. Once we have her in hand, all that remains is negotiation."

"I can see how well you negotiate." Quince lowered his aching head into his hands.

Hillary unclasped her seat belt, rose. "Martini, anyone?"

"It would help if you stayed sober," Jensen said.

"It would help," Hillary said, "if you stayed professional. Stayed." She stopped, struck a pose, tapped her front tooth with a long nail, studied him. "Hell, it would help if you *became* professional." She went on to the bar, mixed her drink in a shaker, poured. "I am suddenly aware, Quince," she said, "that we, too, may be 'expendable.' I want out of the whole deal."

Quince scowled at her. "It's a little late for that."

She studied him. "You're turning out to be an even bigger disappointment to me than Eddy," she said. "At least Eddy has balls."

She picked up her glass, drained it, poured another. "I want out. Okay. You won't let me out. At least start trying to think of a way for us all to live through this."

Quince made a show of looking out a window. "You can get out any time you want, big sister. But it's a long way down."

"Shut up, Quince! Just shut up!" She slammed the glass down. It shattered. She pointed at Jensen. "All we have, now, is to go on, to go through with it. You'd better start thinking about what Eddy's going to do to us. He *told* him we were involved! *Told him*. You can forget buying him off. You can forget everything except avoiding him. If we can." She selected a new glass from the counter. "Personally, as soon as our part is over, I'm leaving the country."

"With Barbara?"

"With her, without her. I really don't care. Not anymore." Hillary fixed herself a new martini, returned to her seat. Her leather jumpsuit was soft, supple, moved with her figure. Quince noticed that Jensen's eyes followed her movements closely. He was repulsed. Professional, he thought: bullshit.

"Have some more coffee, Quincy. Looks as if you could use some," Hillary said.

"What if . . ." Quince asked, then rubbed his face with the palm of his hand. "What if it doesn't work."

"What if what doesn't work?" Hillary asked.

"What if the program doesn't work? It's been over two years since anyone's tried it."

"It works. I know it works. I've seen it work," Jensen said. "If things hadn't gone awry to begin with, it would be working now. It will work."

"If it doesn't work," Quince continued, "the deal's still on. Right? We don't have to guarantee anything."

"Doesn't matter," Hillary said. "Our deal was to set up Eddy. We've done that. Our deal was not to see if anything works. If it doesn't work, that's just tough." She crossed her legs. "I'm not negotiating that any further." A pause. "Neither are you, Quince." The plane was flying level and smooth. They had been in the air for nearly an hour. "The one thing I'm not clear on is the final terms."

Jensen looked up. "We've covered that," he said. "You get the girl. If you want her."

"Beyond the girl," Hillary said.

"And the money. I think that's clear enough."

"And you have the cash?"

Jensen looked up, serious. "We have the cash. Cash is easy. Do you want cash?"

"Of course we want cash," Quince said, struggling to sit upright. The chair, comfortable as it was, was downsized, didn't fit his large frame. "If the program works, you think we'd trust you with anything else?" He looked at Hillary. "You'd clean us out ten minutes after we made a deposit. Don't be ridiculous."

"Don't look at me," Hillary said. "I'm not about to take a check."

Jensen nodded. "Whatever you want."

"And what about the payoff there? To Cole's people," Quince asked. "You have money for that, too?"

Jensen pointed to a large, black leather case on the floor by his chair. "Yes," he said. "A little more than half a million."

"So, we land there when?"

"Eleven o'clock. We'll be about fifty miles away, through the mountains."

"Mountains? In Texas?" Hillary asked. "How amusing."

"We'll have a car waiting. Mr. Fletcher will provide a large van.

"Goody," Hillary said. "Just like a field trip."

"We should be there"—he consulted his watch—"just after noon, with luck."

"Grand," Hillary said. "We can do lunch."

"Shut up, Hillary," Quince moaned.

For a while they didn't talk. The hum of the jet was the only noise except for the clink of ice in the shaker on the bar.

Quince broke the silence. "I wonder how I ever got involved in this."

Hillary studied him briefly, disappointment in her eyes. "I never wonder, Quincy," she said. "I never do."

Eddy slammed the pay telephone receiver back onto its switchhook, stood still for a moment, rubbed his temples. His broken finger ached from the impact.

"You okay?" an irritable voice behind him asked.

The cashier of the Hill Country Tavern, a mousey blonde with bad acne, was giving him a severe, disapproving look. He nodded. "Well, don't go banging our stuff around," the girl responded. Pale blue eyes flashed. "Lot of people depend on that phone." She spun back to her work, cast a bright smile on two elderly tourists flashing their AARP cards in her face, demanding discounts. "You know," she announced to the elderly couple, "I don't know why we put up *signs*. Folks just *ignore* them. There's a definite problem with *literacy* in this country." She shot Eddy a nasty sideways look.

He ignored it, walked with forced control back to the booth where the buck-toothed waitress was delivering a to-go order of bacon and egg sandwiches for Hedge. Two new thermoses, purchased from a small stand of curios, and travel supplies were also present, one filled with coffee, the other with orange juice. It was Eddy's idea. Hedge had lost a lot of blood. Eddy stood, waited until she left. "Let's go. Now."

"Something wrong?" Moria asked.

Eddy had said nothing about any phone call. He was supposed to be in the men's room. He wasn't sure Moria would agree that making a call was wise. Now, Eddy wasn't so sure, either. "Just talked to a friend of mine," he said.

"Who?" Moria's eyes swept the room. The crowd had thinned since they arrived. Now, only local coffee hounds lingered: swapped stories, postponed work. "On the phone. Called a friend of mine. . .Monica. Let's go."

Moria's eyes settled on Eddy. "Know about her," Moria said. "So does Princess. Jealous as hell. Wish you'd blow one of them off. Drives me nuts." Eddy nodded. Nothing was a surprise anymore. "So what happened? The rabbit die?" Eddy felt a prick of anger. Monica was a friend. Whatever else she was was none of Moria's business. He turned to leave. "We got to go."

"What?" Moria said. "What's the deal. Sit. Damnit: sit."

"She's been trying to reach me," Eddy said, perched on the edge of the booth's seat. "Had no idea where I was. Am."

"Yeah. That's okay. So?"

"She had a call this morning. Couple hours ago."

"Yeah. So?"

"From Barbara."

Moria looked blank.

"Barbara. My daughter."

Moria's face set. "Jensen?" Eddy shook his head. "Well. What, then?"

Eddy went through it: Monica had only been in bed a short time—"hard night," she told Eddy, "all one-timers. Short stuff." She was groggy when the phone rang: girl's voice, asked for Eddy.

"So who was it?" Eddy demanded.

"Your daughter. Barbara."

Eddy's mouth went dry, sweat formed all over him. "You sure?" He knew Monica hadn't spoken to Barbara in years. But the girl on the phone said she was "Eddy's Barbara, Eddy's daughter."

Monica let that sink in. "Guess that's who it was. Think?"

"When did she call? Exactly?"

"I don't know. Didn't look at the clock," she shot back. "I'm not a fucking secretary," she said. Eddy didn't react. She softened. "She's in trouble, Eddy."

Eddy's mind leaped. It was a ransom call. Jensen wanted to turn up the heat. "Go on."

"She. . .well, I really don't understand all this."

"Tell me what she said," Eddy spoke in a cutting whisper. "Exactly." The cashier cleared her throat. A sign above the telephone asked patrons to limit their calls to three minutes.

"She said she's okay. But she needs your help."

Another pause. "Go on," Eddy hissed.

"She talked about somebody named Vicki. Vicki's the one in trouble, she said. Who's Vicki?"

Eddy's mind swirled a minute, then settled, remembered. "Vicki's a friend."

"Of whose? Look, Eddy. I don't mind helping you out, give you a place to stay now and then, watching your stuff for you. And I can understand about that bitch-kitty you live with over at the Sheraton. I mean, I'm no angel, and we got no *specific* arrangement, but—"

"Where is she?" Eddy demanded.

"—you've got a thing or two to learn about little Miss Princess, though. I called that bitch trying to find you. She's a tramp, I can tell you that! You know she screws every cowboy in Dallas when you're gone?" Monica asked. "She's got a thing for rodeo riders. Picks them up out in Mesquite—"

"Where is she?"

"At the Sheraton. Right there in your bed! Some guy named Randy answered the phone. Big as all get out: 'This is Randy,' he says. 'Who you want—' "

"Not her. Barbara. Damnit, Monica, where's Barbara? I don't give a shit about Princess." He didn't. He realized all at once he didn't care about Monica, either.

"Well, that's not the way it looks from where I sit. Looks to me like you give—"

"Barbara," Eddy hissed. He slapped the side of the phone box in frustration. The cashier coughed again, louder. "Where's my daughter, Monica?"

"How should I know? Where the hell are you? All I have is a number where you can call her. She said she wouldn't be there long—"

"So, what's the number?" He had trouble controlling himself. He was rushing all the way across Texas to try to save her, and here she called him up, asked for help. What *was*

going on? Monica read the number off to him. He repeated it
mentally, said it back. "Where is that?"

"Beats me. She said if you can't reach her there, you need
to meet her."

"Where?"

"She also said to tell you she's not alone. Somebody named
Sanderball—"

"Sandobal," Eddy corrected, feeling some relief but no less
confusion.

"Well, he's with her. And she's got her present with her,
whatever the hell that—"

"Where? Where does she want to meet?"

"Sounds like a club or something. I don't think it's in the
Metroplex. I never heard of it. Where the hell are you,
anyway?"

"Name?" Eddy asked. "Give me the name."

"Yeah, just a second. I wrote it here someplace." He heard
her shuffling papers in the background. "Place called Balmorhea. She made me spell it. You want me to spell it?"

"No. I got it." He breathed out.

"When you coming back? We need to talk."

Eddy hung up. He dialed the number Monica gave him, got
a motel in Ysleta. The manager said they checked out that
morning, but they left no word.

"You get a name?"

"You a cop?"

"No."

"Jealous husband?"

"No. You got a name on them?" Silence. "I'm the girl's
father," Eddy said. "Just need to locate her. Family business."

"They paid cash. So no name. But the guy had a badge of
some kind. Not local. Said his name was Sandobal."

Moria took in the story, looked around the emptying restaurant.
"So, who's Vicki?"

"Some friend of hers. Actress or something."

"And Sandobal's a cop?"

Eddy nodded. "From New York. New Jersey. Someplace. California, now."

"Cops complicate things, wherever they're from."

"He's a kind of boyfriend, I think."

"Boyfriends complicate things, too."

He pulled Eddy's pack of Camels over, shook one out, began playing with it. "Let's think this through a second. She wants you to meet her at Balmorhea."

"Right."

Moria shook his head fast. "Right." He ripped the cigarette apart, let the tobacco spread across the Formica table. "What kind of game is this?"

Eddy looked around helpless: no answer. Then, something else Monica said struck him. He looked into Moria's small eyes. They compelled as they did the first time he saw them: a quiet demand. Moria was confused. He was not a man who liked confusion.

"There's one more thing," he said.

"Yeah?"

"She told Monica she had her 'present.' "

"Present?"

"A gun. S&W .38. I bought it in Dallas, FedExed it to her."

"Ought to buy stock in that company," Moria sighed. "So, she's looking for trouble?" Eddy shrugged. "Okay. I got it. Let's check out of this joint. We got some miles to make up."

Back on the highway, Eddy said nothing, focused on bringing the Mercedes up to speed: eighty-five ought to do it, he thought. Barbara was waiting. But for what? Rescue or help? Hedge sat up. His breath was heavy, rasping. He had the food on his lap, fresh blood was visible through the bandages. He was eating. A good sign. "You guys took your time," he said.

When Eddy checked him a few minutes later in the rearview, his head was back, his eyes hidden again behind the shades. It was the longest speech he had ever heard him make.

*   *   *

The Alpine airport looked about the way Quince expected it to look: small, run-down. Two runways striped through yellow sand, rocky desert between volcanic mountains. A couple of gray metal hangars baked in the sun, all overseen by a two-story control tower built in an era when jet aircraft were still science fiction. Terry touched down easily, taxied to a stop far from the tower, as instructed. Before he shut down, a navy-blue Chrysler sedan pulled out of a gate, approached them. The port to the cockpit opened, Terry emerged: crisp uniform, sharp haircut, square jaw. Nice-looking guy, Quince thought: young, virile. Probably can fuck all night long.

Hillary gave him a woozy smile. Quince figured she had downed three, four stiff martinis on the trip. "Nice flight, Terry," she said.

"Thank you, Ms. Lovell," he said, then frowned. "They're going to want some information. We didn't file a flight plan out of Houston. Came out of nowhere. They've been barking at me on the radio all the way in."

"Let me handle it," Jensen said, looked out a window. "Where is Mr. Fletcher?" He went to the other side, looked.

"Things not going so well?" Hillary asked. "Another little miscalculaton?" Her speech slurred.

"Shut up, Hillary," Quince said.

Jensen extracted the large black case from the area next to his seat, rummaged briefly through it, then pocketed a wrapped sheaf of bills. He then opened another, smaller case, removed a leather wallet, stood, checked to make sure his pistol didn't show. "Open up," he ordered Terry, glanced at Quince. "You look like hell," he said. "Come up here and stay just inside the door. Let them see you, but not too well."

Quince followed Jensen to the open door, peeked out into the brightness. Desert smells invaded the small plane. High country, cool and dry.

Jensen stepped down the ladder. A western suit and a khaki security uniform got out of the Chrysler, came to meet him. The guard was armed, dark, heavy.

Jensen opened a wide smile, kept one hand on the button on his suit. "Gentlemen," he said in a loud voice, nodded back toward the plane. He pulled the wallet out, flashed it open.

"United States Department of Justice. That's the deputy secretary in the aircraft. I apologize for our unorthodox arrival. I'm certain that we've upset your morning, but it couldn't be helped. I'm afraid we're on official business of the Federal Government."

The two men stared at Jensen, at Quince. He wondered if he should wave. Settled for a nod. Jensen's voice dropped. Their heads were together briefly, then the money changed hands, the suit smiled, guard gave Quince a short salute. The two returned to the sedan and drove off. Jensen came back to the plane. "They might think to make some calls later, but for now, we're okay." Quince stumbled back to his seat. His headache was worse than ever.

"Did you cut them into our little deal?" Hillary asked, smiled. The pilot stood dumbly beside her, sipped coffee, looked protective.

Jensen gave her a hard look, shifted to Terry. "I want this plane gassed and ready to go." The pilot looked at Hillary. "Don't look at her," Jensen ordered: "Look at me. We'll be returning in two, three hours at the most. We want to be in Houston as quickly as you can get us there."

"Should I file a flight plan this time? Houston won't be bullshitted so easily. Or bought off." He gave Jensen a quick, ironic wink. Hillary reached up, took his hand.

Jensen smiled. "Yes. File a plan. Now, you can leave." He pulled a small fold of currency from his pocket. "Get something to eat. See a movie. Be back here ready to go." Terry stiffened a bit.

"Go on, Terry," Hillary said. "His bark is worse than his bite, but I'm assured that he can indeed bite." The pilot gave her hand a squeeze, then set down his cup, took the money from Jensen, left the plane.

Quince looked out the window: panic. "They're coming back. With a van."

"That's for us," Jensen said. "Mr. Fletcher is obviously not here to meet us. I've arranged for an airport shuttle to take us where we need to go."

"Another little miscalculation?" Hillary asked. Jensen glowered at her. "I think I'll stay here. You don't need me for this."

"I think you'll do exactly as you're told."

"Let her stay," Quince said. "We don't need her. She's sloshed anyway. Goddamn embarrassment. And you really don't need me—"

"You're coming," Jensen said. "You're both coming. Now." He picked up the large case.

Hillary rose unsteadily, gathered her balance. "Quincy. Be a dear and mix some drinks. For the road. I'm going to freshen up." She moved to the head, swayed slightly, went inside. Quince sighed, went to the bar.

"You're not going to do that, are you?" Jensen asked.

Quince picked up a bottle of vodka, poured it into a large metal shaker along with two handfuls of ice, then added a quick dash of vermouth, screwed down the lid, shook it once. "I always do what I'm told," he said, picked up a clean glass. "I'm the only Lovell who does."

21

Balmorhea

Vicki awoke: daylight. She was in the rear seat of the Suburban, and at first felt lost, confused. She sat up, looked around. Morning light swirled, fell into place: Day Two with Pancho and Lefty. Too bad about Cisco.

Al still drove, both hands firm on the wheel: road-weary. Red, in the middle, kept fooling with a small TV screen mounted on the console. The picture was lines, static, kept fading in and out, no sound. "Can't get shit out here," he complained, turned tiny dials.

Vicki looked out the window. Dawn spread across an arid landscape. Not quite desert, but close. Small mountains lined the horizon to the south. Occasional cedar trees, prickly pear were visible alongside the interstate.

"Want to stop for smokes?" Al called back. "We're nearly out."

The thought of stopping "for smokes" chilled Vicki. In the past two days, she had learned to dread any stop, no matter how short. Stops meant hope, for a time, then disappointment. Stops meant death.

Vicki had never seen a dead person before, except on TV. Both her parents' funerals were closed-caskets. She'd once met a girl named Irene Blakely, an actress who made a career playing dead people. ''I've been a corpse seventeen times,'' Irene proudly announced her credits. ''Shot four times. Burned up once. One suicide. Knifed twice. Once in a coffin. The others were disaster movies. Twelve were nude, but always face down. They said I had a good butt.'' Irene said it paid well. ''They have to shoot death scenes several times. You can get eight, ten days' work. Hell, walk-ons with lines are lucky to get two.'' At the time, Vicki laughed. She'd do that, she thought then. No more. She'd experienced enough death for a lifetime. It wasn't the same as the movies. It was ugly.

The big problem was that the people she most wanted dead wouldn't die. They just kept on going: Energizer Bunnies.

''So?'' Al asked. ''You want to stop or not?''

''We've stopped too much,'' Red barked. He seemed to read Vicki's thoughts. ''Every time you stop, something happens. People get killed. You're a maniac.''

Al chuckled. ''I'll try to do it right this time.''

''We got any money left?''

''Couple sawbucks.'' The bag she grabbed from the liquor store had not been the money sack, Vicki learned: Blackie's food. She and Red yelled about that for a long while.

Roadsigns indicated they were deep into Texas. Vicki rubbed her eyes, tried to move, couldn't. Her ankle was cuffed to the seat's floor bracket. Her bladder needed relief, but she didn't want to stop. She agreed with Red. Better to wet herself. What difference did it make?

When the storm finally broke the night before, they were overwhelmed with muddy rain. The road was slick: visibility zero. Lights from passing vehicles flattened out in the dense atmosphere, sprayed white beams everywhere at once. Vicki was sure they would lose control, crack up. They finally pulled off for a while into a deserted tourist trap's parking lot.

It was dark, cold, raining. Al parked behind a collapsed billboard: chocolate shakes, cheeseburgers, fries, $1.99. Al broke out the bottle she had taken from the liquor store. They drank it, talked about friends they had in other places, things they would do with the money. Red talked about somebody named LeRoy. The liquor hit them hard. Red cried. Al laughed, sang along to the CD player: Johnny Mathis, Righteous Brothers, Johnny Rivers.

They didn't offer Vicki a drink of anything, just some chips, hot links, cheese and crackers. She was ravenous, choked it all down dry. They paid no attention to her after that. After a while, she lay back, closed her eyes, thought of Gary and California.

Sometime during the night she felt something on her leg, moving up her thigh. At first, it tickled, then it grew stronger. She was sure there was a hand on her breast. She opened her eyes, sat up, looked around: nothing. Red sat in the front seat, awake, his eyes open in the rearview. Al was nowhere in sight. The back door of the Suburban was ajar, open. Vicki looked through the rear windows into the inky night. Nothing.

The rain was diminished to a crawling drizzle, dripped out of the clouds, washed away the mud. Vicki focused on the blackness. A figure appeared, about twenty-five yards off, occasionally lit by the headlamps of a passing vehicle: Al. She was naked, her body white, waxy, obese in the frequent flash of headlamps from the highway, then brightly illuminated by lightning overhead. She stood with her back to the Suburban, faced the darkness of the desert beyond. Her flabby hips sagged beneath a roll around her middle. Huge chunks of flab-rippled thighs splayed downward past thick calves to broad, flat feet. Muscles stood out in relief on her arms. Her hands were high, over her head, palms flat, upwards to the rain.

Vicki scooted down, peeked through the crack in the door. She watched Al lower her arms, wipe her entire body clean with the rainwater. She turned slow, caressed herself, ran her hands over large misshapened breasts, in between her thighs. Her face turned up toward the rain, allowed it to wash over her. In the flash of passing headlights, Al's face contorted, her mouth open, drinking in the rain. She cried out into the storm, her hands worked faster now, one moved from taut nipple to gelatinous stomach, then up to her stretched-out neck, then back again, the other buried in her crotch, worked furiously between her huge legs, massaged herself.

Vicki could not look away. She bit her finger to keep from being ill.

Al climaxed. Her mouth, open to the falling drops, stretched wider. A roar, low and bestial, bellowed from her. Her free hand wrapped itself around her head, the other pushed and pounded on her crotch. She cried out again, a higher pitch this time, her bare feet shuffling slightly on the muddy ground, her knees half buckled. She arched her back: another cry in the rain.

Then she collapsed, bent forward, knelt, forehead down to her bent knee, both hands now grasped the back of her neck. She shuddered, shook off the water that ran down her broad back, made her slick and smooth in the white glare of passing headlamps. At last, she stood, straightened, then wandered off, out of sight into the darkness.

Vicki pulled the rear doors together softly, tugged until she heard them click, dropped the plunger lock. Cold sweat formed a sheen beneath her clothes. Nothing like this on TV, she thought.

She checked Red. He hadn't moved. After a bit, the front door of the Suburban opened, she heard Al shift back into the driver's seat, smelled a cigarette. Red said something soft. Al grunted in reply. It took a long time for Vicki to stop shivering, go back to sleep. Reality crept away into the night.

Now, they were back on the road. "Nothing but shit," Red said. He twisted dials. "Need some news. Need to know if they've made us. Anything on the radio?"

Al leaned forward, pushed buttons. Tejano music, loud singing popped through for a while. "Just Mexican shit," she said. "Can't get nothing out here." She snapped off the music. "Shouldn't've whacked Teach," she said. "That's going to come back on us."

After a while, they slowed down. Vicki saw an exit sign: Balmorhea. At the intersection was another of the ubiquitous roadside gas station-grocery-cafes. Beyond it, there was nothing but rocks, sand, barbed wire, an occasional windmill. Al guided the Suburban off the ramp, turned right onto a state highway:

290, Vicki read: Fort Davis, Alpine. In a few minutes, she spotted a water tower, Texaco station. Her heart beat a little faster. This was it: escape.

Hope died quick. The town was comprised of two operating gas stations, four closed ones. Something that looked like a combination hunting lodge-cafe dominated one side of the highway. That was the main street, a few tacky houses lined the other side. Vicki knew what Texas-rural looked like. She grew up with it. They passed these junk-laden yards, rusty trailers, broken-down vehicles jammed up against the weedy fences. She decided that she might be better off with Al and Red than walking up to the home of some deranged inbred and shrieking for help. Every yard seemed to be home to a pack of snarling dogs, furious that the Suburban was gliding along right in front of them.

Al slipped up beside a small grocery, left the engine idling. "Smokes," she said, climbed out.

Red scowled, picked up the revolver. "Don't do nothing stupid."

Hope once again pushed itself forward in Vicki's mind. Then an omen in the station's window caught her eye. The same orange-skirted señorita from the billboard appeared on a poster-sized ad. "I need to pee," she said.

"Hold it," Al ordered. "We ain't got far to go now." She left the Suburban, stretched high when she got out, stomped her feet a bit, then strolled into the store. Vicki held her breath. In a few moments, she was out, a carton of Marlboros under her arm. Through the glass, Vicki saw the attendant still behind the counter. A noise came from Red: a slow exhalation of air. He had been holding his breath, too.

Al puffed happily back behind the wheel. They pulled out, passed another set of small buildings, then a more modern but no more inviting L-shaped motel, the town faded away behind them. Panic replaced hope.

She was surprised by the emotion. She wouldn't have believed herself capable of feeling anything but the dull ache from her bladder. If they weren't stopping in Balmorhea, then where were they going? A set of orange letters scrawled on a restroom door rose in her mind's eye. How could anyone find her now? She had thought of nothing but this town. Now it disappeared in the sotols and sandy gravel behind them. The city limits sign went by. Red noticed that, too: surprise. "Hey," he yelled. "That was it."

"That was what?"

"That was fucking it. The place. Thought we were going there."

"We are."

"But that was fucking *it*. Turn around."

"Keep your shorts on, asshole. We ain't going to the town. Going to the park. Few miles down the road."

"Park?"

"State park. Motel, everything. Cole picked it personal: nice and quiet." She made a kissing noise. "Prom Queen'll love it. Great swimming pool. We can go skinny dipping!" Vicki felt bile rise, swallowed hard.

Red sat back. "I'll be glad when this is over."

Al lit another cigarette. "Want a smoke?"

Vicki spotted a rail fence that rose, ran along the road to their left. Al slowed the Suburban. A grove of trees appeared. White stucco buildings were visible. A brown State Parks sign announced, "Balmorhea State Park and Recreational Area."

"There she blows," Al said. "Keep Prom Queen quiet. This could get hinky."

Midge Watkins, Senior Superintendent and Head Ranger at Balmorhea State Park, was a dour, pinch-faced woman who had never in her memory passed a completely pleasant day. Short, flat-chested, flabby-bottomed, she spent most of her time trying to figure out a way of beating the house odds in Vegas. Most of her salary went to pay for past attempts. Most of her life was as big a waste as each try. Midge's job did have pluses: benefits were good, demands small. But the pay was poor, and retirement was a long way off. Midge wanted to move to Vegas permanently. She had an idea for a new system. All she needed was money.

One morning two months before, Bob Cole stepped into her office and offered Midge a deal. She went for it: ticket out.

She took one look at the bright-eyed man in the five-hundred-dollar suit, knew what he was. He was working a game, and he wanted privacy. She said no until the price was right. She didn't know the details and didn't care. A hundred thousand bucks would go a long way toward a setup in Vegas. Midge was already packed, had a full list of Vegas-based plastic surgeons, had sold her mobile home. Her letter of resignation was in the desk drawer.

Remote, isolated, well off the interstate, Balmorhea State Park was the best-kept secret in Texas. It was built by the Civilian Conservation Corps during the Depression and boasted the largest, coldest, most attractive natural swimming hole in the western United States. San Solomon Springs fed twenty-six million gallons of cold subterranean water a day through a system of locks and canals into the giant half-moon-shaped pool. In one end, out the other. An oasis in semi-arid waste. The pool was surrounded by juniper, live oak, cottonwood, and hackberry trees: hand-planted. The runoff fed a canal where two endangered species of fish found no place else in the world swam, mated, survived.

In the summer the pool was frequented by the most obnoxious collection of tourist-dipshits Midge could imagine. They stopped by to picnic, party, and swim from May through Labor Day. Midge hated all of them. They were rich, young, or both. From the string-bikinied teenaged girls to the fat men in boxer-short-style trunks to the show-off college boys in Speedos, they disgusted her, made her feel like a frump, a failure.

Travelers could put up at the San Solomon Springs Courts, an eighteen-unit strip of motor-court-style cabins built at the same time as the pool and mostly left alone since. Air conditioning and two-channel television were added. Kitchenettes were available. Each cabin had two entrances: a front to the parking lot, and a rear to a canal with the strange fish. But the heavy pine bedsteads, threadbare throw rugs over hardwood floors, oversized, splintery Adirondack chairs testified to the indifference of the Texas State Park Service's plans toward modernization. The only evidence of changing times was the PVC used to replace worn plumbing, the acoustical tiled ceilings, the thick layers of dark paint, inside and out.

Midge's headquarters were in a cottage at the park's only public gate. There wasn't a lot of business after Labor Day. Mostly picnickers, occasional ecology nuts dropped by to stare at the Pecos mosquitofish and the Comanche Springs pulpfish. The cottage had an outer office, a back room that contained a cot, a toilet, a gun closet.

That Friday morning, her last as a Park Ranger, Midge arrived early, made a pot of coffee, started a Kitty Wells CD, took up her post behind the desk of the park office. The window to her left looked out over the entrance, a chest-high counter divided the desk area from the registration area. She kept the gate locked, would all day, in direct violation of park policy. Those were Cole's instructions. Midge was already working on a blackjack system she was sure couldn't be beat.

She hadn't heard from Cole in ten days, but he said he wouldn't call unless plans changed. Otherwise, she could expect to see him in person Friday evening. She planned to fix a home-cooked meal for him: venison stew. She planned to give him a bottle of malt Scotch she'd been holding onto since an old friend—a hunter—dropped by for a visit and left it in partial payment for Midge's special attentions. She planned to see if Cole wanted any of those special attentions after a sip or two of that premium whiskey, after he came across with the payoff. Cole might be some kind of crook, Midge thought, but he was also one good-looking cowboy.

She dealt another hand, noted idly that last night's rain had flooded the parking lot—again—and that this might bring out Jerry Brady, the proprietor of the park's combination bath-house-concession stand: a lease. Jerry was also the park's chief Mr. Fix-It. He was also Midge's regular Friday fuck. Unless he went fishing. She didn't know how she could keep Jerry out, but she would have to do it. She always gave the superintendent, other employees off-season Fridays off. There wasn't much to do—why not take a long weekend "on the state?"—she covered for them. Jerry covered her. But Jerry was also a deputy sheriff.

That didn't bother her too much. Half the local able-bodied men she knew were deputy sheriffs. It was a big county. Still, Jerry had an office. Midge didn't know what to expect that afternoon, but she was pretty sure Cole wouldn't like to have even a part-time deputy lawman poking around—either in the park or in Midge—while it was going on.

Her instructions, though, were simple. Wait for Cole. Let him in. Get the payoff. Lock things up good and tight, leave her resignation letter on the desk, haul to Vegas. She figured to make Gallup by noon tomorrow.

Kitty Wells wailed off, Midge got up, poured herself another cup of coffee, popped in a Willie and Waylon disk. Leftover rainwater dripped from the trees onto the tin roof of the office. The walls were covered with black-and-white and sepia-toned photographs of the park in better days. Midge straightened a couple—she always straightened a couple every morning, noted they were dusty. Dusting was not in Midge's job description.

A big blue Suburban with whipping antennas and a TV aerial came down the highway from town, turned abruptly into the park's drive, stopping at the single heavy-gauge wire strung across the opening. The driver honked twice—long blasts— Midge looked out the window and frowned. Tourists, she thought. Cole had told her to expect him late in the day. This was not Bob Cole.

The "Park Closed" sign was prominently displayed, dangled on the wire. She decided they could damn well read it for themselves. She sat down behind the desk, calculated the odds on taking a hit with eighteen when there was only a two-deck shooter, three-fourths dealt, and the dealer showed eleven or less. Another honk.

"Shit," Midge swore, rose from her chair. Normally, she wore civvies to work. Regulations at Balmorhea were lax, especially in the off-season. She liked skirts. Today, though, following Cole's suggestion, she had on the full uniform: green blouse, gray trousers, black boots, mesh gimmecap with the seal of the Texas State Parks Department. A bright gold badge sat right where her left nipple should poke out, if she had had enough breast behind it to poke. She killed the CD, took one more sip of coffee, listened to one more angry blast, stormed out the door.

The Suburban was decked out: luggage rack, chrome grill, fog lights. Red-and-white pinstriping ran the length of the vehicle. "CABRITO," the license plate read. Midge hated it on sight. She made her way up to the wire, ten yards in front of the Suburban. The tinted windows reflected the morning sun. The shadow behind the wheel told her a heavy-set man was driving. One hand was propped on the outside rearview mirror, cigarette smoldering in fat fingers.

"We're closed," she yelled. She pointed at the sign. "Annual Maintenance," she added, turned back to the office. The horn sounded again. She spun, angry. "I said—" she started. The hand outside now waved her to come forward. "Christ," she muttered. She went to the heavy wire, contemplated the best way to negotiate it, stepped over, walked up to the window, stopped. The man was a woman.

"Open up."

Midge narrowed her eyes. "We're closed."

"We've got a reservation," the woman said. She smirked, laughed almost, winked. Midge had a thought, suppressed it. Naw, she thought. These people wouldn't have anything to do with a man like Cole—or he with them.

"No, you don't. We're closed. Annual Maintenance."

"Fuck it," a voice in the back yelled. "I'm tired of this shit!" The back door window hissed down. Midge found herself staring into the barrel of a small caliber revolver. Behind the pistol was the unshaven face of a red-haired man, his eyes bloodshot, angry. "Open the gate: *now.*"

Midge swallowed hard. "I think there's been a mis—"

"Open the goddamn *gate!*" the redhead yelled, stepped out of the truck, raised the gun, hit her on the head.

Midge slumped to the ground. Lights flickered in front of her, a black cloud surrounded her vision. Pain seared down her forehead behind two long trails of blood. She felt pressure on her throat: the revolver's barrel.

"Listen, bitch," a voice came to her ear. "Get up and open the gate right now, or I'm going to blow off your fucking head and read your fucking mind." Midge tried to twist around to look at him, opened her mouth to speak. "Say one word. Please. Just one. Please," he begged. She knew what he meant. "I'm in a bad mood," he said. "I'm having a bad day. I'm going to say this one more time: Get up and open the fucking gate. Now!''

With the gun still pressed into the back of her neck, Midge gathered her feet under her, stood, staggered over to the gate. Her throat was dry, constricted. She pulled the key ring off her belt, opened the padlock, dropped the wire. The Suburban passed over it. Her head cleared. This was *not* part of the deal. She felt a push behind her, walked up to the idling Suburban. The redhead kept the pistol on her, now jammed her ribs. Inside the vehicle, in the backseat, she saw another figure—a woman. The TV was on: snow. The gun nudged her.

"Inside the office," the redhead said.

"Just go ahead and whack her," the woman behind the wheel yelled.

"You don't know who you're dealing with," Midge said. "I—"

"And I don't give a shit. Inside, now."

"Do you know—"

"Move, lady. Don't talk. I'm too fucking tired to hear anything you got to say." He pushed her ahead of him into the office, made her sit in a chair, used a pocketknife to cut the electric cord off her CD player, another off her coffeemaker. He studied at the antique PBX machine with its multiple plugs, wires. "No direct dial?" She glared at him, furious, afraid.

He tied her ankles to the chair, wrapped her hands with duct tape he found in the desk. He stuffed a wad of paper towels into her mouth, wrapped more tape across her lips to hold them in place. Her eyes begged him, but he ignored her, ransacked the outer office, dumped out drawers, overturned files, made a mess.

Her purse lay open on the desk. He went to it, dumped it out, found her wallet. "Twenty bucks," he commented, more to himself than to her. "Why the fuck is it everybody we run into is broker than we are?" She made no movement, no sound. There was nearly five thousand in hundreds rolled into a brown plastic prescription bottle amidst the cosmetics, keys, other junk. He glanced at the label, discarded it with a shake of his head.

"Just stay quiet, you can go home after while," he said. His voice was full of fatigue, pain. "Maybe we all can." Then he studied the peg board on the wall, selected a key to a cabin, went out. She heard him yell. "Cabin One. Get inside."

Midge struggled. The wires around her ankles held. Her mouth was dry. Her eyes were watered. She wasn't afraid. She was pissed off. She had let that punk take her so easily. Vegas wasn't worth this. Blackjack wasn't either. Cole was going to hear about this. Then they would see what they would see.

Red opened the door to Cabin One, entered. Al shoved Vicki in ahead of her, shut the door. The parking lot-side entrance opened into a narrow hallway. A tiny bathroom was on the left, then steps led down to two bedrooms, one small one straight ahead, the larger other with the rear exit to the right. The right one had a double bed and two chairs. The other had a twin bed, there also was a rusty stove and a refrigerator shoved into one corner.

"I want to go," Vicki said. Al had set her on the bed. Her hands were cuffed again. "I need to go."

Al ignored her, turned and slammed into the tiny bathroom. "No goddamn toilet paper," she yelled. "Red, go get me some toilet paper."

Red tried to tune in a channel on the larger bedroom's TV. He came into the hallway, shot Vicki a look. "Don't move." He went out.

Vicki wasn't sure she could move, even if she wanted to. Her body ached, head throbbed. She had bruises and scrapes all over. It would take a week of therapy just to put her in shape to go to work.

"You there?" Al's voice came from the other side of the door.

Vicki started to say something, but didn't. Her limbs were dead. Only her breathing continued. She sat still, holding one hand in the other, staring at them. Three nails broken, another chipped, another threatening to split. Both wrists red, chafed, bruised. There was an ugly purple mark on her left forearm. Her elbow hurt, gums itched, eyes burned. She was galled inside her legs, her bladder throbbed, begged for release. Her feet were moist, itchy inside the sneakers. She felt in touch with every part of her body, as if it was someone else's skin. She inventoried herself. The total wasn't worth much.

"Hey?" Al yelled again. Then: "Red? You there?" In a moment, the door opened, she waddled out. She held onto the waistband of her jeans up around her thighs, her panties bunched in the fabric's folds. Her biker tee-shirt fell blessedly down over her crotch. Vicki started, stared, then looked away, then back again. She couldn't help it. A word came to her: gross. It was inadequate: grotesque.

Al moved to the door, peered through a small window cut at eye level. The tee-shirt rode high in the back. Massive flabby hips rippled when she moved in tiny little hopping steps. A death's head tattoo grinned from the left buttock. "Where the fuck'd he go?"

"Toilet paper," Vicki said. "I got to go."

"You ain't going nowhere, Prom Queen," Al said, turned, stretched slightly. The tee-shirt rode up. This time, Vicki didn't avert her eyes. Al's dark bush fanned out over the inside of her thighs, spread upwards. A roll of fat draped down from under her black shirt: hairy navel. "What you looking for, Prom Queen?" Al said. "Well, it ain't there. Used to be. Not anymore." She winked. "Bet you're disappointed, huh? Put a liplock on my love muscle? Well, times change. But where there's a will, there's a way. I may be a changed man, but I ain't given up all my old tastes. We might have a little time before your friends show up." She smacked her lips, ran out a tongue, licked the air.

Vicki's stomach twisted. She didn't think it could. Not anymore. She thought she had seen too much, heard too much, to be shocked, sickened. There were depths of disgust she hadn't begun to plum. Her throat closed.

The door banged open, Red shoved through. Al retreated into the bathroom. Red had a roll of toilet tissue in his hand. He cracked the door, tossed it inside, went into the other bedroom. In a moment, Vicki heard the TV again.

"All free," Al said, coming out. She flicked water from her hands. "Your turn."

"I'm all right," Red said.

"Your turn, then," Al turned to Vicki. Vicki rose, offered her hands. Al looked at her, grinned. "Want me to help you?"

Vicki shook her head, pushed her shackled wrists forward again. Al went to the other room, came back with the key, unlocked the cuffs. "You're sure, now?" Vicki shook her head. She went into the bathroom. Once inside, she leaned over the toilet, heaved until urine ran down her legs, puddled on the floor.

"You all right in there?" Al's voice penetrated the throbbing in Vicki's ears. It was the third or fourth time she asked. She didn't want her to ask again, or to come in. "Christ! She's ralphing again."

"I've . . . I need to take a bath." Vicki choked, gagged. The small room reeked.

Silence. "Okay. Good idea. You're getting a little rank. Want me to scrub your back?"

Vicki reached over, pushed the lock in on the door. It was too flimsy to keep Al out, but at least she would have warning. A kissing noise on the other side of the door was all she heard until Red's voice stopped it. "Knock it off, for Chrisssake," he yelled.

She turned on the shower. It groaned, banged, yielded a sluggish stream of rusty water. Vicki unwrapped a bar of soap, toed her sneakers off, stepped under the thin spray fully clothed. At least it was hot. She gave in and cried.

22
Exit Vicki

Vicki came out of the bathroom barefoot, soaked. She waited in the entrance hall.

Red was in the large bedroom, sprawled across the bed, eyes closed, .22 revolver in one hand, the other across his bare stomach held a Sprite. She stepped down to the other room, stripped off the doused sky-blue sweatpants, underwear, bunched them up, squeezed water out onto the floor, pulled them back on, repeated the procedure with the top: deliberate motion, blank mind. The bra she discarded. She flopped down on the twin bed, stared at the ceiling: *End of the Road,* she thought, starring Vicki Sigel as the road.

From the beginning, she assumed something good would happen. Someone—anyone—would take her out of the scene, write her out of the script. Now, after something like a bath, with sopped hair, cheap soggy clothes draped on her body, she gave in. She was empty, hollow, everything was wrong. She was done.

She rolled her head to one side, saw an old-fashioned rotary dial phone on the bedside table. Red remained in the other room, a wall between them. A rush of emotion filled her. She sat up, looked around: no Al. No handcuffs, either. With energy she didn't think she had, she scooted near the phone, held her breath, waited: nothing. She picked up the damp towel, pretended to rub her hair dry with one hand, lifted the receiver with the other. It was heavy compared to modern phones. A grating dial tone hit her ear: Bingo. Her finger poised over the dial.

The pause released panic. She breathed, short. She replaced the receiver, looked at the door. No Red. She lifted it again, inserted a chipped nail into the nine hole of the rotary, started to pull it around, then changed her mind, eased it back: 9-1-1? Out here? Her heart boomed beneath the dank sweats. She shifted to the zero, noting the word "Operator" was almost worn away, pulled it around to the metal stop: slow, silent. Gentled it back. A warbling tone sounded in her ear. A pause. Then another. Another.

"C'mon," Vicki breathed. Two more rings, two more. "C'mon, answer." After ten rings, she gave up. Sweat poured from her, mixed with the water in her clothes. She replaced the receiver on its cradle, moved over, away from the phone.

"Switchboard," Red called from the other room.

Vicki started to reply, profess her innocence, ignorance. Her throat clogged. She cleared it. "What?"

"They have a switchboard," Red called. "Operator's tied up right now. Can't connect you." She doubted he ever opened his eyes.

She moved farther from the phone, rubbed the towel over her head again, this time with vigor, anger. Red appeared at the landing, stood in the doorway between rooms, shirtless, gave her a short grin: crooked, yellow teeth. She saw his skinny chest, protruding ribs, pale, thin skin. Purple veins raced across his biceps. They seemed too large, out of proportion to his arms. His carrot-colored bristle stood up, blue eyes danced. He went to the doorway's tiny window, peeked out. Pistol in hand. Humphrey Bogart with a short red crew cut.

"No cops yet, Lefty," the dialogue echoed in her mind. "Maybe we lost 'em. Then we can ditch the broad, go on the lam." Red said nothing. He just looked outside, checked his wristwatch. What was he waiting for? Who? Old question. The grime the shower should have washed away was still there.

She doubted she would ever get rid of it. The bruises on her face, her mouth, her arms hurt, throbbed. If Red gave her the gun, she'd just shoot herself, save them the trouble.

"Al's gone for groceries," he said, strolled down the steps toward her. "Coffee. Something to eat. If she can find anything. If she can *buy* it this time. Not shoot up the whole country. Which I doubt. You hungry?" Vicki didn't answer. "Al doesn't want to give you up," he said. "She's got plans for you." He winked.

Vicki stared at him, mouth open. "I thought there was money—" "Oh, there is. Lots of money. Al says we can have both. Or she can. I'm not so sure. Al screws up more than she don't. You probably noticed that."

"I—" Vicki started, stopped. The last thing she wanted to do was appeal to this little prick, cast him in the role of some kind of savior. But who else was there? She had no idea who was coming with a bag of money to exchange for—for *Barbara*!

The name settled over her like a chill. She had forgotten, shoved it aside. She was so sure somebody would stop this madness before it came to this, she hadn't fully considered what might happen when they found out she wasn't Barbara. In the back of her mind, she had presumed that Barbara herself would show up sooner or later. If Barbara didn't rescue her, she would take her place: stand-in out, lead in, she thought.

But Barbara wasn't on the set, not even in the studio. Vicki adopted Barbara's name, played her part, answered when they called her, forgot she was Vicki: understudy to the star. Stand-ins never turn their faces to the camera, never say lines. She was about to have to do both. A *Star Is Born,* she thought. She was about to be in some serious trouble. So were Red and Al. And they didn't have a clue.

She put three fingers to her mouth, stifled panic, forced her thoughts to order. Here they were, where somebody who wanted Barbara was about to arrive. What would happen then? She sat still, detached. They'd be pissed off, whoever they were. They wouldn't pay. Al wouldn't want to walk away empty-handed. Al'd want something for her trouble. Vicki glanced down at her soaked sweats, ruined body: her.

Fear rose again. She remembered the night before: the open

door on the Suburban. The sense that someone touched her breast in her sleep. Al's naked form in the rain, the macabre ritual: Earth Mother Al. Vicki's imagination conjured the monster, no longer worried about a hostage's welfare, no longer protecting her because she thought she was worth something. No way to stop it.

Mistaken Identity, starring Vicki Sigel as Barbara Lovell. The story begins on Broadway in New York City. It detours some, moves to LA, but now races toward a conclusion as surely as a reel spins to the last frame: Pretty young heroine raped by butch biker transsexual. Body on floor. Gallons of blood. Cue theme. Fade to black. Roll credits. "This film is dedicated to the loving memory of Vicki Sigel." She shuddered, shook all over.

She couldn't bear it, couldn't live through it. And why should she? No studio would touch her after that. Gary wouldn't touch her after that: over. She lay back, closed her eyes. Who could save her? Think, damnit! Nobody. She had to save herself.

Red proved clairvoyant again. "Don't worry, sweet-meat. Long as I'm okay, you're okay. Al's a freak. I know that. So do you. But she'll listen to reason. She won't hurt you."

"I saw—," she started. Took a breath. "I saw her last night. In the rain. She was . . . naked. In the rain. She was . . ." Vicki trailed off.

"Yeah," Red nodded. "That's something she does. Got it from some goddamn Indian someplace. Real Indian. Not some goddamn blankethead. Supposed to get her ready for some serious fucking. 'Anticipatory karma,' or some shit. Goddamn freaky. Rain sets her off. She used to be okay. When she was a he."

Vicki's lip curled. She couldn't help it.

Red grinned. "Crazy world, ain't it?"

"How did you . . . ," Vicki asked. Keep it going, she thought, keep him talking. She needed a friend, even him. She sat up, swung her feet over the side of the bed—sexy feet—rested her elbows on her knees, chin on her hands. ". . . you know, meet?"

Red gave her a long look. "Well, if you're wondering if *I'm* a fag: the answer's no. Neither was LeR—was Blackie. Oh, what the hell. His real name was LeRoy." He glanced away, sad. "Him and me, we grew up together. Bakersfield." He came over, sat down in one of the Adirondack chairs, no cushions, deep slanted seats, high backs, thick coats of dark brown paint. He stretched out, put his bare feet on the bed next to her, scratched his inner thigh with the barrel of the pistol.

She looked at him. The top button on his jeans was undone, light red hair traced its way up to his navel. Could she fuck him? The thought repulsed her. Nothing appealed, nothing. But he might save her. He might be the only thing standing between her and Al. The notion convinced her. Maybe he'd settle for a blow job. Anything to keep Al at bay. She scooted closer to him, cocked her feet up on the broad arm of the chair, twitched her toes a bit, used one to scratch the instep of the other, let him get a good look. "Gives me a hard-on just looking at them," Gary said. Be right, Gary, she thought, just once, be right.

"So," Vicki said, inched closer to him. "He—Blackie, uh, LeRoy wasn't gay?"

"LeRoy?" Red laughed. "No fucking way. I don't know why they hooked up. Al was a deadhead, stone freak queer. LeRoy was always straight. They were into heavy metal, heavy drugs. Al could always score. Always had a job working. Brought me in. Then me and LeRoy got caught, went away, got out, got caught again. That's about it." He yawned again. "Do I win anything?"

"But you were friends?"

"Yeah. Me and LeRoy. Tight. Not me and Al. No love lost there, as they say." He laughed, opened his eyes wide, checked her, relaxed. Then, serious: "Al was LeRoy's friend. Till yesterday. I don't know how—never mind."

Keep him talking, she thought. She leaned on her hands, arched her back, stuck out her chest. "And Al? She—he—never got caught?"

"Once. Killed a guy. Caught her easy. She jumped bail, went to Mexico for a while. That's when the sex thing—the change. Down there. You can buy anything in Mexico." He shook his head. "After that, Tuscon, worked Vegas, Denver, I guess."

"What kind of . . . work?"

"Strong-arm stuff. Butch muscle. Dyke joints, mostly. Some hooker clubs. Don't like to have a lot of men around. Chicks work better when a woman looks after them. Because Al's the way she is—he is—she could handle things. That's what she said, anyway. Things got hot for her, so she went east. Did a little work in Texas someplace. Houston, maybe, Dallas, I don't know. That's where she met this guy Johnny, a nigger pimp. He connected her with Cole, a high roller of some kind out of Dallas. Then she come back to Arizona, got back in touch. When this gig come up, we were out again, looking for a number. She called us, and here we are."

"Yeah. Here we are." She didn't know what else to say. She wanted to flirt with him, make him think she liked him, give him some ideas. He didn't seem interested. She must look like hell on toast, she thought.

Red lay his head back, closed his eyes. "You know, the toughest part of this gig is staying awake. Feel like I could sleep for a fucking week."

"What'll you do now?" Vicki asked: Shirley Temple, she thought, maybe Jodie Foster. No Juliette Lewis, and no Sharon Stone. He looked like the type who liked little girls, easy girls. He cracked his eyelids, checked her. "I mean, when you get the money?"

"South America." Red smiled. "That was the plan, that stays the plan. Rio solo. Guy we met in the joint was from down there told us all about it. Beaches with naked women running around, begging for it. Toot for sale on every corner. Half the people from somewhere else. Nobody's going to notice one more gringo with a pocket full of money." He closed his eyes. "The only thing I'm sure of is that if you got enough money, you'll make it. Too bad LeRoy missed it."

She glanced around, dreaded the sound of Al's return. "And Al?"

"Who gives a shit?" he asked, casual. Then he frowned. "I've about had it with that perverted motherfucker. Maniac. Hell, this was supposed to be easy. Snatch your ass, keep you healthy, get the payoff. I didn't know we were going halfway to hell and gone to do it. I didn't know enough. That's a fact. I swear, only reason I think Al pulled me in on this was because

I knew how to blow that car." He thought. "And that was a fuckup. That truck wasn't supposed to go up like that. Then, she killed that cop," he mused. "State fucking trooper. That was bad. Nearly as bad as making LeRoy kill that girl."

"Making him—" Vicki cut herself off. Don't argue. "Yeah," she said.

"Well, she *made* him do it." He sighed. "We could've boosted a cold set of wheels. Easy. Al's always doing things the hard way. Like that liquor store. Had 'wrong' wrote all over it. And like this." He waved his hands. "Why couldn't we be in some Holiday Inn someplace? Why we got to be in this shit hole? She gets her kick from it, I guess."

"I guess," Vicki said. "She scares me."

He opened his eyes: hard look. "I don't give a flying fuck what happens to that queer son of a bitch. Once I get paid, it's sigh-yo-nara and kiss my ass. But you can be sure. Nothing's going to happen to you till I've got my cut—and LeRoy's cut—and I'm out of here with lots of miles between me and the whole fucking deal. After that, you're on your own." He smiled, lay back, closed his eyes once again. "Now you got the whole picture, sweet-meat. But you can forget any ideas about giving me a ride."

"What?" Vicki snapped to, sat up, mentally sagged. Ahead of her again.

"I know your game. See right through it. You don't move your ass through the joint without knowing when somebody's scoping your buns, thinking what you might do for a little ride. You're sitting there trying to talk yourself into it. Don't shit me. Gives you the red-ass just to look at me. The last place I'm going to put my cock is between your teeth. I like it too much to lose it." Reminded, he reached down, scratched his groin, kept his eyes shut, chuckled.

Vicki didn't think about her next move. If she had planned it, thought about it, he would have read her mind, been ahead of her. She just did it, as if it was scripted: automatic, ad-lib. There was no chance to question, to rehearse: action, cue Vicki.

All in one movement, she reached out, picked up the heavy old telephone, in her left hand, stood up. With her right, she dropped her damp towel over Red's closed eyes, unshaven face, then smashed the base of the weighted black instrument on top of it. Bell rang a solid tone. His nose crushed with a wet splat. Red's legs lifted, knees bent, tried to rise. She threw herself astraddle his thighs, pinned his hand with the revolver between them, clamped them tight on the thick boards of the chair's seat. She lifted the phone, brought it down again. Something hard crunched, yielded beneath the black weight. Red's right hand flailed at her. She ducked it, lifted the telephone, smashed it down again, and again. Each time, she felt bone, cartilage, teeth smash, vibrate through the sharp ring of the phone's bell. The towel stained scarlet, Red's free hand dropped. He was out: dead out.

"That's a wrap!" she gasped, heaved. "Everybody take five." She used both hands, lifted the phone again, hit him once more: he didn't move.

Vicki gulped air. Red's legs were limp beneath her hips. His free arm hung down. Blood soaked the towel, but she didn't raise it. Might be faking. She lifted the phone, poised. Out, maybe dead, she thought, didn't care. At once, she dropped the phone, leaped off of him, danced up the small steps to the entrance way, the front door, looked out the small window. The parking lot was empty. Al could be back anytime. Not that way.

She turned, went into the other, larger bedroom, spotted the back door: escape. Then she saw Red's shirt, shoes. Shoes! She turned, went into the bathroom, found her sneakers, splattered with her waste. She tried to heel them on. They wouldn't go. She'd have to sit, loosen the laces. No time. She carried them out into the hall, started again for the door, stopped again. She should take the pistol. She didn't want to; it scared her. But she had to take it. Al had the shotgun, the police pistol. She'd come after her. No time. She returned to the hallway: froze. What if Red came to? What if when she turned into that room she found him there, face smashed, bloody, furious? She swallowed, took a small step. That was it: no go. She couldn't force herself around the doorjamb into the other room.

"Shit," she said. "Next scene, Vick. Take your exit! C'mon! We're rolling." She couldn't will herself to move. The sound of a vehicle prodded her. She leaped up onto the landing, still

afraid to look behind her into the smaller bedroom. Through
the door's window she saw the Suburban wheel through the
drive, stop. Al got out, stalked over to remove the wire gate.
Without thinking, Vicki raced down into the room. Red was
where she left him, bloody towel on his face. Thick trails of
gore ran down the sides of his neck, onto his chest. His ribcage
rose, fell slightly: alive. "Jesus," Vicki prayed. "Give me
strength."

His hand was still between his thighs. She pulled them apart:
empty. Then she spotted the .22 on the multicolored rug,
beneath the chair. Again she froze. One second, two, three.
She counted, then held her breath, fixed her eyes on the bloody
towel, reached between his calves, snatched the revolver, all
the time expected him to grab her. Suddenly he gasped in
breath, the towel concaved over his mouth. She snapped back
the hammer, aimed it at the bloody towel, backpedaled against
the bed, stumbled, sat, held him in the long barrel's sight. He
exhaled, bubbled the towel red, didn't move.

Then she was on her feet, toes dug into the worn rug's fabric.
Up the steps, around the doorway, past the double bed. She
jammed the gun under her arm, snagged her sneakers with one
hand, grabbed the doorknob with the other, jerked it open,
leaped outside: free.

The autumn-killed grass was rough, prickly beneath her feet.
She looked around. To her right was the parking lot, pool area,
concession-bathhouse, a maze of high chain-link fences, open
ground. To her left, the cabin complex swung in a lazy arch
away from her. Volleyball pit, a rack of croquet mallets, baseball bats stacked in a corner. Directly before her was the canal,
green in the midday light. Beyond it another strip of grass, then
cover. That way, she thought. The canal was too wide to step
over, curbed by gray fieldstones. Long jump. A footbridge was
farther down: too far. She didn't look back, raced forward,
leaped to the other side, stumbled, rolled, found her feet, moved.
She scooted into a narrow grove of trees, underbrush—a wind-
break—running parallel to the man-made stream. She cut her
feet badly on sharp rocks, cacti seemed to be everywhere.
Brambles tore at the wet sleeves of the sweat-suit, caught her

hair. Then she was through the bushes, beyond the thicket, shielded by the trees' sparse fall foliage.

She stopped, panted, collected herself. She sat on the ground, loosened the sneakers' laces, jerked them onto her feet, tied them tight. Then she raced down a slight incline of broad, sharp-edged rocks, knee-high weeds where her progress was stopped by a breast-high barbed-wire fence. She stumbled against it, tore a triangular rip in the top of the sweats, pricked her hand.

Fingers holding onto the top wire, she swayed, gulped air, took her bearings. To her right at the end of a path along the fence line was a long, open field, plowed: another fence, then another. Beyond them, she could see mountains shimmering in the near distance, maybe two miles, maybe less. Best thing: mountains. Places to hide there. But the field looked soft. She'd be visible the entire way, even if she could run that far in fresh-turned earth.

Her muscles were cramped, tight from three days of atrophy. They'd come, she knew, would be there when she had to have them. But the last thing they needed was several miles of broken field running to warm up. She looked around. There was the back of a building with a tall sign out front: a store, but it was way off to the right, on the highway, beyond the pool, and two, three twelve-foot fences. And it looked deserted. Forget it.

To her left was the empty RV park. Weedy concrete spaces, each marked by a utility pole. There were thin, head-high weeds between her and it, then a utility shed, probably locked: no good. Al would find her in ten minutes.

Directly ahead of her, across the barbed-wire fence, a grassy pasture spread out in a pie shape, rose to a knoll. She couldn't see beyond that, but in the distance there more mountains, more purple sunlight. No choice, she thought, then looked down the fence, searched for an opening. The wire was taut, barbs sharp. *The Great Escape,* she thought. Where's James Garner? Where's Steve McQueen and his motorcycle?

She pulled at the top strand: no give. She put a sneaker on a lower wire, tried to balance, held the pistol out away from her. Plenty of slack. She fell backwards, her right buttock hit a rock. A sharp pain knifed all the way down one leg. "Shit, shit, shit!" she yelled.

Behind her, she heard a bellow: "Prom Queen! Where you at? You think you got away with something?" A laugh followed. Loud and long. "You sure made Red see red! He ain't dead, though, and he's coming. You can run, but you cannot hide. Not from Big Al!"

Vicki scrambled to her feet, teeth locked against the pain in her hip, looked back toward the strip of cabins. Only the red-tiled roof was visible through the trees between.

"Proooom Queeeen!" Al's voice boomed out. "Come on back here! I got the next daaaaance." The last word blew away on the morning breeze. The blast of a shotgun chased it. In a few seconds, Vicki felt heavy pellets rain down on her, she dropped. The gun boomed again, she heard the pellets fall away to her left. Al couldn't see her. She fired into the air to scare her. It worked.

She took one more look at the fence, tried a lower strand again: hopeless. Too much give to stand on, not enough to squeeze through. She remembered a trick she learned as a child on the farm, one she would never have believed any adult could accomplish—then only in the movies—a real Arnold Schwarzenegger move. She tossed the pistol over, put both hands on the top strand between the barbs, took a short skip, vaulted herself over the tight top wire. Her wrist twisted, but she landed rough on the other side, rolled to her feet, scooped up the .22, and was off, covered the rocky ground in a steady trot, tried to ignore the stinging pain in her hip, a burning tear on the heel of her left hand caused by a barb. "Try that, Arnold," she panted. "No stuntman on this set." No stand-ins, either. Not anymore.

"*Wonder Woman,*" she gasped: "Starring Vicki Sigel. Does her own stunts." Takes her own chances, Vicki thought. She looked at the wound on her hand. Lynda Carter never had it so bad. More shots boomed behind her. She ran in an easy lope, sought her stride. Her muscles protested at first, then they gave in, stretched out, except for the bruised hip, felt good. Her lungs cleared, found a rhythm. Every step took her farther from Al.

Her gait lengthened when she hit the top of the knoll, picked up speed, rushed down the other side. Her eyes widened. There was a steady decline for a hundred yards into a rocky chasm, an arroyo, a jagged edge fronted with thorny mesquite, brambles. The other side was ten, twelve yards across a red tear in the yellow, grassy weeds. She had momentum, rushed on, strained for more speed, stretched each step. Her eyes found a flat space, a clear spot on the other side. Dead center a flat, orange-colored rock—orange! she thought—lay brilliant in an errant ray of sun.

She built her pace, pushed harder, angled toward it, her knees, arms pumped, lungs filled. Susan Clark in *Babe*. She glanced up, sought her angel: inspiration. The arroyo yawned, red and raw. She could see brown water in the bottom, far below. She would have to *be* Wonder Woman, Superwoman, to fly. She sighted her orange target, judged a foot pad for the launch, gulped a final breath, landed on her toes, propelled herself across the open space. Her legs bicycled, sought purchase, reached for the shale platform on the other side, arms up, pistol gripped tight. The balls of her feet struck the target. She emptied her lungs, ready to shout in triumph, to gain balance, to pitch forward, roll, when the flat, orange rock beneath her sneakers cracked, crumbled beneath her. She fell helpless into the hollow, empty air below.

23

Standoff

"So, where is she, exactly?" Jensen asked. He sat in one of the Adirondack chairs in the small bedroom of Cabin One, smoked a cigar. Red lay on the bed, his face a mangle of gore, rendered flesh under towel-wrapped ice. Jensen provided the ice. Or Quince had, when Jensen ordered him to. Jensen was in charge now. That much was clear. Such clarity made Quince nervous.

They had been there thirty minutes, found the cabin door open. Jensen went in first, gun out, head down. Quince stayed behind, dawdled. Hillary remained in the van, passed out. Jensen finally called Quince inside. Red stumbled around the room: bled, raved, weaved: smashed nose, broken teeth, lips shredded by their jagged stubs. One eye was crushed beneath a hammered optical orbit, the other badly damaged: blind.

He had a lot of names for Barbara. None pleasant. None entirely understandable, either. "Guckinh Itch," was the only one Quince could comprehend. Quince did not believe his niece capable of such violence. But there was Red. There was the bloody telephone. Believe it or not, he thought. Now he felt like Hillary. He wanted out. He envied her stupor.

Quince tried not to look at Red. Or at Jensen. The lawyer

stood in the landing by the door, elevated, leaned on the door-jamb to the other bedroom, arms in front of him: casual, impassive. He wished he was anyplace else in the world. He looked at the double bed in the other room, found it inviting.

Quince also refused to look directly at Al, who occupied the other Adirondack, the one where she had found Red an hour before, then left him, battered, unconscious, while she searched for the missing Barbara Lovell. Nothing in Quince's experience prepared him for Al. She was monstrous, unnatural. The legs of her cracked leather pants were covered with burrs, cactus spines, stickers. Sweat rings draped beneath her arms to her waist. Moisture poured off her nose, and a pistol-gripped, sawed-off 12-gauge rested between her thick knees. An automatic was jammed in her jeans' waistband. Quince decided she was not real. He believed that.

"Are you telling me," Jensen asked, calm, low, "that you allowed her to escape. After all this? Is that what you're telling me?"

"I didn't 'allow' shit. But she ain't here," Al said. "You can see that for yourself."

Red moaned, tried to say something. It came out: "muggh idl fitsh."

"Just shut up," Al said. "Do us all a favor. You stupid fuck."

"That man needs a doctor," Quince said.

"No shit?" Al replied. She kept her face toward Jensen, her small, dark eyes focused. She lit a cigarette. "Where the fuck is Bob Cole? That's what I want to know. Supposed to do business with Cole. Nobody said nothing about some fancy nigger with a nickel cigar."

Jensen's face was impassive. "Mr. Cole delegated us to handle this."

"I don't give a flying fuck who 'delegated' what. I ain't dealing with nobody but Cole. I don't even know who the hell you are. Or him." She jerked her chin in Quince's direction. "Smells like a lawyer, though."

Quince assumed the role. He pushed himself off the doorway. Gain strength, he told himself. "Bob Cole is dead." Jensen's head snapped up, his eyes narrow, mean. "Let's put all the cards in place," Quince said. His voice was steady, cool. Jensen shrugged, sat back. Quince continued, "Cole is dead. Period. You're dealing with us, now. Where is Barbara Lovell?"

Al looked at the ceiling, laughed: a bellow. "That's great! That's just fucking wonderful! We grab this bitch, drive her halfway across the world, keep her in one piece, and you come to tell me the guy who wants her is dead. 'Oh, gee. I'm sorry. The deal is off.' Oh, great. Just great."

"Nobody said anything about the deal being off," Quince said. He turned, looked out the door's small window. The airport van was in the parking lot, next to the Suburban. It had three bench seats, a six-cylinder engine: worthless shit. Hillary was still out. She was a piece of shit, too, he thought. He wasn't sure if it was vodka or indifference that finally overcame her. Or fear. She'd lay down, went to sleep forty miles out of Alpine. It pissed him off. She started this.

"Without the girl, there won't be a deal," Jensen said. "There wouldn't have been with Mr. Cole, either. Where is she?"

"The girl. . ." Al said, stood up, rested her shotgun against the bed, passed Quince on her way to the bathroom, deliberately brush against him. He could smell body odor, sour, fetid. ". . . is gone."

"We can see that," Quince said. "What we want to know—"

"I don't give a fuck what you want to know," Al shot back from inside the open door. "Counselor." Water ran in the sink. In a moment, she was back, double chin dripped. Quince studied the heavy earrings on her fat lobes. She took a position on the top step. "Look at him. Damnit. Friend of mine. Partner. Look what your little Hollywood cunt did to him. Beats any damn thing I ever seen. Good people are dead because of her."

Jensen rested his cigar on the arm of the chair, stood, looked up the small steps, faced the pair. "We came to make an exchange. We have the money. This is a simple business transaction. We can be done in five minutes, depending on how long it takes you to count."

Al grinned. "Oh, you're a pretty one, you are. I'd like to get you—"

Jensen pulled his pistol from under his coat, pointed it casually at Al. Quince gulped, stepped back to the wall. "This is a *business* transaction," Jensen said. "Either produce the girl, or we'll be on our way."

"Ott fout pay!" Red gurgled. Blood ran out of his mouth. He pulled the bloody ice pack away, revealed a smashed cheek, gaping mouth, tongue bit half in two. Tried to sit up: couldn't. There was a deep purple dent above his eyebrows. "Haunt— haunt fughngh oney! Who huner—who huner ran. Eash! God—" His arms lifted uselessly from his side. "Hurs, Al! Hurs!" He collapsed against the pillows, sobbed.

Jensen stepped over to the bed, put the muzzle of the pistol on Red's battered forehead, crossed his bandaged wrist over the top of the pistol, shielded his face. "Do you have the girl?" Red sobbed, shook his head. "Do *you*?" Jensen's eyes trailed to Al.

Al shrugged. "Not at the moment. But running a bluff—"

Jensen pulled the trigger: twice. Red's body jumped slightly, arched, went slack. Blood saturated the pillow beneath his head, ran to the floor.

Quince turned away, faced the wall. Bile bubbled up, filled his mouth. "Goddamn," he said, swallowed, fought nausea. "Goddamn." His ears rang, eyes watered, nose burned. The room slowly filled with thin gray smoke, the smell of feces, cordite. Quince gagged again, his stomach heaved again, cramped.

Al didn't move. A small smile creased her ugly face. An eyebrow arched. "You're good, lover. Real good."

Quince made himself turn, look. Jensen smoothed his creamy suitcoat, stepped away from Red's body, resumed his chair, exchanged the pistol for his cigar. He seemed unconcerned that Al might pull a weapon. The bandages around his wrist were dotted with splattered blood. "This is no bluff," he said. "This is business, and I fully expect you to conduct yourself accordingly. You are in no position to make demands. Where is the girl?"

Quince put a hand to his mouth, bit his fingers. Take a stand, he ordered himself. "This," he started, bit his fingers again. "This is not supposed to happen. Not—"

"Please be quiet, Mr. Lovell," Jensen said. Then gently, "Please."

Quince slumped against the wall. He groped for a chair. There was none. He never felt so sick.

"Mr. Lovell?" Al asked. "You her old man?"

Quince shook his head. "Uncle," he said. Why? he thought. Why explain anything to this huge, ugly woman? Idiotic! Get a grip, Quince, he commanded.

"No shit? Cole said her old man was the one wanted her. You a 'funny uncle'? She's one nice piece of ass."

"Suppose you tell me exactly what happened here?" Jensen interrupted.

She shrugged. "I go for some groceries, leave Red here to watch the girl. I get back, he's in that chair there, face bashed in, out cold. Prom Queen's split."

"Prom Queen?" Quince asked.

"The package," Al said. "The cunt." Her eyes stayed on Jensen. "Prom Queen. Barbara Sweet-Meat. That's who you want, right? That's who Cole was going to slip us six hundred long and green for. Right?"

Jensen nodded. "You let her get away."

"*I* didn't let her do shit. When I left, she was in the shower. Hosing down. Freshening up. Been a long ride. To be honest, she don't travel well."

Quince looked at her. His head wanted to explode. He wanted to go somewhere dark, lie down.

"I don't know what went down. I don't got the details." Al glanced at Red's body. "And you sort of canceled out the chance of getting them. Anyway, I get back, she's gone: shazam!"

"How long ago?" Jensen asked.

Al shrugged. She went over to the bed, careful to sidestep the shotgun, picked up Red's limp wrist, checked his watch. "Don't know. Hour, maybe. Two. I was out there a long time. Checked out the forest and the hills. Come back for a drink when I seen you drive up, let you in." She looked at Red's ruined face, shattered skull. "Man, you *are* good. I never seen nobody that fucking good. Nobody straight, that is. Coldblooded motherfucker, ain't you." She gave Jensen a narrow look. "You're not on anything, right?"

Jensen gestured with the cigar for Al to move away from the bed. "So, you looked for her?"

"Fucking-A. Shot up the whole place, thinking maybe I'd flush her out. But she's a stone fox. Like you. Bitch don't scare easy." She glanced at Red's corpse. "She don't bluff, either."

"What do we do now?" Quince asked. He didn't want to ask, didn't want to know.

Jensen put his injured hand to his temple, remembered, scowled at it, lowered it. "Look for her, I guess. I don't believe we have a choice."

Quince walked across the room. Movement felt good. He peered out the back window into the dying afternoon sun. He saw the canal, the line of trees beyond: brush, thicket, mountains. "Where?"

"Out there," Jensen said. "She can't get far. Not on foot. Very well. Al, is it? I don't suppose you have a last name."

Al shrugged, grinned. "Al'll do."

"Here's the situation. Ms. Al," Jensen said. "We have a contract for you—as a subcontractor for Mr. Cole—to deliver one Barbara Lovell, alive and in good condition, in exchange for a sum of money."

"Two hundred grand. Times three." Al smirked. "That's the deal, Rastus."

"*This,*" Jensen continued, "you have yet to do. She apparently has eluded your capture and is free somewhere in the vicinity. What are the chances she might have made it to a house, a telephone?"

"Nil and none," Al said. "Nearest place is back in town, except for that store over there on the highway. It's closed, locked up. No outside phone, either. I already checked to the west. She didn't go that way. Whole park's fenced. Barbed wire, high and tight. She might have crossed someplace, but I doubt it. Too pretty to be much of a Girl Scout."

"So we'll assume she's out there. Possibly hidden in the park somewhere. And we must find her. I'm injured, as you can see, but I will join in the search. So will Mr. Lovell." Quince felt something break inside him. He didn't want to do this. "So will you. Time is now a factor. Split up: Mr. Lovell, you will go in one direction. I'll take another, and Ms. Al here will take a third. We can presume she'll try to make it to the highway. If you locate her, do *not* harm her. That's very important." He glared at Al. "Do you understand that?"

"Roger Wilco," Al smirked.

"I'm very serious about that," Jensen said. "If you have to use force, be certain that it's not deadly. I want that clear in your mind." He inflected the word in such a way as to cast his doubt that Al possessed such an organ.

"Oh, yeah," Al said. "She's got Red's piece. Twenty-two. Cap pistol, but it's still a gun."

Jensen nodded once, glanced at Quince. To Al: "Do you have a weapon Mr. Lovell can use?"

Quince was stunned, He opened his hands: innocent. "Weapon? I don't need a weapon. That's my niece—" Surely Jensen didn't expect him to shoot Barbara, or anyone.

"You'd better take this." He picked up Al's shotgun.

"Hey," Al said. "That's mine. Even paid for it."

"She's frightened, exhausted," Jensen continued, checked the load, put the pistol grip of the big gun in Quince's hand, "and armed. She may not recognize you. If you locate her, fire two quick rounds into the air. Are you familiar with this type of weapon?"

Quince nodded, relieved. "I can handle it." He doubted it.

The big, burnt orange Ford F-150 Supercab idled past the entrance to Balmorhea: third time. On the first two passes, Barbara kept the speed at twenty, Sandobal studied the small park. This time, he drove. She was in the bed, crouched low against the side, peeked over.

They had been on the move since picking up the rental. She had hoped to hear from Eddy before she left. No luck. Monica, whose number Eddy gave her, sounded too dumb to live, more than a little pissed off. Didn't know where Eddy was, how to reach him.

Sandobal slowed. Once they reached the end of the park's property, he sped up, U-turned in front of a small store, drove back to the edge of town. He pulled into the gravel parking lot of the Mule Deer Lodge, a dismal, L-shaped motel with no pool. He stepped out, leaned on the bed, next to her. "What'd you think? I didn't see anybody."

"Park's closed, but there're people there."

"There's a Suburban. It's got to be the one stolen in El Paso."

"Not really. They're common as dirt here. 'National Truck of Texas.' "

"That doesn't make sense. A state can't have a national anything."

"Sandobal, Texas is different from any place you've ever been," Barbara sighed.

His eyes wandered the distance beyond the tiny town. To the north, the interstate, then rock-strewn desert. To the south, mountains, sotol, sage, dust. The afternoon sky was too blue, too clear to look into comfortably. Last night, it was yellow with dirt, then raining mud. "It sure ain't Kansas," he said.

Barbara raked the bangs from her eyes, irritated. "We're not sure it's the park, not the town."

"We're not even sure this is the right town, right place." He pushed up the cheap sunglasses, kneaded the bridge of his nose. "We're not sure there is a right place. Face it, we're not sure of anything."

For once, she didn't argue. They had stopped three times in the diminutive hamlet, once at the Texaco Food-Mart, once at the Trans-Pecos Lodge, once at the office of the motel. Only the FoodMart attendant had been helpful, directed them to the state park. A guy outside the Lodge said they didn't open until late afternoon.

"We don't know who they're meeting or when. All we know—" He broke off. "All we *think* we know is that this is where they were headed."

" *'Think'* we know?" Was he backing out again?

"All we know is what you saw—in about thirty seconds— scribbled on the back of a restroom door at a gas station in Arizona. We assume it was a message from Vicki. We assume you read it right—"

"I read it right."

"—that you *remembered* it right. We assume that this is the only place it could be. Could have been some college kids, playing games."

Barbara scowled at him. Resentment snarled. "What are you doing? Chickening out?"

Sandobal glanced at her, sighed. "No. I'm a cop, Barbara. I'm trying to look at the whole thing. I saw that Suburban back there. That's the one from El Paso. But who's driving it?"

"All right," she said, tense. "What do we do?"

He thought for a second. "Park is closed. Gate's locked, and the Closed for Maintenance sign is up."

"Makes sense. If something's going on, then they wouldn't want a lot of tourists running around."

He nodded. "Yeah, well. The Suburban's there. And there's a van. A different van. Right?" She nodded. "So that means the payoff is going down."

"Or they could have stolen the van to replace the Suburban. Every cop in the state's looking for it."

He looked up the highway into the center of town. "Wonder where the police department is?"

"Police?" Her eyes widened. "You aren't thinking of bringing in the police?"

"Sooner or later."

"What're we going to do? Just walk in: 'Hi, officer. My name's Sandobal and this is my friend Barbara. We're chasing kidnappers from California, and we think they're out at the state park having a picnic. They're armed and dangerous, tristate killers, so you might want to bring a gun. Oh, and by the way, we killed this guy who said he was a cop back in Arizona, but we can explain that.' Right."

He looked at her. "We're going to have to face up to that, too. If something's going on out there, we need to let the local authorities know about it. Otherwise, if somebody gets hurt—or killed—we could be in more trouble than we are right now." She sniffed in reply. He slammed his hand flat on the bed's side, snapped her attention back toward him. "Look: I'm a cop! Not to sound like a broken record, I have *no* jurisdiction here. This is Texas. I'm just a citizen. I'm already breaking nine kinds of laws running around with a gun under my coat.

A dozen more by letting you do the same thing. I might get away with this. *If* we find bad guys. You—"

Her dark eyes flashed. "You're not *letting* me do one thing."

"You know what I'm talking about. And you know I'm right. We got to find the local cops, let them handle it if they can."

"What if they botch it? What if they see them coming, just kill Vicki, take off?"

"We'll have to take that chance." He went around to the cab, got in behind the wheel. "You coming?"

She held her position for a two-count. Then reluctantly swung over the edge of the truck's bed, got in beside him. "If they screw it up, I'm going to blame you." She slammed the door. "And so is Vicki."

"My only question," he replied, "is who do I get to blame?"

"Me," she said.

Unable to locate anything that looked even remotely like a police station, Sandobal and Barbara pulled back into the lodge, now open. There they learned that Jerry Brady, deputy sheriff, whose office was in the basement of the building, had gone fishing, wasn't expected back before dark. They sullenly drove back to the park, said nothing. Barbara drummed her fingernails on the metal briefcase on the seat between them. She kept it unlatched, open, the gun resting, ready.

Barbara broke the silence. "Tell me what you're thinking."

"I'm thinking I should go back, call the state police or somebody."

"But you're not, are you?"

Sandobal shook his head.

They cruised one more time past the park entrance. The van, the Suburban hadn't moved. They reached the small, closed store a quarter mile past the entrance. Sandobal turned, steered down State Highway 17 on the other side of the store. To the south, its gray strip trailed straight toward distant peaks. They studied the park from the west. A new angle. The back of the pool structure, sundeck, then the other side, picnic area, concession-bathhouse complex, then the alabaster strip of white cabins beyond. Soon they crossed a small bridge over a deep arroyo. Sandobal spun the pickup around, returned.

"They see us scoping them out, won't it scare them?" Barbara asked.

"I don't know that anybody's even looking."

He hit the brake, threw Barbara forward. She banged her forehead on the dashboard. "Shit!" Same spot she injured the night before.

"Shh," Sandobal ordered. "Look." He pointed. Barbara, one hand held her injured forehead, stared.

"Jesus," she gasped.

Shimmering in the morning sunlight, visible from the waist up in the waving grass next to a line of trees running parallel to the stark, white cabins of Balmorhea, was a tall black man in a cream-colored suit. He was far away, but one feature stood out prominently as he moved slowly through the grass, head down. In his left hand, held high, was a gun.

24

Walking Wounded

Vicki came to. She opened her eyes, blinked against yellow light reflected off a Columbia-blue sky, focused on a jagged, dead mesquite limb, thick as her wrist, tapered to a lopsided point, jutted directly out of her body. Several sharp shards of wood bristled from the end of the rotten stob. Some ugly, pincered insect crawled over the rugged tip. I'm dead, she thought.

She remained still, understood that her buttocks rested in the thorny branches of a large mesquite tree on the narrow, graveled banks of a shallow stream. Yellow water only three, four feet below her, ran over sharp white rocks, all pointed up: natural blades. Now she remembered falling, grabbing air. So much for Superwoman.

Smashed, snapped branches told her the tree broke her fall, saved her back. She was caught by an exaggerated V in its trunk. Sharp pains told her that the thorns of the wild tree stabbed through her sweats, her skin. Breath was painful: broken ribs, she thought. "What's next? Heart attack?"

She studied the dark, ugly point that protruded through a rip in the sweatsuit's top under her right arm, next to her breast. She gasped, winced, the rough bark of the stob pulled against her skin. She noticed there was no blood. There ought to be blood. She shifted her weight. Pain rippled through her torso. She relaxed, understood that the broken branch was between her body and her arm.

She wrestled against a web of hurt, maneuvered around in the V of the tree, then ripped herself free of the branch, left the sleeve and a hunk of the top of the sweatsuit raggedly hanging. She tried to pull up straight. The thorns pulled out of her back, side, hips She lost her balance, dropped to the wet gravel below, jolted her left leg. She took stock. Her hips were bruised, punctured, screamed at her. Her left leg wouldn't bend, her right shoulder hurt too much for her to bring her arm close to her body. Her head throbbed. Big surprise, she thought.

She sat on the gravel below, looked up. The tree grew straight out of the side of the arroyo, then turned, twisted, formed its V. A few feet either way, she would have missed it, fallen on the sharp stones below. A few inches either way, she would have run onto the rotten, broken branch, sent it through her like a spear. Heart-and-lung shish kebab, she thought. She pulled open the ripped shirt's top, inspected her stomach, sides, breasts. Deep red fingers ran across her skin, puncture wounds seeped blood. Her right breast was red, scraped raw. Prickling pain told her that her thighs, calves were also stabbed. Her right hand, already wounded by the fence's barbs, bled freely. Her left was also covered in scrapes, bloody holes. Her wrist was sprained. She was hurt inside someplace. Every breath was a torture. But she was alive.

She looked up at the high edges of the natural ditch, remembered: Al.

How long had she been out? The sun was setting, she had no idea of direction. Panic moved her. She eased to her feet, scouted around, spied the .22 in a bed of prickly pear. She extracted it, mindful that the cactus's spikes drew more blood from her lacerated fingers. She cocked it, then eased the hammer down, counted: four rounds. "Pistol-Packing Mama," she whispered. Was that a film title?

To her right, the stream widened slightly, flowed from under a thick knot of spiny brush: tumbleweeds, mesquite. The way toward the plowed field, and mountains beyond was blocked.

To her left, the water narrowed, but the bank flattened out, rose slightly, trees provided cover from above. *"Danielle Boone,"* she muttered. "Starring Vicki Sigel: Farm girl goes to the big city to seek her fame and fortune. Winds up back in the country, defends herself against the Red man, falls off a cliff, slogs down a wet trail, fights for her life against a humanoid freak of nature."

She smiled grimly at the mixed projection, limped down into the water, grateful for the cool soak through her sneakers, then slogged downstream. Every step hurt. She pushed the pain aside. She needed to get up, on the side opposite the park, then make her way to the mountains. Anywhere away from Al.

The stream flowed silent, no gurgle, no babble. She reached down, cupped her hands, filled her mouth. "Don't swallow," she remembered childhood lessons in woodcraft—prairie craft. She sloshed the water around her parched mouth, spat it out, collected two small stones, tucked them into her cheeks, scraped against her teeth. "Caps, for sure," she said. "No choice, now." Saliva flowed.

Vicki's splashing, wading steps unnerved her: echoed. She moved to the bank, looked up now and then, each time expected to see Al's grin peer down. She pushed on, brushed errant, thorny branches out of her way, pulled her wet, sweaty hair out of twigs, brambles. "Got to keep going, Vick," she lectured herself, "got to move." *Danielle Boone: Frontier Woman*, she thought: star billing, for sure.

Sandobal drove past the park once more, but this time, he parked the pickup close to the closed store's porch, got out, went to a window, peered in. "I don't see a phone," he said. "Closed for the season. Guess we do this ourselves." Sweat ran down his forehead, temples, but it wasn't hot: Fear, Barbara thought. "What's the plan?"

"First," Sandobal said, "you're not going in there with that."

Barbara looked at her hand, at the .38. "Why not? They've got guns. I'm not going in there naked."

Sandobal looked across the pool area, past the cottage-office, toward the cabins in the distance. "You'd probably do better naked," he said.

"I'm a good shot. Better shot than you."

"If we do this right, nobody has to *get* shot."

She opened her mouth to protest, saw the determination in his dark eyes. She slumped. "Okay. You're the boss. What's the plan? How're you at climbing fences?" Sandobal peeked around the corner of the porch. Around the perimeter of the park's northwest side, an old CCC-constructed chest-high fieldstone fence crumbled away. A yard wide, it formed a barrier for a twenty-yard strip of yellowing grass, which in turn surrounded a twelve-foot-high chain-link barrier, topped with razor wire. Beyond that was the oddly shaped swimming pool. No gate. The park was built like a frontier fort.

"I don't intend to," he said. He explained his plan: Crouch down by the fence, sneak past the pool, then go through the main entrance on foot, use the sparse shrubs around the cottage-office for cover.

"What do I do?"

"Stay here," he said. He put up a palm to halt her objections. "Get in the truck and wait. Keep it running. But wait. If I spot Vicki, I'll either come back, or, if I can, I'll grab her, then we'll run like hell for the highway. It's a straight shot through the gate. You see us coming out, you haul ass, pick us up. Don't stop. We'll jump in the back. Then, we run."

"What if you don't see her?"

"Then I'll come back. Rethink it."

Barbara put a finger to her lips. "I don't like it."

"I'm not real happy with it myself. But they don't know we're here."

"You don't know that."

He shook his head. "No. I don't. Maybe . . ."

"Maybe she's dead," Barbara finished. "That's what you're thinking."

He shook his head. "I doubt it. Unless they've figured out she's not you. If not, there's no motive to kill her. The main thing is we don't know where she might be. Hell, she could be in the Suburban, in the van, in one of the rooms, tied up, handcuffed, gagged. I have no idea. Go in there like the Marines, all we'll do is get her killed.'' He looked around the corner again. ''There's something else: we're not sure these are the same people, that she's anywhere near here.''

''They have the Suburban.''

''Could have found it. Could have bought it. Who knows?''

''What about that guy? He had a gun.''

''Hunter, maybe?''

''Sandobal.'' Barbara shook her bangs out of her eyes. ''You don't hunt with a pistol, in a suit. You're not *that* much of a city boy.''

''Well, you keep telling me things are different in Texas,'' he grinned. She loved him again. Hot and cold, she thought. C'mon, Barbara. Make up your mind. ''I go in alone. I can't work if I have to worry about you. Besides, somebody's got to cover my ass.''

Barbara considered. ''You spot her, can't get her, come back in a hurry.''

Sandobal pulled his .357, checked the load, stepped away. Then he turned, came back, kissed her. It wasn't a passionate kiss, not a sexy kiss: no tongue, mouth closed. He held her close, pressed his lips hard against hers: movie kiss—quick, clean, memorable. She was surprised, off guard, but she gave in, moved close to him, smelled the cheap motel soap on him: nice.

He pushed her out to arm's length, held her shoulders. Their dark eyes locked. ''I love you, Barbara Lovell. I know you don't love me. But I love you. I want you to know that.''

''Everybody's got to love somebody,'' was all she could think to mutter. He gave her shoulders a nearly painful squeeze, jumped off the porch, moved out. She stood where he left her. Then she smiled when she saw him duck-walk down the stone fence, keep low, out of sight. She *did* love him, she thought. She wished she had said so. He came upon a huge sotol plant at the base of the fence, stepped gingerly through it, lifted his leg high. It would have made her laugh if she wasn't so scared.

With every limping step, pain shot from Vicki's hip into her thigh down past her knee. Her back ached. Her right breast exposed through the ripped fabric throbbed with alarm, but her arm, shoulder seemed more flexible. Walking wounded, she thought. *Battling Bastards of Bastogne*—James Whitmore, Van Johnson, Robert Ryan. No women in that one, except a whore or two. They even changed the title for wide release: *Battleground.* The League of Decency didn't like "bastards." Vicki didn't either.

The arroyo bottom ascended sharply, the stream petered out under a deadfall of mesquite, the going got tougher, sweatier. She stepped careful, moved through knots of dead tree limbs, piles of tumbleweeds, ignored devil's claw, burrs that stuck to her pants, shoelaces. She emerged into a low thicket of wild plums. Every joint protested every step. Her knee was too stiff to bend. "Well, Mr. Dillon, there's just nothing else I can see to do," she croaked, hobbled. She crouched, scooted through the prickly brush, found a clear field of vision. Her heart sank.

She was now adjacent to the RV park, fifty yards to the north across a frost-killed meadow. Another high barbed-wire fence—a new one—blocked her way to the east. To her right, farther south, mountains still beckoned, but they now seemed far away: impossible. She spotted two lines of fence posts between her and an open field in the near distance. She could never jump another fence.

She looked back toward the line of trees, the cabins. The incline back up the hill toward the main park, pool area where she had run down, jumped the arroyo, was clear but steep. Had she angled this far over, she could have circumvented the canal, made it around: easy. She'd be safe now. Not hurting. The thought made her tired. She stared at the grass, the tree line, the cabins: no Al.

She hobbled into the grass, moved slowly toward the RV park. In places, weeds grew up out of the cracked concrete, but in the center it was wide open blacktop. At last, she reached the utility shed. A stout padlock secured the door. She slumped down the far side, panted. Around the side, she caught a view of the canal and the rear of the cabins.

Two men, one black and one white, both in suits, carried guns, stood on her side of the canal. They had just crossed the footbridge near Cabin One. They had come for her, she thought.

Or for Barbara. Didn't matter. Neither was present or accounted for. She smiled in spite of herself. "Surprise, Al," she whispered. She imagined the ugly woman's rage. She hoped it would only be something to imagine.

Another idea: Maybe Al was dead. Maybe these guys were cops. Maybe a rescue party showed up at last. The thought excited her, forced her to her feet. She peeked again. They moved out, separated. Then she saw the familiar sight of Al's sawed-off shotgun in the white guy's hands. "Nope," she whispered. "Cops don't use those."

But maybe Al was dead, anyway. Maybe they showed up, found Vicki—Barbara—missing, just put her out of her misery. Maybe Red was dead, too. Maybe, she thought with a jerk, maybe she had killed him after all. Now, they would kill her. If they found her, that was sure. She was worth something to them: revenge. It wouldn't matter to them whether she was Barbara or not.

Frustration built. Tears threatened, but she fought them back. "Shit, Vick," she said. "This is a piece of cake. Walk on the beach. Just like Annette Funicello." And, she added, the last thing she needed: Frankie Avalon.

She pulled her head back, discovered she was hyperventilating against the pain. Every breath brought a stab, a tearing deep inside her, a scary liquid rattle. She pushed matted hair out of her eyes, looked again. The men split up. The white man—big guy with short, curly hair—moved slightly toward her at an angle, shotgun held awkward, high above the grass. He scowled, stared right at her. She held still. Didn't breathe. His eyes swept the RV park, then he moved on, slanted away, headed toward the brush pile at the mouth of the arroyo. The other man passed into the line of trees.

In the distance, beyond the pool, through a maze of chain link and barbed wire, Vicki spotted an orange pickup pass on the highway, moving slow. A farmer, she thought. She hadn't seen that highway before. Then she realized: orange! Salvation! If she could get his attention. Too far away. She came to her feet anyway, thought of running. Weight on her leg hurt. Then she saw Al. "Nope, not dead. Nine lives, old Al has."

Al moved slowly along the side parking lot, looked at everything. She approached the concession-bathhouse next to the pool. She also carried a pistol, the automatic they took from the trooper in Arizona.

Vicki breathed deep, challenged her pain. It didn't ease, but she handled it. She waited, looked again. The white man continued slowly on his arch, the shotgun high across his chest, eyes surveyed the ground in front of him: uncomfortable. Soon, he would be in a position to see her again if she didn't move. She scooted around the base of the shed, worked her way to the front, kept the small building between them. She spied the pickup again, parked by the small store. Al would be able to see her if she moved directly toward it. But the big woman had disappeared into the concession building. The pickup was too good a chance to pass up.

She tried again to bend her knees, run. The left one wouldn't bend. Leg wouldn't run. During the short rest, her entire body had stiffened. She walked slowly, upright, limped, protected by nothing but luck. Across the RV park she spotted the faux rail fence. The canal blocked her way to that. She couldn't leap it, wasn't sure how deep it was. There was only one way out. The way she came in. The front entrance. She would have to go back, circle the cabins, go past the wire gate. Then down the highway, toward the pickup. It was pointed in the right direction to see her if she could get outside the park, wave to them. She had no idea who might be there. Didn't matter. She knew what was here.

She moved in a world of hurt, slow, noticed her shadow on the ground, wondered if her hair looked worse on her head than it did in silhouette. She also wondered if her body would ever recover. She felt like a cripple. *Cripple CoEd Ranger,* she thought, starring Vicki Sigel: poster girl for kidnap victims everywhere. Long way from Superwoman.

The thought took shape, worked her mind. Hell, she thought, if Raymond Burr could make a second career in a wheelchair, why couldn't she do it on a cane? Might be innovative. Gary would like it. He liked all kinds of shit that had weird twists. She'd wear miniskirts, show a lot of thigh. She limped on.

A new thought struck her. There's a *switchboard* in the office. Red said so. The operator was "tied up," he said. That meant alive. Might have a gun. At least, might know what to do. The idea gained form, pushed her. "First the canal, then the cabins, then the parking lot, the office, the highway," she said. Measurements. One at a time. Only way to fly.

On her side on the hard tile floor inside the park's office, Midge Watkins was furious. She had twisted, turned so violently, the chair she was bound to turned over, she banged her head. Her hands were asleep, feet, too. Her arms ached, head hurt. More, her pride throbbed for revenge.

Her breath whistled through her nose. She was sick of the sound of it. Her jaws ached from the gag. From the start, she wrestled with the cords on her feet, the tape on her hands: no give. Since she fell over, though, she found some slack. She worked it: tugged, pulled, twisted. She had no idea what was going on. Didn't care. Cole's ass was grass.

Before she fell over, while she sat, seethed, the switchboard lit up: Cabin One. She squirmed, cursed while the panel buzzed. The sons of bitches were trying to call out! What were they doing? Ordering pizza? The buzzing ring it made filled her ears, made her eyes water, infuriated her. Then the ringing stopped. In a bit, the light on the switchboard came on again: phone off the hook. Same cabin. It made no sense. Damnit. *Goddamnit!* She had had it with things that made no sense.

Then she heard the shooting: Shotgun, she thought. Were they hunting? Or were they killing? Was she next? That was when she turned herself over. Then she waited, heard nothing. She tugged viciously at the tape, at the cords on her legs. Her hands, wrists had no feeling. Tears filled her eyes. This sucks, she thought. It just plain sucks! She would *not* die like some kind of animal, trussed up, waiting for slaughter. She would not!

All at once, she jerked hard with her left hand. The tape ripped free. She couldn't believe it. She held it in front of her eyes, stared. The skin was white, shriveled, wrinkled with impressions from the sticky binding. Her fingers tingled as circulation returned. She made a fist, then tore the tape from her mouth, spat out the gag, and breathed. Now, she thought, we'll see.

She ripped her right hand free, worked it a bit while her left tore at the cords around her ankles. At first, she couldn't stand. Her feet wouldn't work. She wiggled her toes inside her boots to hurry the blood back.

Finally, she came to her knees, crawled over to the window. A big white van was parked in the middle of the parking lot, nose to rear of the Suburban. "Alpine Airport Shuttle," she read aloud. "What the hell?" She fought her way to her feet, stamped them back to life. Anger swarmed all over her. Fool! Cole came in that van. She'd bet on it. He knew where she was, knew what they'd done to her. He was inside now. Laughing at her. She had had enough. Fuck Cole. Fuck Vegas. "Party's over," she said.

She went to the switchboard, called Jerry Brady. His machine picked up: still fishing. She dialed his pager number. That could take a while, she thought. Midge took a breath. Nearest other cop was Van Horn. Maybe a highway patrol car in between, but not likely. It was up to her. She could run, she could hide, or she could do her job. She'd made this bargain. Now she needed a way out. The deal with Cole—okay, it was wrong. But this wasn't part of it. Cole was past tense. She went to the door that led to the back room: locked. The punk had her keys. Anger swelled anew. She took a step back, kicked the flimsy barrier open, stalked in. The punk was meat, too.

Inside, the cot blocked a closet. She shoved it aside, opened it: gun rack. She removed a Winchester pump. Midge shoved shells into the shotgun, knew what she had to do. She stalked to the outer office, took a position behind the counter, waited, boiled. She felt better already.

She glanced at the switchboard. Somebody had hung up the phone in Cabin One. What did that mean? She felt her knees weaken, her grip on the shotgun tighten. "C'mon, Jerry," she said. "I can't do this by myself." Yes, she thought, she could.

"State Park," Moria said. He waddled out to the Mercedes parked in front of the Trans-Pecos Lodge. Eddy's ears pricked up. He turned slightly away. A maroon sedan turned off the highway from the interstate, the driver looked over the lodge, then U-turned and headed back toward the interstate.

His rage was gone. He knew he had to be cool, calculating, play it right, or he would blow it, could wind up hurting Barbara himself. For the past four hours, he'd made up scenario after scenario. But now, they were in Balmorhea. His adrenaline levels peaked again. He felt sharp: ready. There was only one question: where was Barbara?

"Not the town, the State Park," Moria panted. "Motel of some kind out there. It's supposed to be closed today. Perfect. I always underestimated Cole. Son of a bitch was smart!"

Eddy looked once more at the highway: clear. "Where's the park?" Barbara was close. He felt it.

"Mile and a half, the broad inside said. That way." Moria pointed to the west. "One road in, one road out. Can't miss it."

Eddy got in, glanced in the back seat. Hedge was still out, forearm across his chest, the other dangled. Blood crusted on crude bandages. "Go slow," Moria warned.

"Slow, hell," Eddy said. He pulled out, sprayed gravel.

"Slow," Moria insisted. "Let's don't blow this."

"I won't blow it," Eddy said. "Not this time, I won't."

"What the hell?" Midge breathed out the words, fogged the glass in the cottage office. A man sneaked around the cedar trees flanking the drive, stayed low, crow-hopped from bush to bush. Soon he was beneath the window, paused, scampered away. He wore a worn baseball cap, a battered, stained corduroy coat, jeans, sneakers with no socks. What held her attention was what he carried in his right hand: an ugly, nickel-plated revolver.

"Who the hell are you?" Midge asked in a whisper. "Another one of Cole's 'people'?" She moved to the office door, cracked it open. He passed across the sidewalk to the drive, stayed low, reached an oversized live oak, slid down behind the trunk, panted, watched the cabins. "Cop?" Midge wondered aloud. "Or crook?" She shook her head, gripped the shotgun, waited, watched him watch the cabins. Didn't matter. Son of a bitch was about to meet the Law on the Premises.

Sandobal's legs were cramped from walking in a crouch for over a quarter mile. He peeked around the trunk of the tree, held his pistol in a professional grip, studied the vehicles, the cabins, waited.

Insects buzzed in the bushes, trees around the pool. He started to ease forward when he saw a well-dressed but rumpled man come around the corner of the cabin. A pistol-gripped sawed-off shotgun dangled from his hand. Sandobal cocked his pistol. This was a big man, well built, handsome in a way, even familiar, but he looked sick, weary: suit dirty, full of burrs, stickers, tie loose, expensive shoes covered with dust. His eyes were tired, face red, crumpled in worry. He didn't fit the description of anyone Sandobal expected to find, but he carried a dangerous weapon, and he wasn't dressed for hunting, in Texas or anywhere else.

The man went to the van, opened the passenger door, leaned in, talked to someone, gestured. Then he slammed the door. He shook his head, passed the Suburban, entered Cabin One. Sandobal breathed. Someone was in the van. Safe bet: Vicki.

Barbara had a clear but distant view of Sandobal. Her angle on the van was blocked by trees, but she sensed that he could see someone inside. She bit her lip, stamped her foot against the soreness from last night's wreck. Her forehead throbbed where she hit it on the pickup's dashboard.

She was antsy, couldn't stand it, edged down off the porch, held Sandobal in sight. She scooted behind the pickup's wheel, turned the engine over. It rumbled to life, she eased it forward toward the rock fence. Then she left it running, climbed into the bed. Sandobal eased away from the tree. "Vicki's in the van," she whispered to herself, then said aloud, "Get her."

* * *

Midge watched while the large man in the suit went to the van. Who was *this* guy? she demanded. Maybe *he* was a cop of some kind. Then she shook her head. No. Too well dressed, and that gun was straight from TV. The guy looked into the van, then went inside the cabin. Baseball Cap left his tree, crept toward the van. That did it, Midge thought: enough. She opened the door wide, checked her badge to make sure it was visible over her tiny left breast, stepped outside.

Sandobal bent his knees as low as he could, crept toward the rear of the van. He reached the right rear wheel. Took a moment, looked at the cabin's door, raised himself to peek inside at the rear seat: nothing.

He looked to his right, toward the pool, then to his rear, toward the office. He noted the door was open—had it been before?—couldn't remember. Phone in there. He started to retreat, call somebody: highway patrol, somebody. Then he saw the burnt orange nose of the Ford pickup creep forward, out from behind the store. He raised his arm, waved her back. The pickup stopped, waited. Then he saw her bright-red figure in the bed, raised up behind the cab. "Impatient little bitch," he hissed. Wait, he mentally commanded her, please.

He had to move quick, now. He crept along the side of the van exposed to the cabin's door. If the suit came out, he'd see him clearly. He took a deep breath, cocked his pistol, stood, gripped the passenger door, jerked it open. No one in front. He put his head inside. "Vicki?" he said in a loud whisper. "Vicki Sigel? You in here?"

A fall of blonde hair framed a mature, beautiful face raised up, mint-green eyes blinked at him. He stepped back, pushed the door open wide behind him: not Vicki. "Uh . . . ," he said, confused.

"Who the hell are you?" the blonde said, irritated. Her voice scratched. She wore a green leather jumpsuit like a second skin, unzipped far enough to expose expensive underwear, pushed up cleavage. Her makeup was stale, sweaty, the fabric of the seat on which she had been lying was impressed into one cheek. She lifted one long, red middle fingernail to her smeared lipstick. "I asked you a question, cowboy."

Sandobal gaped at her. She looked at the pistol. "Are you planning to shoot me?" the blonde asked. "I have such a headache, I really don't give a damn. You might be doing me a favor." She traced her finger over her lips, smoothed out the jumpsuit's fabric across her knees, smiled at him, noted his eyes on the exposed tops of her breasts, smiled. "You wouldn't have some vodka on you by any chance?"

"Freeze, mister!" The command came from behind Sandobal. He spun around, struck the van's door with his shoulder hard enough to make it spring back, push him forward. He stumbled. From the corner of his eye he saw a short, sour-faced woman dressed as a park ranger. He also saw a shotgun aimed directly at him. He opened his mouth, reached for his shield, but the weapon spoke first. The wadding struck him in the hand: stung. Both knees went numb. He dropped his pistol, fell, unable to stop himself. Blood spurted from his lower body but he felt nothing but the sting in his hand. The boom hit his ears before everything went black.

Midge stood for a moment, watched the guy fall, studied his lacerated jeans. Her ears rang from the shotgun's blast. The air smelled of cordite. "Birdshot," she said aloud. "Goddamn birdshot. Should have put in double-ought for a job like this. I *know* that." She stepped toward Sandobal, kicked the Python away from his outstretched hand under the van. He was bleeding badly. She hit him lower than she meant to, but the effect was good. He was down, out of commission. That was good. Now where was the suit? Where was the punk? Where was that godawful ugly woman? Where was Cole?

She stepped up over Sandobal's body, had a good look at the woman in the van. She ducked down when Midge fired, but now she sat up again, gave Midge a cold smile. "And just who are you?" she asked. "A waitress, I hope."

Midge studied her face a moment, checked the cleavage, felt

briefly envious, turned, looked around: bitch. The real problem was elsewhere. Anyone with hair that severely bleached couldn't be much of a threat, she reasoned.

She stalked past the van, marched up the side of the Suburban toward Cabin One. Fuck Jerry, she thought. He could sort out this mess when he got here. The door to Cabin One was open. The suit stood there without his weapon. He had a shocked, surprised look on his face, eyes wide, wider. C'mon, Midge thought. I'm not *that* intimidating.

"All right—," Midge started, then she spun around: instinct. Her ears still rang from the shotgun blast, masked the noise, but now she saw what the suit saw. "Oh, shit," Midge said.

She planted her feet, stared at the burnt orange pickup bearing down on her, the shock of dark hair on the girl behind the wheel. She lifted the shotgun, pulled the trigger: nothing. Forgot to pump out the spent shell. She looked down at the gun, stepped back against the side of the Suburban, then looked up again. She saw the elliptical blue FORD emblem bearing down on her gold badge. Blackjack, she thought when the pickup mashed her into the heavy Chevy truck's passenger door.

Vicki hobbled to the footbridge, stopped. She had flopped down in the tall grass between the canal and the RV park twice: once when the black guy came back, stalked the length of the canal, then veered off toward the RV park behind her, again when the heavy white guy shuffled by, cursed, went around the side of the strip. Al was still out of sight in the pool area. She regained her feet: a struggle. She promised not to do it again.

The bridge was a pretty little arching fieldstone structure, wide enough for two to walk abreast. At its apex, she could be seen clearly by anyone who looked. It was chancy. The pickup was out of her sight line. Office, she now thought. Office, a telephone. Maybe she'd call Gary. "Hi, sweetheart. Any calls while I was out?" She was nearly home. Fuck Gary, she thought. Time for her to have a real agent. She looked like hell, hurt like hell, but still had her stuff. Her right breast ached steady, throbbed, the other pains matched its tempo. She didn't have much left. One last push.

She cast her head around painfully, searched the cabin windows: empty. Then the other direction, toward the pool, watched for Al. The .22 remained in her hand, forgotten. She reached the bridge, took a breath, put a torn sneaker toe on it, prepared to go as fast as she could, heard the blast of a shotgun. Not close, but close enough.

"Seen me!" she whispered to herself, crouched down, forcing her injured knee to bend. After a painful, breathless moment, the noise of smashing metal and glass struck her ears. Without a thought, she pitched the gun over the side of the fieldstone arch, placed both injured hands on its surface, cartwheeled over into the canal. Water flooded over her head, hurt flooded her body, she fought to stay conscious.

Got to quit this Wonder Woman shit, she thought: hard on a girl.

25

Judgments

"What the fuck?" Moria shouted. A column of steam, dust, dark smoke rose in front of the white strip of cabins as they rounded a curve in the highway, approached the park. Eddy sped up, sailed past the entrance. The nose of an orange Ford pickup was jumbled in the wreckage of a Chevrolet Suburban. He glanced over, spotted Jensen, pistol in hand, rushing toward the wreckage. A large man stood beside him holding a tall blonde woman by the arm.

Eddy's anger surged. He almost lost control, then swerved back to his lane. "That's him!" He braked hard, twisted the wheel, shoved the car into a U-turn.

"I see him!" Moria said. "Drive on." Eddy ignored him, continued the turn. Moria reached over, grabbed the wheel. Eddy swatted Moria's hand away, continued to turn. Moria made a blade of his fingers, brought it down hard on Eddy's elbow, breaking his grip. He shoved Eddy hard against the door, grabbed the wheel, straightened the car. "Drive on!" he ordered. "Don't be stupid. Let's get a look at this."

Eddy's teeth clenched, fists formed. Moria was looking behind them. "That your daughter?"

Eddy straightened up, put his hands back on the wheel, fought to stay calm, glanced back. "No." He knew who: Hillary.

They reached the store, blocked from view. "Turn here," Moria ordered, pointed left. "Follow that highway."

Eddy felt something slip away. "You're crazy! I'm going back. I'm—"

"Turn here," Moria insisted. "Let's get a good look. They're not going anywhere in those heaps."

"I'm going back! It's not your daughter," Eddy shouted, glanced into the store's parking lot, judged the angle for another U-turn.

"Turn, damnit," Moria insisted. "Make a turn down that highway. Now!"

"Fuck you!" Eddy yelled. He swung the car into another arch, then felt the barrel of a pistol on his temple.

"Turn now," Moria said: calm, cold. He clicked back the hammer.

Furious, frustrated, Eddy coasted past the store, wheeled down the highway. They passed the blocking structure around the pool: nothing.

"I'm going in," Eddy said evenly. "Barbara's in there."

"Wait. Turn around now."

They passed a narrow bridge over an arroyo, Eddy pushed the Mercedes into a wide turn. Panic climbed his back, his neck. "I'm going back, now."

"I said, we wait and look," Moria repeated in a low tone. Eddy eased up on the accelerator, shaking with anger. "I know what you're thinking," Moria said evenly. "I lost a daughter, remember?"

"I don't intend to lose mine."

"Be cool," Moria said. "Pull over. Let's take a good look." A pause. "I'm on your side, Eddy."

Eddy nodded. Sweat ran down his face. He eased the car onto the shoulder, far side of the bridge, idled forward, stopped. They were now shielded from view by the thicket alongside the arroyo's southern edge.

"She's either okay or she's already dead," Moria said. His gun still pointed at Eddy's temple. "That's cold, but that's the way it is. You got to live with that. Got it?" Eddy nodded again. "We bust in there now, no clue what's happening, where she is, what's going on, won't do shit but get us both killed. And," he lowered the gun, "if she's alive, it won't help her stay that way."

Eddy stared straight ahead. Said nothing. Moria studied the thicket, high grass across the fence. "Let's go in from here," he said. "Come from the rear."

Eddy pulled out his own pistol, popped the slide.

"Ready?" Moria opened his door.

"Moria," Eddy said. "That's my sister in there, my brother. So you'll know. I'm going to kill them." A pause. "Both. Whether Barbara's okay or not. It's not what they did. It's what they tried to do." Moria nodded, but Eddy wanted it clear. "You try to stop me. You try to make a deal. You're dead, too."

Moria's eyes softened, but they were flat. "Don't threaten me, Eddy. You haven't got the balls to threaten me: not now, not ever."

"It's not a threat," Eddy said. "It's a fact."

Moria sighed. "You never killed a man, have you?" Eddy stared into Moria's eyes. They challenged him to answer. He couldn't. Didn't matter: Moria knew. "It's not as easy as you think. Especially when you know him." Moria looked away slightly. "It's harder to kill a woman. I know."

"This won't be hard," Eddy said. "I got one thing I care about, and she's in trouble. It's their fault, and this won't be hard."

Moria nodded once. "It's your call." For a moment longer, they studied each other's faces. He saw the familiar compelling softness in his boss's eyes. Then Moria broke, glanced at Hedge. His shades were off, eyes open. Snake, Eddy thought.

"We're going," Moria said. "You okay?" Hedge didn't move or change expression. If his huge chest didn't rise, fall, Eddy would believe he was dead. "Let's go," Moria said. He pushed open the door, crossed the ditch, eased himself through the lower strands of a barbed-wire fence into the weeds beyond. Eddy followed, vaulted over the top of the fence, followed into the neck-high growth and into the trees.

* * *

The canal wasn't deep, maybe three, four feet of clear water. Flowed smoothly over slippery, moss-covered concrete. Vicki half stood, half floated, pushed against the light current, kept her head beneath the surface, came up only to grab a searing lungful of breath. She now understood that the shots she heard weren't meant for her, but the crashing noise perplexed her. Sounded like the end of the world. She came up once more, breathed slow, listened. A cloud of dust, smoke rose over the cabins from the other side.

She pulled herself up, peeked over the canal's edge: Al. The big woman moved across the blacktop from the concession area, circled toward the front of the cabins, pistol up. Vicki went under, half floated, comforted by the safety of the cold water. Her hair swirled around her face: auburn seaweed. Her muscles, grateful for the chilly bath, felt stronger. The worst of the aches eased, the throb in her hip lowered to a dull regular thud. She could bend her knee better.

She looked again: nobody. Her feet fished around on the bottom, searched for the pistol. The water was clear, but the greenish-brown moss obscured her vision. Finally, the toe of her sneaker struck something on the smooth concrete, she reached down: the .22. Would it work after being wet? They always worked in the movies, except when the bad guys had them. She remembered Sylvester Stallone in one of his major macho flicks: he emerged from a long swim in a river, machine gun in hand, bandanna around his head, grease all over his face, sneer on his lips, killed Oriental soldiers by the score. Kevin Wong, her upstairs neighbor, was an extra in one of those movies. She invited him over for a drink one afternoon. He bragged about his big role, said he died fourteen times in a single scene, half the time as an officer: good money.

"It's all in the camera angles, baby," he said, grinned, exposing crooked teeth. "We all look alike, except naked." Then he hit on her. When she said no, he called her a racist. She kicked him out: skinny little gook.

Light filtered down through the reeds, water plants next to the canal, glittered on the surface. She debated. If she stayed put, she'd soon be chilled through, numb. Had to move. But she lacked the strength to pull herself out quick, scramble over the side. She would be too exposed.

She pushed up the canal toward the pool, bobbed on the bottom. The narrow ditch sluiced beneath the blacktop drive, covered by a grate. There was enough clearance to come up, breathe, so she dove under, pushed herself along. *Creature from the Green Canal,* she thought. There had to be a way out, she reasoned, had to be.

On the other side, the canal deepened, turned abruptly to the right, then emptied into a rectangular well, ten, twelve feet deep. Three sides were mossy slick, too high to climb. The fourth side was a lock, open two feet from the bottom rear of the concrete diving platform top, formed a partial wall to the huge swimming pool's deepest end. Water flowed under the platform, six, eight feet, then slid over the lock's gap, filled the well, then emptied into the canal. She looked around: no way out.

Vicki eased herself over into the well, dog-paddled across to the lock, forced her aching legs to tread water. She was never a good swimmer. West Texas girls don't swim. But she was athletic. She filled her lungs, endured a bubbling pain behind her right breast, then heaved herself over the lock like a sea mammal: slick. *Free Willy III,* she thought: *The Dive for Freedom.* Her weight carried her deep, the current pressed her below the surface, against the inside of the lock. Panic filled her eyes, she opened them, saw swirling water. A fish floated by. All her strength gathered, she pushed against the lock's inner wall, forced a kick against the rushing current beneath the ugly, mossy platform, then struck something: a gate.

She almost gave up, released herself to the current, died. It would be easy, she argued with herself. Her lungs pulsed, wanted release. The heavy gauge wire of the gate wouldn't budge. Then she opened her eyes, saw a latch through the swarming bubbles. With one hand, she pulled herself over to the rusty clasp, fingers tore on the rough, heavy metal. On the other side she could see light: fine, sharp rays filtered through the pool's surface. Must reach the light, she thought.

She tore at the latch. It was firm, designed to be opened from the other side. Her lungs were bursting, insisting. Pain knifed through her right side. She pulled, pushed, hit it with the pistol: no effect. She put the barrel of the .22 on the latch, cocked the hammer, pulled the trigger: twice, three times. The gun blasts sounded sharp, metallic in the water, like a spring. Smoke-filled bubbles obscured her vision, but when she pushed again, the latch was open, the gate gave. She pulled herself through, kicked twice, pushed her head upwards, broke the surface of the pool with a gulp, a gasp, pulled air, light into her lungs, eyes.

It took her five minutes to find the strength to climb up the poolside ladder, flop down on the concrete diving platform. She lay on her back, heaved air, her injured breast exposed. That was the least of her worries. Overhead, the sky's evening-deepened blue mocked her with its depth. She thought of Charlton Heston lying on a futuristic beach in a bad movie. "Charlie," she said to the sky. "You've got nothing on me. Right now, I could go for a couple of well-armed gorillas."

Her breath slowed, still hurt. She hobbled up, pulled a scrap of torn fabric across her chest, tried to tuck it in. She inspected the high fence topped with razor wire between her and the highway. Behind her, a sidewalk led between shrubs, well-trimmed trees away to the bathhouse-concession area. *"Huis clos,"* she said aloud. "At least your brain is working, toots."

She limped behind the diving boards, looked into the parking lot in front of the cabins. The two men she saw before and a tall, blonde woman stood viewing the destruction before them, the wrecked Suburban, the smashed Ford. So much for orange angels, Vicki thought. Hope she was wearing a seat belt.

Al moved into view. Vicki stepped back. The big woman carried a body over her shoulder, moved toward the office. The ranger, Vicki decided, noting the gray trousers. A regular shotgun dangled from Al's free hand. Another body sprawled on the ground next to the van. Al stopped, looked her way. Vicki crouched, endured scalding pain in her hip, knee. She peeked up, but Al had passed on, out of sight. When she looked at the wreck again, the man, woman were still there. But she now saw something else. A bright-red bundle lay stretched at their feet. The big white guy was kneeling over it. Not it:

she. She recognized the crimson wind suit. "Barbara," Vicki whispered. But she didn't know if she felt relief or regret, or just pissed off. Barbara wasn't moving at all.

She looked again at the other body. Sandobal, she guessed, the things we do for love. Al returned, stood over him. "Shit," Vicki swore. "Nothing is working out today." She moved further to her left: exposed. But she had to see, to know what was happening.

The heavy man stood, pulled Barbara up, lifted her over his shoulder in a fireman's carry, made his way toward the cabin. The woman and black man followed them inside. Barbara was apparently alive. But she was badly hurt.

She had come for her. It was Barbara in the pickup, the orange pickup. Her angel was working after all.

She looked at the .22 still in her hand: no choice. She had one bullet left. But one or none, strength or no strength, hurt or no hurt, it was up to her to save her savior. Enter the Duke, Vicki thought. "Well, Pilgrim," she drawled. "Reckon it's time for the cavalry."

Something cold, wet covered Barbara's forehead. A sour, strong odor filled her nostrils. Directly in front of her eyes behind a snap of ammonia was a familiar face: Hillary. Barbara gasped, swatted at the vial.

"I think the little whore is awake," Hillary said, stood up, backed away a step.

Barbara's breath caught, her mind spun once, settled. She stared into Hillary's icy, mint-green eyes. She tried to raise herself, but Hillary put a hand on her shoulder, pushed her back. She felt weak. Her whole body hurt.

"You're going to be fine, darling," Hillary cooed. "You had a teensy-weensy little accident: totaled two cars, half a motel, murdered a policewoman of some kind. You'll be fine." Barbara remembered the terrified face of a uniformed woman just below the slope of the pickup's burnt orange hood. She closed her eyes, forced the memory back.

"Shut up, Hillary," a familiar male voice out of Barbara's line of vision said. "You never know when to shut up."

Hillary's finger drifted up, curled a strand of blonde, studied Barbara, then she moved out of sight. "I simply do not *believe* that there's nothing to drink here," she said. "I thought this was a resort of some kind."

A black man's face appeared: strange, sinister. Darkness behind his eyes. "Are you feeling better?" he asked. She looked at his mouth. His teeth were slightly pointed. "It would be a disaster if anything happened to you."

"Sandobal?" Barbara said. Her throat was dry, crusty.

"Ah, yes. Your police officer," he said.

"Your boyfriend wasn't so lucky," Hillary quipped.

"For God's sake, Hillary. Can't you see that—oh, never mind." Barbara knew that voice: Quince.

"Do you feel well enough to sit up?" the black man said.

Barbara's vision cleared. She pushed herself up, away from him, onto her elbows. Her head raged, everything was framed by a hazy cloud. "Sandobal?" she said again, pulled her bottom up onto the pillow.

"Officer Sandobal is, uh, in good hands," the man said. He stood fully erect, extended his left hand.

"You might say he's in God's hands," Hillary chuckled.

"He's dead, isn't he?" she asked: "Tell the truth for once, Hillary."

"Hillary? What happened to 'Aunt Hillary.' My, we are all grown up, aren't we?"

"Is he dead, or isn't he?"

"Like a herring, as your uncle is fond of saying."

Barbara's face clouded. Tears welled. She fought them back. "You bitch," she said. "You evil bitch."

"He was a good-looking stud. How was he in the sack?"

"For God's sake!" Quince shouted.

The black man set a poker face toward Barbara. "I think I should introduce myself. My name is Jensen, Mitchell Jensen."

She ignored the proffered hand, noted the blood-spattered ace bandages around his right wrist.

He withdrew the gesture, smiled at her. "Like father, like daughter."

Barbara shook her head. She looked around the room. Hillary's well-maintained buttocks were neatly positioned on the edge of a large, brown Adirondack chair. She smoked. Quince stood beside her, agitated.

"When Eddy hears about this, he's going to kill you."

"Mr. Lovell," Jensen said, "is well aware of the circumstances surrounding your . . . your presence here."

Barbara's dark eyes flashed, cleared completely. "I doubt that," she said. "You don't know Eddy."

"Oh, he *knows* Eddy," Hillary put in. "Met him last night. *He* shook hands with you, didn't he, Mitch?"

Jensen stepped away, went to another, identical chair, sat down, extracted a fresh cigar from his suitcoat. The room stank: open sewer. Barbara wrinkled her nose, looked around.

"I'm afraid you've been a great deal of trouble," Jensen said. "Running away, then coming back in the manner you did. Someone could have been killed. In fact, someone was."

"Saved your uncle's bacon," Hillary said. "I'm shocked he didn't mess his pants." She wrinkled her nose. "Smells like he did, anyway. What *is* that?"

"That," Jensen smiled, "is another one of your niece's unfortunate victims. He's in the other room. In repose."

Hillary rose, stepped up through the doorway, glanced into the other bedroom. "Quince, are you aware that there's a dead body in there?"

"Mr. Red," Jensen said before Quince could respond. "Or such was the name I was given. I'm afraid he left us while you were resting, Ms. Lovell."

Hillary shrugged. Quince turned away. His face was white, Barbara noticed, pale. She'd never seen him that way. She also didn't care.

"What I don't understand is why you came back," Jensen said. Barbara stared at him. "If your gallant officer found you, offered you rescue, why didn't you just run away?"

Suddenly, Barbara realized that these weren't the kidnappers. There was no red-headed Malory, no strange woman around. She knew all these people. All but Jensen. They didn't know that Vicki was the one who had been kidnapped. The kidnappers were gone. Somehow, Vicki escaped.

"What do you want?" Barbara asked Jensen. "Money? How much is she paying you to have me kidnapped?"

"I'm afraid that you've missed the point," Jensen said, tented his fingers over his cigar. "You were invited here—"

"I was kidnapped." Barbara eased into Vicki's role, imagined her ordeal. "I've witnessed a half-dozen murders, an armed robbery. I've seen cars blown up, cops shot, and now, for some reason, you've forced me to run over a woman."

"Forced you?" Quince said. "Nobody—"

"You left out another little killing of your own," Jensen said. "Our red-headed friend in the other room."

"I didn't—" Barbara started, caught herself: *You're Vicki.* Vicki must have killed the guy, escaped. "I didn't mean to."

Jensen looked at her curiously. "Well, actually, I had to finish the job for you. But I probably would have had to do it anyway.

"It doesn't matter one way or another," Jensen went on. "Unless you cooperate, you will be in worse condition."

Barbara directed a question to Quince. "Tell me, Uncle Quince. What's—"

"You've been abducted, you ungrateful little bitch," Hillary cut in, stood. "You spat in my face, ran off on your own, so I decided to make what use of you I could. We are about to trade you to the one person you want most in the world to see, to be like: your worthless father."

"Trade me? For what? Eddy doesn't have any—"

"Money?" Hillary said. "Of course he hasn't. What in the world would he do with money? But he has something better. We've struck a bargain. Or we shall. As soon as we get back to civilization. Which reminds me." She looked at Jensen. "Isn't it about time to go? I need a drink. I want a bath."

"We've a bit of unfinished business," Jensen said.

"Not with that. . .that freak of nature out there?" Hillary exclaimed. "I am truly disappointed in you. I thought you would engage a better class of gangster."

"She was Mr. Cole's choice. Not mine."

Hillary sat back, lit another cigarette. "Well, what about her—or him—or whatever it is?"

"You talking about me?" a husky voice burst into the room ahead of the ugliest woman Barbara had ever seen. "My ears was burning." Barbara gasped, blinked her eyes. She came into the room, stacked the shotgun in the corner, pulled a bent cigarette out of a pocket, lit it. Her clothes were filthy, covered with fresh, sticky blood. She forked the cigarette in two stubby, blood-encrusted fingers, blew smoke out her nostrils, looked at Barbara, then at Jensen: "Okay, who the fuck is this and why ain't she dead?"

Vicki crawled under the low branches of a huge cedar tree, close to the parking lot. Every few feet, she had to stop, gather strength. Then Al returned from the office, weapon in hand. Shiny, wet blood stained her clothes—her "colors," Vicki remembered—her arms, hands. She stopped, listened. Vicki held her breath. Loathing knotted her stomach. She wasn't human. Al swiveled around, trained the sawed-off shotgun on everything in sight. She hunched her shoulders, stepped off, walked away

Vicki pointed the knobby sight of the .22 at Al's large back, then on the back of her head, couldn't fire. She bit her lip. Why? she demanded. Why can't I do this? If Al turned around, if she could see her eyes, her ugly mouth, she knew she could kill her. But she couldn't shoot her in the back. Al didn't turn around. She looked over the wreckage, walked out and looked up and down the highway, shrugged, then went to Cabin One, walked in.

Vicki told herself she should run, get out. The way was clear now. The entrance open. Maybe there were keys in the van. She could take it, back it out quick, hit the highway, find some cops. There had to be cops. Or not.

Barbara came without cops—Sandobal didn't count. If he could find help, he would have brought it. No. It was up to Vicki. She had to go in, save her. It was the only way.

She crept forward on her stomach, wriggled across the parking lot. The ragged, wet sweatsuit tore beneath her. She felt gravel rake her exposed belly, scratch her wounded skin. It'll take more than oils and bubble bath to fix this, she thought. "Oh, Gary," she hissed, "if you could see me now. Julia Roberts or Demi Moore couldn't do this." This was a part for one of the Redgraves: the skinny, tough one.

She reached the small lawn lining the walk along the cabins'

entrances, rolled over beside the white buildings, wriggled
under the large bedroom window of Cabin One. She pulled up,
looked inside: Barbara was on the double bed, talking to the
black guy. The white guy stood in the opposite corner. No Red.
Al was in the center of the room, waved her fat arms. Vicki
couldn't see the blonde. She could hear their voices. Everyone
shouted, pointed fingers, weapons. Vicki lowered herself to the
ground, heaved air, collected what strength she could find.
Okay, in quick, use the gun to scare them, shoot Al if you have
to. Bunch them up, get Barbara, get out.

Then, she reassessed. What if Barbara was hurt too bad to
walk? What if she panicked? What if somebody shot back?
She looked at the .22. One bullet left. One chance, three, four
bad guys: hopeless. Not even Clint Eastwood would try that.

She pushed the problem away, next to the pain in her body.
Barbara came after me, she told herself. She crossed three, four
states. Came after me. Just like I hoped she would. She ran
that pickup right into the stolen Suburban. Risked her life.
She's my angel. Can't let an angel down: bad luck.

And she brought her gun.

Vicki knew it. Was certain. They might have found it, might
have taken it when they carried her inside, but maybe not. She
took a deep breath, heard the rattle in her lung, then crawled,
stumbled over to the open door of the pickup. She pulled up
on the seat. There was the familiar, battered metal case, latches
open. She dropped the .22 onto the ground, stretched across
the seat, opened the top, found the S&W, glanced at the two
CDs in their form-fitted holders. "Okay," she panted. "Here
comes the judge."

"You ain't going to tell me shit," Al yelled, pointed the SIG
Sauer at Jensen. "This is *not* the same cunt. This is *not* Prom
Queen! This *is not* Barbara Lovell. Just what the fuck you
trying to pull?"

Barbara studied the argument. Jensen was visibly upset, com-
posure ruined. His only cool: he ignored Al's weapon. "I have
no idea what you people are talking about," Barbara said. "My
name is Vicki Sigel. I'm an actress—"

"Shut up!" Al shouted. "I *know* who the fuck Barbara Lovell is. I spent three days hauling her prissy little ass from California. Two good men are dead because of her. Who the fuck are you?"

"Vicki Sigel," Barbara insisted, looked at Hillary, smiled.

"Oh, Barbara," Quince said. "Shut up, for Christ's sake. You're only making things worse." He stepped forward, put a hand out.

She shied away. "Don't touch me!"

"What're you trying to pull?" Al demanded. "Thought you were her uncle."

"It's *I Love Lucy!* " Hillary said: a bray. "My God, I woke up in the middle of *I Love Lucy.*"

"Don't anybody move!" The shouted order came from the landing. "I've got a gun, and I know how to use it!" Everyone froze: tableau. Quince stood with one hand extended toward his niece. Hillary, cigarette halfway to her mouth, stared straight ahead, her eyes waxy. Jensen sat where he was, a half-smoked cigar fixed in his left hand. Al smiled.

"Prom Queen!" she said, spun around, stepped forward. "About time!"

Vicki shot her in the face.

Al didn't fall back, didn't move. A bloody hole tore out the back of her head, her knees buckled. She sat down, hard, collapsed face forward. Barbara grabbed a breath, rolled off the bed, looked up: Vicki. Her tall, beautiful friend stood at the top of the steps of the entrance way, frozen in a three-point stance, legs locked, eyes wide, thumb cocking the pistol for a second shot. She had never looked worse. Her hair was plastered to her head, one arm bare, scratched, torn beneath the threads of a sopping rag of a sweatsuit, a naked boob thrust out: Amazon, Barbara thought.

Everyone now moved at once. Jensen spun around, reached inside his coat.

"Watch it!" Barbara yelled. Vicki fired the .38 again and again. Jensen dove to the floor on the opposite side of the bed.

"Goddamn," Quince grunted, surprised. He folded in half, stumbled over Jensen, collapsed on top of him. Jensen pushed Quince off, tried to rise, but Vicki fired again, shot the gun empty. Bullets tore ragged holes in the antique plaster, smashed through the rear window, splintered the back door. Hillary stayed precise, her back to Vicki, a bemused expression on her face, her burning cigarette poised in her fingers. She jumped, blinked with each blast of the pistol. The .38, now empty, clicked. Vicki lowered it slowly, stared. Quince moaned.

Jensen stood, shaken, his suit smeared with Quince's blood, his automatic pointed at her. "I take it you are not Barbara Lovell, either."

"God, I wish I had a drink," Hillary said.

Vicki fainted.

26
Reunion

Vicki Sigel came to for the second time that afternoon. She was dumped in an Adirondack chair, directly across from Barbara, slumped in its twin. The blonde woman, ironic smile on her scarlet lips, her generous figure accentuated by skin-tight green leather, sat gingerly on the edge of the bed, next to the white guy, propped up where Barbara had been before.

He was bad. Fingers pressed tight against his stomach, blood bubbling between them. He stared at the wound, watched life pour out of him.

Vicki remembered she had shot him, wondered who he was. She shuddered. She was a killer now: Dead-eye Vick. Hell on wheels with a telephone or a pistol. How's that for casting against type? Her eyes found Barbara's, who stared back. She's grateful, Vicki thought. Big fucking deal, we're still in deep. The bad guys are still alive.

Vicki ran her fingers over her body, took inventory. Everything hurt. Behind Barbara, the black guy stood in the far corner, automatic pistol in his left hand, the S&W .38 on the floor at his feet next to the SIG Sauer. Al's shotgun leaned on the wall next to him. His eyes rested on her. She glanced down, but made no effort to stretch the torn fabric across her front.

Al's body sprawled, floated face down in a young lake of blood. Vicki surveyed it with a short look, but felt no responsibility, only relief.

"A tragedy, isn't it?" The black guy saw her look around, asked. "This all could have been so simple."

"Who're you?" Vicki heard her voice. She no longer felt afraid. She wasn't even dazed. Mostly, she was weary. And, she thought, she was hungry, ravenous. How odd.

"I think the question," he said, "is, who are you?"

"Another fuckup?" Vicki sighed. "I've had it with fuckups. You people really screwed up my career."

"You okay?" Barbara asked softly.

Vicki nodded at her friend. "Nothing six weeks on the beach won't cure." She managed a grin. "You owe me, girlfriend. I gave up a lot to be here."

Barbara raised her eyes, gave a grim smile back. "That's a matter of opinion, who owes whom."

Vicki glanced at Quince, then up at the black guy. "It's all in the timing," she said. "I never had the timing for farce."

"I," the black guy interrupted, "am Mitchell Jensen. The lady is Vicki Lovell's esteemed aunt, Ms. Lovell. The gentleman dying on the bed is Mr. Lovell." He put the remains of a smashed cigar in his mouth, rolled it around. "I hope we are all finally met. I'm not sure I could tolerate another surprise visitor this afternoon."

"That's the trouble with these vacation hideaways," Hillary commented. "People just keep dropping in." She moved over next to Jensen, put a set of long fingers on his shoulder. "Can we go now, Mitch?"

"Oh, shit," Quince groaned. "Why didn't I see this coming?"

Jensen ignored him, gave Hillary a dark look. "There seems to be some question about identity," he said.

"What question?" Hillary said. "I think I know my own—"

"I've been double-crossed enough on this operation. You think I'll trust you?"

Hillary looked hurt, pouted. "That's ridiculous."

Jensen's eyes moved between the two young women. "Which one of you is the real Barbara Lovell?"

Vicki and Barbara looked at each other. *"What's My Line?"* Vicki snapped. " 'Will the real kidnap victim please stand up?' " She smiled slyly at Jensen. "You're so fucking cool, Superfly, you figure it out."

"It's *not* hard to see," Hillary said. "There's even a family resemblance, more's the pity."

Quince began weeping. The flow of blood continued, increased. "I'm such a goddamned fool," he wailed.

Hillary glanced at him, sneered. To Jensen. "Mitch, this is absurd. The brunette is my niece. I have no idea who the other one is." She glided away, picked up a small purse, opened it. "Does anyone have a spare cigarette? Isn't it about time we were on our way?"

Quince raised his head. "You are one cold bitch," he said, frail. "You might do something."

"What do you want me to do? I shouldn't even be here. Neither should you. But here we are. Don't blame me if you've managed to get yourself killed by this . . . this whatever she is wherever she came from. Where *did* you come from, anyway? Why are you even here?"

"Beats hell out of me," Vicki said. "Somebody want to tell me what's going on around here? I think I deserve to know."

Hillary smiled. "My brother's dying. You shot him." To Jensen: "She's not only pretty, she's dumb, too."

Quince spoke up: a gurgle. "I'm not dead yet, Hillary. But he'll . . . if you don't stop him. I've seen what he—" Quince's mouth snapped shut. His eyes focused on the wall separating the bedrooms. "Don't let him near me," he said, shook. Tears began anew. "For God's sake, Hillary. For once in your life . . ." One gory hand pawed at the lapels of his suit, streaked it with his own blood.

"God, you're pathetic," she said.

"Relax, Mr. Lovell," Jensen said. "I'm content to allow you to expire in peace." He paused. "Or to recover, if you can."

Hillary smiled at Jensen. "The deal's still intact, big brother. Except it appears that Mitch and I are the only ones left to deal with."

"Barbara!" Quince cried out. "Help me!"

"I don't know how, Quince," Barbara said.

"Quince?" Vicki asked. "I thought he was your father."

"Quince?" Barbara laughed. "That fairy wouldn't make a wart on Eddy's butt."

Jensen looked at her evenly. Nodded at Barbara. "So, *she's* your niece?"

"That's what I've been telling you, yes," Hillary said. To Barbara: "We'll be leaving shortly. Mitch and I have an appointment in the Bahamas. We'll need something decent for you to wear. Then we'll be on our way."

"On *our* way?" Barbara looked up. "I'm not going anywhere with you."

Hillary looked at her. "You may change your mind."

"In your dreams," Barbara said.

Barbara turned her eyes toward Jensen. "How much did she pay you?"

"Pay me?" he asked. "She paid me nothing. We are planning a rather large business transaction," Jensen said. "You might say we're partners."

"You might say they're lovers," Quince said bitterly. "Why didn't I see that?"

Barbara bit her lower lip, cast her eyes down, brow furrowed.

"I can't believe it," Quince moaned. "Jesus, Hillary. You and this—" He stopped, looked at her.

She feigned shock, recovered. "Who do you think was smart enough to put this together? You? Whose idea was it to abduct her, to dangle her in front of Eddy? Yours? You think I wanted this ungrateful little whore back?" She pointed at Barbara. "For what? I don't need her, Quince. I never needed her. She was a way, that was all. Means to an end. So long as I controlled her, I controlled Eddy, I controlled my future. Of course, if she had played it straight, she could be married to a millionaire now, sitting pretty in Newport or Palm Springs. Instead, all she wanted to do was spread her legs for the first nobody-prick who smiled at her."

"Runs in the family," Quince said. "Had a great role model."

"Oh, Quince. You don't know me. Don't know anything about me. All we needed you for was logistics. For the gangsters. You were good at that. But your usefulness is past, Quincy darling. To be honest, it wasn't worth much to begin with. Put him out of his misery, Mitch. I'm sick of the sight of him.''

Jensen shook his head. "Let him go on his own. He's expendable."

"That is such a *nice* word!" she exclaimed, smiled at Quince. "But what about her?" Hillary asked, nodded toward Vicki. "Isn't she—'expendable'?"

"She's not important. She did prove valuable, though. I would never have thought of using bait to bring Miss Lovell here on her own."

Vicki bristled. "Bait! Who's bait? Those bozos thought I was her." She pointed at Barbara. "They—they screwed up. That's all. So have you. When the cops get here—"

"Cops?" Jensen's eyebrows raised a fraction. He glanced at Hillary. That got him, Vicki thought.

"Yeah, cops. You don't think I came back here without calling the cops? Highway Patrol. Texas Rangers! The local sheriff's rounding them up right now. You're probably surrounded. What kind of—"

"You're quite correct," Jensen said, glanced out the window. "We have a plane to catch." He took two strides to the bed, raised his pistol, put the barrel on Quince's forehead, "Sorry, Mr. Lovell. It's been a pleasure."

"Oh, my!" Hillary said.

Barbara launched herself out of her chair, stepped on Quince, causing him to scream out, broadsided Jensen, knocked him backwards.

Vicki moved toward Hillary, but she couldn't stand. She scooted forward to the floor. Hillary scrambled away, out of reach. Jensen tried to recover, lift himself and Barbara at once. His pistol waved around the room. Barbara sunk her teeth into the back of his neck, he dropped the big automatic on top of Quince, who grabbed it in a bloody paw.

Hillary crouched on the other side of the room. "Get off him you silly little bitch," she yelled. She tripped over Al's body, fell. Vicki hoisted herself to her feet, used the chair as a prop. Nothing worked, legs useless. She eyed the shotgun in the corner, pulled herself up onto the bloody mattress, pushed forward, fell on top of Quince, who was trying to lift the pistol. Jensen was on his feet now, wore Barbara like a heavy coat, danced in the narrow space between the bed and the wall. He banged against the chairs, whirled around, his unbandaged hand seeking purchase on her head, shoulders. Barbara's nails raked his face, smothered his eyes.

"Hang on," Vicki gasped. "I'm—" She tried again to rise, collapsed backwards. "Shit!" she yelled. Her legs wouldn't support her. Pain raced up and down her whole body, blinding her.

The door burst open: splintering wood, glass. A huge man crashed into the room. His eyes wide, looking everywhere at once, his hair wild, spraying away from a sweat-covered face. But what Vicki mostly noticed was the enormous pistol in his hand.

"Eddy!" Barbara yelled. "It's about time!"

Deus ex machina, Vicki thought.

Eddy, out of breath, windbreaker torn and scraped by the thicketed brambles and tree limbs he had crashed through when he first heard shooting from the cabins, stumbled over the threshold, the Desert Eagle held out in front of him. He hardly knew what to do, didn't think. He was on the opposite side of the arroyo when he heard the first shots, leaped down into the sluggish water, scrambled up the other side, ran hard for nearly two hundred yards, his tar-coated lungs protested every step of the way. Somewhere behind him was a fence with shreds of his windbreaker in its barbs, but all he recalled was Moria's voice behind him yelling that he would "cover him." Eddy didn't care. He was going for Barbara.

Eddy took another step into the room, scanned it. Jensen danced around in the narrow space next to the bed, Barbara hung on his shoulders. Jensen wheeled, tried to smash her against the white stucco wall. Her forearms wrapped around his head, fingers ripped at his eyes. He was blind, screamed in rage, pain. Eddy raised his pistol, tried to get a shot.

"Kill him," the figure on the bed yelled in a gurgling voice. "Kill him before he kills all of us." Eddy recognized Quince. And he had a gun. He waved the big automatic generally in

Jensen's direction, then toward Eddy. Eddy brought his pistol up, aimed at his brother, touched the trigger, hesitated.

In light seconds, a train of thoughts slammed through Eddy's mind. He had never killed a man, not in cold blood, not in anger, not at all. He hated Quince. Wanted to kill him. Needed to kill him. But he was his brother. Eddy saw himself in Quince's tortured face, saw the outline of his own fingers on the pistol's trigger, saw his own blood flowing out of Quince's stomach, saw his own eyes in Quince's eyes. He couldn't do it.

The high sharp blast of a small caliber weapon raked against the pulse pounding in Eddy's ears. Quince jumped once, the pistol he held fell to his side. Eddy dropped to one knee. Moria, he thought. Jensen screamed, Barbara's hands all over his face, fingers deep in his eyes, teeth buried in his neck, blood ran down his cream-colored collar. Eddy stepped back, looked for an opening. He saw another woman on the floor, and Hillary's figure in green was off to one side. How many people were in this room? Where was Moria?

Before Eddy could count them, Jensen whipped around, Barbara's weight still on his neck. He crashed her against the white wall, dislodged her grip. Then he spun, rolled to his right, dumped her onto the floor. Off balance, he reeled, struck the wall again, upset a bedside table. Then, his eyes running blood, he reached for a sawed-off shotgun against the wall.

This time, Eddy did not hesitate. He pointed the big automatic at the middle of the dirty, stained suit, pulled the trigger once. Jensen flew back against the wreckage of the table, hit the wall, collapsed. Blood spouted from a black hole in the suit. Eddy moved over to him, shot him again. Eddy stepped back. So much for Batman, he thought.

He felt Barbara grab him around the knees, looked down. "You're late," she said, tears in her eyes. "Why are you always so goddamn late?" He let himself breathe. His ears rang, eyes burned, body tingled. He felt alive.

For a moment, no one moved. Gunsmoke hung heavy in the room. "Hi, Eddy," Hillary called out. "Got a cigarette on you?" He looked steadily at her. She was standing against the far wall, swaying slightly, her hands at her side. Eddy gathered more breath, pulled Barbara to her feet, held her close to him.

He could feel her pulse. He was calm, now. His own heartbeat was slowing to normal. "It was nice of you to drop by," Hillary said. "Saves time."

Eddy studied his sister. She was still pretty. Her hair was mussed, makeup smudged, but she was still Hillary. He then looked at Quince slumped on the bed, a small, red hole in his temple, eyes open, vacant. The other woman—a girl, he saw, but older than Barbara—sat up, spent, hurt. Vicki, he guessed. Looked like a drowned cat. What a fucking mess.

Eddy looked at his sister again and saw that she held a small black automatic. Moria hadn't come, hadn't shot Quince. Hillary did it. A phrase came to his mind, words from the past, from his long-dead father, words Eddy had heard so often when Hillary came home, pregnant, strung-out, broke, in trouble: "Hillary," he breathed out, "what have you done now?"

A shrug. "I had to do it, you know. Quincy never could stand violence. He might have hurt someone."

"Any reason why I don't just shoot you, now?"

"I could use a drink," she said. "That's not much of a reason, but it's all I have. Did you come empty-handed, or did you bring a house gift?"

Anger flared, he pushed it back. He had planned to kill her, just as he planned to kill Quince. But looking at her, he couldn't. He glanced at Jensen. That was all the killing he wanted to do: ever. He had Barbara now, it was over. He lowered the gun. "I'll give you your worthless life," he said. "It's not much, but it's what you made of it." He sighed. "But this is over. You've lost."

"Shut up, Eddy. You're boring me more than usual," she snapped. "Maybe you've got it all wrong. Maybe this was the way I planned it."

"I don't think so," Eddy said. "You might have started things, but you can't finish them. Never could."

Her tone changed: sweet. "There's a lot at stake here. I've got a lot of money. Right here. I don't suppose we could make a deal?"

Eddy gripped Barbara tight, shook his head. "Not with me."

"Guess that's it." She smiled. "Every now and then, you just run out of options." She sighed, looked at Quince, at

Jensen. "Jesus. They're all dead." Her mouth twisted, made her ugly. Then she slumped. "Damn," she said. "It was all going to work out. Are you sure we can't make a deal?"

"The ride's over, Hill," Eddy said quietly. "No deals, no nothing. I'm out of it. Forever."

"You're sure? Lot of money. More than you ever dreamed of." Her voice was soft.

"I'm sure. I'm leaving. We're leaving." He paused. "I never cared that much about money. You never understood that, did you?"

She looked at him steadily. Then her eyes became weary. "No, I guess not. So, it's over. I'm ruined." She raised the small pistol. "I could make it a family day, just kill you, too."

Eddy nodded, tightened his grip on Barbara. She looked up at him. "Go on, Hill. Now's your chance. I'll just stand here and take it. Like a good 'little accident.' But do it now. Otherwise, I'm just going to walk away."

Hillary aimed at Eddy's head. "No," Barbara said. Then: "You'll have to kill all of us. Or I'll follow you. I'll kill you myself. You're old, you're ugly, and you're phony. I'll never let you rest. Have you got the guts to kill all of us, Aunt Hillary? If so, you better start."

Hillary's eyes moved from Eddy to Vicki to Barbara. "You could have had it all," she said.

Barbara's eyes were steady. "No," she said. "*You* could have. But the truth is, you'd rather play than win." She tried to stand, used Eddy for support. "The truth is," she said, "that no one—no one—ever, ever loved you."

"Game's over, Hill," Eddy added. "You lose. I don't think you'll ever play again."

Hillary's eyes enlarged, then set, like twin jade stones. Her mouth made a hard line, she drew a breath. Then her shoulders sagged, and for a moment, she was beautiful again. "You know," she sighed, "for once, I think you're right. God, I could use a drink." She bent her elbow, put the barrel of her pistol into her mouth: pulled the trigger. The room lit with Vicki's screams.

Barbara went limp beneath Eddy's arm. Eddy stared at his sister's body, tried to feel something. She was now just a cruel memory. A noise outside caught his attention: Moria. The small man kept his word, left Jensen to Eddy, but he stayed outside, out of harm's way: Coward, Eddy thought. Big surprise.

He half carried Barbara, still limp, and turned to the open door, stepped out. All he saw was a yellow ash oval as the words "Louisville Slugger" moved straight toward his eyes: home run.

27
Players

"So where are they, Eddy?" Moria asked.

Darkness receded. Bright blades of light stabbed Eddy's eyes. Tried to focus. He occupied one of the big wooden chairs. Moria the other. He could feel the knot on his forehead: Rhino, Eddy thought. He looked around: Barbara and the other girl in the doorway, handcuffed together. Barbara looked bad, the other girl—Vicki, he remembered—worse. Hillary's body splayed against the far wall like a broken doll. The other corpses lay where they were. The room's floor was slick with blood.

Eddy started to rub his forehead. He couldn't. His hands were tied to the chair's arms with the old-fashioned telephone's cord. He tested the bonds: loose, but there. "He made me tie you," Barbara said. Her eyes were apologetic.

"Smells like a morgue in here," he said. "Butcher shop."

"I've been in worse," Moria said. "Won't be here long, if you'll just hand over the discs." He held his Desert Eagle in his hand. Eddy's own automatic was in the short man's waistband, looked ridiculous. The other weapons, the SIG Sauer, Barbara's .38, even Hillary's small automatic were piled under Moria's chair. Al's shotgun remained in the corner. Moria noticed

Eddy's eyes on the guns. "Something, ain't it? Hell, I've seen less hardware in a combat weapons squad."

"Why didn't you just ask me?" Eddy questioned, mouth dry, tongue swollen, head aching.

"Tried that," Moria said. "Couple times. You're not exactly the cooperative type. You know that?"

"Why should I cooperate with you?"

"Hello!" Moria smiled. "Earth to Eddy. Big stakes here, Eddy boy. Big stakes. This is business. You've cost me a lot on this deal. No fault of yours, but no fault of mine, either. Somebody's got to pick up the tab. Those discs are valuable. I don't know why, don't know to who, but they're worth a lot. See?"

"Enough for all this?"

Moria shrugged. "You don't know how to take a loss. Figured you'd do anything to save your girl. She's kind of pretty, Eddy. No resemblance to you." He smiled. "You know the funny thing." Moria shook his head. "I think Jensen was wrong. I think Cole was playing it straight. I don't think he was double-crossing anybody."

"Salt of the earth," Eddy said. "Just lost his head."

Moria's eyes widened briefly, settled. "Account closed." He sighed. "Now we're all here. We're not supposed to be, apparently. But here we are. And everybody but us is ready for the meat wagon."

"So, what now?" Eddy asked, his gut tightened. He knew.

Moria picked up his pistol. "Lot of people are dead because of this. Take them years to figure it out. One or two more bodies won't make any difference. There's a pile of money at stake here. I intend to have it."

Eddy looked at Jensen's body. "Without him?"

"Him? Who's he? Somebody's gofer. Somebody's boy. I'll find the somebody. I can do that."

"Yeah," Eddy said. He tested the cords again: looser.

"So," Moria asked, "where are the CDs?" Eddy stared straight ahead. "I'm not fucking around, Eddy," Moria said. "I'll kill all of you. Where?"

Eddy hesitated, looked at Barbara. "LA."

Moria's eyes widened. "You're lying."

"They were in a case. Briefcase. I sent it to her. With that."
He indicated the S&W, still on the floor, then looked at Barbara.

Barbara was stunned. "Those? Those *blank* CDs? *That's*
what this is about?" Eddy nodded.

"It's a nice act," Moria said. "But it won't play. I don't
believe they're in California."

"Well, I don't know about the rest of you," Vicki said,
straightened, winced. "But I, for one, am *not* ready for another
road trip. I need a doctor."

Moria stood, pointed his weapon at her. "I think it's time
we added to the body count. Let you know I'm serious." He
reached out, put the barrel of the pistol on Vicki's head. "Where
are they, Eddy?"

Vicki looked up at him, impassive. "You think you're scaring
me, shorty? Hell, you're nothing. You want tough: try Hollywood. They'll eat your lunch."

"I hate to kill you, sweetheart," Moria said. "You're
spunky."

"Fuck you, fat stuff." She spat on the floor.

Moria's face darkened. "Say good-bye, whoever you are."
He aired back the hammer. "Last chance, Eddy boy."

Barbara spoke up. "They're here." Moria lifted the pistol.
Vicki sighed.

"All right. Where?"

"Don't tell him," Vicki said. "He'll just kill us anyway. I
know his type. Can't get it up without dirty movies."

"Don't push me," Moria warned.

"Outside," Barbara said. "In the pickup."

"In the wreck? You're kidding."

"Or they were," Barbara said. "I don't remember much."
Eddy gaped at her. "I didn't have time to plan anything," she
said, shrugged. "I wanted my gun, so I grabbed the whole
case. They're still there."

"Sit tight." Moria stood, frowned, went out.

Eddy pulled at his bonds. More give. "You okay?" Eddy
asked Barbara.

"Sore ankle, knee. Vicki's the one beat up."

"Hell, I'm fine," Vicki said. "Just fucking fine. All this
was about some CDs? Music?"

Moria returned. He held the battered briefcase high. "Got it!" He sat down in the chair, case across his knees. His eyes lit when he opened it. "Abracadabra."

Moria held the CDs up to the overhead light. He turned them in his short, stubby fingers, checked for scratches. "Perfect," he said. "I love technology."

Eddy looked through the bullet-smashed window. It was dark outside. "So let's go. You got what you wanted."

Moria shook his head, replaced the discs. "There're people waiting for these someplace. People with a lot of money," Moria said. "I don't know who they are, not yet, but it's an odds-on bet they won't like loose ends."

Eddy looked around the carnage in the room. "Sloppy," he said. "Not a player's work."

Moria looked at him sadly. "You're a sucker, Eddy. A patsy. You bought into the whole thing. I'm sorry for that. You did me a good turn once, but I repaid the favor. Now, I have no choice. You tend to think with your heart, not your head, can't tell business from personal." He stood, slipped the discs into his white suit pocket, raised the pistol. "So long, Eddy. Thanks for the dance. It's been real."

"No!" Barbara screamed. Moria turned his head. Eddy placed his feet on the floor and exploded upwards. His wrists were still bound to the heavy chair, but he spun on one leg, used the reclining back as a battering ram, slamming Moria up against the wall. Eddy lost balance, fell on top of the women. He felt their fingers tearing at the phone cord, heard Moria yell behind him, expected the slam of a bullet into his spine at any second. Then he was free, stood, lifted the chair with him, dumped it over onto Moria.

"Gun!" Eddy yelled. "Where's a—" The handguns were too far. He spotted Al's shotgun in the corner, dove for it. Moria slithered out from under the chair, grabbed the sawed-off weapon, shoved it under the bed, then rolled away out of Eddy's grasp, tried to aim. His Desert Eagle banged, hard, metallic, deafening. Once, then again. No clear shot.

Eddy was on his feet. He vaulted over the bed, felt his foot sink into Quince's body, tripped over Al's corpse. Moria fired again. Eddy leaped to the landing just as a slug from Moria's pistol clipped his right arm, spun him around and into the doorjamb. He bounced outside, tripped and fell against the orange pickup's open door. Behind him, he heard Moria coming. He rolled over, ignored the stinging in his arm, scrambled on the gravel beneath him. His hand struck something hard, familiar: a gun.

He pulled it to him. Long-barreled .22 revolver: gift from God. He cocked it, Moria appeared in the doorway, his huge pistol scanning the area. Eddy pointed it at the short man, put the stubby sight on Moria's chest, just below a strange pencil point of dark red light on Moria's white suit, pulled the trigger: sharp pop, like a balloon bursting.

Moria staggered back against the door, his hand flew to his chest, came away bloody. "Fuck!" he said, calm. Eddy saw the same tiny red point, now on the bridge of Moria's nose, between those dark, compelling eyes. "What the hell was" Moria's head evaporated in a red cloud. He sat down in the doorway, as if too tired to stand.

Eddy never heard the shot. He lay where he was, the empty .22 in his hand. Moria's headless torso sat in the doorway. A geyser of blood spewed, stopped. "Shit," Eddy said, tried to sit up, dizzy. He had no idea who'd shot Moria, didn't care. He only wanted to grab Barbara, get away. He staggered up, moved past Moria's body, pushed it over, made his way past the bloody killing floor to Barbara, Vicki. "Let's get out of here."

"He's got the key on him," Barbara said, holding up their shackled wrists.

"Sorry," Vicki said. "Don't think I can stand up."

Eddy tried to pull them up together, a mass of legs, arms, groans and sharp cries.

"Relax, Eddy," a voice behind him spoke. "We'll take it from here."

Eddy stopped, turned. Standing on the landing, surveying the human wreckage below through his green eyes, shaking his head, was the impassive dark face of Moria's bodyguard: Hedge.

* * *

In a few moments, they were outside, near the canal. Hedge, torso still covered with blood, somehow stood upright, healthy, solid, flanked by a familiar form: Federal Marshal Theodore Billings. The big ugly lawman carried Vicki in his arms, placed her on the grass. Barbara staggered out on her own, dazed, spent. She pushed him off, tacked unevenly over next to the canal, sat down, pulled off her sneakers, lowered her feet into the water.

"Keep your fucking hands to yourself!" Vicki's voice sparked in the darkness. "Hey! That hurt!" Eddy turned.

Billings stood up, shocked, then recovered. "She'll make it," he called over. "What about her?" He nodded toward Barbara.

"I'm fine. What I needed," she said, indicated the canal's cold water. She reached down, scooped up a palmful, washed her face.

Billings walked over to Eddy. No longer dressed in his rube cop getup, he now wore blond camo, desert combat boots, a knit cap covered his head. He also carried a 9-mm Glock in a holster and had a short ugly rifle with a laser scope slung across his huge back. Hedge stripped off Eddy's windbreaker, ripped open the sleeve on his shirt, tied a rubber tourniquet on Eddy's arm, daubed it with a foul-smelling ointment, put a bandage on it.

Billings studied Eddy's wound. The bullet passed through clean. It hurt, but would heal. He looked at the lump on Eddy's forehead. "Looks like somebody popped you a good one." He chuckled. "Couldn't happen to a nicer guy. Wish it'd been me that done it."

"Check out the office," Hedge said. Billings scowled, left.

Hedge smoked, grinned at Eddy. "He hates your guts."

"Feeling's mutual," Eddy said.

Hedge grinned again. "Been on your ass since the start of this."

"You're a cop?"

Hedge shook his head. "Not so you'd notice." He stuck out his hand. "Lawrence Guetierrez."

Eddy, hesitated, shook hands. "Thought you were Vietnamese: something." He was thoroughly confused. "Gwen, something. Long. That's what the cops—uh, Billings. That's what he said." He began to understand: cover.

"Billings," Guetierrez smiled, "is a racist redneck. But he does good work."

"For who?"

"Never mind."

"I thought he was a fed. Marshal or something."

Hedge/Guetierrez frowned. "We get a little help from our friends. He was—let's just say he was." He shifted his weight: change of subject. "I'm Samoyan. Or my mother was. Samoyan and Hispanic American," he said, grinned. "We figured Moria would buy into a gook quicker than a spick. Or a redneck. Felt sorry for that Houston detective." He grinned again. This was eerie. Eddy had never seen him smile, make any expression. "What was his name?"

"DaCara."

"Right. He'll never figure this out. Cost a fortune to keep him quiet."

"You think he can be bought?" Eddy's opinion of DaCara was high.

"Everybody can be bought." A pause. "He gambles." Guetierrez held up the discs. "They're intact," he said. "That's the important thing."

"You wanted them, too," Eddy said.

Guetierrez nodded. "Been tracking them since the van robbery. Been tracking you. Tracking your accomplices."

"Dodd and Henderson."

Guetierrez nodded. "Followed them to Brazil. That was their plan, by the way, case they didn't tell you. Sell the stuff to an arms dealer named Sorrello. He wasn't too happy when they showed up empty-handed. Left them on meat hooks in a São Paulo slaughterhouse." He dropped his smoke, ground it out. "Wasn't pretty."

Eddy looked into the room: "Neither was that." Anger came up behind his eyes. "My daughter, her friend. Could have been killed." Guetierrez nodded. "So could I."

"Naw. We had you covered."

"So, what were you waiting for?"

"These," he said. Lit another cigarette. "Truth is, we didn't know a thing about your daughter. Her friend. The kidnappers were independents. Rank amateurs. Bungled it so bad, we didn't connect to this at all. Not the way Jensen normally works. He's slick. Or he was." He glanced at Barbara. "Think he was losing it. Can't believe he gambled on a broad."

"That broad is my daughter."

"I was talking about your sister." Guetierrez grinned again. Eddy couldn't get used to it. Anyway, that was all on the side. Your sister's idea. Rope you in. It wasn't till this morning, listening to you and Mendle, I put it together. I had no way to let Billings know until you stopped to eat. That was touchy. I was dying, remember?"

Eddy looked at the blood-stained tank top. Guetierrez pulled the shirt up. An ugly bullet wound puckered. He reached down, clipped a fingernail beneath one edge of the suppuration, peeled it off to expose ordinary, uninjured skin beneath. A small, flesh-colored tube ran down into his jeans. "Hollywood," he said, pulled on the tube, pumped out blood. "I used to work as an extra in action movies. Helps to know the trade."

Eddy looked at Barbara. She sat on the canal's edge, her injured knee soaking. "Why'd you bust in last night? Why save our ass?"

"Wasn't Moria's ass worried me. It was yours. You had the discs. Or knew who did. Jensen was ready to deal direct. Get the discs, blow off the kidnappers, make the deal, drop out. Screw Hillary. And Quincey. Whatever it took. It was time to take him out. Damn near got there too late. You almost took him out yourself. Those two with him were better than they should have been. Main thing, though, we didn't want to lose you, or these.

"So, anyway, we knew where it would go down—thanks to you." Eddy looked a question. "The phone message in Houston. Came right to me. Unbelievable. Confirmed it at Pap's Cafe. Dummied the arrest, my shooting, my getaway. Gave me cover."

"You let the cops know."

"Right. We didn't know what Jensen's contacts in Balmorhea had to trade. 'Disney can deliver,' they said. But what? The discs? Had to be. But who had them? Cole's getting hit threw everything out of joint. Jensen was paranoid.''

Eddy stepped away, rubbed his face. ''What happened to Raul?''

''Castillo?'' Guetierrez frowned. ''Found him—or what was left of him—sixty miles north of Laredo. Next thing we know, Cole has set up a deal through a pimp named Johnny Ribbon and a guy—we think—named Alvin Lawton. That's him in there. Only now, he's a she. We still didn't know what the deal was. Not till today.''

''So you show up just in time.'' Eddy remembered what Jensen told him about the explosive bullets, Moria's head. Jensen wasn't lying about that.

''I called Billings this morning when you stopped to eat.'' He pulled a cell phone from his pocket. ''He flew out on his own. Waited. Nobody was supposed to get killed,'' Guetierrez said.

''Blew that.''

''Yeah.'' He held up the discs. ''We had to pull out some stops. Break some rules. Too important.''

''Who's 'we'? You Feds? FBI?''

Guetierrez only smiled. ''Let's just say these are important.''

Eddy lit a cigarette, shook one out to Guetierrez. He took it. ''So how could you let someone like me wind up with them? How could a couple of jerks like Dodd and Henderson. . .and Raul,'' Eddy said.

''Long story,'' Guetierrez said. Eddy waited. Guetierrez sighed. ''Lot of people out of work these days. They know one thing, one job: covert espionage. Lot of guys. But now, Cold War's over. So what do they do? Can't go home. Can't get unemployment. Hell, they were lining up their bosses against walls. So they went into business, used what they knew. But they were bad at it. They're clumsy, obvious, heavy-handed when it comes to off-the-rack criminal stuff. Did what they could to get by.''

''Loan-sharking?''

''Didn't have the contacts. Didn't have the know-how. Didn't have a clue. But they knew what was going on inside.''

"How?"

"Jensen. He was inside. Hey, our people go bad just like everybody. Get greedy. The business ain't what it once was. And he had old friends. Politics, international banking, investments."

"Hillary?"

"You're getting it. They get together, accident, really. They bump uglies a little, cook up the deal. Then pull in Quince, who brings them Cole, Dodd, and Henderson. Told them to find a patsy. Somebody who'd stand up. Somebody they could wipe without a trace. You, in short." Eddy looked away. "They were supposed to leave you looking good for a busted robbery."

"Almost worked," Eddy said.

"Not without the goods," Guetierrez said: grim. "Dodd and Henderson wind up dead. Castillo drops out. You're downstate with a hole in your liver."

"Kidney."

He shrugged. "The CDs are gone. Jensen's out in the cold. Cole's all over him. Jensen thinks Cole's double-crossing him. He takes Cole out, decides to screw everybody, deal direct with you. Meanwhile, we're going nuts trying to find the discs."

"No copies?"

"Sure. But they're still dangerous in the wrong hands, they work too well." He paused. "They're worth a lot."

"Yeah," Eddy said.

Billings came around the corner of the building. "One of the stiffs in there's got a California shield. The other's the ranger. Or the rangerette."

"That's not funny, Teddy," Guetierrez said. "We know about the ranger. Who's the other guy?"

Barbara's head snapped around. "Sandobal," she said. "Detective Sergeant Louis Sandobal. Santa Barbara Police Department."

"No shit?" Billings said. "How come?"

"How come what?" Barbara's eyes flashed in the light spilling from the cabin. She pulled herself to her feet. She stood, but her leg gave. She almost collapsed, but then found her balance and hopped on one foot over to the men. Her face was angry. "How come he's from California, or how come he's here?"

Billings put his hands on his hips. "How come he's dead?"

She looked into Eddy's eyes. "Because he loved me," she said. To Billings: "Take me over there. I want to see him."

Billing's mouth opened to speak, but the determination in Barbara's eyes stopped him. "Here," he said, "lean on me." They hobbled off.

When Barbara left, Eddy felt jealous. Even from her position on the ground, Vicki could see it. He reminded her of a football player she dated in high school. The name came back: Jacky Dee. Her first steady guy. One night at a postgame dance, she left him in the parking lot to "go talk" to Bobby Bailey. Jacky didn't like it. Stood there, smoked, stared after her. He knew what she was going to do. She lost her cherry that night, always felt sorry for Jacky Dee. Things might have been different if she'd stayed with him. Dance with the guy that brung you, she thought. Screw the guy who fucks you. She should have stayed and danced. Jacky Dee had a future. Wound up owning his own company. Bobby wound up in a paper mill. Jacky Dee: smoking in the dark.

A brilliant moon now appeared over the trees, lit the whole scene. All Eddy needed was a smoke to be Terry Dee. All she needed to hear was some old-time rock and roll. Complete memory. *Sweet Sixteen,* she thought. Was that a Molly Ringwald title? She couldn't remember. Didn't matter. She'd never be that young again.

She raised up on an elbow, felt groggy, shook her head. The fat guy who carried her outside put her down on her stomach. Before she knew it, he had her sweat pants down, jabbed a needle in her hip. Copped a feel, drugged her up all at the same time. Then he put them up again. What did that mean? Didn't like what he saw? Her right boob still hung out. She touched it. Sore as a boil, purple as a raisin. Least it was still there. She still had her equipment, no matter how damaged. And her feet were okay. Walk her right into a role. She now had real

experience, she thought. Screw method acting. She was the
real thing.

Eddy then stepped toward her. She smiled at him. Yep, she
thought. Just like Jacky Dee. Eddy reached in his pocket, lit
another cigarette.

"Got one of those for me?" she asked.

Eddy checked. Pack was empty. "Last one," he said. He
handed the one he just lit to her, she took a deep drag, felt it
lift her, returned it. "Keep it," he said. Barbara's father, she
thought. How old? Forty-five, fifty? Hard to tell. He had a
body under that windbreaker. Worked out. That she could see.
"That's okay," she said. "Trying to quit."

"Why?"

"Good question," she laughed. "Give it back." She accepted it, took another deep hit. Their eyes met. He straightened
up, stretched.

"Glad you're okay," he said, gave her a smile. "I'm grateful
for what you did for my girl. For Barbara."

"Nothing to it," Vicki said, laughed. "A walk-on."

"Yeah, well," he said. "I'm grateful anyway."

He turned, walked away. Now he seemed old, tired. Something inside her deflated. Maybe he wasn't like Jacky Dee after
all.

Eddy returned to Guetierrez. "Any reason why we can't
leave?"

"Three or four counts of murder," Guetierrez said.

Eddy stiffened, stepped away. The vision of prison rose in
his mind. "Thought you weren't a cop."

Guetierrez laughed. Then, serious: "There's going to *be*
cops. All over the place. We got a lot of bodies to bury. We
don't want any profile on this. Officially, what went down here
was a drug deal gone sour. We'll spread around some snow,
handle the paperwork. None of this happened. It's over, Eddy.
Get out of here."

Eddy stood for a moment. The night was cool, chilly. He
pulled the ragged windbreaker around his shoulders. "Take the
Mercedes?" he asked.

Guetierrez glanced around. "No. Sorry. It was Jensen's, traceable. Take the airport van. Leave it in Alpine. I think you'll find a pretty nice plane waiting. Hillary's. Pilot's name is Terry Something. At the moment, he's balling a hooker he picked up at the Best Western motel. You can't miss it. Only one in town. Oh, he was screwing your sister, too. So break the news gently. And carefully. If he asks. Go where you want, then blow him off. Stay the hell out of Texas. Let this cool off."

Eddy started to move away. "I . . ." He didn't know how to finish.

"Get the fuck out of here," Guetierrez said. He replaced the famous shades. "Now."

Three hours later, they were airborne, off to LA in Hillary's jet. Eddy made some stops, picked up fresh clothes, pain killers, bandages, bags of ice, smokes, couple of pizzas. Vicki ate one all by herself: pepperoni and anchovy. "You got to love anchovy," she said, licking her fingers. "It's not pizza without it."

Terry took the news about Hillary easier than Eddy thought he would. Or maybe not. He looked scared, ready to run. But he agreed to fly them to LA after Eddy said he could keep the plane. "I don't give a shit what you do with it," Eddy said. "Let's go."

As they lifted over the southern Rockies, the plane's bar gave them all a drink. Eddy felt himself relax for the first time in days.

Vicki lay on the silk sheets of the pull-down bed, sulking. She couldn't walk at all. Eddy had to carry her on board. He was gentle with her, surprised that she seemed so light, so soft. It was hard to believe she was capable of all she had done. When he lifted her, she put her arms around his neck, her head on his shoulder.

"Don't get any ideas," she said, as he put her down. "Soon as I get back to Hollywood, I plan to kick butt. They got nothing I can't play." She gave him a smile, tapped out a cigarette, indicated that she needed a light. He obliged. "I'm quitting again," she said. "Soon as I get back."

Then she used the plane's phone. She listened, asked who was speaking, threw it across the room. "Can you believe that shit?" she demanded. "He's in bed with some bimbo! Says 'he's tied up' and giggles. Giggles! I'm beating people to death with a damn telephone, he's banging some gum snapper! He doesn't know who he's fucking with. I'll call David Lynch. Tarantino! Bob Altman! I'm telling you: I've got something to sell!"

Barbara sat in one of the starboard chairs, a beer open next to her, cigarette smoldering in the ashtray, her knee was a deep purple, ankle red, swollen. Her forehead bruises covered by her bangs. Her eyes were heavy, dark with fatigue and grief. She took a drag, sipped her beer, looked up at Eddy. "I can't help feeling that it's all my fault," she said. "That he got killed." It was a statement, not a question. There was no bid for sympathy, no self-pity.

Eddy stared at her. First time he'd seen her in years, but she was no longer his girl, his anything. She was a woman. There was beauty: Ellen, then with a wince: Hillary. Then, no. Not either. Barbara—defiant, he thought: certain, grown. She stunned him.

"He believed in me," she said, shook her head. "It's hard to find anybody to believe in you."

"I don't know much about that," Eddy said after a moment. "I never met the guy. But I do know one thing. People don't do things they don't want to do, no matter what they say, no matter how they act. He did what he wanted to do. You can't take the blame for that. It'll eat you up." A pause. "It wasn't your fault."

She nodded, sipped her beer. "Well, one thing's for sure. This does it for my plans to be a cop." She gave him a wan smile.

"I never much liked that idea," he said. "It's dangerous."

She laughed, a short, dry bark. "Well, one of us is going to have to make a living. You're out of a job, you know."

Eddy agreed. "I'm out of work, out of money. I got twenty-five grand stashed. That won't go far."

"Not in California, it won't," Vicki spoke up. "Hell, parking alone will eat that up in a month."

Eddy felt himself sinking. He'd lied to Hillary. He always cared about it. All his life: money. The enemy forever. Now, again, he felt the old pinch, the desperation. How would he make it? Not he: they. Some things never changed. Barbara was his responsibility again, and she needed some kind of life. What then? Back to truck driving? Back to hard labor? He was still a con with a sheet. What else could he do? The small of his back ached where he wore Moria's gun. No, he thought: not that. He was no longer a player. He never would be again.

Costa Rica, he thought, shook his head. *Stop dreaming, Eddy. Stop.*

He swiveled around, kicked a laptop computer out of his way. Fucking computers, he thought. He saw the large black case next to it. He found it in the van, brought it aboard: "Leave nothing," Hedge/Gueticrrez had warned him. "Wipe down the van. No trail."

"I wonder how much I was really worth?" Barbara asked idly. "How much those CDs were worth."

Eddy picked up the case, opened it, saw the neatly bundled bills inside: he knew.

Epilogue

Six Months Later

The telephone on Detective Sergeant Greg DaCara's desk was, as usual, covered with papers, reports, files, scraps of meals, Styrofoam containers. His mouth, as usual, held a cigarette. Ashes littered the floor next to his chair. Deep scowls, as usual, shot his way every time he expelled a blue-gray breath out over the crowded, noisy squad room. The phone rang.

"DaCara," he said when he found the receiver, jammed it into his ear. "Homicide."

"This is Lawrence Guetierrez," the voice on the other end spoke clearly. "Washington, D.C."

DaCara sat back, dropped his butt into a half full cup of cold coffee, pulled a smoke from his pocket, put it between his lips. "Yeah, so what?"

"I need you to put a little light on something, Sergeant."

"They call me 'Sunshine' around here, and I'm not even black," he said.

"I'm seeking information about an officer who worked with you about six months ago." The voice sounded official, all business.

"Not with me," DaCara said. "I don't work with nobody. Loner. I smoke," he added.

"Name was Billings. Theodore Billings. United States Marshal."

"This is Houston PD. You want the Federal Building."

"Our information is that he was attached to your squad. Investigation of the murder of one Robert Cole. Maybe an arson, bombing as well."

"Bomb Squad's number is—"

"Our information is that he was your partner."

"Yeah?" DaCara blew smoke out of his nose. "Well, your fucking information's wrong. Never heard of him."

"Robert Cole or Marshal Billings?"

"Neither one.

"How about Moria Mendle?"

"Dallas businessman, I think." He leaned forward, spoke quietly into the receiver. "Dead, I think."

"What about Eddy Lovell?"

"Astronaut? Think there was an astronaut named Lovell."

"Eddy Lovell," the voice repeated.

"Nope."

"Thanks. That's all I needed to know."

"No problem," DaCara said. He hung up, reached forward, picked up a racing form for Louisiana Downs. He lost ten grand the previous weekend. If he hit the trifecta this week, he'd be even for the month.